The Extraordinary Anna Parke

Melanie Murphy

For my boys-my husband Brian,

and my sons, Jack and Max-

who inspire me each and every day.

Older and wiser and larger than humanity, unencumbered by timelines and logic, the trees that rise from the dusty Earth, tall and straight and sure, have a sense of magic and beauty beyond the comprehension of mortals. They have seen both the delights and atrocities that mankind has perpetuated decade after decade. They are the quiet bystanders of our history and future, the true witnesses of our legacies and failures.

The forest is a sacred place, nature's last stronghold on a starving planet. Maybe the trees should be permitted a voice, a say in the direction in which our world turns. Maybe we humans need to listen more intently to the experts who have been here long before and will remain here long after our fleeting existence.

Who are we to say what trees are and are not capable of? They must laugh at our naive assumptions of their grandeur and majesty, humans dwarfed by giants. Maybe it is our logic as humans that has closed us off to their chuckles and whispers. What stories would those trees reveal had we the consciousness to listen? What magic courses through their very roots, hidden underground in vast networks of complex mazes? What secrets are held within their gnarled and ropy limbs?

Chapter 1

Now

On a worn, thrift-store corduroy sofa, caddy cornered in a tiny apartment above Lee's Chinese Kitchen, Anna Parke sat. Despite the open window, the air was laden with the scent of stale pan fried noodles; no matter what she did, she could never quite rinse her hair clear of that pungent, oily scent. Her Main Street apartment was a wreck: empty beer bottles littered the small, oak coffee table and laundry was piled in almost every crevice of the one-thousand square-foot loft. She couldn't even tell whether the clothes were clean or dirty anymore. And if she was being honest, who really cared?

Her mother would be horrified to see the state of affairs: the clutter, the wine-stained, sticky countertop, the dust bunnies lined up like an army underneath the wobbly, metal kitchen stools. But, if she lived her life according to her mother's ideals, she would be confined to a sterile, sanitized box that smelled like lemon floor cleaner. Her head pounded and throbbed, betrayed by the five Coors Lights that felt so fresh and cool trickling down her throat last night. She gazed into her bedroom.

From her vantage point, all she glimpsed was the foot end of her full-sized mattress, and the naked feet that shirked the comforter in the drunken throes of last night's sleep. Brief visions of the evening danced upon her mind. She had met Ken, (or was his name Keith?) at Don's, the local watering hole that has served Windsom's drunks for decades. He had never specifically mentioned her birthmark. Doing so would have been rude, but Anna could tell he noticed it. Of course he noticed it. Everyone noticed it. Who could possibly ignore the maroon blotch that covered most of her cheek? Shifting from her cheek to her eyes and then back to her cheek again, his gaze was almost palpable. But the heaviness of his stare lessened with each sip of the cold liquid that filled her glass and then her belly, and once the alcohol took her away, Anna no longer cared what he thought about the unsightly blemish.

They had slowly danced to the sound of The Rolling Stones' "Wild Horses' echoing from the old-fashioned juke box, which contained no album newer than 1985. Most modern establishments don't even have jukeboxes anymore, but instead rely on the more trendy and space-efficient digital media players that can customize entertainment with any song imaginable. But Don Redmond, the bartender and owner, couldn't give two hoots for modern convenience. He bought that jukebox thirty-five years ago for $750 dollars, a lot of tip money at the time, and it has done him just fine ever since, thank you very much.

Anna remembered the lyrics. They seemed so meaningful and profound in the wee hours of the night when the haze of alcohol makes the world swirl like creamer in black coffee. But now, as she gazed into her bedroom, hungover and tired, the magic of the evening was gone–replaced with a fuzzy mixture of shame and disgust. Her breath tasted stale, her hair was a tangled mess, and the mascara that she hadn't bothered washing off last night, felt clumpy and heavy on her lashes.

Anna cringed at her recollection of the clumsy walk back to her apartment, the fumbling undressing, the sloppy, wet kisses full of need and urgency, the intermittent sleep where strangers spend an unnaturally intimate night fighting for blanket and pillow space. She hated what came next: the sober morning eyes and the awkward small talk, the half-hearted *I'll call you soon* promises never to be fulfilled, the *Sorry, I have to run. I have an early meeting to get to* lies uttered through stiff lips and averted eyes. Anna wasn't proud to admit that she had done this dance and played this game many a misty morning. She always wished they would just wake up before she did, and leave silently without the pretenses they thought necessary in the morning sunlight. Even worse than the uncomfortable goodbyes and the pathetic excuses was the suggestion of breakfast. She always declined the insincere offers of a coffee and an egg sandwich at the local diner. After all, they didn't mean it; they were just trying to be nice. Small talk is hard to come by once you have seen the other person naked.

Anna stared out the small front window, one of only two in the entire apartment, at a sleepy row of shops: a deli, Hoen's shoe store, Stitch and Sew, Windsom Cinemas. Each stall darkened against the six-am fall sunshine. In about fifteen minutes, Lacey Macquade would race past Lee's Chinese kitchen on her way to open up the small downtown post office; Randall Knowles would pedal his metallic red Schwinn on his daily fifteen-mile, pre-work bike ride. Did he make his daily exercise routine so public on purpose? Just to make other people feel bad? Who wakes up this early to go bike riding for God's sake? By seven-am Windsom would be awake and Anna dearly hoped that no one would be present to witness her guest's departure; the last thing she needed was to fall victim to small-town gossip.

The new Town Hall building blocked her view of the Adirondack Mountains, the main, but definitely not the only drawback of this sleazy apartment in which she spent the last five years. Yet on the other hand, maybe not having those trees in direct vision was a good thing. She had spent years contemplating and subsequently avoiding the puzzling waves they emanated, the magnetism that seemed to draw her to those woods, the vibrations they sent out making the tiny hairs on her arms stand at attention sending shivers down her spine.

Either way, her apartment was within walking distance of The Food Mart, where she earned her pathetic paycheck–here she was at 29-years old still scanning groceries like her pimple-faced teenage co-workers–and close to the bar in which she spent it, but the sink leaked, the windows were old and drafty, and the landlord was persistently stubborn when it came to rent collection and consistently absent when it came to making the needed repairs on what was clearly an old, run-down building.

Anna tiptoed to the bathroom, trying to avoid the creaky spots on the floor, making as little noise as possible to avoid waking up her guest and having to actually talk to him. She carefully closed the door and sat down on the frigid porcelain toilet. A feeling of anger rushed through her at that moment and she felt her face turn hot and red. Here she was, walking on eggshells through *her* apartment, trying not to wake this guy about whom she honestly couldn't care less. She imagined herself storming into the bedroom and confronting him.

"Keith.. How about you get up already. It's time to go."

He would slowly rouse himself in that groggy, unwilling way that most people have when being pushed awake by a shrill angry voice.

"Hmmm? Good morning."

Then would come that shit-eating grin that men always wear after having conquered a new one-night-stand.

Keith would begin, "Last night was——-"

"Necessary," Anna would finish the sentence. "Last night was necessary. You could even say it was adequate, but that's about it. And now it's over. Time to go."

"Well, that's not what I was going to say."

He would seem wounded, but Anna would see through his charade.

"Don't bother," she would shoot back, throwing his shoes at him as he would sit up in her *bed bare-chested and sulking.*

"Wait a minute," Keith would respond, slowly coming to the realization that he was in fact being kicked out.

He would have faintly hoped for some morning sex to complete the experience. He kind of liked Anna and thought she felt the same way, in spite of the magnetic pull of the alcohol. But now his anger would be growing alongside her's and he would feel suddenly defensive. He was a good guy. He wasn't some chauvinist pig. SHE *was the one who had invited him home and* SHE *was the one who told him to spend the night.*

"Just gonna use the bathroom," he would say, shifting as he began to move the blankets aside.

"Nope," Anna would answer. "Use the bathroom in Lee's."

He would glare at her as he got up, not even bothering to cover up his nakedness. His outrage would make him look at her with more scrutiny and the strange mark on her face that hadn't bothered him last night would now become the object of his focus.

"How about getting that thing lasered off or something. Maybe it would make you less of a bitch," he would say as he brushed past her and out of the apartment.

Anna wouldn't know that Keith or Kevin (or maybe it was Kyle) would, in reality, never have said such a cruel comment; he thought Anna was pretty despite the mark. Nor would she know that he was actually a decent human being because she never actually had the conversation. This back and forth didn't actually exist. She often invented scenes such as this in her mind; mentally she had confronted at least a dozen men, getting more and more brazen with each imaginary exchange. But instead, she decided against flushing the toilet- too much noise- and went back to her place on the sagging couch

After settling back down again and contemplating the lackluster view the front window offered, Anna's eyes were drawn begrudgingly to the brown cardboard boxes, stacked against the far wall of what passed for her living room. She hadn't gotten around yet to unpacking the items and the memories that were surely tucked away in the shadowy darkness within them...or maybe "gotten around to it" is less accurate than "had been avoiding" unpacking those items and memories. The boxes accumulated a fair amount of dust, yet Anna had unsuccessfully attempted to ignore their menacing presence ever since she made the pilgrimage back to her childhood home on Ackerly Lane to retrieve them just a few weeks ago.

While her apartment wasn't more than three miles from her childhood house, it felt light years away–a distant planet only encroaching on her periphery at certain points of its path around the solar system. She made the trip back home only after that disconcerting phone call she received a few weeks ago. That phone call that shook her solitary world to its very core–that phone call that changed the very course of her life forever. Amazing how death will do that. Every single time. It's one of the few things that can be counted upon in this life. Death has a way of turning the world on its head, knocking the breath out of us, forcing us to re-envision our futures and reconcile with our pasts. Anna remembered the words that issued out of the phone's receiver on that fateful day and reverberated through her very being.

"Hello?"

"Is this Anna Parke?".

"Yes. Who is this?"

"Oh good. I heard somewhere that you were living in Lee's rental. It's Mrs. Douglaston."

"Oh. Hello Mrs. Douglaston. How can I help you?" Anna asked, surprised to hear this friendly voice from her past.

"Sweetheart, I'm sorry to call you with bad tidings…"

Anna cast one more fleeting glimpse at those boxes and couldn't help but feel the ghosts of her past rise up around her. She didn't know if she could ever bring herself to open up those cubes–open up her history. But one thing became quite clear as Anna intentionally averted her gaze, her past had come calling, and no matter how much she tried to outrun it, it had caught up to her at last.

Chapter 2
Then

Anna Parke was born in the sleepy little town of Windsom, NY, located in the outskirts of Warren County, surrounded by the rough edges of the Adirondack Mountains, jagged like a serrated knife along the horizon. Those mountains loomed large and fantastic in all her childhood memories. There was nothing remarkable about her birth; it was a perfectly normal affair. After a few pushes and grunts Ms. Parke–she was always Ms. Parke, never Beverly or Bev or Bebe like other women of the same name–forced Anna out of her comfortable water world and into the bright sunshine and sterility of reality. Ms. Parke looked over her daughter, took note of Anna's auburn hair, slimy with umbilical fluid, her pink wrinkled toes, and a purple wine-stain birthmark that stood out like a smear of blood on her milky, creamy newborn cheek. Ms. Parke frowned imperceptibly when she laid eyes on the unsightly blemish and handed her child over to the nurse, careful to keep her perfectly manicured hands free from the natural gooeyness associated with the messy business of childbirth.

Her dead-beat father was not present. His absence was unsurprising; he left months ago. Ms. Parke's pregnancy was unintentional, an unfortunate result of a completely out-of-character effort to keep her wayward new boyfriend from straying any further than he already had. God knows why she wanted him to stay. He wasn't anything special, just another two-bit wise guy who thought he knew what he wanted. Maybe it was loneliness that pushed Beverly to maintain the relationship. After all, she didn't have much contact with people; in fact, she couldn't stand them. And the feeling was mutual.

Ms. Parke knew that she was not liked by the members of her small, country community. But she felt a certain pride in her reputation and looked down her nose at her neighbors. She viewed their trivial lives with disdain. Ms. Parke was immune to the whispers of the women in Gerald's grocery store, the comments made about the "frigid woman whose icy personality probably matched her bedroom performances." She averted her eyes from the beauty parlor stares that smilingly and secretly said, "What does Johnny see in that goody-two-shoes Beverly anyway?! She's so prude she thinks it's a sin when the wind blows at her skirt!" These shameful encounters were not fully unwarranted. Beverly Parke always had a way of coming off snobbish...not only to the women in the tight-knit community of Windsom, but to her own boyfriend as well. She never socialized with her neighbors, a quality on par with treason in a town where people prided themselves on that good old 'love thy neighbor' maxim. Beverly Parke did not attend the Fourth of July barbeques, nor did she volunteer at the local soup kitchen. She declined all invitations to parties and Mahjong games; who would want to sit around with a bunch of middle-aged biddies swapping tiles with foreign symbols on them and exchanging meaningless chit-chat? And most unnaturally to the other Windsom residents, she did not partake in the pomp and circumstance of cheering on the high school football team at their weekly games; Beverly would have rather stuck needles in her eyes than sit on those metal bleachers in the cold and watch acne-filled adolescents beat each other up over a brown leather pigskin. Although it is not a crime to be a loner, in Windsom, New York it was.

Beverly Parke simply did not have any desire whatsoever to befriend her neighbors. She much preferred the quiet company of her tabby housecat Minnie, who purred softly at her feet as she sipped her nightly green tea, dressed in her prim white, cotton nightgown that laced up to her chin. Minnie never asked stupid questions. Minnie never made boring observations. Minnie didn't chew with her mouth open or wear ripped denims or make idle small talk about uneducated matters. Beverly had been alone for as long as she could remember; she had inherited the house from her own parents who suffered a tragic end in an unexplained camping accident. No one ever knew of the exact circumstances; Beverly was always vague and closed off when discussing her own family history. Regardless of what happened, the 'incident' left her with enough money to live comfortably albeit not luxuriously, and allowed her the privacy that suited her personality.

Even though Beverly had no use for the company of others, she was not immune to the allure of the opposite sex. Her neighbors would be surprised to learn that as a child, Beverly dreamed of flirtatious encounters with boys. Her stringent upbringing forced her to install internal breaks on most of her physical impulses, but she enjoyed the attention she received from her male classmates and allowed herself to be kissed a few times by Greg Dorman behind the maple tree at the back of the schoolyard. These kisses and the subsequent “attentions" she received from boys didn’t last long. A combination of bad luck, awkward pre-pubescence and a general case of not-fitting-in dulled any interests the opposite sex felt towards Beverly. Additionally, early on, her playful nature had been curbed by her parents, who instilled within her a sense of fundamental snobbery, and as a result, she had limited experience with men, and knew next to nothing about bodily pleasures.

And because Beverly Parke considered herself to be above the typical Windsom man, who was unworldly and provincial and generally beneath her, and because she never left the town in which she grew up, which afforded her no opportunity to meet outsiders, when Johnny Hart, a traveling salesman from Manhattan, came to town, she put on all the charm she could muster, along with a fair amount of the rose-colored lip gloss she purchased at Hoen’s drugstore, and worked her feminine charm as best she could.

Although Johnny played a small part in what would become the story of Anna Parke, he assumed a large role in the life of Beverly Parke from the summer of 1982 through the winter of 1984. His crisp downstate accent, and the nonchalant way he wore his shaggy brown hair made him chillingly attractive to the thirty-year old, conservative, righteous and decidedly virginal Beverly Parke. Johnny was sophisticated; no country bumpkin, he drove a shiny red Ford Escort that stood out amongst the pick-up trucks like a tulip among weeds. What Johnny thought was to be a small stint upstate to pursue a new career in sales–and perhaps more importantly but less vocalized, to escape a small scandal involving a younger girl and her angry father in Manhattan–turned into an almost two-year relocation to a place he neither wanted to be, nor to which he would ultimately commit.

While Johnny's new job peddling magazine subscriptions led him to Beverly Parke's front door on a humid summer afternoon in late July of 1982, his charisma and dimples led him to Beverly's bed a week later. A few months later, he was no longer living above Wainright's garage, but had become a permanent resident of 43 Ackerly Lane. Beverly's house looked like a palace compared to his dumpy apartment and Johnny was happy to save his weekly paycheck instead of squandering it on rent. The haste of the move did not go unnoticed by the Windsom residents. The women gossiped and judged and snickered behind Beverly's back. But who cared what they thought? They were probably just jealous that Beverly had found someone better than their own hillbilly husbands. The men wondered only how Johnny had managed to get himself into Beverly's skirt. But all of Windsom's residents agreed that it would never last, that Johnny would get tired of the 'ice queen' and turn tail. They were cruel...and they were right. Johnny and Beverly's relationship unraveled as summer turned into fall and fall turned into winter and 1982 turned into 1983 and 1983 turned into 1984.

One autumn evening, Beverly Parke paced back and forth, back and forth across the red woven throw rug laid carefully atop the old oak floors of the living room. The aroma of dinner hung in the air: meatloaf with roasted red-potatoes and cole-slaw set out on the kitchen table. On this night, Beverly made an effort to prepare Johnny's favorite meal–the most she could muster in terms of an apology after a particularly ugly disagreement they had earlier this afternoon, the topic of which had faded as the sun traveled across the sky in its daily path. Usually Johnny was the one to apologize, never Beverly, a fact in which Beverly felt a sense of misplaced pride. But something about their earlier disagreement left Beverly feeling edgy, and that anxiety crept back into her mind as the meatloaf turned cold and the potatoes turned brown in their oily bed.

Finally, Beverly heard the familiar sound of her boyfriend's boots stomp up the front steps. She also detected the slight shuffling of his footsteps indicating that he may have stopped off at Don's after work. She put on a chipper facade as Johnny walked through the door, careful not to bring up the fact that he was late or that he was drunk.

Usually, Johnny started the after-fight conversations; he was the one to smooth things over between them and he was the one who usually accepted the blame.

But when he didn't speak, Beverly uttered, "Hi. How was your day?" She couldn't prevent the twinge of annoyance from creeping into her voice.

"Fine," he sighed without further elaboration.

Instead of kicking off his boots–Beverly never allowed him to enter her home with his dirty shoes–he moseyed right past her, heading towards the white Frigidair. She heard the clanking sound of bottles before he pulled the single Budweiser out of the refrigerator. He began to drink in long, greedy swallows.

"Can you at least take off your shoes?" Beverly couldn't resist.

Johnny didn't make any move whatsoever. He just stared at her under his heavy lashes.

Again, "Johnny. Take. Off. Your. Shoes! You have no idea what kind of germs you are dragging in here from outside."

Johnny's lips turned into a smile that did not quite reach his eyes. He almost said something. He opened his mouth and Beverly expected some sort of sarcastic retort followed by acquiescence. But he didn't say a word. Boots on, he simply walked down the hallway and into the bedroom leaving the door open behind him. Beverly heard the creaking of the bed springs under his weight.

Standing in the kitchen, fuming with rage, Beverly scraped the congealed remnants of dinner into the silver mouth of the garbage can.

The truth of the matter was, Johnny no longer found Beverly's aloofness appealing, and the bedroom routine had soured and turned stale. And maybe there was something else too that discomforted Johnny about

Beverly Parke, some well-concealed fuzziness–that was the only word that came to mind when Johnny tried to pinpoint what frightened and unsettled him about his girlfriend. He began spending more and more time at Don's,drinking Coors until two o'clock in the morning and finding warmth with whomever expressed a fleeting interest in his accent.

While Beverly began to tire of Johnny's boyish frivolity, she was not ready to admit defeat. Some part of her didn't want to be alone forever, and she knew that this might be her one chance. She made a last-ditch effort one night in December of 1984. She pulled out the black satin negligee (with the $19.99 price tag still attached) that she never quite mustered up the courage to wear. She styled her hair and dug the scarlet lip-gloss out of her purse. She dimmed the lights and waited for Johnny to return home from Don's. As she heard his thick-soled shoes thumping up the stairs, her heart pounded, her whole body in a heightened state of excitement and anxiety. Swaying on his feet from too many cold beers, he opened the bedroom door to find Beverly, assuming the pose of a 1950's pin-up girl. She looked out of place and pathetic in the gloom. They made love quickly and without enthusiasm. Usually, Beverly's love-making was silent and still, but tonight she called out his name at the very end as if she knew that this would be the last moment of intimacy they would ever share. Beverly Parke fell asleep as Johnny zipped up his jeans, laced his thick soled shoes–the same ones that announced his entry just an hour before–and stole out of the house and out of Beverly Parke's life forever.

The next morning, Beverly awoke to snow quietly falling on her windowsill; the old glass frame was cracked open a bit last night in attempts to let in some air, and the fresh, piney scent of trees surrounded her. She did not have to check to see if Johnny's car was parked in the driveway; she knew he was gone. She did not yet know that a part of Johnny was still there, within her. Pulsing in her throbbing womb was what would soon become the extraordinary Anna Parke.

Chapter 3

June Barbury, the attending nurse, eyed Ms. Parke with something like shock as Anna Parke was abruptly thrust back into her arms.

"Here, take her," Ms. Parke said.

"Are you sure Ms. Parke?" June uttered in surprise.

Over the course of the past ten years as a nurse in the maternity ward, June regularly witnessed hundreds of new mothers weep tears of joy as they first beheld their precious babies; she heard their whimpers of relief after they pushed their screaming newborns into the world and their soothing whispers into tiny pink ears: *Don't cry anymore sweet one, Mama's here*. But she never saw a reaction quite like the one she observed as Beverly Parke relinquished her freshly birthed baby girl into June's open arms with eagerness. In the three days following, as Ms. Parke healed, June Barbury changed the tiny Pampers, the ones with blue and pink ducks and teddy bears adorning the borders, and tended to Anna, the whole time wondering how this woman could be so detached from such a beautiful gift from God. Could it have been the unusual marking on the tiny cheek that caused Ms. Parke to act so strangely?

"Can you take her into the nursery tonight?" Beverly asked June. "I would like some uninterrupted sleep."

"Normally we suggest that newborns remain with their mothers in the beginning," June Barbary explained to Beverly, *you know, to love them,* she thought in her head, but didn't dare say out loud. "It is easier to establish bonding and breastfeeding."

Her patient scoffed, "I have no intention of nursing. The sooner the baby gets used to formula the better."

June didn't know how to respond to Ms. Parke's abrupt tone, so she simply said, "Well..if you're sure."

"I'm sure," Ms. Parke said, rolling over in her white hospital bed as if to say that the matter was closed.

Aside from her refusal to breastfeed and her disinterest in bonding with her new baby girl, Beverly Parke had no visitors, none at all. Another anomaly in a hospital wing where friends and family insistently and oftentimes overwhelmingly flood their loved ones, bearing flowers and balloons and fluffy, stuffed teddy bears purchased at the shop in the hospital lobby, not caring how intrusive their presence might feel to exhausted new parents. Ms. Parke's room boasted none of the usual oohs and aahs of admiring onlookers ogling the tightly swaddled newborn bundle sleeping in the rolling crib. Instead, room 4B in the maternity ward was quiet and somber. And the more and more June watched Beverly interact with her child–or maybe the lack of interaction is more appropriate–the more concerned she became. There was something off about the woman, something cold and unnatural. Many new mothers struggle to redefine their lives once they hold their bundles of joy for the first time, but Ms. Parke put forth no effort, expressed no love, no motherly instinct whatsoever.

June continued to try to foster bonding during Beverly's five-night stay, but for some reason Ms. Parke seemed closed off to any display of motherhood. June thought that perhaps Ms. Parke was experiencing the throes of postpartum depression and didn't try to force the issue too hard. Anna was a sweet baby who was easily consoled and comforted; therefore, when the time came for Beverly to be discharged from County General Hospital, Anna did not protest, but instead closed her tiny first around her mother's collar and allowed herself to be carried out of June Barbury's life for good.

Over the course of the next few years, June Barbary found herself thinking about Beverly and Anna quite often. She couldn't quite put her finger on it, but something about the mother troubled her deeply and there were times that June felt a stabbing guilt for not, at the very least, referring Ms. Parke to the counseling center. Something about the way the mother looked with disgust upon such a sweet little baby. Could 'disgust' be the correct word to describe how Ms. Parke gazed upon her daughter? About how Ms. Parke's calculating eyes lingered upon that purple mark marring an otherwise flawless little face? June thought that she must be remembering wrong. Memories and emotions often have a way of transforming themselves into tall tales under time's relentless passing. Surely, if the mother had disturbed her so, June would have spoken up, right? And yet, her mind kept returning to the pair. There was something about that little baby girl swaddled tightly in the hospital issue blue and pink cotton blanket...

Chapter 4

What Beverly Parke didn't notice as she left the hospital after her brief stay in the maternity ward–she might have, had she paid more attention, maybe even a cursory glance into the rearview mirror after she hastily secured her daughter's carrier in the back seat of her sedan–was the way the trees that lined the main thoroughfare and then the meandering roads in her small development seemed to bend towards the car as it huffed along towards Ackerly Lane. At certain moments during the fifteen-minute ride home from the hospital, some of the branches came so close that they almost grazed the roof of car.

Beverly thought she heard scraping sounds as she pulled into her driveway, a sound indicating that her car had brushed up against something–which was odd because the nearest object to the driveway was the maple tree positioned at least twenty feet away–but by the time she exited her car and then hastily retrieved her daughter, the branches of that maple tree snapped to attention to avoid Beverly's calculating gaze. The tree looked on with silent approval as Anna Parke was carried up the front porch and through the door. After much anticipation, she was finally home.

Chapter 5

Beverly adjusted to her new daughter as one might adjust to the taste of a new and foreign food: slowly, gradually, and with some cringing. Anna Parke was a mild-tempered, easy baby who did not demand (nor was she given) much attention. The needs she had were met in a halting and grudging manner. She was bathed and changed and kept clean. She had a new crib and soft bedding depicting smiling farm animals. She was given creamy Gerber jarred baby foods and powdered Similac formula.

But even an easy baby needed everything done for it. It bothered Beverly to think about why human children couldn't be more like animals, who were basically self-sufficient a few days after birth. Beverly's baby managed to ruin all of the bedding with its spit-up, and any outfit Beverly wore was sure to be stained with the same off-white, sour smelling vomit that stained the bibs and tiny onesies piling up in the laundry basket. On top of the mess, was the sleep disruption. Beverly was used to going to bed promptly at 9:30pm, and sleeping uninterrupted until 8:00am. Now the baby destroyed her regimented rest and Beverly found herself leaving Anna screaming in the crib until she could no longer drown out the sounds of the breathless sobs. Sometimes, Anna would simply exhaust herself and the screams would muffle into gurgling sobs and eventually lead her back into sleep. But on the occasions that the cries only intensified in pitch, Beverly would stomp into the nursery to perform the cursory feeding and changing routine only so she could quickly drop Anna back onto the crib mattress to get a few more hours of rest.

So it's safe to say that from early on, Beverly began to resent her rosy-cheeked daughter with her blighted complexion. She resented that good-for-nothing, smooth talking salesman who waltzed into her home and ruined the silent and solitary life she had so strategically carved out for herself. She hadn't asked for diapers or sleep deprivation or motherhood. And so it was, that before Beverly even tried to love her new daughter, she retreated from her.

And it was, in this way, that along with the growing trees, time passed. Although she was well-cared for, in a practical way, Anna's childhood was loveless and melancholy. Even though all of her practical and material needs were met, there was something missing that she couldn't quite put her finger on. Anna ate well and had plenty of toys, even Surfs-up Barbie who wore a shiny pink swimsuit and plastic glitter-encrusted sunglasses that actually opened and closed, just like real sunglasses.

Anna's prized possession was a dollhouse made by a grandfather that she never met. One day, while exploring the attic, Anna's eight-year-old eyes alighted on this beautiful treasure, and after acquiring begrudging permission from her mother (*Sure, let her have something to keep her busy)*, she dragged it out of its hiding place, down the wobbly, creaking ladder and into her sunny bedroom. It was apparently her mother's, when she was a child. Anna couldn't ever imagine Beverly Parke engaging in what she would have undoubtedly considered childish frivolity.

She gently dusted off the cobwebs and was delighted to find that the dollhouse was the mirror image of her own home that nestled next to the woods on Ackerly Lane. It had the same wallpaper, a real porcelain bathtub and toilet, the same sturdy brown front porch on which she often took her lunch in the summertime, and in one of the tiny replica bedrooms, Anna joyfully discovered a set of dolls: a father, a mother, a little girl and an older brother.

Anna spent long, lazy afternoons enacting scenes where the father (Mr. Billingsly she named him), would come home from work to a home-cooked meal of meatloaf and mashed potatoes, where the mother (Anita), cuddled and snuggled and read bedtime stories to her young daughter and helped her teenage son with his homework, where the family would sit together on the green velveteen couch in the living room and play Monopoly or Yahtzee or some other wholesome board game. Anna yearned for the family she held in the palms of her hand as the lazy afternoons wound their way towards dinnertime and she would be called away from her fairytale world by the smell of supper. How wonderful to have a big brother, Benjamin, she decided his name would be. How wonderful to have a father who happily looked forward to whittling away the evening hours with his children tucked by his sides on the overstuffed living room sofa.

"Mom, can you come play with me?" Anna would plead with her mother.

"Absolutely not Anna; I'm busy."

No *I'm sorry honey, but I'm busy now.* Just an *Absolutely not.* Not that Anna was surprised by such abruptness. She came to expect it from her mother.

"Just for a little while? I need help designing a new bedroom. I have this idea that the brother and sister can switch rooms. I think the furniture would look better–"

Beverly Parke immediately cut in, "It's just a silly toy Anna and I refuse to waste my afternoon staring into that old thing with you."

"Well can you at least–"

"No. Go play," Beverly responded with finality.

So Anna gave up asking her mother to play with her; the answer was always the same. Sometimes when Anna went to bed at night, these very same dollhouse scenes would play out on the insides of her eyelids tempting her back to sleep even when the morning light played upon her gingham curtains.

As Anna continued to grow into herself, Beverly Parke continued to retreat into herself. Ms. Parke, always a stickler for order, became increasingly insistent on cleanliness and organization. Almost as if by throwing herself into the intricacies of maintaining a spotless home, Beverly could avoid some other, scarier aspect of her life. Anna always wondered what exactly it was that her mother was compensating for by the tidiness upon which she adhered so desperately. What was she hiding? After all, no visitors ever walked through the doors of 43 Ackerly Lane. What was the point of such rigidity if no one were to ever see it?

"Come on now Anna," Ms. Parke would scold, "Remember the folded laundry must be put away immediately to preserve its freshness."…"Anna, your dolls should be placed in size order, and should always be seated upright on the shelf. See? Like this. There is a place for everything," Beverly Parke would order.

Anna, who couldn't understand the purpose of her mother's intense need for order, would do as asked. Each tiny request for attention that Anna dared utter was met with a brief "No Anna; I'm busy" or Beverly's favorite, "Absolutely not." So gradually, Anna stopped asking her mom to braid her hair, to fix her an after-school snack, to read with her before bed.

Ms. Parke spent hours sorting various household items, dusting and then rearranging the small trinkets that lined the mantle above the fireplace, always muttering to herself, *A place for everything and everything in its place*. Dinnertime was always a quiet affair, filled with a menacing silence that was amplified by the clinking of the ice cubes against glass tumblers, heightened by the scratching sound of forks upon plates. But lately, Ms. Parke began cleaning up dinner before Anna was even finished with her meal: sweeping an already crumbless floor around Anna's feet and wiping an already shining table around Anna's elbows. Anna began to feel as if her presence in her own home was an unwelcome intrusion. She felt that the divide between her and her mother was increasing every day. Of course at eight years old, Anna could not vocalize any of these feelings, but she was insistently aware of feeling like an outsider, feeling as though her very person was a source of aggravation for her own mother, feeling as though the notion of family meant something more than her own paltry experience allowed her to know.

Throughout the years, Anna viewed her mother with a mix of fear and idolatry. She relished those few and fleeting moments where her mother expressed approval. Ms. Parke's approval typically came in the form of a slight smile and a nearly imperceptible nod, usually as a result of a report card displaying a neat row of A's, or a floor mopped to a gleaming shine. Anna desperately sought this meager show of affection and basked in the aftermath as a new blossom soaking up the sun's warming rays.

Anna began to instinctively avoid her mother; life just seemed easier that way. After school she closed herself up in her room and into her dollhouse dramas that continued to evolve as elementary school turned into middle school. She wouldn't have admitted to the few friends she had that she still played with dolls, a notion that would have been bitterly sneered at by young tweens with newly developing bodies and the first bursts of acne sprouting on unsuspecting cheeks. Yet, the dollhouse was Anna's escape, a world where The Billingslys ate together and played together and loved one another openly and affectionately...a world where Anna was welcomed...a world where Anna belonged.

Chapter 6

Now

Soft snores from the bedroom reached her at this moment and Anna contemplated making some loud rattling sounds in the kitchen–possibly an upturned pan–to wake her unwanted house guest. For how long could this stranger possibly sleep in an unfamiliar bed? From the sound of it, Ken or Keith (or maybe Kevin) had no thought whatsoever about making the hasty departure for which Anna so dearly hoped. The departure which Anna had imagined a few minutes earlier.

Sex was one thing, especially the kind of rash, brazen unapologetic sex that proceeds a drunken night at the bar, but sharing a bed in slumber felt much more intimate to Anna, much more personal. She desperately wanted her apartment to herself so she could freely shower and go about her day. Anna might have had the guts to actually wake the sleeping man, she thought about the imaginary exchange–she played in her head–had she not such an aversion to the small talk that would inevitably follow.

Anna got up to open the front window of her apartment; she felt suddenly dizzy and was desperate for some fresh air. The apartment was too warm, too stuffy and smelled too much like a frat house, which is acceptable in the nighttime, when the buzz of alcohol casts its dreamy haze, but unbearable in daylight when the memories of the drunken night seem sordid and shameful.

The boxes in the corner seemed to glare at her and call out to her as she walked past them. *Open us*, they taunted. *You can't avoid us forever.*

Sure I can, Anna thought to herself. *Watch me.*

Using some extra strength to pry open the screenless glass pane, sticky and uneven from too many coats of paint, she glimpsed the very tip of the trees that surround Windsom and not for the first time, she wished she had a better view. From her childhood bedroom window, the trees seemed an arms length away and now she had to search for their friendly greenery above the cement and stony buildings that encompassed Windsom's Main Street.

But then again, maybe she was better off being farther away from the strange and strong pull of the trees. Didn't that trite old maxim say, *Out of sight, out of mind?*

At the moment, Anna wasn't so sure that she agreed with that.

She glanced at her phone, which now read seven-sixteen, and for a moment, eyes closed, she relished the cool breeze that wafted through her apartment.

A discordant snort from the other room roused her from her revelry and she stood up quickly, thinking that her bed-mate had finally awoken. But, when the snores returned to their soft even drone, she realized that she had no such luck.

Plopping down on the sofa with a sigh, her eyes once again alighted upon those boxes. She didn't know if she could summon enough strength to open them, to face her past, her childhood, her mother. After all, she was perfectly content in her current life, wasn't she? Why did she have to go rifling through those demons from her past? Anna thought about hauling those boxes right out of her apartment and throwing them, unopened, into the dumpster behind Lee's Kitchen. But something stopped her. She couldn't put her finger on exactly what, maybe some desire, some urge to see what remained of her old life.

Who was she kidding? She wasn't content. Not at all. How could she be? She was 29-years old, working at a supermarket, still trying to outrun her past. *Later…*she silently told the boxes. *Later*…she thought as she picked up her phone and started scrolling through her unread emails. There is always later.

Chapter 7
Then

The Adirondack Mountains, the majestic rise and swell of craggy bluffs and trees and wildlife, the stuff of fairy tales and legend. The apotheosis of awe and fantasy. Even though travelers from around the world regularly visit to observe the epic grandeur of this region of New York, to the people in Windsom, the expansive Adirondacks lost their luster long ago. To the typical Windsom resident, the Adirondacks mean tourists and intruders. They mean fabricated wooden chairs and lumber and honky tonk hotels and arcades.

Yes, the mountains bring their share of city folk. People who feel that it is their duty to expose their children to the "country" by loading their fancy Mercedes or BMW monstrosities to the hilt with toiletries and hiking boots and taking the drive "upstate" to scoff at the locals who drive mud-splotched Chevy pick-up trucks or Dodge Rams. They ask each other questions like, "Could you live here?" and they marvel at how anyone could find himself satisfied in such quaint surroundings. Many outsiders come simply to gaze at the fall foliage, with their thousand dollar cameras with the telescopic lenses that look like submarine periscopes, as if the trees are some sideshow circus act at which to be ogled and photographed. They come with their maps, and their itineraries, and their inflated wallets and egos. And after spending an extended weekend in one of the tourist hotels, the ones with hired celebrity chefs and indoor swimming pools, they pack their SUVs back up and head home, feeling good about themselves for having braved the backwoods of America and for having rubbed elbows with the local hicks, who are undoubtedly in need of a good dentist.

But, even though Anna Parke resigned herself to the notion that the nature outside her door was to be shared by these obnoxious and demanding tourists, she was not jaded to the beauty surrounding her The mountains called to Anna. They enchanted her. From a young age she would stare out her window fascinated by the way the trees on the mountains changed their wardrobe from season to season...lush and emerald in the spring and summer months, rusty and golden in the fall, brown and melancholy in the winter. For as long as she could remember the trees loomed outside her bedroom window; they observed her tears and longings, always constant, always stable.

Anna's usual visits to the mountains were solitary and quiet. She spent time hiking the trails, running her hands over the jagged rocks, listening to the flow of the streams trickling over branches and boulders, weaving fragrant honeysuckle wreaths and then tossing them into the roving stream in hopes that some other little girl would discover them and believe them to be magical haloes.

Ever since that disconcerting conversation with her mother three summers prior, the conversation about her father and his whereabouts, she came to rely more frequently on the nature surrounding her. These mountains became her safe haven, her home. She did her best thinking here, sitting cross-legged on the soft forest floor littered with pine needles. The wilderness accepted her, heard her, welcomed her.

As a child, she spoke to these trees that seemed to bend towards her as she meandered through the woods; they spoke back, whispering the secrets of the past. At first she thought it was just her imagination, but as she got older the trees continued to communicate with her in an intangible way. She heard them not with her ears, but with her soul. They had a friendship. They guided her into the hidden alcoves of the forest and showed her unfathomable beauty.

She remembered the first time she heard them, really heard them. They always spoke to her, but one day–maybe when she was about six-years old–their murmurs became more concrete, more palpable. She was playing with her Suzy doll, alone in the neatly manicured backyard. She had been shooed outside so that her mother could mop the floors; the scent of lemon Pine-Sol wafted out of the open kitchen window. On this gorgeously sunny spring day, Anna had brought two tea cups and a large sheet outside with her. As she raised the teacup to Suzy doll's lips to give her a taste of the imaginary lavender tea imported from France, she heard her name on the breeze, an echoing mantra, a million voices in one, *Anna... Anna... we are here.* She turned around to see the trees fringing the perimeter of her yard swaying and dancing in the light May wind.

Anna rose from her seated position on the sheet, her Suzy doll protectively tucked against her chest and said "Who said that?"

We did, We did, she perceived them to say.

"But who are you?"

Your friends. Come to us.

Anna walked over to where the voices seemed to originate, to the edge of the dense line of trees a few feet away.

Just as Anna was about to reach out her trembling hand that had not yet lost the baby fat, to touch the lush, green underbrush, she was interrupted by her mother's shrill volcanic voice booming through the kitchen window.

"Anna! Get away from the woods!"

"It's ok mom," Anna called back. "They're calling me."

"Don't be ridiculous Anna.Collect your things and get back inside. Immediately!"

Anna acquiesced. Her six-year-old self didn't have much other choice. She said a hushed goodbye to the voices she heard calling her, summoning her. But ever since that moment, the forest lured her, pulled her with a magnetism that was both beautiful and terrifying.

As she got older, she became more adventurous in exploring the woods behind her home. When she was headed into an area that could prove potentially dangerous, it almost seemed to her that the trees blocked her passage with ropy branches, a gentle reminder not to stray too far from the path on which she safely roamed. The trees also seemed to show her the way back home, their soft brambles catching her hair in an attempt to keep her here with them, as if they believed her more fully protected in the serene woods than in her orderly home. Anna could communicate with them as well; they would shower their leaves down upon her when she sent out the hazy request. The trees would lower their branches and entwine their flexible limbs around Anna's ankles and wrists, as a cat wrapping its quivering tail around its owner's feet. She couldn't have described the magnetism she felt to the trees if she tried. It was a dull thrumming in her core that was reciprocated by those tall figures as though an invisible thread connected them, weaving them together in solidarity.

At the time, she didn't realize that she had an extraordinary gift. She merely viewed the trees as she viewed other living creatures, as spirits with needs and wants. But one day, in fourth grade, her teacher, Ms. Ring gave the class a writing assignment. They were working on a persuasive unit and each student was required to write a letter to a friend in an attempt to convince him to either take some sort of action or adopt some new belief. Danny Wu wrote a letter to Justin May in an effort to persuade him that MTV was better than Vh1. Jessica Trankel wrote to her best friend Sarah Hagins about Aurora being the most beautiful of all the Disney princesses.

When it was time to peer edit, Jamie Gibbs, Anna's desk-mate, giggled as she read Anna's letter, which was written to a silly maple tree convincing it to keep its leaves instead of shedding them this winter. After all, leaves would keep it warmer during the snowfalls that were particularly brutal in this part of New York.

"You were supposed to write to a real person, dummy," Jamie teased. "Trees can't think. Maybe you should write to your doctor and convince him to remove that mark from your face instead."

The comment stunned Anna. Over the years she had become accustomed to the way her classmates' gazes drifted from her eyes to the birthmark on her cheek, but usually that was the extent of it. Just stares of curiosity. So the cruelty and meanness of Jamie's statement brought a deep scarlet blush up to Anna's face accompanied by a feeling of utter embarrassment.

Aside from that, her classmate's remark made her feel dumb and stupid, but it was too late to rewrite the assignment so she ashamedly handed it over to Ms. Ring. She never forgot the odd, tilted way her teacher looked at her when she was called up to Ms. Ring's desk the next day to discuss a more appropriate topic for the assignment.

"Anna," Ms. Ring said, "This is a very creative concept, but this is not the assignment."

Anna tried to avert her eyes, which were brimming with tears as Ms. Ring hungrily searched Anna's face for a response.

Ms. Ring tried again, "Anna, sweetheart, did you hear me? You were supposed to write a persuasive piece... to a person."

Pause, no answer. As Anna's gaze remained affixed to her shoes, she wished she could melt into the green-tiled floor. At this point, her classmates caught on to what was happening in front of the room, and even though Ms. Ring was whispering, Anna could hear her classmates giggling and she could hear Jamie quietly filling them in on Anna's stupidity. Telling her peers how Anna had written to a tree. How silly!

Ms. Ring must have seen the tear trickle down Anna's cheek and fall clumsily to the floor, leaving a splat mark.

Finally, Anna squeaked out, "I'll do the assignment over. Sorry."

"Good idea Anna. You may go back to your desk now."

Anna felt her classmates' eyes boring holes into her crimson, blistering face as she walked back to her seat.

She quietly crumpled up her persuasive essay into a tight ball. It was soft and damp in her clenched fist. Tearing a fresh, clean sheet of looseleaf out of her notebook, she decided to write her assignment about Converse being the superior sneaker. After all, everyone wore Converse, didn't they?

So, Anna stopped talking about the trees and she certainly stopped writing about them in class. But even though Anna never told her friends or teachers about her ability, her relationship with the trees continued.

On one haunting visit to the woods, Anna ventured too high up the ascending slope of a mountain in an attempt to tackle a trail that was far more advanced than her ability. She had her eyes on this particular slope for many months now and finally gathered up enough guts to try it. Putting one shaking foot in front of the other, she climbed her way precariously to a small ledge wrapping around a gray, mossy boulder. When she stopped to take a breath, she realized that she was shaking and quietly regretted her decision. Looking down, Anna gauged that a misstep would result in a fall of more than fifty feet. The ledge upon which she found herself was barely the width of her shoe. She remained frozen in place, too afraid to go either forward or backward, trembling in her pink summer shorts and sneakers. She visualized herself falling, mangling her body on the rocky outcroppings that she would certainly hit on her descent. Tumbling over and over again in the air and then finally hitting the ground; the impact would surely paralyze her at best. She sent out a silent plea through clenched eyes, “Help, please.”

At this very moment of peril, a blue spruce,one that was surely unreachable the last time Anna blinked–at least fifteen feet away and well beyond her grasp–appeared closer. And after one more blink, the tree materialized closer yet. When Anna reached out her shaky hand, she found that her high altitude positioned her parallel with the top quarter of the ancient evergreen and she was able to wrap her fingers around a thick gnarled branch, almost near the very top of the tree. Cautiously, while gripping the rough outcropping, Anna tentatively placed first one foot and then the other on a solid branch. She was then able to pull her vibrating body fully onto the powerful wood. Anna slowly climbed down the tree, descending with each careful step; she somehow knew that she wouldn’t fall, that the tree would protect her as she cascaded down its irregular body. The tree branches seemed to position themselves perfectly to catch each of Anna’s footfalls and graspings. When she finally reached the ground, she offered up a hushed thanksgiving as she wound her way towards the exit leading back to her house. What was this strange gift? And was it a gift? What did it mean? Was she a freak? ...destined to be misunderstood and ridiculed? Or was it something beautiful and special? Anna didn't know.

Anna's childhood self accepted what happened, the possibility of magic hadn't yet been beaten out of her consciousness by adults and reality. If Santa Claus and the tooth fairy were real, why not talking, moving trees that acted as the guardians of a lonesome girl?

Even though Anna knew that discussing the trees with peers or teachers would be met with jeering and skepticism, she still searched for someone in whom she could confide. She tried to tell her mother about the friendly trees and how they serenaded her on her daily visits and helped her in times of need. Maybe her mother would believe her? How foolish.

As Anna was in the middle of relating the terrifying incident on the ledge, her mother abruptly dismissed such fantasy, and with a sharp vehemence that was uncharacteristic of Beverly Parke, she spat out, "Don't be foolish Anna, trees are trees, not friends. How could you be so silly and stupid? I thought you were smarter than that!"

"But mommy, odd things happen in the woods sometimes. Sometimes the trees---"

Her words were put to an abrupt halt with Beverly's continued disgust, "I do not want to hear anymore about this. The matter is closed."

This was another of Beverly's favorite sayings. Along with "Absolutely not," her mother loved declaring matters closed when Anna was nowhere near done.

But this time, Anna couldn't quite bring herself to accept that this conversation was indeed over; she still had so much to say and so many stories to tell her unyielding and closed-off mother.

"Please, mommy...can I just finish telling you---"

"Stop talking Anna! I already told you that you are never again to talk to me about this topic. Grow up already," Beverly shrilly screamed directly into Anna's upturned and eager face. Beverly remained frozen in place, glaring down at her daughter, daring her to go on. And in the harshness of that gaze, all of Anna's hopes-her hope of finding someone to understand her, someone to listen to her, someone to acknowledge and support her experiences–faded, leaving her with a feeling of soul-crushing emptiness. "And one more thing Anna," Beverly whispered so softly and with such exposed and raw rancor that Anna cringed as she spoke the words, "If I ever find out that you have gone into the woods again, I will make you sorry you were ever born."

In the entire galaxy, no person has more power to inflict pain upon a fellow human than a mother on her young child. No form of rejection hurts more, stings more. It is a fact that mothers oftentimes exploit, sometimes knowingly and most often accompanied by extreme guilt. But Beverly Parke felt not a drop of guilt as she wielded her rigidity and cruelty against Anna at this moment in time. In fact, she felt entirely justified in doing so. And the power that Beverly Parke inflicted upon Anna at this key moment in her life, left the poor girl breathless and confused.

This exchange solidified a few thoughts in Anna's mind, the most significant being that she could never again share her secret with anyone ever again. No human could possibly understand her bond with those primeval beloved lifeforms that inhabit her thoughts and dreams. If her own mother couldn't, wouldn't understand, how could anyone else?

For a while Anna reluctantly adhered to her mother's ruling and avoided the forest. Beverly's mannerisms and words during that forbidding conversation frightened Anna in a way that she could not quite verbalize nor understand. But even as she got older, even when she was sure that fairy tales and magic couldn't possibly exist and even when she began to doubt the notion that trees could speak and move, Anna still heard the persistent calling of those trees; the whisperings arriving on the breeze wafting through her bedroom windows. So Anna's small and only act of defiance while growing up, was disobeying her mother's order to, at all costs, avoid the woods behind Ackerly Lane.

Before coming home after school, she would sneak away and lose herself in the mazes of trees behind her home. She would tell her mother that she had stayed late at school for extra help–as a straight A student, Anna certainly needed no tutoring–or for a Student Council meeting–a club that appealed little to Anna's sensibilities. Anna would carefully straighten her clothes and remove the twigs and leaves from her hair before entering through her front door, careful to keep her secret hidden, safe.

She relished the cool comfort of the trees; she continued to tell them her stories. And they continued to listen and whisper and provide. Sometimes in the clarity of the next day, those visits to the woods seemed dreamlike and far away and she doubted that what she saw and heard and felt ever truly occurred.

Chapter 8

One day, years later, Anna came to the mountains, this time accompanied and for a different sort of visit. She came with two high school classmates–friends. At sixteen years old, Anna finally realized and accepted the fact that she would never get the love nor attention she desired from her mother, though she continued in a frenzied desperate way to attempt to please her. She maintained a nearly flawless academic record, kept her room perfectly dusted and tidy, took on not only her scheduled chores, but went above and beyond to sustain the pristine condition of the house. However, no deed, no act at all, was met by her mother with any more than the briefest of nods, the tiniest of smiles. So, Anna began to look elsewhere for approval.

She found that her teachers and her peers were much easier to please. All teachers required was a good grade on an exam, which came naturally and easily to Anna. A simple "Yes, Mr. Goldman" or a "Thank you Mrs. Smith" worked wonders. All her peers required was loyalty, which Anna gave freely. So it was that Anna got her fix from them and quickly became addicted to the ease with which peers and educators endowed her with acceptance. And this need for approval, this drug-addict desire for her next score is what led her to the woods on this crisp mid-November Friday afternoon.

"My parents would kill me if they knew I was here! I told them I was sleeping at your house, Lex," Dani said.

"Yeah, we definitely can not get caught. My mom almost had a heart attack when I walked in 15 minutes late from school the other day," Lexi added.

Anna walked next to Lexi and Dani silently, butterflies playing on the insides of her rib cage. In her hands, she carried a small duffel holding a sleeping bag, flashlight and water bottle. She thought fleetingly about her sleeping bag, a childhood relic featuring the characters from *The Little Mermaid* adorning the entire top side. What would her friends think when they saw it? Would her worth dwindle in their eyes? The friendly pine trees stood guard as the three girls walked deeper into the woods and the sun sank lower in the sky. Twilight would soon be upon them, followed thereafter by darkness.

When her mother saw Anna leaving the house earlier that day, she hadn't asked many questions. Beverly resorted to a 'don't ask, don't tell' policy with her daughter. As long as Anna achieved good grades and didn't raise any eyebrows, Beverly didn't much care what

Anna did during her free time. Beverly did not know any of Anna's friends; Anna never brought them around and to be frank she didn't much care to know them. But even though she hadn't personally or physically met them, Beverly knew them enough. They were loud, giddy, giggling girls–young and stupid–who thought only about the current make-up and fashion trends. Some of them were no doubt experimenting with boys already for God's sake. Well, they'd better hope they don't end up like Beverly herself did, with some unwanted surprise growing inside of them. Bikinis don't look so cute with huge distended bellies and stretch marks.

Ms. Parke's disinterest was viewed by Anna with sadness and regret. Anna was a bright, perceptive girl and her mother's slights were not lost on her. She didn't expect her mother to protest when she left the house with her sleeping bag in tow; she told her mother only the vague lie that she was sleeping at a friend's house and would be back in the morning. Anna dimly hoped that her mother would object, that she would have some excuse to back out of the plan to which Lexi and Dani had anticipated all week, and the plan to which Anna herself had only feigned excitement in their presence. She could almost see herself calling her friends to report, "Sorry, my mom won't let me leave. Have fun though." However, there was no such luck, and here she was, trudging through the woods leading up to the mighty Adirondacks fearing what was to come when the darkness finally arrived.

"This is fine," Lexi abruptly said, "If we go too far into the woods they won't be able to find us."

The three girls dropped their duffels and spread out their sleeping bags on the soft forest floor. Anna tried to hide her nervousness as Dani and Lexi prattled on. They had done this many times before, had ventured into the woods and found solace in the comfort of their boyfriends. This was Anna's first time; she wasn't excited about being here, nor was she content to share her safe haven with others, but she did want it to be over. She wanted to put this night behind her before it had even truly begun. Long ago, Anna abandoned voicing her own doubt in the face of her friends and learned that being agreeable and going with the flow produced a more desired result.

"Are you nervous?" Lexi playfully teased, "This is your first time alone with Aaron."

"I'm not nervous," Anna lied, her quavering voice almost giving her away.

Good thing for Anna that the air was brisk and the evening chilly; the chatter of her teeth would not have gone unnoticed on a still summer evening. She had known Aaron basically all her life; she had known all her peers basically all her life. That's both the beauty and tragedy of growing up in small-town U.S.A: everyone knows everyone else and for good or ill, can trace each current day relationship back nearly to pre-school. So the same kids who sat together in the sand-box ended up making out under the bleachers in high school. Many of them will end up marrying one another because people who are born in Windsom tend to stay in Windsom.

However, it wasn't until a few months ago, when Anna found herself sitting next to Aaron on the cold metal bleachers of the high school football game that she conceived that their relationship could be anything more than strictly platonic. As their hands grazed lightly against one another, Aaron's fingers lingered on Anna's exposed wrist. Her pulse quickened under the warmth and she felt his gaze lingering on her slightly parted lips.

Over the course of the following weeks and months, Aaron tended to show up at the parties, games, and other social events at which Anna found herself. They whispered quietly in corners together, and once, Anna was sure that Aaron would try to kiss her, but they were interrupted by Peter Daniel, their clownish classmate who drunkenly stumbled into them, knocking Aaron's nearly empty beer can to the floor. Anna became increasingly aware of how Aaron looked at her, the hungriness in his eyes. He was good-looking in a conventional way: blue eyes and light curly hair; he was sweet and charismatic when it suited him, a popular 11th grader and athlete.

"Aaron told me that he doesn't even mind your birthmark," Lexi continued with a stifled giggle, "He actually thinks it's kinda cute. Last week, he told me it's the same color as Barney the Dinosaur."

Is he kidding me? Anna thought to herself. *Barney the dinosaur? Really? Some stupid purple puppet that dances around on stage for kids.*

The fact that Aaron apparently equated the color of her port-wine stain to this foolish character who was the star of a 80's children's television show, did not make Anna feel pretty nor desirable.

Dani, glancing at her watch, interrupted Anna's musings by saying, "The guys should be here any minute."

At that very moment, as if on cue, the girls heard the distant crunching of leaves and branches and the rise and swell of laughter and voices. The sounds grew nearer and a few minutes later the group of boys emerged into the clearing. Ryan, then Joey, and Aaron behind them. They dropped their bags next to Dani as the sun dropped behind the horizon. Anna avoided Aaron's searching gaze.

By 10 o'clock Lexi produced a large bottle of vodka filched from her parents' liquor cabinet. Tomorrow, she would add tap water to the mostly empty bottle and gingerly return it to its rightful place. Her parents never drank. Her father acquired a liquor collection as a result of corporate gifts and unbeknownst to him, the Kahlua bottle was mostly filled with diet cola, the Johnny Walker Scotch filled halfway with iced-tea, and next would be a watered down liter of Greygoose that the six teenagers passed around from one set of hungry lips to the next. One day, they might find out, but that day was surely in the future and to teenagers the future is not a concept that functions in their daily reality. If and when that day does come, Lexi will feign ignorance. Afterall, what could she, an innocent young girl possibly know about alcohol?

When the bottle came to Anna, she gulped down a mouthful of the burning liquid; she thought about faking it, pretending to take a sip, but she was caught doing so a week ago and thought it best to conform. Besides, the spirit would help raise her own; she would need some courage once the group became groggy and tired.

As the stars above burned white through the navy blanket of the sky and the wee hours of the night turned into the wee hours of the morning, the group paired off. Lexi and Ryan ventured off to find their own alcove of privacy, Dani and Joey did the same. Aaron came over and sat next to Anna, his face inches away. She could smell the sweet scent of liquor on his breath as he leaned close to press insistent kisses below her ear. She could feel his calloused hands groping greedily underneath her sweatshirt. She thought about how little she knew of him.

Anna imagined getting up and walking away from Aaron. In her mind, she played out the scene:

"You know what Aaron, I think I'm over this."

"What do you mean?" he would say. "I thought we were having fun."

"Well, maybe you *were having fun, but I'm definitely not," Anna would respond back.*

Aaron would look at her with those puppy dog eyes that had probably gotten him into the pants of many of her classmates. He was not used to rejection, certainly not from someone like her.

"Come on Anna," he would urge. "Don't be that way."

He would continue pressing his mouth against her throat; his hands would recommence their path up her body.

"I said, ENOUGH, Aaron."

He would look at her with a dawning understanding. He would know that his desires would not be met tonight.

Anna would stand up, gather her belongings and walk back down the wooded path through which she had entered just a little while earlier, not caring what Aaron would tell his friends when they returned, not caring what Dani and Lexi would say about Anna's abrupt departure.

But instead, Anna allowed Aaron's fingers to explore her chest, permitted his kisses to trace a path down her neck. She knew what was expected of her here, in the quiet woods with only the moon and her trees as witnesses.

This wasn't how she had imagined her first time would be. She was conditioned by the likes of *CosmoGirl* and *Seventeen Magazine* to believe that losing your virginity should be special, intimate: something experienced with the boy of your dreams, the boy you loved, the boy who brought you flowers and jewelry and chocolate. Aaron was none of those things. She didn't love him, or even truly know him. She didn't think he loved her either, nor did she expect him to. Aaron was known for his flirtatious ways with the girls of Warren Bailey High School and was better educated than she in the ways of high school relationships. Anna was Aaron's fleeting interest, his newest conquest to be savored for a time, but only until the next girl showed interest. And maybe that was the way it was supposed to be. Anna never would have dared broach the subject with her mother. Had she the courage to even ask about sex,

Beverly Parke surely would have imbibed her daughter with her detached notion of intimacy and its association with humiliation and disappointment. Lexi and Dani viewed sex as an amusing ride to be enjoyed frequently and for personal gain. So, Anna's first real and personal sexual knowledge, aside from learning about the biology of it in Health class, was experienced with this needy, drunk, teenage boy, a boy with his unyielding and expectant hardness pushed against her open thighs. Instead of saying no, Anna let herself be taken. She gave herself over freely and willingly, albeit regretfully. Only the trees whispered their disapproval.

It was over quickly, Aaron never even got around to fully undressing; instead his jeans and underwear remained snaked around his ankles, as did Anna's. He didn't ask permission, nor did he make much effort to help Anna find pleasure. While Aaron was experienced in finding his own orgasm, he knew little about female arousal, nor did he care. The selfishness of seventeen still clung to him like a heavy cologne that hadn't mellowed yet. There was a sharp pain, which instinctively brought a swell of fresh tears to Anna's tightly clenched eyes. She heard the distant sounds of Lexi and Dani, engaging in similar, yet based upon the sounds, slightly more enjoyable activities. When Aaron finally rolled off of her, and the weight of his body and the pungent scent of his breath no longer pervaded her senses, Anna felt an unfathomable emptiness, like an abandoned cave filled only with the echoes of the howling wind. She wiped between her thighs; her hand came away sticky and warm. She quickly pulled her underwear and jeans back to their rightful position and noticed only the soft snores of the upturned face lying next to her. At least one of them had come away from the encounter satisfied.

Anna feigned sleep when the rest of the teens came back to the clearing to settle down for a few hours of slumber before the sunrise. Despite her throbbing abdomen, she finally drifted off to an uneasy sleep. Anna dreamed of the mountains and the trees, but instead of the moon and its friendly cast, looming bright and large in the sky of her nightmare were the disapproving eyes of her mother.

Chapter 9

A few years later, when it was time to make a serious decision about her future, Anna couldn't quite bring herself to say goodbye to the Adirondacks that brought tranquility to her soul and the trees that continued their soft dialogue, so even though her grades were stellar, and she concluded high school ranked fourth in her graduating class, she chose to attend a local community college rather than accept some of the more prestigious offers from NYU and Columbia University. She was at peace with her choice, but there was no excitement as she accepted the rolled up scroll that was her diploma presented to her by Principal Corgan on graduation day. A meaningless paper: a formality.

Anna was hurt though unsurprised that her mother didn't attend the ceremony. But then again, maybe it was better that Beverly didn't come; her presence would have made things more awkward. They would have both been forced to put on a sort of charade, pretending that their relationship was much more than it actually was. The loving mother, the doting daughter.

Beverly had more practical things to do: laundry that needed folding, dishes that needed scrubbing, floors that needed mopping. She didn't organize a graduation party or a celebratory dinner. Beverly didn't believe in the fuss that often accompanied such milestones. Graduation was simply an expectation for Beverly Parke, the logical conclusion of a high school experience.

So instead of spending her graduation afternoon with a doting family, Anna tagged along with Lexi's family. Mr. and Mrs. Donaldson planned an elaborate luncheon at Matteo's, an upscale Italian restaurant in Sioux Falls. Sioux Falls, located about fifteen minutes away, is a bit more developed than Windsom and boasts a trendy downtown area that appeals to a younger clientele. Local realtors proudly refer to the town as "up and coming." A nomer that many in Windsom wished their town boasted.

Mrs. Donaldson spared no detail for her daughter's special occasion. From the tiny pink roses arranged neatly in sparkling glass vases to the charcuterie table laden with creamy cheeses and decadent Italian sliced meats, dotted with blackberries shining like jewels interspersed throughout the display, Mrs. Donaldson's pride in her daughter literally radiated throughout the dimly lit room. And even though Mrs. Donaldson provided

Anna an identical tiara and matching sash that sported the word 'graduate,' that her own daughter wore, and even though Anna's name was added to the cake directly below Lexi's in scalloped pink buttercream, Anna felt like an unwanted guest, an intruder. A polite afterthought. That's what she was at this party, wasn't she? The supporting actress, alone and unimportant in contrast to Lexi.

When Anna came through the doors of 43 Ackerly lane at 6 o'clock pm, still wearing the blue graduation robe, the sequined tiara and sash and holding her tasseled cap under her left armpit, Beverly gave her daughter one of her tight-lipped smiles and went about reheating their dinner of leftover chicken casserole from the night before, a perfect meal for the occasion. Leftovers seemed to speak volumes. Beverly didn't ask about the ceremony, nor did she inquire about the luncheon. They ate in silence, both pondering the life that lay before them, unraveling like the spool of a kite gradually beginning its journey upwards.

As Lexi and Dani prepared for their exciting journey of college, Anna began applying for a summer job. Her two friends would be rooming together next year at Siena College–a small private university located about an hour and a half away from Windsom. They insisted that Anna come visit often, and Anna half-heartedly promised she would, but as they drove away, headed south, with a car packed to the hilt with extra-long sheets and shower caddies and Ramen Noodles, Anna knew that it was the beginning of the end of their friendship. All three of them knew it. New places, new faces; out with the old, in with the new. They were moving on; Anna was staying put. It made Anna momentarily sad to think that her own life held no such excitement nor adventure, but after all she had made her choice. She must live with it.

Anna secured a job as a cashier at the local Food-Mart and dwindled August away dressed in a maroon apron ringing up the groceries belonging to those faces that she had seen all her life. She learned all about Mrs. Lycan's arthritis and Mr. Sheehan's multiple grandchildren, scattered all throughout the country. She heard all about the blue-sequined dress Mrs. Casey would wear to her daughter's impromptu wedding (it was currently at the tailor–too big in the bust), and Mr. Tulley's bad left hip (he was scheduled for a replacement surgery at Mercy Hospital in Albany in early march).

People haggled with her over expired coupons and tried to procure discounts on yogurt that was set to expire the next day. She learned to double bag milk and not to bag the eggs. In her early days at The Food Mart, she committed the sin of placing the eggs in the brown paper bag first and then loading the remaining grocery items on top. As soon as Mr. McCann picked up his parcel, the telltale crunching sound informed her of her misstep. It took her a solid hour to clean the gooey egg whites off the grocery belt and floor. But Anna learned quickly, if only to avoid complaints and conflict. She took no pride in her job title, but valued the steady, although meager paycheck.

As the days wound away, Anna found herself bored and lonely, unfulfilled and on edge. On pay day, she would walk over to Chilly Scoops and eat her double fudge sundae at the counter, watching the tourists plan their schedules for a day out on Lake George or an afternoon exploring Fort William Henry. These people didn't want to secure a room in the hustle and bustle of Lake George Village, a major tourist destination boasting lake-front resorts and honky-tonk souvenir shops about forty-five minutes away, and instead thought that they would save a few bucks at a Windsom hotel. She would then go home to a silent evening spent with her increasingly quiet and faraway mother. Wasn't there more to life than the predictable day-in and day-out routine she experienced?

On the rare afternoons when she found herself with some free time (most of her days were spent at The Food Mart), Anna retreated to the woods, careful to avoid the clearing where she spent that fateful and disconcerting night with Aaron. The thought of that night made her feel dirty and cheap. She had spent one additional evening with Aaron and his eager hands two weeks after their initial encounter. After that he began to tire of her, and his hungry eyes alighted on a sophomore named Jamie Wheeler. This was just as well. She had no intention nor desire to pursue anything of substance with him.

She came to accept the hushed discourse of the evergreens and the favors they seemed to bestow upon her, and as she came to view the oddity more logically, she tried to attribute the murmurings to her wild imagination and the physical assistance they provided to the weather. That bent branch that served as a perfect handrail must have been put there by last night's storm.

The soft leaves that cushioned her landing when she took a particularly precocious tumble over a high bluff must have been a result of the wind. Now that she was approaching twenty, she couldn't possibly still believe that trees could talk, and move, and communicate and help her...could she?

As August ran its lazy course and September blazed, hot and hazy, Anna began her classes at Windsom Community College. At her high school guidance counselor's urging, she declared a major in Business over her initial desire to pursue Sociology or Ecology. Ms. Gibbons told her that Sociology was a foolish and inauspicious choice, unlikely to lead to much success and Ecology was even worse. On the first day of classes, Anna sat in the back of the palatial lecture halls and lost herself in the drone of the professors. After class, Anna retained her job at Food-Mart, saving up her bi-weekly paychecks for no foreseeable financial goal. And so it was that Anna's days became an endless stream of school and then work. School and then work.

In the beginning of the school year, she exchanged a few phone conversations with Lexi and Dani. They told Anna all about dorm-life and the college boys with whom they spent time. The conversations dwindled as September turned to October, and by the time the winter holidays came around, and Lexi and Dani decided to spend Christmas with their sorority sisters instead of returning home to Windsom, Anna barely heard from them at all.

Jenna Sawyer, the second cashier at Food-Mart, requested time off for the holidays, so Anna found herself, on Christmas Eve, in an empty grocery store, eating a ham and cheese Lunchable right out of its plastic tray seated at a small stool, gazing out the storefront window, watching snow accumulate on the car windshields parked out front. Every so often, Anna caught a glimpse of her own reflection in the misty glass. She thought that she looked decidedly older, a frowning 19 year old, pretty, but plain. She had a slim, but curvy figure hidden underneath her work uniform, and her auburn hair, once frizzy and dull, now had soft, shiny waves if she were to free it from the elastic tie pinning it to top of her head. In Anna's perception, it was not her figure, nor her hair, or even her shining hazel eyes that stood out in the gaze of her reflection; in Anna's mind, her only truly striking feature was an embarrassing mark scarring her rounded cheek.

Anna's mother didn't have any objection to Anna working both Christmas Eve and Christmas Day. They had no engagements to keep nor family to visit. They hadn't even bothered to decorate the house this year, so 43 Ackerly Lane was the one plot of darkness against a sea of festive, twinkling red and green and yellow lights. Beverly actually preferred to spend the holiday alone; she was gearing up to re-organize the kitchen pantry, muttering to herself *A place for everything and everything in its place*. She purchased a brand new tag creator from Walmart last week and couldn't wait to color code and label each shelf. And Anna preferred the quiet contemplation of work to an awkward, unfulfilling, and assuredly disappointing Christmas with her mother. So the holiday passed quietly by for the Parkes, each one solitary in her own solitary world.

As the clock struck midnight on New Year's Eve a few days later, Anna was engulfed in a deep slumber. She no longer tried to engage her mother in the traditional pomp and circumstance associated with this night. When she was a child, she used to write her New Year's Resolution on a piece of loose-leaf paper and as the gleaming ball made its way down its electric path in Times Square, she would grip the piece of paper in her sweaty palms and close her eyes, praying for a new year filled with happiness, for a new year filled with love. During her small tradition, Ms. Parke always said, “Anna, aren't you getting too old for this foolishness?” As each year peeled slowly away, and Anna found her life always the same, the fairy tale of December 31st and all of its resplendent promise seemed a cruel reminder of reality. So tonight, wrapped up in the cozy, comfortable cocoon of her bed blankets and sheets, Anna dreamed of colors and light and love. Beverly Parke sat up in the living room, watching *Dick Clarke's Rockin' New Year* on ABC. Neither woman–because Anna Parke was at this point indeed a woman–knew that this year would be different. Neither woman could possibly know that what was soon to come, would change Anna Parke in the most extraordinary way.

Chapter 10

January seemed to stretch out forever. Anna finished her first college semester and was in the process of adjusting to a new schedule of courses including English Literature and Psychology. She was barreling through the general requirements before her business classes would officially commence. She wasn't overly enthusiastic about her business courses; she couldn't quite imagine finding anything of interest in an Economics or Accounting textbook. In contrast, she much preferred learning about the internal workings of the human mind, or the nuances of Romantic poetry. The poetry of Byron appealed to her, with its melancholy and defiant hero, Childe Harold; Percy Shelley surprised her with his visionary imagination and interchanges with nature. She imagined him pondering the Adirondacks and composing some beautiful ode to the beauty that cast shadows on her own small backyard.

Anna started to avoid the woods, even though she yearned to immerse herself in the solicitude of their safety. The trees and their discourse became too puzzling for her adult mind to absorb. She was too old to believe in make-believe, and yet the magic that she experienced there in the peaceful greenery, though it had significantly faded over the years, was still there. This is an unfortunate result of growing up. As the years progress, the wonder of childhood and all life's infinite possibilities diminish as reality sets in. But now, as an adult, the trees began to frighten her and there were times when Anna lucidly wondered whether or not she was losing her mind.

When she wasn't in class, Anna maintained her job at The Food Mart. The endless scanning of groceries and the mundane activity of bagging and sorting food, was broken only by her customers' attempts at friendly conversation. However, even though the questions asked by her neighbors were kind and well-intentioned in nature, all they did for Anna was highlight her loneliness. They asked her about college and her mom; they asked if she was dating anyone; they asked what her career plans were and whether she still kept in touch with Lexi and Dani. "I heard they are studying abroad in Rome this semester," said one well-meaning shopper. When Anna had to respond that "Yes, college is fine," "My mom is well, thank you," "No I'm not seeing anyone, and I have no specific employment path in mind," and finally "No, I haven't really spoken to Lexi and Dani in a while," she was left with a feeling of endless emptiness. For Anna, the new year began as inauspiciously as the last one ended.

The cold seeped into the crevices of 43 Ackerly Lane; it seeped into Anna's bones. She had trouble envisioning a future for herself and was unsatisfied both mentally and spiritually, but couldn't quite find a solution.

Beverly Parke gradually ran out of things to itemize and organize and clean around the house, so her latest crusade was centered around harassing Anna. Beverly Parke never took much interest in her daughter's appearance. As long as Anna's face was washed, hair was combed, and shoes were free of dirt, Ms. Parke basically left Anna alone. However, as the winter winds blew, icy and severe, Beverly's attention was drawn to her nineteen year old daughter's pale face.

One evening in early March, as the two women sat down to their usual quiet dinner, Anna still wearing her maroon Food Mart apron, She felt her mother's intense gaze upon her. She was used to her mother's scrutiny, but learned to live under its heavy-handed judgment years ago. But this night felt somehow different.

As the meal ended, and the last bits of crumbs were emptied from the blue plastic dustpan into the garbage can, Ms. Parke said, "Now really Anna, you will need to look for a more promising job soon. You can't work forever at The Food Mart. No respectable establishment will hire a girl who looks like her face has a mud splotch on it. It's time to have that ugliness removed."

The comment stunned Anna into silence for a variety of reasons. On one hand, Anna had difficulty believing that her mother was truly concerned about her future employability. Beverly had never before shown an interest neither in Anna's education nor in Anna's career goals; in Anna's mind, her mother always assumed that her daughter would simply benefit from the inheritance left by her grandparents. And even though Anna never intended on relying on this inheritance and always planned on having an independent career–even though she hadn't yet figured out what her career would be–she never expressed this thought to her mother. On the other hand, Beverly Parke had made off-handed comments about this birthmark on a few occasions that stuck out in Anna's memory like shiny pennies.

Anna didn't respond to her mother's remark at first; she wasn't overly fond of her birthmark. She had, over the years, contemplated asking if it could be removed, but ultimately she accepted it as a part of her, good or bad. Over the years she grew accustomed to it, maroon in hue and about the length of a thumb held up against her cheek. Anna opened her mouth twice trying to form some words of acknowledgement in return to her mother's command. All she came up with was a timid and hesitant, "I don't know mom; I've kind of gotten used to it."

"Don't be ridiculous Anna; it's ludicrous. I am going to put a call through to Dr. Hammond tomorrow to get a referral for a local dermatologist," retorted Beverly. Unused to anything but complete compliance from her daughter, the tone of Ms. Parke's voice raised a notch, but only a notch as she delivered her decree. She folded the dish towel neatly next to the sink, tied the white plastic garbage bag closed and hauled it outside, closing the front door behind her as she went. To Beverly, the matter was closed. To Anna, the matter was only beginning.

Anna imagined voicing some of her doubts:

"No mom. You're not going to 'put a call through to Dr. Hammond tomorrow.' You are going to leave me the hell alone and learn to love me the way I am."

But of course Anna said none of this. She had no doubt that her mother would follow through with her promise to find a dermatologist, so when Ms. Parke informed her late the next day that she had an appointment with Dr. Susan Richmond this coming Wednesday, Anna was melancholy, but unsurprised. Anna had a few days to think before the appointment and decided that she wouldn't put up a fuss. There was a fleeting moment where protest entered her mind, but what would be the point? The birthmark had become her mother's latest obsession. Ms. Parke surely would not relent until Anna was clean...until her face shone like the gleaming kitchen floor. *A place for everything and everything in its place.*

The night before the appointment, Anna took the sheet off of the dollhouse that still remained in the far corner of her bedroom. Maybe she was longing for the simplicity of childhood, looking for traces of the fleeting magic it held. The room retained its girlish feel. Beverly Parke never allowed Anna to adorn the plaster walls with the posters that she purchased a few years back from the vintage record shop on Main Street. *No way are you poking thumbtacks into those walls*, she said. *And that tacky putty, that will take the paint right off.* So the posters depicting Pearl Jam and Nirvana and Stone Temple Pilots remained rolled up in their shiny cellophane luster, tucked away in her compact closet.

She admired the dollhouse with a fleeting sadness. The comforting and musty smell brought her immediately back to her girlhood, so much of which was spent lovingly in front of this relic, enacting her fairytale world of love and security. Anita, the mother figurine, certainly would have loved her daughter in spite of a tiny imperfection. Mr. Billingsly, the brown-haired patriarch wearing a tawny tweed suit and hat, surely would have played a game of catch with his son and daughter when he returned from a full day of work at the office. Brother Benjamin and sister Anna would surely have playfully argued over who would act as banker and dole out pink and blue and green and yellow paper money in their nightly Monopoly game. Peering into the lovingly furnished rooms, she saw the small pile of remains: the crumbled porcelain head of the little girl doll, Anna, with her decapitated body lying nearby. She vaguely remembered the gratifying crunch she felt as she buried her heel into this beautiful figurine. The guilt returned full-force. Such a pretty, delicate thing, destroyed by her immature anger. How much this antique had cost her late grandfather, she couldn't be sure. But it most certainly wasn't inexpensive. Poor little Anna, crushed under the boot heel of life. She gazed momentarily out of her window. The light breeze gently ruffled the edges of the woods that bordered the back end of 43 Ackerly Lane. The trees looked on in tranquility as Anna hastily replaced the sheet and covered her precious dollhouse once again.

Chapter II

"It's not just a case of carving it out, stitching you up, and being done with it, but it is a relatively simple process," said Dr. Linda Richmond as she examined Anna's cheek on a Wednesday in March.

She had gone through this same conversation dozens of times over the course of her career and had spent countless hours discussing with her patients the benefits and drawbacks of the elective cosmetic procedure about which Anna inquired. It presented no challenge to her, and if Linda was being honest, she had grown tired of giving so much attention to what she viewed as mere vanity. She should have been helping patients cure their late stages of melanoma and treating more severe and pressing skin disorders. These cosmetic procedures–blemish removal, skin lightening, Botox–were quite frankly beneath her.

Dr. Richmond found herself droning on, "It is port-wine stain; the medical term for it is nevus flammeus. Three out of every one thousand children are born with similar markings, so they are relatively uncommon. The mark can be treated with a pulse-dye laser to gradually lighten the color over time. It's a relatively new technology. The red blood cells in the area should absorb the laser and gradually lighten with each treatment."

"Will it hurt?" her patient asked.

They always want to know if it will hurt. The degree to which they must submit in order to attain that flawless complexion, that wrinkle-free smile. They all wanted perfection, but very few wanted to pay the price that comes along with it!

Linda droned robotically on, "The treatments can be quite uncomfortable and many patients choose to be put under general anesthesia for the process, which should take no longer than eight to ten minutes. The area will be sore and raw for about three weeks following the procedure, but nothing too terrible."

"Ok," mumbled Anna. "How many laser treatments will I need?"

"Probably about 7-10 over the course of the next few months, depending on how well your nevus responds to the treatment."

The doctor answered all of Anna's questions and felt the young woman becoming more and more discouraged as the conversation progressed. Maybe there was more to this case than she had originally thought.

Linda noticed Anna Parke glance around the room, taking in the framed degrees proudly blazing the names of prestigious schools: University of Chicago, University of Pittsburgh Medical School. She probably wondered why a person with such credentials found herself with a minor dermatology position in no-man's-land Windsom, New York. Dr. Richmond often found herself wondering the same thing. Why had the course of her life led her here when she was destined for far greater prospects? But what Anna couldn't know, and what Dr. Richmond would certainly not reveal, was that Linda grew up five miles away from Windsom, in an even more remote town, one with only one traffic light and one gas station. Anna didn't know that Dr. Richmond's mother was currently a patient in the local nursing home suffering from the late throes of Dementia. Dr. Richmond would have far preferred to accept the more appealing job offer she received from NYU–an offer that could have skyrocketed her budding career–but she couldn't possibly have moved so far away from her mother. She was all her mother had. Her only family. Not that her mother even recognized Linda anymore; the Dementia had taken too strong of a grasp on her mind. Family has a way of inhibiting a person's freedom in many ways, and the doctor was momentarily angry and defensive for her life choices that landed her in this very exam room.

Had the two women met and conversed under different circumstances, they would both have been surprised to learn how similar their relationships with their mothers truly were, how much comfort they could have offered one another, how thoroughly they could have empathized with one another's plight. But maybe that exchange is reserved for a different life, a different reality, a different tale. And now, instead of taking comfort in Anna, as a woman with a shared experience, Linda Richmond felt simply indifferent and mildly frustrated–feelings that the doctor kept in check as she went through the motions of this appointment. After all, she had a long day ahead of her.

Chapter 12

The medical paper that lined the exam chair crinkled under Anna's jeans. The phrases "simple process," and "nothing too terrible" stood out like a blinding glare on her retina. Anna weakly hoped that Dr. Richmond would report that the surgery would be a complicated affair, rendering her face deeply scarred; had the doctor replied in this fashion, she would have had an excuse to return home from the appointment without a date for the first laser treatment. Her mother may have relented in her pursuit had Anna truthfully been able to report that the treatments would leave a more discernible mark than the one already there. Maybe not. Maybe her mother would have expected Anna to go through with it anyway. Over the course of the past few days, Anna became more and more sure that her mother's campaign had less to do with the birthmark and its impact on Anna's future and more to do with Beverly's compulsive need for order and dominance and maybe something else also that Anna couldn't quite put her finger upon. Whatever her mother's true motives were, there was something unsettling about the relentlessness of her pursuit against the birthmark. How could such a small imperfection spur such a reaction in a mother. Or perhaps 'How' is the wrong word. Maybe the more precise word is 'Why.'

Therefore, when Anna handed over her credit card so the front-desk attendant could process her co-pay, she turned her attention to the next window with the sign announcing 'Scheduling' printed in blue. She left the office and emerged into the bright coldness with a receipt for her copay and a small white card reminding her that she had a laser appointment scheduled at the local out-patient facility in Chester, the neighboring town, in exactly two weeks from today.

When she walked into her home on Ackerly Lane, her mother said, "So, what's the plan for removal?"

It sounded to Anna like her mother was talking about an old piece of furniture that had to be carried out or *removed*. Something unwanted, unloved...something disgusting and useless.

Anna relayed the information along with the date of the first scheduled procedure and was met with Ms. Parke's usual slight nod.

"Better off Anna. The sooner the better. Now I can look at you when I eat dinner instead of averting my eyes."

The harshness and abruptness with which Beverly Parke spoke those words almost knocked Anna off her feet. Anna knew that the mark was blatantly noticeable, but the fact that it evoked such feelings of nausea and disgust within her mother was a new notion that Anna chewed on as she turned on her heels and walked directly out the front door she had entered not five minutes earlier.

Anna visualized a different ending to this conversation. Instead of allowing her mother to insult her, instead of walking out the door giving her mother the last word she concocted this screenplay:

Anna– dripping with sarcasm: Wow mom. That's a nice thing to say to your daughter.

Beverly– in a matter-of-fact tone: Better to know the truth.

Anna– her anger growing: The truth? The fact that I disgust you? The fact that you can't even look at me while you eat? The fact that you have been a judgemental, unloving bitch my entire life and that I hope to God I don't grow up to be anything like you?

Beverly Parke's silence echoed through the empty house.

Who was Anna kidding? Even imagining this exchange felt foreign and uncomfortable to Anna. But more so, it was unrealistic. Anna didn't stand a chance of coming out victorious in a battle against her mother. She remained outside the front door of her home, fuming with unspoken rage and embarrassment.

Beverly Parke, still relatively young, only fifty-eight years old, began to display increasing sharpness and bitterness as the years progressed. The emerging strands of gray hair and the deepening wrinkles around her eyes and mouth were not lost on Anna. Beverly Parke, usually agile and light on her feet, took to her daily and welcomed chores as of late with increasing deliberateness and slowness. Anna guessed that this is simply what happens with age. Of course she could never ask her mother about it. The unbridled anger that Anna felt regarding her mother's insensitivity pushed all concern for Beverly's well-being out of mind.

Anna raced towards the woods, even though logic told her not to, her heart needed some comfort. And she knew where to find it.

The Adirondacks materialized before her sporting their winter white coats. Her breath puffed out in clouds as she forced the icy air deep into her lungs; it burned as it hit the back of her throat, but she welcomed the cold rush it gave her. She ran until her legs began to tire at which point she sunk down at the base of a pine tree, buried her face into her knees, and wept in loud, heaving sobs. The sound of Anna's cries echoed in the stillness. Even the trees and all the solace they offered, couldn't stop her tears from falling.

Chapter 13

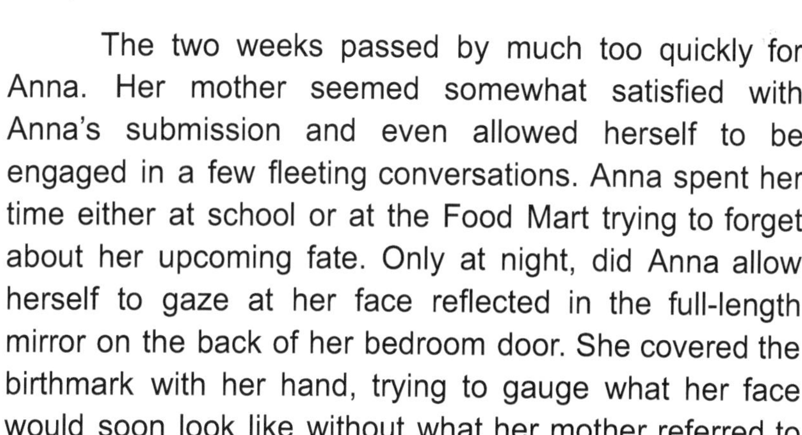

The two weeks passed by much too quickly for Anna. Her mother seemed somewhat satisfied with Anna's submission and even allowed herself to be engaged in a few fleeting conversations. Anna spent her time either at school or at the Food Mart trying to forget about her upcoming fate. Only at night, did Anna allow herself to gaze at her face reflected in the full-length mirror on the back of her bedroom door. She covered the birthmark with her hand, trying to gauge what her face would soon look like without what her mother referred to as that "nagging wine stain." She would look pretty, she decided…generic, but pretty. Maybe being generic wasn't so bad. Like that go-to black dress that every woman owns…simple, plain, forgettable, but able to blend in with the crowd.

The morning of April 2nd was warm and clear. One of those days that tricks Windsom residents into believing that Spring and warmer weather is closer than it really is, like a lover giving a taste of what is to come because to experience it now is too sweet, too overwhelming for the senses. Anna was scheduled to check in for her procedure at 9am and since the clinic was located in the next town over, Ms. Parke consented to drive her daughter the 12 miles east down Route 17. Of course she did. Would she drive Anna ten blocks to a friend's house? Certainly not. But to remove this blemish? To exert her will over her daughter and make sure it was done right? Absolutely. The trip was a pleasant one for Beverly Parke. Anna couldn't have said the same.

The ride to Chester Surgical Center was quiet; neither of the Parke women made an attempt at conversation, not that Beverly ever made the attempt. Most conversations started as a result of Anna trying to escape the unrelenting awkwardness between them, even if only for a few paltry minutes.

Beverly pulled up in front of the gray, stony building and informed Anna, "I'll wait outside. Come out when you are done. And don't make a big fuss about it." Beverly Parke certainly wasn't going to make "a fuss" about it. She much preferred the solitude of her car to playing the role of the concerned mother in the waiting room.

And with those words of encouragement, Anna opened the passenger door of her mother's silver Buick Century and walked through the entrance.

Anna was directed to the "check in" desk at which she gave her name and identification to the slight, red-haired woman with a name tag labeled 'Michelle' seated behind the counter. In return Anna was given a clipboard and instructed to complete the attached paperwork. She printed her name and address neatly on the allotted lines albeit without enthusiasm and filled out a list of questions about family history as best as she could; Anna knew next to nothing of the health of her ancestors-she didn't even know their names. She returned the paperwork to 'Michelle' and sat down, with her purse on her lap and her legs crossed at the ankles to wait.

The twenty minutes before a young nurse called her name seemed interminable. She envisioned her mother, seated comfortably behind the steering wheel of her car, quietly reading the morning newspaper and sipping the green tea she had carefully poured into her dusty pink travel mug this morning before leaving the house. Safe and secure in her car, knowing her daughter was doing her bidding. Beverly must be feeling small pangs of triumph in the minor battle she had waged against the birthmark. Anna herself felt defeated.

Anna allowed herself to be escorted to the small surgical room. She was given a few moments of privacy to remove her faded blue jeans, burnt-orange knitted sweater and undergarments, which she buried in the folds of her discarded denim, and attire herself in the thin, papery medical robe. Goose pimples popped out all over her exposed arms and legs. The harsh lighting made her appear pale and veiny in its unforgiving glare. She waited for Dr. Richmond to walk through the breezy doorway and begin her poking and prodding and lasering. Anna's mind wandered to the woods, but kept returning to the image of Beverly Parke, warm and toasty in the sedan, sure in the knowledge that life was in order: neat and tidy on a tilted planet.

Chapter 14

Dr. Linda Richmond breezed through the doorway, already wearing her green surgical mask and cap.

"Ready to go Anna? Don't look so scared...your face will be flawless in no time at all," she said in a light, airy tone intended to make Anna feel at ease in the sterility of this wintery medical room and to hide her own feelings about the futility of such a procedure.

Linda had a particularly rough evening last night with her mother, who was becoming more and more difficult and agitated as the Dementia ate away at her sanity. Her mother insisted that the night-time nurse was trying to steal her jewelry from the black lacquered case resting on top of her bureau. The orderly had to call

Linda, which he didn't like to do, to try and talk some sense into her deranged and confused parent. When Linda arrived at the facility, she found her mother, red-faced and screaming, threatening to phone the local police station to report the theft. Even when the poor accused nurse opened the top drawer to show everyone that the goods were in fact misplaced and not stolen, her mother was inconsolable. At some point, Linda signed off on forced sedation, and while her mother slept the drug-induced sleep of Diazepam, Linda herself had slept the night in the stiff easy chair in the corner of her mother's room. Now, she couldn't quite ease the tension that had developed in her neck and shoulders.

Nervousness was to be expected, but in Linda Richmond's experience, usually for the types of procedures she performed, the feelings of excitement and anticipation diminished all negativity. But there was something different in the air of the room today. Maybe unease, fear, resignation. Dr. Richmond couldn't quite put her finger on it, but as she looked at the pale young woman seated on the table in front of her, she once again suspected that perhaps the case of Anna Parke had more substance to it, more than meets the eye.

Linda couldn't know that her simple question and following comment produced a feeling of near panic in Anna. Anna didn't know if she was ready, if she really wanted this, if this procedure would make her mother love her, if she should have a flawless face when inside she felt defective and broken.

As Dr. Richmond waited for her patient's reply, her gaze locked with Anna's. The doctor noticed a perceptible change move into Anna's stare; her eyes sharpened. It was almost as if Linda heard a 'click' and a new girl was sitting in front of her. Gone was the anxiety and hesitation, and in its place, the doctor perceived a newfound defiance, a confidence that hadn't been there a moment ago.

Linda asked again, "Ready to go, Anna?"

"No. I don't think I am."

Chapter 15

Anna's breath came in short, shallow, ragged gasps; her heart beat insistently on the insides of her rib cage, a trapped bird desperate to be free.

Anna felt dizzy, light-headed. "No, I don't think I am," Anna whispered.

"Come again sweetheart; I couldn't hear you," Dr. Richmond responded looking up from her clipboard.

"No," Anna said, "I'm not ready. I think I've changed my mind," clearer this time.

What was she doing? Her internal alarm system was blaring as she said those confusing and contradictory words.

"Alright," the doctor said, minor surprise playing in the depth of her smiling eyes.

Dr. Richmond talked on about rescheduling in case Anna should reconsider, but Anna didn't hear most of what the doctor said. She knew there would be no next time. She had a sudden and profound defiance come upon her like a strong wave smashing into an unsuspecting shore. She thought about her life up until now, a life of saying yes, a life inhibited by quiet and melancholy consent. She felt a sudden solidarity with this birthmark, this deep mahogany blemish augmenting her pale complexion; she felt a protectiveness steal over her that was as intense as it was unexpected.

She quickly disrobed, not even bothering to hide her nakedness from Dr. Richmond, who was still explaining the intricacies of medical billing, dressed quickly, relishing the feel of the cold metallic zipper scraping lightly on her outer thighs as she pulled her jeans to their rightful place on her hips. She didn't even make an attempt to close the brass button at the top. She threw herself into her sweater, stuffed her bra hastily into her purse, grabbed her winter coat, and raced out of that room just as quickly as her feet could take her.

Anna fled that building as though she were running from the plague; with each step she felt the burden bearing down on her shoulders easing a bit. By the time she reached her mother's car, her eyes were glowing, every nerve in her body trembling and alive. She didn't have time to anticipate her mother's reaction; she felt liberated for the first time–empowered by her ability to make a decision for herself, unencumbered by the desires imposed upon her by others. When she went to enter the car, she found the door locked against her; her mother's wide eyed countenance blurred by the thick glass passenger side window.

Rather than unlocking the door with the automatic mechanism, Beverly Parke rolled down the passenger window and said, "What happened? Did you get the date mixed up?"

"No mom, I don't want to do it. I'm not going to do it! I know the birthmark bothers you, but it doesn't bother me; it's part of me!" The words poured from her mouth before she had time to think them back in.

"Anna," her mother shot back, "it's a disgusting blemish. You could be quite pretty if you had it removed. People could look in your eyes when they talk to you instead of being drawn to your cheek. We agreed that this was the best course of action! You cannot just recklessly change your mind."

"But I *can* change my mind! I never agreed. I don't care if other people find me gross or ugly; can't you just accept me for who I am?" It was said. It couldn't be unsaid. Anna couldn't be sure why she felt so suddenly emboldened to finally speak her mind. Maybe she didn't even quite know her mind until she started speaking. Maybe a person only gets a certain amount of 'yeses' and she had maxed them out, used them all up. Maybe she simply reached her quota. But she felt a sudden protectiveness over the mark and for the first time in her life, she was not going to back down.

Beverly Parke's face was unreadable. She didn't yell, she didn't try to force Anna to reconsider. She opened her mouth as if she would speak; she almost said something. Maybe Anna would have been given a more solid sense of closure if she had. But instead, Beverly Parke rolled up the window, put the car into gear, and tentatively exited the parking lot, leaving Anna alone and behind in the chilly morning.

Anna didn't quite know what to do. And she couldn't quite believe that her mother simply left her. She didn't exactly know what to expect, but it certainly wasn't this. Anna stood in the middle of the parking lot of the Chester Surgical Center for quite some time clenching and unclenching her fists and trying to form a cohesive plan in her head. Should she go back into the surgical center and beg the doctor to perform the procedure? If the doctor couldn't take her now, she could certainly reschedule for another date. No. She was not going to withdraw back into acquiescence. She hadn't yet even had the chance to enjoy her newfound voice. Should she go home and try to talk the matter out with her mother? Maybe later, not now. They both needed some time alone. She rummaged through her purse and was luckily able to produce a crumpled up twenty dollar bill and some assorted loose change. She vaguely remembered passing a Diner about a mile or so down Route 17, so Anna began walking, grateful for the temporary destination.

"One," Anna said when the waitress standing behind the shiny red counter asked her how many people were in her party.

Anna dimly thought about how all diners feel exactly the same–how they all have the same chrome mirrored facade, the same glass display featuring the decadently iced, glossy and sprinkled cookies and individual cake slices. Is there some special wholesaler that specializes in the mass production of scalloped butter cookies with rainbow sprinkles? How come they all always have a small metal bowl containing green and white chalky mints that dissolve like antacids on your tongue?

Anna was brought to a small rear table with a wonky base; some previous customer had obviously found the movement annoying and had unsuccessfully tried to fix it with a few cardboard coasters jammed beneath one of the legs protruding from the center pole. Anna sat down and stared out the window; she almost didn't hear the server ask for her order. She didn't think she could choke down a single, solitary crumb of food, so she ordered a coffee.

"Is that all?" asked the waitress.

"That's all," Anna replied.

The thought of facing her mother seemed daunting to Anna as she reflected on the consequence of standing up to her mother for the very first time in her life. She wasn't sure if she could face her mother, but at least, she thought, she had begun to face herself.

Anna drank her coffee black, relishing the smooth feel of the white ceramic mug against her lips. The bitter liquid warmed her soul as the morning unfurled around her.

Chapter 16

Now

As Anna gazed at these ominous boxes piled up less than five feet away from her, the memory of that morning in the Diner and everything both leading up to it and following it flooded her senses, like uninvited intruders making camp in enemy territory. She spent the last five years trying to forget, but gazing around her cluttered apartment she came to realize that in trying to banish her past, she had become trapped by it. Her messy living conditions were so clearly a rebellion against her mother's clean-obsessed ways; her sexual promiscuity and nights of drunken revelry at Don's sat in stark contrast to her mother's prudishness. She had become a bad cliche: the antithesis of the woman she both idolized and feared.

At the time, Anna thought that her rebellion would make her life better, freer, happier in some way. But, as she gazed around her small apartment, where she could measure her life in the scant and impersonal possessions scattered around, she wasn't so sure. Would she have been better off going through with the surgery, living in the tidy home on Ackerly Lane? Or would her mother have found some other small scar to protest? Some other blemish with which to contend? Even though Anna suspected that the latter was a more likely possibility, she did not know the answer to these questions that swam around her heavy brain as the hangover took a more localized form: a throbbing headache at her temples.

She remembered her cab ride home from the Diner that fateful afternoon. She remained at that wobbly table for three hours and four cups of coffee, mustering up the courage to go home. She wished she had another option, a family member's house or a friend's, but she had no place else to go and nothing else to do, and the few remaining dollars in her wallet could only buy so much time. Between the caffeine and the nerves, her stomach was a rumbling mess. By the time the cabbie dropped her off at the corner of Acklerly Lane, Anna's stomach was gurgling and burbling, the hot liquid sloshing around like water in a metal bucket. She gazed longingly at the woods gathered behind the row of neat houses and well-kept lawns. They stood tall in quiet solidarity. At that moment, she wished that she could go to them, disappear into their comfortable shade, but didn't dare delay the inevitable conversation with her mother a moment longer.

Anna remembered how she had rehearsed a million conversations in her mind on the walk down the street to her house. Her favorite scenario was a dialogue in which her mother understood and actually apologized for forcing the issue in the first place. But it became quite clear that this was solely a fairytale when Anna pushed open the front door; it was already nighttime: 7pm. The house was dark and quiet; her mother had already retired to her bedroom, as evidenced by the closed door. Anna flipped the lightswitch in the hallway and the harsh glare of the living room fixture projected uneasily into the gloom. When Anna's eyes came into focus, she perceived a large duffel bag filled to capacity in the center of the room. On top of the duffel lay a single piece of paper displaying her mother's flowing script:

> *Since it is quite clear that we no longer see eye-to-eye, I have arranged with Mr. Lee, the owner of the Chinese take-out restaurant on Main Street, for you to take immediate occupancy of the small apartment he has for rent directly above his storefront. It has been untenanted for months and he is happy to have a renter. You will find the accommodations meager, but acceptable. I have enclosed 2 months rent in the front pocket of the duffle bag. The rest is up to you. I believe this is for the best. I have notified him that you will be arriving tonight. I have taken the liberty of packing some of your clothing and possessions. Should you need to return to pick up more items, over the course of the next few days, I will be boxing up your room. I will be leaving those boxes on the curb this coming Wednesday. Whatever you do not want will be picked up by the Salvation Army Wednesday evening.*

Legs trembling, mouth agape, Anna needed to sit down on the floor as she read, and then re-read the simple letter. She felt a warm flush creep up into her cheeks; her mouth went dry and her breath tasted stale;

nausea threatened to take hold of her as disbelief turned into shame, anger and finally a cruel acceptance. While she was drinking away her anxiety with coffee, her mother had gone and edited Anna out of her neat and orderly home, out of her neat and orderly life, the way a writer might edit a manuscript, mercilessly cutting out superfluous characters, words, and storylines that no longer fit, no longer belonged. So that was it. One offense and she was kicked out of her mother's life? It seemed harsh, even for Beverly, and Anna wondered if there was some deeper reason for such a permanent and jarring action. She momentarily thought it all a tasteless joke, a cruel prank, but Beverly Parke never joked, nor did she go back on her words. Anna briefly thought about storming into her mother's room, forcing her to at least have this conversation face-to-face, at one point Anna even stood directly outside the closed bedroom door, shifting back and forth on the balls of her feet. But, in that instant, something became clear to her–a dawning realization that nearly knocked her off her feet. Her mother must have had this arrangement worked out in advance. No one could lease an apartment with such short notice; there was no way Beverly could have contacted Mr. Lee, and signed a contract within the few hours that Anna had sat at the Diner. Anna wondered how many conversations Beverly had engaged in with Mr. Lee about Anna's leaving, conversations completely hidden from the one person whose life it would most effect. It was merely convenient that Beverly was able to use Anna's refusal to go through with the laser treatment as the excuse for such a dramatic move. As Anna lingered outside her mother's bedroom, the door closed tight against her, this clarity, along with a deep seated feeling of betrayal and shame moved her to sling the bag over her shoulder and walk out of 43 Ackerly Lane without looking back.

She shed no tears as she left and emerged into the cool April evening. Nor did she cry when she arrived at what would be her new home. It was only when she closed her eyes for the evening, when she tried to find a nook of comfort on the bare full-sized mattress left by the previous tenant, that the tears came–flowing freely and insistent, like the moving stream through the mountains.

Chapter 17

Even five years later and at almost twenty-nine years old, looking out the very same windows of the very same apartment, the feelings of rejection, shame and bitter disappointment felt fresh and raw like a nagging scab that never quite heals and continuously opens revealing fresh blood. Anna never went home; she never went to pick up any of her bedroom possessions that were left on the curb like discarded candy wrappers blowing in the wind.Going back would have shown a weakness and vulnerability that she was too angry to reveal to her mother. She wanted to at least put on the facade of strength, a display that she didn't need her mother; she wasn't going to crawl back like a drowned rat and scavenge for the scraps of her life that her mother had left carelessly on the front curb.

She told herself that she was giving her mother space, time to think, but as the days turned into weeks, and the weeks turned into months, she never quite got up the nerve to face her mother in person. Anna knew where Beverly Parke shopped for her weekly groceries and where she purchased her few personal necessities and she instinctively avoided those locations as one might avoid a patch of poison ivy lurking in the forest. Beverly Parke spent most of her time at home; she had no friends nor did she pursue any recreational activities, so Anna was unafraid that she would accidentally run into her mother at the restaurants, bars, and delis that she frequented.

But living in the same town as her estranged mother, knowing that she was so close, took a toll on Anna. It made her paranoid and nervous. For the first year since that dreaded evening, Anna thought that her mother would surely reach out, but her hope dwindled when no phone calls were made nor letters received. This silence was what finally pushed her to fully unpack her duffel bag, hang her blouses up in the tiny closet, and settle into this new and unfamiliar loft, with its alien smells and noises.

Anna missed the view of the mountains and the fresh smell of the trees, but she didn't miss her mother. When a child misses her mother, she misses the warmth, the unconditional love, the hugs and gentle caresses.

Anna's mother never gave her any of that, so there wasn't much to miss. She certainly didn't long for the feeling of scrutiny and judgment–the awkward dance in which the two women engaged on a daily basis. Anna wasn't happy, and she felt a nagging sense of guilt, but there was a peacefulness about her new life that she hoped she would one day learn to appreciate.

What Anna did miss, was being so close to her trees even though she was actively fighting against the magic that lurked in those woods.

So for the past five years, since she took her birthmark and her duffle bag from Beverly Parke's immaculate world, Anna found comfort in the bottles that littered her apartment and in the male bodies that occupied her bed. She sometimes walked past her childhood home, only when she knew her mother was sleeping. She sometimes walked past the entrance to the woods. The trees implored her to visit; she felt their pleading in her very core, but she never went any further than a few tentative steps. She was actively trying and failing to leave her old life behind. She thought briefly about packing up and leaving town. Perhaps life would be better somewhere else? But where would she go? She had no relations outside of Windsom, no prospects nor opportunities elsewhere. In Windsom she had a job at least, albeit not a good one.

Maybe over the past few years, Anna had retained a secret hope of reconciliation with her mother. Had she known what was soon to come, would she have tried to reconnect? Would she have picked up the phone and dialed that familiar number? But that ever fading possibility was put to a final close when she received the call from her Mrs. Douglaston three weeks ago.

"Hello?"

"Is this Anna Parke?".

"Yes. Who is this?"

"Oh good. I heard somewhere that you were living in Lee's rental. It's Mrs. Douglaston."

Mrs. Douglaston was the elderly widow who lived at 45 Ackerly Lane, directly next-door to Beverly. The women were never friends, but they nodded to one another while gardening and exchanged curt waves while clearing their cars of the winter snow.

"Oh. Hello Mrs. Douglaston. How can I help you?" Anna asked, surprised to hear this friendly voice from her past.

"Sweetheart, I'm sorry to call you with bad tidings, but..well. I guess it's better if I just get to it. Your mother, dear, your mother Beverly–has passed."

This news hit Anna with the weight of a freight train and knocked any words she may have been forming in her brain temporarily out of her consciousness.

"Hello–?" repeated Mrs. Douglaston. "Are you there Anna?"

"I'm here." A barely perceptible response.

"I don't really know all the details. Something with her heart from what I understand. You can ask the coroner, but I'm so sorry to be the one to deliver this news."

It was a short conversation and after a few more exchanges, Anna put the phone back on its cradle and sat in stunned silence for a long while. Feeling weak and dizzy, Anna's breath came in quick, uneven gasps as she placed her head in her hands. Surely the pounding of her heart was audible in the quiet, echoing apartment. *Something with her heart* Anna thought. She didn't even know her mother had a heart.

Anna couldn't bring herself to cry, even though she tried. She thought that crying would help jumpstart some form of emotional response within her, but her eyes remained dry as she processed what she was just told. Anna tried to feel something for her mother: love, regret, despair, but all she could muster was a dull pity for a relationship that could have been, but never was. Sadness for a mother that was really no mother at all.

The coroner told Anna that Beverly had experienced some sort of heart event and likely felt no pain. Her body was found in the kitchen. Beverly was found with her blue dishrag in hand as though she wanted to ensure a spotless house for the policemen that were called to the house by a nosy neighbor who only knew something was amiss because the trash cans were not returned to their rightful place after garbage day. The neighbor knocked on the front door to make sure nothing was wrong. After receiving no answer, the neighbor went home only to come back later on in the day. After two days of knocking, the neighbor finally phoned the authorities. Beverly Parke likely passed four full days before that call was made.

The image of Beverly Parke laid out, pale and still in the morgue would haunt Anna for a long, long time to come. Finally quiet, no more judgment, no more righteous frigidity, no more condescension.

Anna decided on cremation; there was no family to attend a funeral, no friends. She couldn't bear to hear the petty sympathies from the gossiping neighbors who would surely show their faces, if only to have some juicy bits of news to share at the next town barbecue or Bridge tournament.

Anna banished the urn containing Beverly Parke's ashes to the far right corner of her closet. The shiny copper receptacle, so small in stature, compared to the woman who loomed larger than life in Anna's mind. Sometimes it called to her in the middle of the night; it woke her from her quiet solicitude, jeering and taunting reminding Anna that *there's a place for everything and everything in its place.*

Anna thought the whole business behind her, until it came time to clear out 43 Ackerly Lane so she could put it on the real estate market. Technically the house was her's. Apparently there was some clause in the deed signed by her grandfather, who was the builder and original owner, that the home must remain in possession of the family.

The housing market was booming, she was told by her agent and she would certainly receive over-market value on a property kept in such pristine condition. Anna thought briefly about moving back into her childhood home, a notion that was quickly dispelled. She couldn't possibly go back; it contained too many memories, too many nightmares. It was too close to those beautiful and terrifying woods that continued to whisper to her on the evening wind.

She hired Sal's Moving Company to clear out the rooms and donate the clothes, furniture and practical items to the local Salvation Army. The owner of the company, Sal, phoned her three weeks ago to inform her that the job was done. All that remained of two decades of Parkes were four cardboard boxes containing personal effects, most of which were found in the attic.

Those very boxes now sat in the corner, relocated to Anna's Main Street apartment...the old encroaching on the new, unwelcome strangers emerging from the shadows.

Chapter 18

Then

Lexi and Dani passed around a hissing joint, the embers glowing orange and bright against the dusky twilight. The three girls had climbed over the large chain link fence separating the schoolyard from the cornfields which provided them with some cover from the cars passing on Route 17. Anna thought it a terrible idea to take such a risk, especially with the promise of graduation in the very near future–approaching like thunderclouds on the horizon. Huddled under the football bleachers, Anna choked back her objections as she clumsily inhaled the fragrant and burning smoke deep into her lungs.

Assistant Principal Shilling, strolling to his car after a late afternoon at work, noticed smoke clouds billowing out from the bleacher seats by the football field. As Anna exhaled, he tapped her on the shoulder.

"Girls," he sternly scolded. "What exactly is going on here?"

Lexi and Dani looked anywhere and everywhere to avoid Shilling's intense gaze, so Anna found her voice out of necessity.

"Um. We were just–" she didn't know how to finish her sentence.

"Anna, I think it is quite clear *what* you are doing."

He ripped the half-smoked joint out of her hands and stomped it to bits with the heel of his brown work-shoe.

He continued, "You of all people Anna! You should know better!"

He was right; Anna did know better. She looked back towards Lexi and Dani who seemed to be silently retreating inch by inch as the conversation progressed. Here were her friends–the ones whose acceptance she craved, the ones who were supposed to support her, help her, be there for her–shrinking away like cowards who didn't even know her at all.

Shilling elaborated, "I'm disappointed in you, Anna. I'm sure your mother will not be happy to receive the call telling her that her daughter has been caught with illegal drugs in her possession."

Just thinking about her mother at this moment in time made Anna feel dizzy and nauseous. Anna remained silent, dimly hoping that her friends would help take some of the blame. But they didn't. In fact, neither Lexi nor Dani spoke a word at all. They just stood there with their heads bowed as if in prayer, looking innocent and sorry.

"I will be calling you down to my office first thing Monday morning to discuss repercussions for this infraction. For now, go home girls. Quickly. And you're lucky I don't get the police involved," he concluded.

Once the three girls scurried away out of the earshot of Assistant Principal Shilling, Lexi spoke in a hushed giggle, "Wow. That was a close call!"

"Yeah Anna! Thanks for taking the heat!" Dani added. "My parents would kill me if I got caught!"

Anna hadn't intended to "take the heat" and at the moment she felt betrayed and disappointed that her friends hadn't at least spoken up. In her head, she visualized what she wished she had the courage to say:

"That was so fucked up guys, the way you just stood there! It wasn't even my weed!"

Lexi would undoubtedly have responded, "Whoa Anna. We didn't force you to smoke that joint."

"But you're supposed to be my friends. You're not supposed to just stand there and let me get in trouble with Shilling."

"What should we have done?" Dani would of course chime in. Always loyal and agreeable to Lexi. "Would you feel better if we all sat in detention together? Should we all get grounded? What good would that do?"

"Yes!" Anna would respond. "Yes! We should *all be in this together. We should all get detention* together, *and we should all get grounded* together. *That's what real friends do. They stick* together.*"*

But as always, Anna swallowed those words and said, "No biggie."

What would have happened had Anna said what she truly felt to Lexi and Dani? She would only have hurt herself. Anna needed Lexi and Dani. They filled her free time and took her away from her silent home, if only for small stretches. So Anna buried her anger somewhere deep down inside of her and didn't elaborate on her response.

"Well, good luck with your mom," Lexi called as the girls split ways to head home.

Anna thanked her, knowing that she would indeed need all the luck in the world to face her mother after she got off the phone with Shilling, which, Anna imagined, was probably occurring at this very moment.

Ms. Parke handled the phone call with grace, promising to speak to her wayward daughter when she arrived home. The picture of care and concern. If Shilling only knew the truth.

With much trepidation, Anna approached the mahogany door, adorned with a grapevine wreath of roses, of 43 Ackerly Lane. For an instant, she debated turning around and jogging towards the woods. Certainly the trees wouldn't lecture her about the dangers of peer pressure and marijuana.

She gingerly nudged the door open, noticing for the first time how it squeaked. Beverly Parke rose from the easy chair as her daughter emerged into the living room. She rose agonizingly slowly; no urgency whatsoever emanated from Beverly Parke's rigid posture.

Anna's apology was cut short by a stinging open-handed smack to her cheek. Anna bit back her tears as a blush of shame and anger rose to her face, enhancing the already scarlet finger prints standing out like blood on her raw visage. Her mother had never raised a hand against Anna before; her chastisements up until this moment had been only verbal. Anna's cheek burned hot against her cold hand.

"How dare you embarrass me like that," Beverly Parke shrieked at her trembling daughter, "You disgust me."

And there it was. Embarrassment. Disgust. It was not concern for Anna's health, safety, well-being, or future; it was all about the fact that Anna had brought shame to Beverly.

"But mom–" Anna tried to say.

But before Anna could say any more, before she could plead her case, or extend her words of remorse (although Anna didn't feel overly sorry), her mother stormed off to the kitchen to scrub the already pristine white-tiled floor.

Anna didn't dare pursue the matter any further, and instead retreated to her bedroom where her dollhouse still stood in the corner, a reminder of a childhood that was drastically receding, like the ebbing tide. She gazed into the rooms of that dollhouse, remembering how the miniature furniture and tiny mugs and plates painstakingly painted by the loving hand of her grandfather bewitched her imagination all those years ago. She picked up the little girl, with her blue gingham dress and painted porcelain face–a pink smile completing her ensemble.

With the red marker lying on her wooden desk, she drew a long jagged birthmark on the doll's cool, smooth cheek. She then dropped the figurine on the beige carpeted floor and felt the satisfying crunch as she brought the heel of her foot down hard on its face.

After this act of aggression, Anna's guilt urged her to sweep the crumbled pieces of broken porcelain into her palm and lay the fragments in a small pile in the tiny little girl bedroom, which looked eerily like her own. She turned the dollhouse away from her so she could not see the headless doll and slowly forgot about what she had done.

Aside from this small hiccup, Anna's high school experience unfurled mostly without incident. At least without any outward display of turmoil. Yet, inside Anna's soul raged and burbled like a stormy sea.

Anna continued to engage in occasional and unfulfilling sexual encounters with bumbling high school boys, still mystified by the secrets hidden within her own woman's body. She continued to say 'yes.' Her quiet and easy acquiescence earned her acceptance from those around her, (aside from her mother) and Anna was successful in banishing her true self and true emotions to a place somewhere deep within her beating heart.

The woods remained Anna's safe-haven. She never told anyone again about the communication that she shared with those trees. The memory of that conversation she had with her mother years earlier about those trees still brought on a blush of shame to her cheeks. Anna remembered how she tried to tell her mother about the trees and how they helped her. What had her mother said in response? Something about Anna being stupid and childish? Even though the specifics of certain conversations tend to fade, what remains, even after years have passed, are the emotions and insecurities that those conversations inspired.

As the years progressed, the trees' whispering became more muted, but they still sent out their quiet signals right into Anna's core. When she was feeling particularly lonely, she felt their warmth right into the depth of her heart; when Anna was angry, the trees sent waves of cool comfort to soothe her turbulent soul.

The dollhouse remained in the corner of her bedroom, along with the headless figurine. Everytime she looked at it, the guilt and anger returned full-force. Even the soft murmur of the trees couldn't soothe her loneliness as the years continued to fly.

Chapter 19

Now

Anna sat there long after Kyle–that was his name, not Kevin or Keith–led himself out of her apartment. He offered no breakfast nor an exchange of phone numbers, which saved them both the embarrassment of an extended goodbye. There was no argument in which Anna denied him use of her bathroom, nor nasty comment about her birthmark. Instead, he gave one of the expected excuses: a family birthday. It was just as well. She was glad to see him go.

She sat there thinking about the past: her mother, the trees, everything that had transpired throughout the course of her life. She became overwhelmed by the emotions that the recollections stirred within her, and she decided it was time. Or as good a time as any, to perform the task which she had been avoiding.

She walked over to the corner of her apartment, the one that she had been side-stepping for the past few weeks, heaved the top box off the tower, and dropped it on the floor in front of the couch; it landed with a thud. Using an old Alice In Chains t-shirt, she dusted off the top of the cardboard, held her breath and opened the flaps.

She was hit with an old familiar whiff, of dust and paint and age, and she knew immediately what this first box contained. She lovingly lifted the dollhouse up and out of the box. With her elbow she swept the coffee table clear of all the debris, the empty beer bottles clattered to the floor, and gingerly set the relic in front of her. She peered back into the cardboard depths and saw a shoe box; When Anna peeled open the tight-fitting lid, she saw all of the dollhouse furniture bundled neatly inside. Anna slowly and deliberately went about putting each piece of furniture in its rightful place. The emerald velveteen couch in the living room, the brass, four post-bed in the master bedroom, the blue porcelain toilet, sink and bathtub in the washroom, the hand-painted tiny plates and saucers and tea cups stacked in the kitchen cabinets, the miniature toys–a jack-in-the-box no larger than her thumbnail, a diminutive tawny teddy bear, a microscopic set of building blocks–in the little girl's pink-striped wallpapered room. Lastly, she placed the white wicker rocking chair on the front porch.

Underneath all the furnishings, was a smaller parcel wrapped in white tissue paper and secured with a piece of scotch tape. When Anna delicately tore the packaging open, her eyes alighted upon the four figurines: her dream family. Anita, the mom, in her apron, the father, Mr. Billingsly in his work suit, older brother, Benjamin in his denim, and last, Anna–a headless doll in knit dress. When she saw the decapitated figurine, the memory of its destruction rushed back at her tenfold. All of the anger and shame and sadness she had felt years earlier threatened to flood her as she gazed, with her adult eyes, upon the ruined little girl. She placed the mother at the sink in the kitchen, the father on the soft green living room couch, the brother in the den, and the little girl, headless and alone, on the rocking chair positioned near the entryway on the brown, front porch.

She sat, contemplating the dollhouse for a long time. As daylight left her modest apartment, she thought about Acklerly lane; it seemed as if her entire childhood was on display directly in front of her in the tangible miniature replica of her girlhood. How happy her life would have been if the juvenile dramas she reenacted in this dollhouse would have mirrored her reality. At this moment the call of the trees was almost deafening, pulling to her to come back, to come home. She had mostly been able to block their insistent summons and gradually, their voices had faded to a soft murmur in the back of her psyche. But now they called to her, relentlessly and unapologetically. *Come home* they seemed to say. *We are here*.

Anna fell asleep on the couch with her face upturned less than two feet from this childhood plaything. She dreamed vivid dreams of her mother climbing an old oak tree in the forest, looking back over her shoulder at Anna, who remained on the ground, dwarfed by the mighty trunk.

Daylight arrived, bold and bright, shining through the hazy front apartment window and bathing Anna's face and the dollhouse in vibrant sunshine. Anna's shift at The Food Mart started in two hours. After briefly contemplating calling out sick and then deciding against it–what good would sitting home do for her?–she showered, relishing for a few extra minutes, the warm flow of water racing down her back. When she emerged from the shower, she wiped away the dewy mist from the vanity mirror while brushing her teeth and found herself face-to-face with her own reflection. The port-wine stain, that so offended her mother, was as bold as ever on her pale cheek, purple and jagged in stark contrast to her fair complexion. She pondered this mark, its purpose in her own life story, and its role in the crumbling of her relationship with her mother.

Anna had some time left before she had to leave for work, so emboldened and newly motivated, she pulled the second cardboard box off the dwindling stack in the corner of her apartment, and began to unpack its contents. What she mostly found in this box were a few items of Beverly Parke's clothing, including her favorite white, lace-up nightgown, a small silver hairbrush and matching vanity set, a few old pairs of shoes, and two crocheted quilts in striped patterns of muted pastels. The items, especially the clothing, smelled of her mother's favorite perfume, Chanel No.5, such an uppity scent, a fragrance Anna avoided even when stealing the occasional sample from the Macy's perfume counter at Golden Crescent Mall, which was in Troy, about two hours away. It felt strange pawing through her mother's measly possessions, as if she was nosing through a stranger's closet. Anna supposed her mother basically was a stranger to her, an unwelcoming, judgemental stranger who merely happened to share her own DNA.

Anna promised herself that she would finish the business of unboxing when she returned home from her shift at the Food Mart. The sooner she unpacked her past, the sooner she could go back to her solitary world, safe and secure in her much preferred oblivion.

Anna walked back into her apartment at 8pm that evening, carrying a McDonald's take-out bag in tow, which contained two small cheeseburgers and a medium fry. The grease was already soaking through the bottom of the bag. Many Windsom residents were unhappy with the recent addition of a chain fast-food restaurant to the downtown area. They felt that it sullied the reputation of a town that prided itself on being 'off-the-beaten-path.' The "commercialization of Windsom" as many residents called it, was currently a hot topic in the community and Anna was reluctantly drawn in to many conversations by Food Mart customers about the benefits and drawbacks of "gentrification." If she was being honest, she didn't give a damn about the addition of modern establishments to Windsom's old exterior. Sometimes the old has to make way for the new after all.

She pulled the long chain of the ceiling fan and light fixture. The dim phosphorescence didn't add much brightness to the place and Anna briefly contemplated getting an additional table lamp. Maybe it was time to make her Main Street quarters feel more like a home and less like a college frat house. She quickly ate her dinner, peeling off the warm soggy pickles from the thin meat patty. She wiped her salty fingers on the Food Mart apron she still wore and approached the stack of boxes; there were only two left. She could do this.

The third box contained similar goods as the second box. More clothing: her mother's single formal outfit that Anna had never once seen her wear–a satin cream-colored a-line skirt with a matching camisole, a deep purple terry-cloth bathrobe, two torn pairs of Levis that her mother typically wore while gardening. As her hand came close to the bottom, she felt a slinky fabric brush up against her wrist and Anna was shocked to pull out a black silk nightie that looked brand new even though there were no tags attached to it. She turned the delicate item over and over again in her hand, and couldn't imagine her mother ever purchasing, nonetheless actually wearing such a thing. Anna decided that she would donate all the clothing to the Salvation

Army. She didn't want to wear any of it, and the overpowering musky smell brought back too many unwanted memories.

Anna finally saw what she thought would be the beginning of the end of this task as she pulled the flaps of the last and final cardboard box open. She couldn't have possibly known at the time that what she would find hidden in the depths of that final and innocuous moving crate would change the course of her destiny forever.

Chapter 20

Peering into the last box, Anna found none of the clothing or miscellaneous household items that she expected. Instead she saw stacks of manilla folders. She didn't notice these files in her house on Ackerly Lane. Her mother kept no filing cabinets, nor were there errant papers scattered about in the immaculate and clutter-free home. *A place for everything and everything in its place.* They must have been stored in the attic.

The first folder contained her own health records, dating back to the first immunization she received two days after her birth in the hospital for hepatitis through the vaccinations she received before commencing college. She was unsurprised to find a pediatric dermatologist's report. Apparently when Anna was five years old, Beverly

Parke took her to an office to inquire about the removal of the port-wine stain. The only aspect of this visit that was documented was the 'cause for visit,' but not the doctor's recommendation. Obviously the specialist declined to perform the excision for whatever reason because there it remained, glaring on her face.

There were no sentimental items from her childhood saved by a doting mother: no drawings or report cards or curly locks of hair saved from her first trip to the salon, only scrupulously ordered and cataloged medical paperwork. Of course Beverly would have thrown away the hand-made Mother's Day and birthday cards and saved the pediatric documentation. It seemed to Anna at the moment a very Beverly thing to do. She set this thin folder aside thinking that she should probably keep it if she were to become a fully autonomous adult.

The next few folders contained Beverly Parke's practical items: the deed to the home on 43 Ackerly Lane, bank notes and checkbooks, social security cards, receipts for large purchases, like the Kenmore Elite refrigerator purchased about ten years ago, and apparently Ms. Parke had caved and bought a microwave after Anna had moved out, or maybe "evicted" is the more accurate term. Beverly had always been resistant to modern conveniences, so the receipt for this item, which her mother would have scoffed at years ago, inspired a bitter and surprised "huh" to escape from Anna's lips.

The bottom two folders seemed a little older, more worn and creased than the first few Anna that had explored. In the next folder, Anna saw a single newspaper article, neatly clipped, dating back from August of 1957.

Her breath caught in her throat as she read the heading: "Windsom Couple Meets Tragic End During Family Campout." She felt a strange and foreign feeling settle into her bones as she read:

Windsom, New York, 8/14/57

Local residents, Estelle Parke (52 years old) and Irwin Parke (55 years old) suffered tragic and unexpected deaths last night during a camping trip with their two children. Their bodies were found, a little over two miles into the entrance of the woods that surround their home on 43 Ackerly Lane. The police responded to a call made by their younger child, Beverly, at exactly 10:48pm reporting the incident. The cause of death is believed to be a fallen tree branch of tremendous size; however, the exact circumstances surrounding this bizarre occurrence remains open for investigation. Both children, Jacob Parke (17 years old) and Beverly Parke (15 years old) were brought in for questioning and examination. The Warren County Police Department asks that you respect the privacy of the Parke children during these trying circumstances. No funeral arrangements have been made as of yet.

Questions buzzed around Anna's confused mind as bees might swarm their woven hive. THAT was how my grandparents died? A fallen tree branch? Was this the "camping accident" to which Beverly had so vaguely referred? Who is Jacob Parke? My mother had a brother? I have an uncle? Where is he now? How could a tree branch kill two people? Is that even possible? She read, reread and for good measure read yet again, even when she was sure she had the puzzling information correct. Thoughts slammed against the inside of her skull as she devoured this information for which she had yearned ever since she was a child. This was tangible proof, evidence that she actually had a family, that her mother wasn't dropped out of an alien spaceship above a random town in upper New York.

But there were so many troubling aspects to mentally unpack! Beverly Parke, her own mother, had been present for the deaths of her parents?...had reported their deaths to the police? The deaths of Anna's grandparents had occurred in her beloved woods directly behind her old home on Ackerly Lane? Had she passed over the spot of their deaths in her forest wanderings? That last thought sent a shiver so cold and so eerie down her spine that it almost took her breath away.

But there was one thought that blazed most profoundly, muting all the others: Anna's mother had an older brother? Anna had an uncle? How come she never knew of him before? Anna sat back on the couch, both exhausted and exhilarated, to think over the mystery that had just begun to unfurl around her like a flower blossoming in the springtime air.

After some time, Anna pulled out her cellphone, opened up a fresh Google tab and typed Jacob Parke Windsom New York into the search box. How had she never attempted a Google search before about her deceased grandparents? She clicked on the first link and found yet another small article, this one dated September

18th 1957, just a month after the other news clipping. Her eyes greedily drank up the words that indifferently appeared before her.

> *Jacob Parke, age 17, was arraigned yesterday morning for his suspected involvement in his parents' untimely deaths. His younger sister, Beverly Parke age 15, testified that she witnessed Jacob chop through a tree trunk outcropping on an oak tree that stood perpendicular to their sleeping parents so that the massive limb would fall upon sleeping Estelle and Irwin Parke. The hatchet in question was found in Jacob Parke's duffle bag upon confiscation. He has been charged with manslaughter in the second degree. He is currently awaiting sentencing. Being that he is a minor, he will likely be placed in a juvenile detention facility to serve out the beginning of his time.*

There were two pictures underneath the short report. One picture with a caption reading, *17 year old Jacob Parke,* displayed a teenage boy in a baseball uniform, obviously taken about a year or so before the incident. He was smiling and happy. The photograph captured him high-fiving another teammate on the Windsom High Baseball team. The second picture showed Jacob Parke at his arraignment, dressed in khakis and white dress shirt, looking defeated and scared. Here they were, the before and after pictures of Jacob Parke. The difference between both photographs was startling; the one of the left–the all American boy, clad in sporting attire and triumph; the one on the right–accused felon, somber and morose. However, what both pictures had in common was possibly more shocking to Anna as she scrutinized an uncle she never knew existed; the heart-shaped face, the wide bright chocolate eyes, the long graceful neck of her mother also defined the physical appearance of Jacob Parke. Even a stranger would have thought the resemblance between the two uncanny.

Had Anna's jaw not been firmly attached to her face, it likely would have dropped to the floor as she stared at the images of Jacob Parke displayed on the small screen in front of her. She was stunned into a shocked silence as she thought about how unwilling her mother had been to talk at all about her own upbringing and family. How much vigilance it must have taken Beverly Parke to hide such a scandalous past! Many aspects about her upbringing started to come together like a jigsaw puzzle that finally begins to reveal its hidden graphic. But while the pieces fell into place, a huge gap in that puzzle remained. Multiple gaps. Anna understood why her mother kept to herself and chose to avoid the gossiping housewives of Windsom, Beverly's reluctance to discuss even the most minute detail of her own upbringing. How exhausting to bury the fact that her own parents were murdered by her older brother!

Anna placed her phone gently in her lap and gazed into the dollhouse once again. It looked foreign and out-of-place on her living room coffee table. She picked up the older brother figurine, who now had a real name; he was no longer Benjamin, the name she had invented as a child. He was no longer a fictional plaything; he had a real name: Jacob Parke.

There were more folders in the nearly empty box, but Anna didn't think she could handle any more surprises for the evening. She was exhausted after a full day at the Food Mart and she needed to process what she had just read and seen. Anna forced herself to take a step away from the container, no matter how much it called to her. She promised herself that she would finish up tomorrow. She had the entire day off from work and she would complete the job of sorting through the papers and documents and files that remained. Maybe she would learn more about this mysterious uncle.

Anna stared at the ceiling of her bedroom for a long time. For as long as she could remember, she had ached for a family that extended further than her icy mother. She imagined holidays filled with laughter and voices and warmth instead of the silent and awkward dinners that dotted her memory. But now that there was possibly another Parke somewhere out there, assuming that he was indeed still out there, she wasn't sure that she wanted to accept him. How could she possibly accept an uncle who was a convicted felon? A murderer? And how old would he be now, if he was still even alive that is? However, the pull of family was too enticing to ignore, and Anna slept an uneasy slumber tossing and turning in her squeaky mattress trying to morph the pictures of teenage Jacob Parke into an elderly man in her humming mind.

Chapter 21

The next morning Anna found that her head was no clearer nor was she any more at peace with the information she had gleaned last night. In fact, if anything, she was more confused and anxious and shocked by this new pocket of her life that she discovered. She made a plan to finish rifling through that last cardboard box and spend the remainder of the evening trying to learn more about her long lost uncle. She was sure that she could find a few more articles about him if she searched harder, maybe even if she made a trip to the local library.

Anna was disappointed to find that the remaining contents of the box revealed no additional secrets nor did they shed any light on her uncle, her mother or her grandparents' deaths. The last few folders were filled with the manuals that accompany typical household appliances: the directions for the Hoover vacuum cleaner, the assembly instructions for the garden shed that Beverly had put together on her own when Anna was eleven years old, the information for the water filtration system that was installed years ago. Useless. All useless now.

Anna replaced these papers into their folders and laid the folders back into the cardboard box from which they came. She kept the thin folder containing the newspaper article on her lap and reread the words one more time. The phrases “unexpected deaths” and “fallen tree branch” and “bizarre occurrence” seemed to blaze off the thin newsprint straight into her brain. She kept returning to the name: Jacob Parke. Jacob Parke. Jacob Parke.

Chapter 22
Then

One day, late in the summer of 1998, the summer before Anna was scheduled to start Warren Bailey High School, Anna found herself in conversation with her mother. Conversation between the two individuals was a rare event, reserved for only necessary moments where schedules had to be made or chores needed to be discussed. Later on, Anna regretted the questions she asked, felt she had wasted an infrequent opportunity to engage with her mother...felt as though she had squandered the precious few moments she was given.

While seated at the immaculate kitchen table, engaged in yet another quiet and somber dinnertime punctuated only by the clinking of ice against the glass tumbler, Anna asked her mother, “Where is my father? Who is he and why did he leave?”

Up until this moment, Anna had only gleaned a few minor details about Johnny from the scraps her mother slipped to her during the years. She didn't even know his last name. And she was desperate to know more. She knew that he was from Manhattan, which to Anna, seemed a luxurious and exotic location, a city where skyscrapers instead of mountains dotted the skyline. She knew that he and her mother never married, which seemed as foreign a concept to Anna as the algebraic functions she learned about in Math class. She couldn't fathom her mother engaging in any sort of romance, especially participating in the vague concept of conception that was outlined to her in Health class. She never asked for more information, probably because she feared her mother's reaction. However, something in the still summer air piqued Anna's curiosity and emboldened her to ask the question that blurted through her lips during this fleeting moment of conversation.

As soon as the words escaped her mouth, Anna wished she could pull them back, like the bitter brussel sprouts that were at the moment squished between her enameled teeth; she wished she could swallow them and digest them in the depth of her intestines. How would they taste in her stomach? Pungent and acidic? Her mother's head snapped to attention and her eyes turned hard. Beverly Parke had never before yelled at Anna; her reprimands were usually monotone, forced, and said without much conviction or care, which made the venom that spewed forth this time that much more unusual, that much more surprising.

Beverly Parke hissed, "Your father is a good-for-nothing drifter who isn't worth the dirt on the bottom of my shoe. He left me with nothing except a mousy little girl with a stain on her cheek that can never be washed off. Every time I look at you, I see shame and humiliation. Never again ask me about him."

Despite the warning bells going off in Anna's mind, she felt compelled to continue. "Well, what about any other family? Cousins, aunts...anyone? There MUST be someone else besides you and me! We can't be the only Parkes!"

Beverly's face was flushed scarlet as she screamed at her daughter, "There IS no one else, Anna. It's just me...and you. That's all there is. And the sooner you get used to that fact the better off you will be. Family is a burden...if you don't see it now, you will soon."

"But–" Anna began. But before she could say anything else, Ms. Parke stormed off to her bedroom, slamming the door, closing Anna outside alone.

Anna felt the tears, hot and heavy seep from the corners of her eyes. They came quietly, one after the other tracing rivulets down her cheeks and leaving a salty residue on her tongue. She caught a reflection of herself in the hallway mirror. Anna searched her face; she certainly did not have the graceful yet plain beauty of her mother. She didn't have the long, lean neck or heart-shaped face that likely attracted Johnny to Beverly years ago. The purple birthmark stood out, clear and blatant on her cheek. It took up considerable space on the right side of her face, beginning at the bottom of her eye and descending as long as the top of her upper lip.

Anna angrily wiped at this dark, jagged mark, foolishly hoping it would rub off. Her soft brown, shoulder-length hair was tied into a low ponytail. The childhood softness of her face was beginning to melt away and as Anna stood staring at herself she could almost make out what she would soon become: a teenager with straight teeth, hazel eyes, and soft-pink parted lips. But in the next instant, that near-woman was gone, replaced with the awkwardness of the middle-school years, a crying girl, alone in the glare of the hallway light. A girl on the brink of womanhood. A sun setting over the mighty mountains in the fading twilight. She looked out the window and saw the trees gently swaying to the rhythm of her heartbeat. Their presence comforted her a bit, but just a bit as the tears continued to fall.

Chapter 23

Now

Now that Anna contemplated the fact that she was not entirely alone in this world, that there was possibly another Parke out there somewhere, her mind reeled. She had been told so many times that she was alone–that her mother was all she had. But maybe, just maybe, she could locate this uncle. She had to try to find him.

The only clue about Jacob Parke was the offhand comment that he likely went off to a juvenile detention center following his arraignment in August of 1957. A modern day news source wouldn't have dared publish such a vague prediction. Anna typed 'Juvenile Detention Centers Warren County' into the Google search bar on her cellphone. Seven facilities immediately appeared in the stream, not all of them nearby, but all within about a sixty mile radius. Warren Outreach Center was first on the list. She bit back her hesitations, and hit the 'call' button next to the listing, and as she waited for assistance soft jazz music emanated from the speaker.

Finally an answer, "Hello, Warren County Outreach Center, Amy speaking. How may I direct your call?"

"Hi. I'm not too sure who I'm looking for; I would like some information about a patient that may have been placed in your facility in the late 1950s. Is there someone who could help me?"

"Please hold. I will transfer you to Records."

Anna held..both the line and her breath.

Another woman's voice picked up the line, "Records, how can I help you?"

Anna repeated, "Hello. I'm looking for some information about a teenage boy who may have been placed in your facility in the late 1950s. His name is Jacob Parke. He would have been seventeen years old at the time."

"Hmm. Jacob Parke you said? That's a long time ago, and there are confidentiality protocols that would need to be followed. I would need to check the archives first, which is not an easy task. I'm pretty busy now, but if you leave your name and phone number I can most likely give you a call back in a few hours.It would be silly to begin the paperwork until you know for sure that the man in question was actually a patient here," the voice on the phone explained.

Anna gave her name and number and ended the call by saying, "I would very much appreciate a call back. Jacob Parke was…is my uncle" and for good measure she added, "I don't have any other family."

The woman on the line replied, "Sure sweetie. Let me see what I can dig up. I'll give you a call. Goodbye now."

"Goodbye...and thank you," said Anna quickly.

Anna had six other similar conversations, which took up most of the morning and sat back on her worn sofa waiting for the callbacks. She took out a yellow legal pad and wrote the name "Jacob Park" on the top of a fresh sheet. Underneath she listed all the facilities that she had already phoned and decided that she would systematically cross them off her list as she hopefully received the return phone calls. She would call them back if she didn't hear from them by tomorrow, she decided. She unsuccessfully attempted a few more Internet searches hoping that she would gain some additional knowledge on Jacob Parke's whereabouts, but most of the links she clicked on were dead ends...so many Jacob Parkes exist in the world!

The first return call came at 2pm. The man on the line simply reported that no one by the name of Jacob Parke had ever come through the doors.

By 6pm, every single facility that she called had been crossed off her list except one and Anna was no closer to locating her uncle than she was this morning when she first awoke, hopeful and optimistic. It was too late in the evening to put through any more phone calls, so Anna decided that she would try again tomorrow. She doodled on the bottom of the legal pad: pictures of trees and mountains and large bubbly question marks.

Tomorrow she would put calls through to more juvenile centers. She would try institutes in the Albany area. She supposed that it would have made more sense that Jacob be sent to a facility outside his home town. Anna ate a late night dinner of Soy sauce flavored Ramen Noodles before going off to bed, which left a bad aftertaste and salty residue on her tongue. The searching and calling had exhausted her and this night, she slept soundlessly–no dreams at all.

The next day, she did just as she planned. She called ten facilities in the Albany and Dutchess County area. She called any facility that mentioned "residential housing placement" on the website, even if some of those establishments were clearly long-shots. She even called one private, country-club psychiatric facility that was located in a luxury log cabin deep within the Catskills; she called them knowing full well that under no circumstances would Jacob Parke have ever been sent to such a trendy and modern place. This was a place for celebrities and millionaires.

All of the centers had confidentiality protocols that Anna would be expected to follow in the rare case that Jacob was indeed a patient there all those years ago. When did this world become so efficient? So bogged down in privacy and red tape? Didn't anyone care that Anna was on the edge of her seat here…fiending for information? No. No one cared. She was alone.

Some of the centers put her on hold and were able to inform her within minutes that they had no record of a Jacob Parke in their systems. Others took her name and phone number and promised to call back. Like yesterday, she began crossing names off her list and grew more and more disconcerted with each report that, "No. Sorry Miss, We haven't had any patients here with that name." One facility reported that Jacob Parke was still a resident there! But any hope Anna felt with that information diminished when she realized that it couldn't be the same Jacob Parke; the one who was currently a resident at Overlook Home was only twenty-five years old. Finding Jacob Parke, her Jacob Parke, was like finding the proverbial needle in the haystack.

Just when Anna was about to give up for the day, call it quits, her phone announced that a call was coming in with its persistent buzzing on the wood coffee table.

She answered, "Hello?"

"Hi. This is George Madsen from the Half Moon Home for Juveniles, I'm looking for Anna Parke."

"Yes. Hello. I'm Anna. Thanks for returning my call Mr. Madsen."

"Well…it is my job to provide updated information on all patient inquiries. I have a file on the patient in question, Jacob Parke. I just need to confirm some details with you. HIPAA regulations."

Finally!

Anna felt a vague hope begin to build within her again, like a balloon inflating with helium. She didn't want to get her spirits up again, only to have that balloon popped when it was revealed that it was yet again a sad case of a mistaken identity.

"Hello? Ms. Parke?" said the voice on the other side of the phone.

"Yes. I'm here. What sort of information do you need?" Anna stuttered.

"I need to confirm Mr. Parke's home address and names of kin."

Anna replied, "He lived at 43 Ackerly Lane in Windsom New York. His parents were Irwin and Estelle Parke. I'm his niece." That last sentence tripped her up a bit.

This information must have satisfied Mr. Madsen because he responded, "Ok Ms. Parke. It is not our policy to provide patient information over the phone, but we can provide you with a copy of Jacob Parke's file if you come to our facility in person. Our office hours are Monday through Friday 9am-3pm. Please make sure to bring at least two forms of identification."

So it wasn't a false alarm! This was real. There was actually someone who might help her.

"Yes,"Anna replied. "I will be there tomorrow! Thank you Mr. Madsen! I truly appreciate your help."

And with that, Anna pressed the 'end' button on her cellphone, which felt hot and electric from so much use. Tomorrow. Tomorrow she would go to The Half-Moon Home for Juveniles and see what she could learn about her uncle. She felt nervous and jittery as she went about her afternoon and evening routine.

She did some quick math calculations in her head and determined that Jacob Parke would be in his late sixties or or early seventies today, if he were even still alive. There was a chance. She didn't even know what she expected had she the good fortune to actually track him down. What were her goals in locating an uncle who was also a murderer? Did she just expect him to sit down to Thanksgiving Dinner with her? What right did she have to just waltz into his life with her questions and demands?

Her thoughts were hazy and unclear as she tried to fit this new individual into the notion of family that she had already clearly established. She felt a sudden and intense anger towards her mother for denying Anna the truth about her past. Beverly Parke closed her daughter out of so much of her life; Anna felt at this moment, and not for the first time, that she hadn't really known her mother at all. But tomorrow, she hoped to learn something about her, something real, something that she could latch onto. She thought about a line from *Macbeth*, something that she had read in high school, or maybe it was in another universe somewhere deep within the past, "Tomorrow and tomorrow and tomorrow creeps in its petty pace from day to day to the last syllable of recorded time." But unlike for Macbeth, her tomorrow was right on the horizon.

Chapter 24

It was 8:30pm and Anna's body felt electric. She couldn't keep still. She needed fresh air; her body craved movement, so she headed out of her stale apartment with the intention of going for a long walk. Her feet took her instinctively the three-miles distance towards her childhood home. She paused outside 43 Ackerly Lane, which now had a wooden 'for sale' sign staked into the front lawn. The house looked cold and empty in the encroaching darkness. Did Jacob Parke ever take his summertime meals on that front porch? Did young Beverly play with her brother in the fading twilight? Mysteries hung in her mind like spiderwebs glistening in the shadowy corners of her consciousness.

Anna felt that old familiar pull of the trees and heard their familiar callings in her rapidly beating heart. They urged and coaxed and insisted that she seek them out; Anna could feel their branches tangled in her soul, luring her to immerse herself in their comfort. She turned on her heels and gradually approached the opening to the woods. Pulled by an almost magnetic force. Did she dare step in? Did she dare respond to the invitation that those tall oak trees emitted to her? In her own apartment, the whisperings were muted, barely audible, and over the years, she learned to ignore them, live with them so to speak. But, as she stood contemplating the majestic woods that loomed before her in all their grandeur, the trees pleaded with her to return. They had a story to tell her.

It took a great force of will to turn away. Not for the first time, she felt frightened of those trees and what they promised to reveal to her as the night deepened around her. What if they told her something that she couldn't bear to hear? She turned her back to the forest and ran in the opposite direction, legs pounding on the pavement to a home that didn't feel at all like a home at all. After about five minutes of running, Anna's legs began to slow down and her jagged breath burned as she forced it into her lungs. It felt as though she were inhaling razor blades. She walked the rest of the way home and by ten o'clock that night, she collapsed in utter exhaustion upon her unmade bed.

Chapter 25

At 8:45 the next morning, Anna found herself seated on a stone bench outside the Half-Moon Juvenile Facility picking at the buttered roll she purchased from the deli on the corner in an effort to calm her trembling soul. She was not even remotely hungry; she was too anxious to eat. The day was overcast, the clouds above

threatened rain. She had consumed a cup of strong coffee on the hour and a half bus ride from Windsom to Schenectady and her stomach was roiling and turbulent.

She waited for fifteen more minutes on that bench, which felt like fifteen hours; the seconds passed interminably slow. At nine o'clock sharp, Anna stood up and walked through the newly unlocked doors into the lobby, which was really no more than a waiting room. She approached the woman wearing purple scrubs adorned with sleeping sheep behind the plexiglass counter and told her that she had spoken with Mr. Madsen yesterday about picking up a file on a former patient.

"Please have a seat. I'll tell Mr. Madsen that you are here," said the clerk. "Oh, and I'll need your photo ID for our records."

Anna handed over her identification and found a seat, her left leg tapping a nervous tattoo upon the carpeted floor. She picked up one of the glossy magazines fanned out on the glass table in front of her, *Psychology Today*. She tried to read an article titled, "Mindfulness and its Effects Upon a Restless Brain," but couldn't really attend to the words swimming before her. About twenty minutes later, the woman behind the glass divider called her over and directed her to a small door off the hallway behind the reception desk. Mr. Madsen was ready to see her.

Chapter 26

Mr. George Madsen was a middle-aged man with horn-rimmed spectacles, ink-stained fingers and a crop of brown unruly hair on his head that stood almost straight up as if he had been electrocuted. He was in charge of Patient Records, had been for the past 8 years and was frankly too busy to spend his time with a girl looking for answers about some distant relative. Throughout the course of his time as an administrator at Half-Moon, he had dealt with many curious visitors and had pulled countless files. Many claimed to want to help their family members contained within these walls, but once they read the goods hidden in their 4-inch thick file folders, most got scared and turned tail. It sounded noble to want to come to the aid of an "ill" uncle or cousin or sister, heroic even, but mental illness takes its toll on all involved and most of the time, family members pay the highest price.

Not even glancing up from his work, Mr. Madsen said, "Take a seat Ms. Parke."

He almost apologized for the wait, but swallowed the words. He wasn't sorry. Hell, he was doing this girl a favor by even agreeing to help. He had important work to do. But again, this was a part of his job description and he certainly needed the paycheck.

He didn't say anything else, so after a few silent moments, the girl spoke up, "Hi. I'm Anna Parke. We spoke on the phone. It's nice to meet you."

She extended her hand across the desk, forcing George to delicately set his work down on the surface in front of him to give a brief shake and to finally glance at the person seated before him.

This girl, Anna, looked nervous, on edge. There was a restlessness about her that made George uneasy. The way she shifted in her seat, trying to find a comfortable position on the brown, metal folding chair. George hadn't gotten around to purchasing an actual chair for his visitors. He had meant to at some point. She was fairly pretty and plain, younger than he had expected, but what stood out to George as he adjusted his glasses to get a better look was a dark mark blooming on her cheek. What it must be like for a young woman to spend her entire life with that thing on her face George couldn't quite envision. It made him feel bad for her. She looked at him so earnestly, so hopefully that George began to feel slightly less cranky, which was unusual for him.

"I pulled the file that you requested on Jacob Parke. You'll find that he was a patient here from 1957-1963."

George Madsen watched as Anna did the quick calculation in her head. The calculations that he himself had already done, but had been too tired to utter aloud. Jacob Parke entered the Half-Moon juvenile facility when he was seventeen years old and left when he was twenty three years old; six years he spent within these walls, six of his most formative years. While his peers were graduating, and attending college, dating and finding meaningful employment, Jacob was entombed here, isolated and alone. George understood loneliness and he understood rejection, but even though he spent his existence rifling through the lives of Half-Moon's patients, he couldn't possibly begin to imagine what life was like for this girl's uncle nor the others. Most of the time he didn't even try to. He had his own issues to worry about that were depressing enough: a cheating wife, a mortgage that he couldn't afford, and less serious but more pressing, a cracked windshield that needed to be replaced.

After a few moments, Anna spoke again, "So, after he left…that was it? No one here ever saw him again?"

Mr. Madsen responded, "It is our facility policy to follow up with all our patients for five years after their release. Most patients are required to come in for bi-annual check-ins, especially whose initial enrollment is mandated by federal law."

And with that, he handed the thick manila folder across the desk into Anna's groping hands. Even though George had begun to feel for the girl, he was relieved to be done with her. One more box to check off of his 'To-Do' list for the day. He really did have work to do. He made the effort to stand up and motioned to the door, a gesture that for him was over-and-beyond his usual abrupt client dismissals.

Anna stood up also, but instead of walking to the door as George expected, she asked, "Do you happen to have an empty room here where I can look through this folder? I thought I would be able to wait until I got home, but…now I think I can't wait."

He was surprised by her honesty, her willingness to share what was within her. George himself rarely revealed what emotions hid behind his exterior. *An extra room? Does she think this is a hotel? We're bursting at the seams here?*

But instead he said, "I think I can arrange that."

He led her down the corridor to a smaller, dimly lit room with a desk surrounded by old, dusty filing cabinets.

"This is the best I can do, Ms. Parke."

"Please, call me Anna. Thank you so much, Mr. Madsen. This is more than fine."

"Okay then," Mr. Madsen said as he backed out of the door.

"Sincerely. Thank you," said Anna again. "I know you are a busy man and probably have a million other things to do. You have been of more help than you realize."

Mr. Madsen didn't, couldn't realize how much he had indeed helped Anna at this moment in time, but when he walked down the hall and back to his own office, there was a hint of a smile on the corners of his lips. He had to admit that maybe being helpful and wanted felt kind of good.

Chapter 27

Anna gingerly opened the folder. Inside was a large stack of paperwork held together with a black binder clip. She unsnapped the clip, laid it aside and began the job of pouring over the papers held inside. The first document was a physician's report labeled "Physical Examination" and dated September 16, 1957. This must have been the initial exam performed when Jacob was first admitted to the Half-Moon Juvenile Facility. The exam told Anna his age: seventeen years four months, his birthdate: June 12,1940, his height and weight: one hundred and sixty three pounds/ five feet ten inches and his vitals: all within normal limits.mThere were five other physical exam reports, one for each year as a patient.

The next set of documents were psychiatric reports that spanned throughout the course of the six years of Jacob's stay. As she read through the psychiatrist's notes and observations of Jacob Parke, she felt light-headed and dizzy, the way she used to feel when she would playfully suck the helium out of birthday party balloons with Lexi and Dani. They used to giggle when they heard how the hot chemicals disguised their voices into elvish squeaks.mBut this was a different dizzy. An overwhelmed-with-information dizzy that threatened to make her head spin off.

And she did not giggle, nor did she even crack a smile as she read through the densely written notes about her uncle. Certain phrases stuck out in her mind like rocks jutting off a mountain as her eyes studied the reports before her: acute personality disorder, anxiety, Prozac, Abilify, sleep disturbances, withdrawn. She tried to reconcile these words with the image of Jacob Parke, smiling in his baseball uniform, that stared out at her from her phone screen a few days prior. She guessed that she shouldn't be surprised to find that Jacob had been a troubled youth, especially after he murdered his own parents in the woods, but seeing the words neatly typed before her evoked a profound sadness not only for Jacob himself, but for his parents–her grandparents–and even her own mother. Could she truly blame her mother for being so closed off about her history? After all, her own brother killed her parents! And Beverly had watched it happen! Anna could picture her mother as a little girl, gasping through choked sobs on the phone with the police trying to come to terms with what had just happened. With how her life had just been shattered by the very person that Anna was currently trying to locate. Maybe all those conversations cut short, all the concealing, all the secrets were justified.

Anna put both the physical exam reports and the psychiatric reports carefully on the floor beside her feet and continued rifling through this folder; the act was starting to feel more and more like an invasion of privacy. She felt like she was the star of some sensationalized mystery film on the Bravo network and while she was beginning to feel sympathy for her mother–the sister of a murderer–she was beginning to like her own character less and less.

The next paper she came across was the arrest warrant for Jacob Parke, which contained his official charge: murder in the second degree. Seeing that word 'murder' on such an official document left her with a knot in her stomach that never quite eased. Next a grim, black and white mug shot of a frowning and tousled Jacob Parke, with his fingerprints underneath. Following this hideous document was a collection of official court data including Jacob's plea: not-guilty and the judge's ruling from his court case: eight to ten years at Blue-Moon Juvenile Facility. A throbbing headache was starting to develop in the front of Anna's brain. She longingly thought about the un-eaten buttered roll that she had hastily discarded a few hours earlier and vaguely remembered seeing a vending machine somewhere. So, she left the files open and exited the room in search of some sugary snack.

Anna saw Mr. Madsen again as she retrieved her can of Coke from the mouth of the vending machine in the hallway. Instead of immediately cracking it open, she handed it over to Mr. Madsen.

"Here. It's the least I can do."

She rummaged through her bag for a few more quarters to buy another for herself when Mr. Madsen kicked the bottom right of the machine prompting another can to drop loudly into the bin.

"Employee secret," he muttered as he took a long swig from the can Anna had given him.

"Thanks."

"How are you doing in there Ms. Parke? Finding what you need?"

"I'm not so sure, Mr. Madsen. It seems like my uncle was a pretty troubled young man," Anna said.

"Yeah. Well, this building holds many sad stories," Mr. Madsen said as he ambled away.

She contemplated what Mr. Madsen said as she walked back to the tiny room and back to the files containing Jacob''s secrets. Maybe she would have been better off not opening that cardboard box. Maybe she would have been safer not knowing about Jacob Parke, letting that box gather dust in the corner of her apartment for the rest of eternity. She banished these thoughts. She had a right to know her full story, even the ugly chapters.

When she sat down again, she held the can up to her forehead for a minute relishing its damp coolness against her forehead. The can opened with a satisfying hiss; the cool, crisp liquid revived Anna a bit and gave her the pep she needed to complete this difficult task. It was almost noon at this point, and Anna had been in this tiny room for about two hours (aside from her trip to the vending machine). The folder was getting thinner; she was almost done.

The next document she came across was titled 'Patient Release Form,' and dated October, 18 1963. It opened with a terse written report completed by a psychiatrist named Dr. Herbert Dunn:

> *Jacob Parke has made significant progress over the past 6 years since his admission to our facility. He has received bi-weekly counseling sessions and is being treated with clinical doses of both*

Prozac and Abilify. His mood shows improvement and his behavior over the past two years has been exemplary. He has emerged as a leader amongst the patients at Half-Moon Juvenile Facility. I whole-heartedly endorse his early release from our rehabilitation program.

Anna was surprised to learn that her uncle–it still felt odd even thinking of Jacob Parke in these terms–seemed to change his ways over the course of the six years that he was here, *if* a murderer could change his ways that is. Although it still seemed odd to her that an individual convicted of murder should serve such a meager sentence, but she guessed times were different then. And he was a minor. Even though it made her happy to know that Jacob was rehabilitated and that he was apparently capable and stable enough to earn a doctor's recommendation for early release, she couldn't ignore the feeling of anger that all of this stirred up within her. And she couldn't help herself from thinking that maybe Jacob was the reason why her mother was so screwed up, and in turn why she herself is so screwed up. Maybe Jacob was to blame for all of it. But despite all this, Anna had to acknowledge the burning curiosity within her as she thought to herself, "OK. So he got out of here in 1963. Where did he go next? "

The next sheet of paper answered this question. It was an employment record. Apparently Jacob Parke was set up with a full-time government job at Schenectady Lanes, a Bowling Alley in the downtown area. The job was apparently part of a movement to help troubled young people reset their lives after serving time. He was also provided with subsidized housing as indicated on a lease agreement. Her breath caught in her throat as she read the name 'Jacob Parke' signed in a messy script. She ran her thumb over this signature and could almost visualize her twenty-three year old uncle eagerly signing this agreement, knowing that he would be saying goodbye to the Half-Moon Juvenile Facility permanently. She also noticed that he wrote his 'P' with that same little flourish at the loop that she does. Was this mere coincidence? Was she just looking for a family connection with the only family member she had left on this planet?

There were some additional Physical Examination sheets following this; apparently Jacob continued to visit the facility for his mandated bi-annual check-ups. On each sheet, on the empty line where it said "occupation" the attending doctor had written Bowling Attendant Schenectady Lanes.

Anna finally reached the end of the folder. It took her three hours, a can of Coke, and some jitters to unpack six years of Jacob Parke's life. While the information she gleaned satisfied some aspects of her curiosity, she still had so many questions. Specifically, where is Jacob Parke now? Paperwork and data can only reveal so much about a person.

She placed the papers and documents and forms and records back into the folder, careful not to bend or crease anything. She stood up, opened the door, and walked out into the corridor, which seemed unnaturally bright after being encased in dull lighting for so long. On her way out, she stopped back into Mr. Madsen's office, only to find him engulfed in his own stack of paperwork. She thanked him for his consideration and asked him if Schenectady Bowl still serviced the area's bowlers.

"It's called 'Alley Oops' now, but it's still there. If you take the number 3 bus downtown it's about a mile up on Norwood Avenue. You'll see it," Mr. Madsen absently said.

Anna had a new destination. 'Alley Oops,' a cute name for a bowling alley she thought, as she exited Blue-Moon Juvenile Facility. The clouds cleared, revealing a bright and temperate afternoon. She imagined what it must have felt like for Jacob Parke to emerge from these same doors years ago, a free man. Did he walk out truly rehabilitated? Or did he strut through the doors laughing at how easy it was to murder two people and get out scot-free? Did he plan to finish what he started by murdering his sister as well? Anna shivered as she tried to push that last thought from her mind.

She turned to face the large cement building again. She scanned the windows that glittered against the facade in the sunlight and wondered from which one Jacob had peered out. A thought so strong came to Anna's mind at this moment; she realized that she couldn't go back to her old routine unless she knew definitively how Jacob's life had panned out once he was set free from this sad place. How could she wake up everyday and go back to bagging and scanning groceries knowing that her blood was out there somewhere? At least she hoped that he was out there somewhere. She had to follow the path.

Newly motivated and invigorated, she turned back around and scanned her surroundings for clues that would lead her to a bus stop. She had work to do.

Chapter 28

Anna hopped off the number three bus and onto Norwood Avenue, a bustling shopping area with the urban flair that Windsom's Main Street lacked. She headed in the direction she hoped was "up" as Mr. Madsen directed, passing a Greenwood Bank, a small children's department store named Denny's, and an A&S Pork Store with its front door propped open with a black doorstop to the warm, breezy afternoon; she could hear the customers placing their orders at the deli counter, "I'll take a pound of capicola and half pound of store made mortadella." She almost stopped to ask a passerby about the location of the bowling alley, when she looked up and saw the electronic sign, boasting a bowling pin that was at least four feet tall with the name 'Alley Oops" in cursive up the pin's slender neck. It was at the moment turned off, but she could still make out the slogan, 'Serving the Schenectady area since 1940.' How lucky for her.

She walked through the twin metal doors; the bells attached to the handles announced her entrance. Her senses were immediately assaulted by the familiar sounds and smells of the bowling alley. Greasy french fries, stale bowling shoes, the clatter of strikes being thrown and pins rattling helter-skelter on the glossy waxed lane, the urethane resin marbled balls in swirls of red and blue and gold shone dully in the dim light. Bowling alleys have a way of evoking youth and nostalgia, no matter how modernized they have become. Beverly never took Anna bowling, a fact as unsurprising as it was sad; however, Anna visited the local Windsom Alley a few times over the years, once on a school field trip and a handful of times with Lexi and Dani in high school. The high school bowling excursions were less about the sport than they were about finding an inconspicuous place to socialize. Despite the grime and the smoky atmosphere, there is something undeniably wholesome about the experience of visiting a bowling alley; it's as if you are transported back to a simpler and easier time, where a Saturday night consisted of keeping tabs of strikes and spares on an iridescent notepad.

Anna approached the front desk where a young worker with a nose piercing in a navy blue smock was spraying some sort of sanitizer inside the red and white velcro shoes set out in a neat line on the counter top. Could a measly spritz of fragrant mist truly disinfect these shoes that looked as though they were worn by hundreds of feet over the course of the past decade? And those colors! Half red, half blue, velcro, maybe they were so hideously manufactured to prevent some brazen bowler from walking out with them. Anna briefly wondered why no designer ever bothered to modernize the look of such hideous footwear. She asked the teenager if she might speak to a manager about a past employee.

"You probably want to speak to Gina; she's on break now, but she should be back in about a half an hour. She better be back...I've been here for four hours now and haven't even had my fifteen-minute yet," the disgruntled teen informed her.

And because Anna had nowhere else to go, and because she wanted to make sure she didn't miss her chance to speak with Gina, she said, "I'll just wait over there for her to come back."

She sat at the food counter and her rumbling stomach reminded her that she had barely eaten anything all day. She ordered a large hot pretzel that didn't taste nearly as good as it looked and an iced-tea. She didn't think her stomach could handle the normal fried bowling alley fare. Anna sat and waited for about forty minutes until the frustrated front-desk clerk from earlier, Manny, his name tag read, whisked past her on his way out.

"Excuse me," she called to his back. "Has Gina returned yet from break?" Anna asked as Manny rushed past her, cigarette already in hand.

"Oh, yeah. Sorry. I forgot to tell her that you were waiting. She's at the front desk," he hastily replied as he placed the cigarette in his pursed lips; he didn't seem overly sorry...just in a rush to get outside for a smoke break.

Anna supposed that there was some sort of employee entrance in which Gina returned, because she had been eying the front doors since she sat down to wait and saw no one walk through the entrance aside from a young mom with two squirming toddlers in tow. Anna brushed the large morsels of kosher salt from her lap and walked over again to the front desk.

"Excuse me," she said to the woman standing behind the counter, "I'm looking for someone named Gina."

Chapter 29

Gina barely glanced up from the computer screen in front of her. A middle-aged woman, with long turquoise fingernails and a variety of jewel encrusted rings adorning her fingers, she typed insistently at the keyboard, her nails making click-clacking sounds as they met the plastic letter cubes.

"Excuse me, "said a voice. "I'm looking for someone named Gina."

"That's me," Gina said distractedly. She didn't know who this woman was, but she definitely did not have time for idle chit-chat. She had payroll to deal with and food orders to place. Apparently there was a shortage on McCormick's frozen french fries, so she needed to contact the distributor to figure out a suitable replacement. Pete asked for time off next week and that meant that she had to rearrange the entire scheduling matrix in order to have enough staff members working;

there were three birthday parties on the calendar for next week alone and four more before the end of the month. Running a bowling alley was not supposed to be this stressful, and if she had a more reliable staff, maybe her job would have been easier. She thought about Manny, her most recent hire, smoking a cigarette out front, right next to the entrance for all to see and decided that she had to be more discerning when hiring. The problem was, not very many people wanted to work at Alley Oops, so Gina was forced to take what she could get.

"Um," she heard from across the counter.

"What do you need?" Gina asked.

Her eyes flicked momentarily to the face of the woman standing there, opposite her and she immediately felt guilty for having responded with such a sharp tone. The first thing Gina noticed was a huge marking, taking up most of the lady's cheek. The woman was pretty nonetheless, but there was something in those eyes that looked at Gina so earnestly; Gina stopped her typing to hear what she had to say.

"Um. My name is Anna Parke, and I'm looking for information about an employee who used to work here, probably about thirty-forty years ago."

Thirty-Forty years ago, Gina thought to herself. *How old does this girl think I am?*

Clearly the woman had the same thought, because before Gina could answer, she said, "This is silly. I'm sorry. You definitely were not here that long ago."

"Yeah. That's way before my time. Sorry I can't be of more help," Gina said, resuming her typing. She had to finish this schedule.

But this woman, Anna Parke, didn't move. Gina could feel her eyes staring at her from across the counter. The girl let out an audible sigh and seemed to be contemplating what she would say next. Clearly she was not done.

"Well, could there be employee files or records? Maybe W2 forms? Anything?"

"Lady. I'm sorry, but I'm really very busy. I'm short-handed this week and I need to man the desk. Anyway, we haven't kept records since the place switched names decades ago."

Gina felt for her, she really did, but there was nothing more she could do. When the woman didn't leave, Gina added, "If there's not anything else I can do for you, would you mind...I mean, giving me some space?"

The woman opened her mouth, and then it all came pouring out, "I just found out that I had this uncle who apparently murdered his parents. I have no other family. My mother passed away a few months ago and there are just so many unanswered questions. I came in today from Windsom and it seems like I am no closer to having any of my questions answered than I was this morning when I got on that damn bus.``

Her tone startled a few of the gathering customers, and it startled Gina.

"I'm sorry," this woman, Anna Parke said, a deep blush working its way up her cheeks. "I'm sorry. Thanks for your time." And she turned around and began to walk away.

Gina wanted to just let the girl leave, walk out. She *was* busy and had so much to do in order to keep this godforsaken place running, but she just couldn't help herself, "Miss.--hold on a minute, Miss."

The woman turned around. Gina could see the hope rekindled in her sad eyes.

"My father used to own this place. His name is Fred Teemer. He's retired now, but maybe he can help you. He's eighty-six years old and not always lucid in the memory category, but he probably would have known your uncle," Gina offered.

"Oh! Yes! Yes, I would love to speak to your father!" Anna Parke replied.

She seemed grateful, so very grateful.

"He usually comes in to visit on Mondays. I suggest coming back then. I'm sure he would be happy to chat. He loves this damn place."

Pause.

Gina could see the girl taking this in, digesting it.

Finally, "Do you think it would be ok if I went to see him directly? I'm kind of on edge here?

"I don't know," Gina replied. "He's old and he lives alone." *Am I really going to send this woman to see my dad?* Gina thought to herself. *I don't even know her.*

"Please, Gina. I understand that you must be protective of your dad. I mean him no harm. I just want to talk. Jacob Parke, the man I'm looking for, is the only family I have." Anna Parke took a gamble with that last part. She played upon Gina's heartstrings, but it was true, wasn't it?

Well. What's the harm? This girl seems safe enough, Gina mused. *And besides, my dad loves visitors, and God knows I certainly don't go see him nearly enough.*

"Ok," Gina sighed. "I'll give you his address."

Gina scribbled an address on the back of a business card and hesitated before handing it over to Anna Parke who placed the card hastily in the back pocket of her jeans. She thanked Gina once more for her help and guidance.

Gina watched the woman exit the bowling alley and wished her a silent farewell. She hoped that Anna Parke found what she was looking for. Even though Gina had a hard exterior, she was a sucker for a good family reunion story and she was happy to play a part in this one, even a small part.

Chapter 30

On her way out of Alley Oops, Anna glanced at the silver watch on her wrist; It was five minutes to three. She still had a few hours before she had to start thinking about making her way back to Windsom. A lot could happen in a few hours. A whole lot.

She thought about the exchange she just had. Anna almost cried tears of gratitude as she watched Gina write down Fred Teemer's address. She thought that she had reached yet another dead end in her search for Jacob Parke. She also felt a sense of growing pride in herself–an emotion that was as new to Anna as the rising sun. In the past, Anna would have undoubtedly accepted Gina's first answer–and that answer would have resulted in her going back to Windsom without the information she needed. Anna would have been fuming at herself for not pushing just a bit harder, and would have sat on that bus headed towards home ashamed of her cowardice. But Anna hadn't just accepted dismissal. She had advocated for herself just a touch, had pushed herself out of her comfort zone…just a bit, for help. Anna had spent her entire life taking care of herself. Never asking for anything from anyone, trying to make as little of a footprint on this Earth as possible, and in the past she had felt content knowing that. It was a fact she carried around in her back pocket to remind herself that she was independent and ok. But maybe, just maybe, asking for help *was* ok…when you really needed it. Anna chewed on that notion as climbed into the yellow taxi that pulled up next to her as she stood outside the cab stand a few blocks away from Alley Oops.

She gave the driver her destination: 1751 Conklin Avenue, Apartment 3. As the cab pulled away, Anna gazed out the window noticing how the sun glinted off the side-view mirror obscuring her own reflection. The only feature she could make out was her Africa-shaped birthmark, plum and blatant on her right cheek.

When the cab pulled up to 1751 Conklin Avenue, Anna thanked the driver, handed over the fare–nine dollars and seventy five cents–and approached the small squat building. She judged that there were probably only four apartments in the entire property based on the four rickety mailboxes that stood before her. The whole street looked shabby and run down; the grass grew wild and ragged in certain places and the fences were rusty and old. She glanced at the row of mailboxes and sure enough, the name label for number three read: Fred Teemer. She walked up the crumbling cement stoop and rang the bell for number three.

Chapter 31

"Hello? Who's there," Fred Teemer shouted into the intercom. He could never figure this contraption out, which buttons to push when you wanted to talk and when to release the buttons to listen. Modern technology was always more hassle than it was worth.

"My name is Anna Parke, your daughter Gina gave me your address."

The voice was staticky and hard to hear. "Huh? I can't hear you," Fred replied, adjusting his new hearing aid. Damn thing didn't help much despite the doctor's promises. "Oh never mind, come up please." Fred heard the buzz and click of the door opening over the intercom and poked his confused face out of the door of apartment number three. “Who are you?” He asked again as he saw a girl emerge from the stairwell.

“My name is Anna Parke,” she announced. “Your daughter Gina gave me your address.”

“Gina? Is she ok?” Fred asked, confused. He always worried about Gina. No husband, no boyfriend. Who would look after her when she got old and tired like he was?

“Oh Yes. She is fine,” the girl replied. “I had some questions about your bowling alley. Do you have some time to talk?”

Did he have time to talk? About the bowling alley? Of course he had time to talk! He didn’t get many visitors lately. Most of his friends were either dead or shipped off to some old-age home. The thought of that gave him the chills and he was glad that Gina never suggested he leave his place and live in some antiseptic-smelling hospital room. And this girl wanted to talk about the alley. God how he loved that place.

“Ahhh. Good old Schenectady lanes,” he replied, his face lightening with nostalgia. “Come in come in!”

Fred Teemer ushered Anna into his apartment, “I can tell you stories about that place that will knock your socks off!”

Mr. Teemer’s apartment, though threadbare, was spotlessly tidy…Beverly Parke would have approved. The oak floors, while terribly worn and scratched, were crumbless and the couch had a plastic protector covering the upholstery which made sitting on it rather unpleasant, but he never sat on the couch. He much preferred the green upholstered Lazy-Boy positioned right in front of the boob-tube. The plastic covering was his wife's doing.

"Would you like some tea?" Mr. Teemer asked.

"Sure," the young lady, Anna or was it Ava, replied, "Thank you Mr. Teemer."

"Please. Call me Fred," he responded as he set about boiling some water.

He placed two Lipton's tea bags in mismatched cups, sliced up a rather sorry looking lemon and explained, "My wife would be horrified to see me serving tea in two different mugs. She loved matching sets." Then he went on, "My hands shake sometimes and I keep knocking them right off the counter! I bought a few random mugs from a yard sale last year and they have served me well ever since."

"I don't mind at all Mr. T–, I mean, Fred," said Anna as he set a steaming mug on the coffee table in front of her. "Is your wife here too?"

"No, Maria passed away about twelve years ago. Sudden stroke."

"I'm so sorry," the girl stumbled over her words.

He dismissed her condolences with a wave of his hand. Death no longer has the same potency when a person reaches a certain age. He had come to terms with loss. His wife, his friends, his parents...pretty soon Fred himself would go to that great castle in the sky. He didn't want this sweet young lady, Anna–yes, her name was Anna–to think that she was off to a bad start. She obviously had a reason to be here and Fred was happy to have someone to talk to, someone who cared to hear his stories.

Fred took a seat in the sagging easy chair opposite her and placed the tea cup on his lap where the steam rose up like morning fog rising off the ocean. Fred went about squeezing the lemon into his cup and then picking out the errant seeds that had accidentally fallen in, when he looked up, he saw Anna studying him. And he studied her in return. Cute kid...Hah, *kid*. Anyone under the age of 50 was a kid to Fred. She certainly looked young and healthy. No wrinkles, no gray hair, pretty despite the marking on her face.

In contrast, Fred's face was deeply lined and he had no trace of hair at all. He was creaky and achy and stiff. He looked out at the girl with twinkling blue eyes. His plaid button down shirt and tan slacks showed some wear and tear, especially in the knees where the pants were so shiny and thin they would surely rip at any given moment.

"So. Good old Schenectady lanes. Or I believe they call it Oopsie Daisy now, or something like that," he said with a toothless chuckle.

"Alley Oops," Anna corrected

"Right, right, clever name for a bowling alley," he replied. "You know, I owned that place for 45 years! When I first opened it in 1945 it was the only one in the entire central New York vicinity. People would come from miles around to play. There used to be lines that snaked around the block!"

Fred was happy to have someone to talk to about his beloved legacy and he spoke with pride in his watery eyes.

He continued, "On my 75th birthday I signed the lease over to my daughter Gina. My kids had been bugging me to go into retirement for years, but I don't know…I just liked being there. Gina loves that place as much as I do. About once a week I go back and order up some fries from Carla and watch the bowlers."

He had a faraway look in his eyes as he spoke and as he saw the ghosts of his past dancing in his periphery. When his eyes cleared he noticed the girl's foot jiggling, she was wiping her palms on the knees of her jeans like she wanted to ask him something.

Just as Fred was about to ask why she had come all this way, she spoke,
"So I came to ask about a certain employee, who worked for you in the late 1960s. His name was Jacob Parke." And then as if the girl couldn't hold back, "I just found out that he's my uncle and I am desperate to know more about him…his whereabouts. Anything you can tell me would be so helpful." The girl closed her mouth and Fred wondered if she had told him more than she meant to.

And then she asked again, "Do you remember him, Fred? Any information you have would truly help."

"Of course I remember him," Fred replied quickly. "I remember every employee that ever worked for me! Some people, especially my daughter, think that my memory isn't what it used to be, but when it comes to the alley, I remember everything. Jake was a nice kid, troubled but nice and a damn good worker if I might add."

"Can you tell me about him? I would love to hear your story Fred."

Fred began to wonder about this girl...Anna, sitting in front of him. There was a desperation about her.

He went on, "Jake came from some juvenile home; he was on a government employment placement and his paychecks came not from me, but from the government and then I got a cut from the state in return for hiring him. He didn't say much, but he showed up on time every day and sometimes even stayed late to help me close out the register...and he didn't even get any overtime for it."

Anna didn't say anything, didn't interrupt. She just nodded and looked at him with that intent stare as he went on.

"Jake was in charge of loading and oiling the machines, which is a damn dangerous job. One time I had a guy, Roger Clayton, who lost four of his fingers in one of those machines and he's lucky it didn't take his head clean off his shoulders!" As he said this last tidbit, he held up four fingers and gazed at them as if imagining their sudden disappearance.

"How long did he work for you at Schenectady Lanes?" Anna tentatively asked, once Fred Teemer was done reminiscing. They had sipped two cups of bitter tea together and they both seemed more comfortable with one another as time passed.

"A long time," Fred responded. "I can't remember the exact years, but at least through the 80s."

"Through the 80s," Anna repeated with wonder. "Did he ever talk about his life?...his past?"

"Not really," replied Fred. "He was pretty closed off like that."

"Any idea where he is now? If he is still alive?" Anna continued.

Fred Teemer thought about this question and replied, "Honestly Anna, I'm not so sure. He would pop in from time to time after he moved on, but I haven't seen or heard from him since the early 90s. Maybe 1991."

Anna seemed to deflate at this piece of information and Fred hated to see that, so he suggested, "I presume you have already tried Janine Harper?"

"Janine Harper?" Anna replied.

"Yes. Fred and Janine went together, at least they did for the few years before Jake left the alley. They lived together too. Janine was one of my front desk clerks. Cute kid."

"Do you happen to remember where she lived?" Anna asked hopefully.

"Now that's one thing I do remember," replied Fred. "They lived right above Stout's Pub. We used to go there sometimes right after closing and grab a few beers. I suppose we could have had beers at the alley, but I guess we needed a change of scenery. Jake and Janine used to go right upstairs after we all had a few," Fred informed Anna, again with that glint of nostalgia shining in his eyes.

"Stout's is still there too. Oldest bar in Schenectady."

"Thank you so much Fred, you have helped more than you know," Anna said. She really meant it too, and she bent down to give the old man a warm hug before she left the orderly apartment on Conklin Street.

"It was my pleasure. It was nice talking about those days. All those years of owning that bowling alley, they were some of the best years of my life. Are you sure I can't fix you something to eat? I have many more stories to tell."

Fred didn't want Anna to leave. This was the most conversation he'd had in months. Sometimes he went days without speaking to another human being, weeks if you don't count his short phone conversations with Gina. Gina tries, sweet girl, but she has her own life to live, and besides, she already heard all Fred's stories.

"I'm sorry Fred. I have to go. But thank you. I appreciate your time. And your stories," Anna said as she stood to leave.

An absent glare entered Fred's eyes as Anna said her goodbyes. He became fuzzy and confused for a moment. Was his daughter ok? Who was this girl hugging him? His niece? He stood up and walked to the kitchen to help himself to a tall glass of ice water. Ice water usually helped him regain his composure, which seemed to be slipping away from him with an increased frequency during the last few months. But, when Fred found himself, gazing into the cupboard above the sink, he forgot the purpose of his visit to his kitchen and went back into the living room to sit down on the creaking Lazy Boy to watch highlights of the New York Mets' 1986 World Series victory.

Chapter 32

As Anna walked down the stairwell and away from Fred Teemer's apartment, a vague image of her uncle began to form in her head. Her uncle had a nickname: Jake. He was a man who showed up for work on time and stayed late to help his boss with paperwork–a man who committed a terrible crime, but tried to make up for it once he served his time. It made Anna wonder why he did it. The description of Jacob Parke as delivered by Fred, didn't seem to correspond with the murderer she had envisioned–the cruel, blood-thirsty killer. She realized only Jacob Parke himself could answer the questions that buzzed around her mind.

That feeble hope that had been on the horizon was rekindled within Anna as she contemplated what Fred had revealed to her in his apartment. If the pub was still there, could Janine still be there too? Could Jacob Parke have been hidden away in an apartment above this local watering hole an hour and a half away from her home town all this time? She had to find out.

By the time Anna walked out of Mr. Teemer's apartment, it was late–about seven thirty in the evening and the cool breeze began to pick up, causing gooseflesh to pop out on her exposed arms. She knew she couldn't possibly knock on some random door, especially if the tenant was an elderly woman in her late sixties or seventies so late in the evening. Even though she had not anticipated staying the night in Schenectady, she decided that finding a local motel was a better idea than taking the bus all the way back to Windsom and then coming all the way back to Schenectady tomorrow. She walked to the corner of Conklin, where it met Redmond Avenue and stopped at the 24 hour CVS to buy a few toiletries and snacks. She had barely eaten anything all day and she was feeling dizzy and light-headed. After she purchased a few items for the night, a tiny tube of Crest toothpaste and travel toothbrush, a bag of Lays Potato Chips, luke-warm bottle of Poland Spring water and tic tacs, she continued walking towards the sign that read 'Days Inn' on Redmond Avenue.

Once Anna was settled in a small corner room with a full-sized bed outfitted in a maroon and green striped coverlet, she ate her light snack as she watched the evening news on the small television. The perfectly made-up news anchorwoman spoke about a house fire that occurred in the downtown Schenectady area and Anna briefly thought about this unfortunate family and wondered where they would find warmth on this cool early-fall evening. She sent her boss at the Food Mart a quick text saying that she was feeling ill and would not be coming in for her ten-am shift tomorrow. This was the first time in Anna's memory that she ever called out sick to work. She was nothing if not dependable. Anna fell asleep to the drone of the television and the light of the moon shining through the cheap motel blinds. She dreamed about her uncle, the man she never knew...the bowling alley employee, the boyfriend of the mysterious Janine Harper, the tenant above Stout's, the murderer of her grandparents.

Chapter 33

By the next morning Anna was ravenous, and after a quick shower, with her hair still knotty as a result of the cheap motel conditioner, she went down to indulge in the small complimentary continental breakfast. She ate whole wheat toast and some watery scrambled eggs along with a few sausage links plucked from the neat display. Two cups of coffee gave her the push she needed to approach the front desk and ask about a pub named Stout's. She supposed she could have just tried a Google search, but there must be a million pubs with the same name in New York.

The young man behind the reception desk had no idea about the location of the establishment in question, clearly Stout's did not appeal to a younger clientele, but when he asked the middle-aged woman behind him, she was able to provide an address.

"Right up on Jackson Blvd," she directed. "Across the street from the Dairy Mart. They probably won't open for another few hours though."

"Thanks!" Anna responded. She checked out of the hotel. There was no way she could afford another "sick day." Regardless of what today revealed, she knew she had to go back to Windsom tonight to make her 9am shift at the Food Mart tomorrow. Anna did not allow tomorrow's responsibilities to put a damper on today's intentions and as she exited through the electronic sliding doors she was once again on her way.

Jackson Blvd just happened to be within walking distance and with the bright sunshine warm on her face, Anna headed East to find Janine Harper. Hopefully this mystery woman would give Anna some of the answers she craved.

About twenty minutes later, Anna found herself staring at a run-down pub with a stone facade boasting a wooden sign with 'Stout's' carved into the splintered slab. It was clear from the darkened bay window and the locked front door that it was currently closed. But when her eyes scanned upward, she was able to make out two small windows directly on top of the establishment. That had to be the apartment. She didn't see any semblance of an entry, so she circled around the building and in the back, saw a steep set of rickety wooden stairs leading up to an inconspicuous front door. It was ten o'clock in the morning, as good a time as any and she ascended the stairs in pursuit of Janine Harper.

Anna stood on the landing outside the blue chipped door, straightened her light sweater, wishing she had brought a change of clothes with her on her journey, and using the small brass knocker, rapped lightly. No answer. She tried again, harder this time and a shrill woman's voice yelled from within.

"I'll have your rent tomorrow, you know I'm good for it."

Anna replied back with a slightly raised voice, trying her best to sound unassuming and friendly, "Um. Excuse me, I think you have the wrong person."

"Who are you then?" The voice shot back.

"My name is Anna Parke," she began and then didn't quite know how to continue.

The door slowly opened and a set of narrow green eyes regarded her.

"What did you say your name was?"

She tried again, "My name is Anna Parke. I was told you may have known a man named Jacob Parke."

Chapter 34

As the door opened wider, the hazy sunlight revealed Janine Harper, standing upright in the open rectangle. She was an older woman, in her early 70s, dressed in a shabby housecoat and purple fuzzy slippers. Her gray wiry hair and wrinkled neck couldn't hide the fact that at one point, she had been incredibly attractive. Her green eyes glowed with an intelligence, keen and bright. A black cat wound its way around her ankles and purred as it seemed to stare right through this girl at her front door. Janine's sharp gaze wavered to the girl's cheek for a moment, taking in the unsightly mark, but aside from that one small slip, the old woman's eyes never left those of this stranger standing before her. There was something familiar about those eyes. Something about their shape, so wide, so innocent

"You were told I might have known Jacob?" Janine repeated.

"Yes."

"Who told you that?" Janine pressed on.

"Fred Teemer."

"Oh."

"I'm looking for information about him," the young woman continued.

"What sort of information?" Janine asked. Janine was skeptical about this woman's–Anna's, intentions and hesitant to engage in conversation. She didn't often get visits, especially not from young women, just out of the blue. And that name...Parke. It made her feel things that she didn't want to feel.

"Please Ms. Harper. I mean no harm. I just want to know about him. Anything you are willing to share."

"So you are related to Jake I presume?...*Parke*, same last name," Janine said in reply.

"Please, call me Anna. I know it must be weird for you to see me here. I just found out about Jacob. He's my uncle. I didn't even know I had an uncle until recently. I always thought I was just... just alone."

Alone, Janine thought. She could relate to alone. Janine couldn't stop her curiosity from creeping up. No matter how much she had tried to close herself off from ever thinking, much less *talking* about Jake, she was interested to know about this girl and the motives that pushed her to turn up here on this day.

"Ok. Anna. And what exactly did you hope to find?" Janine asked after she listened to Anna relate her recent discovery.

"I guess I hoped to find him…or at least learn something about him," Anna Parke's words seemed to fade into space as she spoke.

"Jacob Parke broke my heart," Janine said quietly as though woken from a trance.

Silence.

"Can I come in Ms. Harper? Please?"

"Well, if I am to call you Anna, you might as well call me Janine."

"Ok, Janine. Can I please come in?" Anna asked again.

"Yeah, I guess so. You don't look like you would take 'no' for an answer."

So Janine held the door open as Anna Parke, Jake's niece, walked through her front door.

As tidy and sparse as Fred Teemer's house appeared, Janine Harper's was cluttered almost to the rafters with knick-knacks and what Beverly Parke would have referred to as 'dust-collectors.' Every shelf displayed ceramic figurines of little blonde-haired girls, glossy lambs and kittens, Hummels, Norman Rockwell plates and various other collectibles. There were stacks of crocheted quilts in all different colors and patterns piled on the stained sofa and food encrusted dishes in the sink. No one else lived here with Janine, there was simply no room for anyone else to occupy this space. Maybe that's why she acquired so much stuff...to fill the emptiness. Janine Harper cleared off a small square of the couch for Anna to sit on and then plopped herself down across from her in a creaking wooden rocking chair.

"Jake and I have a long history, and if I am to unpack it all, it has to be in my way. I'll tell you my story if you'd like to hear it."

"I would very much like that," Anna said as she shifted into a more comfortable position on the overcrowded sofa. The black cat jumped into her lap. *Traitor*, Janine thought as she watched Anna entwine her fingers in Lucky's silky fur. In her gravelly voice, Janine began telling her story, a story she never thought she would ever have had the occasion to tell again. A story that broke her heart, and that continued to break her heart every time she thought about it.

Chapter 35

I've lived in this apartment all my life. It was just me and my mom here; my dad left when I was 8 and never came back. My mom was a bartender downstairs at Stout's and Mr. Hadley, the owner, leased us this place real cheap. My mother passed away when I was 15. Lung

cancer. I dropped out of school to find a full time job in order to make ends meet. That's when I started at the bowling alley. Frank Teemer, I'm sure he told you, had just opened the place. He was young at the time I don't even know how he had the money, some inheritance or something I guess. Frank needed a front-desk clerk and I needed a job. He paid me well and didn't try to lift up my skirt behind the counter so I considered myself pretty lucky.

Anna listened intently as Janine continued to talk about the early days at Schenectady lanes. A soft purring sound emanated from the sleeping bundle in Anna's lap.

The old woman continued.

Lucky likes you. Listen to her purring! So anyhow things went on like that for a while. I spent almost all my time at work, no time for friends or dating or anything like that. And then I met Jake, that must have been around 1964 or so. He was a few years older than I was. Fred had told me that he just got out of a juvenile detention facility, so I was a bit afraid of him at first. But he had these twinkling eyes and a kind way about him. He was the first boy who ever showed any interest in this plain old, uneducated local girl. He was sweet, that Jake. He would stay late and help me organize the bowling shoes…sometimes he would walk me home. I never had a car or anything like that and it was out of his way by two miles or more.

Gradually we became more than friends. Two years after we met he was living right here with me. He told me about his past before he moved in officially, about Half-Moon and about the trial. He swore to me up and down that he never did it, that he never killed his parents. And I believed him. He also mentioned that he had a sister, but he never seemed to want to talk about her...seemed like they had some sort of falling out or something.

This part of Janine's story particularly interested Anna as she listened.She wished she knew the intricacies of Jacob's relationship with Beverly. How did Beverly feel about the death of her parents? How did she feel towards her brother? She was also interested in Jacob's claimed innocence, but of course he wouldn't have admitted what he did, not to his girlfriend. Right?

At this point, Janine rose from the chair and went to the kitchen for a glass of water, asking Anna if she would like anything to drink. Even though Anna's throat was dry, she didn't want to ask for anything that might delay Janine's story any further, so she declined the offer. On her way back from the kitchen, Janine opened up a drawer in the hallway bureau and pulled out a photograph, which she handed over to Anna. The photograph was taken years ago and Anna noticed that Janine, as she expected, was quite beautiful as a younger woman. Staring out at her from this creased and dulled black and white photo was a smiling Janine holding the hand of a young girl wearing a striped bathing suit. Holding the little girl's other hand was Jacob Parke, who was staring not at the camera, but smiling down at the little girl by his side. He was older in this photograph than in the one Anna saw printed in the newspaper, but it was him nonetheless. But who was this little girl? Janine must have seen Anna's confused face because she quickly continued:

That's me and Jake and our daughter, Rebecca. We were quite happy for a long time here. Rebecca used to love coming to the bowling alley with us. Fred even gave her a sparkly pink bowling ball. Gosh, how she loved that thing.

Anna tried to process this information. A daughter? Jacob had a daughter? Anna had a cousin? Anna did more math in her head; she was becoming quite the expert at calculating ages in her mind and came to the conclusion that Rebecca would be about her age...maybe a bit younger…in her mid-late 20s.

"Where is Rebecca now? Where is Jacob," Anna's curiosity was unblunted and direct. She craved answers and was beginning to lose patience with the deliberateness with which Janine was unraveling her life.

It's a sad story and I haven't told it in many years. You have to bear with me. You see, when Rebecca was about 10 years old, Jake didn't think he needed to keep up with his medication anymore. He said that he was feeling well and that the large doses of Prozac and Abilify were starting to make him feel 'muddled'...that's the word he used, "muddled."

Janine took a slow sip of her water as the ghosts of her past danced upon her eyelids.

That's when things started to fall apart for us. Jake started to…unravel; that's the only term I could truly use to describe it. He started talking more and more about the past and about his parents and about his sister. He would rant for hours about his innocence and how he was framed. How he was cheated out of a successful life and how in turn Rebecca and I had been cheated too. He couldn't let it go. The anger. He said he wanted better for us. That we deserved better. Over the next two or three years his rantings grew worse and he was barely comprehensible. He quit the bowling alley. He couldn't quite get out of bed in the morning. He would ramble on and on about the woods and the trees and he would repeat over and over again, 'The tree knows. The tree knows. The tree knows."

Anna's mind snapped to rigid attention with that last detail. The tree? What tree? She thought about her own puzzling relationship with the trees of Windsom. Did Jacob have a similar connection or was this the ravings of a madman, a murdering madman? Was he also drawn to those woody beings that surrounded him? Could there be some weird family connection? Didn't Jacob supposedly chop down a tree branch, thus murdering his parents? Anna's heartbeat quickened with both excitement and fear as she considered these possibilities.

"So what happened to Jacob?" Anna asked as Janine once again sunk into her contemplative silence.

He started to frighten me; he especially frightened Rebecca. I didn't know what to do with him. I threatened to leave him if he didn't try to get himself back on track. He was unwell. I contacted Blue-Moon; I knew at that point he was too old to be admitted there, but I thought that they might have some suggestions. They helped get him into a different facility that could help him.

There was a tinge of defiant embarrassment as Janine told this part of her story, as if she felt like she had to convince Anna that she hadn't abandoned her own partner.

So that's where Jacob is now. Except they weren't able to help him; he has only gotten worse. I used to go visit him, but whenever I would see him in the visiting center, his tantrums were so out of control and violent...his doctors thought it best I stay away, at least temporarily until he could work out his issues. Well, he never did work out his issues. It broke my heart. And it broke his daughter's heart.

That tiny glimmer of hope rekindled deep within Anna. Jacob was alive. But terribly damaged.

After Janine revealed this information, both women sat in silence for a long time. Janine trying to come to terms with her past actions and the demise of her beloved Jacob, and Anna trying to reconcile this new image of her uncle with the one she had in her head. But, the story was not over.

"I'm so sorry Janine," Anna tentatively said...she didn't know what else to say. What words can possibly heal the wounds inflicted by love? "Can I hear the rest of your story? Can I hear about Rebecca?"

Janine Harper inhaled a large breath, as though steeling herself–readying her mind to tell the remainder of her tale.

After Jacob left, my relationship with my daughter began to crumble. Rebecca adored her father and blamed me for betraying him and turning him into what he had become. I have nightmares of the intense fights we used to have. I hit her once, slapped her right on the cheek. I'll never lose the guilt I feel about that. She was almost 14 by the time Jake went away, not a good age for a girl to lose her dad...not that any age is a good age. Rebecca started hanging out with the wrong crowd; she got into drugs. She hated me, hated school, hated everyone.

Rebecca ran away from home when she was 16 years old with her grimy boyfriend. I tried to track her down; I could never nail down an address or phone number. One time she called asking for money. Of course I refused; I couldn't fund her drug habit...not that I even had any money at the time.

Janine took another deep breath before she disclosed the next bit.

7 years ago, I got a phone call from the Buffalo Police Department, telling me that Rebecca had passed...overdose. They said that she had so much heroin in her system that she probably didn't even know it was happening. She was homeless at the time, living in a shelter.

So that was it..the Parke legacy. The weight of Janine's story was almost too much for Anna to process. What a cursed and melancholy lineage.

"Janine...I am so sorry."

The words felt inadequate and forced in the face of such tragedy, but they were all Anna could bring herself to mutter.

"Well. That's my story," said Janine as if she wanted to dismiss the matter entirely, close the book, shut the door on her past, as if she had revealed more than she had ever intended. At that moment, Anna felt guilty for ever having arrived on Janine's doorstep and forcing her to talk about her history.

But Anna also felt something else. She had a keen and nagging feeling that Janine was keeping something from her, hiding some small piece of her story, some small detail about Jacob Parke. Her story made sense of course. And Anna couldn't be totally sure, but something in the sideways, slightly tilted glance that Janine cast in Anna's direction made Anna think that Janine had deliberated and subsequently decided to keep a piece of her tale for herself only. At one point, Janine opened her mouth as if to say more, but instead of speaking, she took a sip of her water. Anna couldn't blame the woman; Janine had been so forthcoming with so much painful minutia about her life, and to a stranger at that. But nonetheless the notion tugged at Anna's periphery, gnawing at her sense of peace.

"And you said that Jacob is still at that facility?" Anna asked.

"Yup. The Ithaca Psychiatric Hospital," Janine replied with a sigh.

"Thank you very much for seeing me and telling me your story. I'd like it if we could keep in touch."

Anna felt very close to Janine, even though she had only spent a few hours in her small home. So far in her life, Janine was the only person to provide Anna with a glimpse into her family, even though there was no blood relation between the two.

"I'd like that. You know where to find me. Now can I ask you a question?"

"Anything," Anna replied.

"Are you going to go see him?"

"I think I have to," Anna said.

"Don't get your hopes up," Janine said. "Jake is a sick, sick man."

Anna once again thanked Janine Harper and wove her way out of the crowded space. She knew she had to go find Jacob Parke, if only to find some sense of closure, but she was terrified at the prospect of facing him. What would she find? A crazy man ranting and raving about trees. Trees...how odd. Again Anna reflected on her own strange history with the trees behind Ackerly Lane. The push and pull she experienced throughout her life: the yearning put up in stark contrast against the fear. Could Anna and Jacob have more in common besides DNA? Her head was spinning at the possibilities and questions that Janine's story inspired within her tired mind.

As she walked down those wooden stairs leading up to Janine's apartment, Anna was struck with an overwhelming sense of melancholy that threatened to drown her. The tears started flowing, large wet pools formed in the corners of her eyes and trickled into the crevices of her lips. Her throat felt thick with salt. She cried for her mother, she cried for the grandparents she never met, the found and lost uncle Jacob–locked away behind padded walls, she cried for Rebecca and Janine and most of all, she cried for herself–a tiny fragile figurine with a shattered head.

Chapter 36

The apartment was quiet again. Janine couldn't remember the last time she talked so much. In fact, her throat felt sore from the effort. She thought about how strange life could be sometimes. Just when she thought that she moved on, fate directed Anna Parke–Jacob's niece–to her doorstep on such a nondescript fall morning. Janine felt something akin to shock to even learn that another Parke existed. One Parke was enough to cause a lifetime of grief. She thought she knew all there was to know about this cursed family. Of course she thought about Jacob and Rebecca. But for the most part, Janine trained her mind to only think about them in fleeting moments. Anything more was simply too much to bear.

Feeling jittery, Janine rose from the sofa and bent down to retrieve Lucky's food dish. That old cat would be wanting her breakfast now. As Janine went about opening the can of chicken-flavored Fancy Feast, her eyes caught a glimpse of the photograph that Anna held a little while ago. Janine hadn't looked at that glossy image in a long time. It was too painful to be out on display; it was better off buried deep within a drawer. As Janine placed the bowl of cat food on the floor she wondered if she should have told Anna the rest of the story. The full story. But what good would that have done? Anna certainly didn't need another fool's errand to run. One was enough. And finding Jacob certainly was a foolish task. Unfortunately, the girl would find that out soon enough.

But even though Janine was able to push the thought out of her mind, she kept returning to it over and over again throughout the course of the following few days. Turning it over and over again. *Oh well*, she thought. *No use perseverating on it.* But still, the thought nagged at her. *If she comes back I'll tell her*, she decided. And with that final thought Janine was able to put the matter to rest once and for all. And that was good.

Chapter 37

Anna found herself on the nine o'clock evening bus back to Windsom, staring out the foggy window, which only threw her own reflection back at her. She looked exhausted–purplish bags under her eyes and pale complexion, which only exacerbated her facial blemish. She almost didn't recognize herself in the darkness. She was one of only six passengers on the Greyhound bus and the soft music playing over the speakers, the gentle sway of the road, and the soft velour seat beneath her made her eyes heavy. Car rides, or in this case bus rides, always made Anna drowsy. She vividly remembered sitting in the backseat of her mother's small sedan growing up, listening to soft jazz emanating from the puny sound system and feeling herself simply drifting off. Dreaming. She relished those car rides. The silence provided her with uninterrupted 'think time.' At least that was how Anna thought of it. She actually looked forward to sitting in the cool comfort of the gray upholstery and having nothing else to do, but think and daydream. Sometimes before she even got into the car, Anna would plan what she would contemplate, what cute boy she would envision or what vacation she would ponder. Young Anna spun out beautiful fairy tales in her mind as Windsom passed in her periphery.

She woke abruptly to the hiss of brakes and the sound of an opening door. Home. As she stepped down from the bus and onto Main Street it was nearly eleven o'clock. The street was empty and quiet, not one business open except Don's Place, which emanated a soft neon glow that was barely perceptible from where Anna stood. She made her way to her small apartment and let herself inside. Last night marked the only night she had ever spent away from this place since she moved in, and even though she was away for only one short night, her apartment seemed stale and foreign. Or maybe it was her...she felt different, changed in some profound way. The apartment seemed quieter and emptier than it ever had. So much had happened in such a short time. She left in pursuit of an uncle, and though she hadn't yet technically found him, she felt like the knowledge she gained about her own bloodline had physically aged her.

She opened the front apartment window and held her hair away from her neck as the cool evening breeze wafted through, cooling her, calming her. As she stood there, with her eyes closed, she heard the whispers of the trees, louder than they had been in a long time. She tried to ignore them, close herself off to their callings, but they continued their incessant summons. They had a story to tell her. Was she ready to listen? They urged her to return, to embrace them as she once had as a child, to accept the connection they shared, to dismiss what was logical and reasonable and nurture what is beyond comprehension, what was magical and beautiful and right.

Despite the temptation to go to them, to sink into the dark and sweet-scented woods behind Ackerly Lane, Anna knew she could not possibly go. She had absorbed too much today, felt too many emotions, shed too many tears, and she needed time to process. She needed sleep. Anna undressed and naked, crawled into her unmade bed, wrapping the thick comforters around her bare shoulders. She let her exhaustion carry her away.

She awoke at 9:25 the next morning in a panic; she was late for work, another first.She hastily ran a brush through her tangled hair, threw on a pair of Levis, a light long-sleeved Henley and her smock, grabbed her purse and raced out the door. It was only when she took her rightful place behind the cash register on lane two that her breath finally slowed and her heart stopped galloping in her chest. She did not enjoy this new jittery feeling that had recently taken up residence within her.

Anna felt as though the predictable life that she had was beginning to fall apart...and the worst part about it was that she was doing it to herself. She could easily stop her pursuit into her past, let Jacob Parke rot in Ithaca, but something in her soul was screaming at her to keep going. Ignoring that screaming would be an impossible feat and Anna knew it.

The mundane scanning and bagging helped Anna regain her composure and the trivial conversations she engaged in with the regulars helped her achieve a semblance of normalcy for the duration of her shift.

At the end of the evening, Anna looked up from her scanning and came face to face with Mrs. Douglaston, the elderly neighbor who called to deliver the news of Beverly Parke's passing a few weeks earlier.

"Hello dear," Mrs. Douglaston said in a tone that made Anna cringe. That tone told Anna that she was about to have a conversation that she very much did not desire to have.

"Oh, hi Mrs. Douglaston."

"Oh sweetie," she replied, her eyes brimming over with tears. "How have you been?"

"I've been ok. Thanks." Anna tried to respond in a way that was both not overtly rude, but that also did not inspire a prolonged exchange.

"I'm really so sorry about your mom. I see the house is for sale. Any takers?"

"Not yet," Anna answered

"Dear, haven't you thought about living there yourself? Your mom took such good care of the property.

It would be a shame to just sell it to someone else, don't you think?"

As innocent as Mrs. Douglaston's remarks and questions were, they made Anna's skin crawl. If she only knew the intricacies of the situation. And Anna certainly was not prepared to have that heartfelt conversation with a woman she barely knew here at the register. Anna nodded and answered in the appropriate moments, and as Mrs. Douglaston droned on, Anna hurriedly bagged the woman's few items to accelerate her exit.

"Anna. Come visit! We can have some tea and chat," Mrs. Douglaston said on her way out of the Food Mart. Even though Anna swore to take Mrs. Douglaston up on her invitation, in her heart she knew that she could never make good on that promise. She had no desire whatsoever to pursue a friendship with Mrs. Douglaston nor expound upon her inadequate relationship with her mother.

As she walked out of the Food Mart at six o'clock on the dot, Anna felt lonely and unsettled. She dreaded a quiet night alone in her apartment. She needed to escape her own thoughts and the whispering of the trees on the wind. For most of her life now she fought against her pull towards the trees. Magic and logic didn't mix in her mind; Anna believed that she could not have both, and clearly an adult must choose logic over magic, right?

So instead of walking east on Main Street, she walked west and in no time at all, Anna sat upon her usual wobbly wooden stool at the bar at Don's.

Don no longer needed to ask Anna for her order; he knew that she always started her evenings with a

Corona (no lime), which eventually led to Tito's and seltzer and then to many more of the same. The smooth bottle was wet and cold and she gradually felt her anxiety melt away as she greedily drank the fizzy amber liquid.

On a Tuesday evening in the fall, Don's wasn't overly crowded, just the regulars and one couple from Long Island, who sat side by side scrolling through the photographs that they took on their cellphones during the day's outdoor adventures–the final tourists before the new wave began in the winter for ski season.

Before long Anna switched to her vodka drink. One led to two and before she knew it, she felt that old familiar humming in her head and her body grew heavy and warm and fuzzy. This was the feeling Anna sought, the dulled and muddled state that stops the relentlessness of logic and thought…temporarily at least. Unfortunately, only temporarily.

At some point in the late hours of the evening, Anna couldn't have recalled the specific time, she stumbled back to her apartment. The dollhouse on the coffee table cast a jagged shadow on the floor, grotesque and nightmarish in the darkness.

The alcohol blocked out the sound of the trees and Anna slept a drunken sleep while the woods waited for Anna to return. Not yet, she wasn't yet ready to hear what they had to say, but soon.

Anna worked another predictable shift at the Food Mart the next day, and when four o'clock came, instead of going to Don's, Anna went back to her apartment to make plans to go to Ithaca. She could prolong the trip no further; she needed to see this through. She put a call through to the Ithaca Psychiatric Facility, and after confirming that Jacob Parke was indeed still a patient there, she asked to be connected to someone that could help her schedule a visit.

The protocol was stricter than that at Half-Moon and Anna was told that she needed to go through a vetting process before she could gain face-to-face access to Jacob Parke. Anna needed to provide the facility with proof of identification and meet with one of the administrators on staff. If the meeting went well, and if her uncle agreed to see her, she would be permitted a one hour, supervised session with Jacob. So many ifs. Again, Anna despised all the red-tape and protocols of such places. She understood they were necessary, but frustrating-as-hell nonetheless.

She scheduled the interview for next week, October 16th, which was the soonest appointment available and even though she wished it were sooner, she thought the delay was probably for the best. After all, Anna needed to request some time off from work, schedule transportation, and find accommodations in Ithaca, which was about three-hours northwest from Windsom. She also needed time to think about what she wanted to say. What she wanted to ask. But then again, Jacob was a wild card. Anna certainly could not account for his capabilities nor his willingness to talk to her.

Anna was both eager and frightened at the thought of meeting Jacob Parke. On one hand she hoped the week would fly by, but on the other hand she dreaded what was to come. She needed to find a way to still her trembling soul until October 16th. At that moment, she never thought that anyone was more right than Tom Petty was when he sang, "The waiting is the hardest part."

Chapter 38

Despite the anxious anticipation, the week passed quickly. Anna worked five more shifts at The Food Mart, one more than normal, to make up for the three days off she requested and was subsequently granted. Her boss, Adam, was surprised by the request and even though he would have to find employees willing to cover Anna's shifts, he was happy to give his best employee, who had never once asked for any days off, the leave she needed. Adam cared about Anna in a fatherly way and when he asked her about her plans for the three days, she gave him only a vague response about family obligations. He was confused by her response and her hazy answers because as far as he knew, Anna had no family, not since Beverly had died at least, but he didn't force the issue, nor did Anna provide any further detail.

Anna arranged to spend the three nights at the Residence Inn, located in downtown Ithaca. It was a short bus ride to the psychiatric facility and walking distance to many of the waterfalls for which Ithaca is famous. She figured that if she had any spare time she might as well see the sights. She had never been to the city before and even though she was terrified about seeing her uncle, her latent desire for adventure relished any opportunity to escape Windsom.

As she turned the key in the rusted nickel lock in the front door of her apartment, a sharp chill raced up her spine, causing her breath to catch in her parched throat. This would be the longest she ever was away from Windsom; her mother hadn't exactly taken her on any family vacations as a child, nor did she have any relatives with which to stay. She wished that she hadn't waited so long to explore other places and it saddened her to think that her first "vacation" was to track down a murdering, mentally unstable uncle who until a few weeks ago, she hadn't even known existed. She tried to push away that last unpleasant thought, as one would sidestep a persistent car salesman, and started her walk to the bus depot to begin a journey with an uncertain destination.

She stepped off the bus in Ithaca on Monday, October 15th at 2:30 in the afternoon; the day was mild and unseasonably warm. The bus ride was uneventful and she dozed in and out of consciousness as sprawling mountains interspersed with tiny towns nestled against the surrounding woods passed outside the large tinted window. Her meeting with the Ithaca Psychiatric Hospital was scheduled for tomorrow morning at eleven on the dot, so she had the afternoon to explore the downtown area, which was dotted with pizzerias, coffee shops, trendy clothing boutiques, and administrative buildings along with the stereotypical establishments that would appeal to the college students attending Ithaca College or Cornell University located at the top of the hill. The storefront windows twinkled in the afternoon sunshine as Anna walked to the Residence Inn situated at the outskirts of the shopping district.

Anna checked into the hotel and used the keycard given to her by the woman behind the front desk. She heard the faint click as she pushed open the heavy hotel room door to her small room with a double bed and mini fridge. She plopped her small duffel on the navy blue textured chair in the corner and went to the bathroom to freshen up after the long bus ride. The cool water felt invigorating as it ran down her face in small, clear rivulets. She freed her hair from the pink elastic tie and ran her fingers through the knotty tangles. She applied a bit of lip gloss from a small metal tub and thought she looked okay, like her mom always said, "quite pretty if it wasn't for the glaring blemish on her cheek." She dismissed the thought; since she found out about Jacob she didn't exactly know how to feel about her mother. She couldn't reconcile the new bits and pieces of information she learned about Beverly Parke with the cold and aloof woman she knew all her life. It was as though she was given all these new puzzle pieces for a jigsaw that had already been completed. Where did these new pieces fit? How did they alter the graphic that was already there? Anna didn't quite know the answer, but she certainly was not going to let her mother's blatant disapproval interfere with what she had to do here. What she wanted and needed and feared to do here.

Anna walked back through the lobby's electric sliding doors, hearing the faint whoosh as they opened and then closed for her. She headed back to downtown Ithaca with the intention of finding something to eat and heading back for an early bedtime. She wanted to be well-rested for her interview tomorrow. After all, if it didn't go well, she would be denied access to Jacob Parke and consequently denied access to her own birthright. When she put it that way it sounded over dramatic, but wasn't it true also? That couldn't happen...not if she could help it.

The warm afternoon had cooled to a chilly twilight and Anna pulled her light jacket tighter around her shoulders against the slight breeze. Upstate New York in the fall is both glorious and cruel; always providing gentle reminders that the unrelenting winter is just around the corner. As Anna meandered through the brick walkways the signs of the season were all around: smiling straw scarecrows tied to the corner lampposts, storefront windows adorned with pumpkins and paper mache autumn leaves in shades of scarlet, amber and gold, advertisements for the upcoming Halloween parade on neon orange poster board. Anna remembered her own childhood Halloweens spent trick-or-treating with the neighborhood kids. Unlike the other local mothers, who dressed up in silly costumes and accompanied their own children on their yearly escapade, Anna's own mother never found it necessary to supervise her daughter during this ritual and once her plastic pumpkin was filled to the brim with candy, Anna would return to her quiet home and retreat to her bedroom to sort through her booty. She wondered if Jacob went trick-or-treating with his own daughter, Rebecca, before he made the decision to cease his regiment of antipsychotic and anti-anxiety medication. Did he hold her hand and look on with pride as she ascended the neighbors' front stoops to politely collect her treats. Was he a good father?

Her thoughts kept returning to Rebecca. A long lost cousin, a little younger than Anna, growing up only a few towns west. Anna surely would have adored Rebecca; Anna, a lonely little girl who longed for any family aside from her icy mother. At this point, she couldn't help feeling as though she had been robbed, swindled out of a family. And now Rebecca was dead. Another relationship that ended before it even began. And here she was, minutes away from Rebecca's father, Anna's own uncle. The last bit of Parke blood locked behind the metal bars of insanity. These thoughts unraveled like an old sweater and raced through Anna's mind a million miles a minute. The thoughts kept coming, faster and faster; Anna thought her brain might burst.

It was evening now in Ithaca, New York and the stars emerged, sparkling like diamonds against the inky black sky. Anna couldn't recall darkness descending; she was too distracted by her own noisy mind. Her grumbling stomach reminded her that she hadn't yet eaten dinner, and she wandered into a small pizza place with a sign in the window that read, *Tino's Pizza–Home of the Original Cold Cheese Pizza.* So many upstate pizza joints brag about being the originator of cold-cheese pizza; it didn't matter to Anna who was first, the slice was always delicious–crispy cheese pizza topped with a handful of cold shredded, thick cut mozzarella. There was something about the hot crispy base paired with the cold cheese that came together as perfection in her mouth. This evening was one of the first occasions she ordered the meal sober and it was just as satisfying. She gobbled down the entire slice interspersed with gulps of an ice cold fountain coke, making sure not to leave behind any strands of errant cheese left on the white scalloped paper plate.

Anna felt much better once she ate, her mind much clearer, and she walked leisurely back to the Residence Inn after she emptied her plate and cup into the trash receptacle on her way out of Tino's. The night was beautiful–cool and clear, a full buttery moon blazing against a cloudless sky. As she lay in the rough hotel bed, she tried to imagine what her meeting with the administrator at the psychiatric facility would entail. She couldn't help but feel that she was going to a job interview; she knew she had to put her best foot forward if she had any chance of gaining access to her uncle. She wasn't even so sure why her need to meet Jacob Parke was so intense. What could he possibly do for her? She had been totally fine up until a few weeks ago, hadn't she? Content in her blessed ignorance. Maybe she simply needed to know that there was some other Parke out there...maybe it was a basic case of curiosity. But what was that old saying? Didn't curiosity kill the cat? She fell asleep pondering these notions that were blowing around in her mind much the same way the autumn leaves were blowing in the wind outside the hotel window.

Chapter 39

Anna popped awake the next morning as the red numbers on the clock positioned on the bedside table blared eight-fifteen. Even though she had a few hours before she was scheduled to be at the Ithaca Psychiatric Facility, no matter how much she tried to fall back asleep, her body felt wired and electric–eager to get the dreaded interview over with. For better or worse. She took a long shower, carefully smoothing the shampoo and then conditioner through her wavy hair, dressed in dark jeans and a dusty rose knitted sweater, zipped up her sensible low-heeled brown booties, and slung her purse over her shoulder. She was all ready to go, aside from the fact that the clock only read nine-thirty. She sat down, dressed and jittery, on the unmade bed to wait, flipping through the channels on the television placed on the bureau.

Finally, at ten-thirty she decided that she could allow herself to get going. She grabbed a banana and a coffee in a styrofoam to-go cup from the complimentary breakfast buffet as she exited the hotel and started for the bus stop. The day was dreary and overcast, the thick gray clouds threatening rain and Anna was glad that she brought along her red hoodie.

She was surprised to find that the number four Ithaca bus spit her out directly in front of the psychiatric hospital; she only had to venture up the short cement walkway to enter the looming double doors. At least something was easy.

Anna allowed herself a minute to inspect the building. It didn't look at all like the insane asylums featured in the horror movies she watched through squinted eyes and instead of the stone, ivy-clad, barred windowed monstrosity that she imagined, she found herself staring at a rather modern, clinical looking two-storied facility with a circular driveway bearing a sign that simply read: Ithaca Psychiatry Institute. It was now or never.

Anna walked through the front door and into a spacious lobby with green upholstered seats and framed prints of Monet's masterpieces. She approached the front desk.

"Hi. Excuse me. My name is Anna Parke and I am scheduled to meet with administration for visitation clearance," she explained.

"Hello Ms, Parke," the stout brassy/haired lady at the check-in desk replied, again that tiny slip of the eyes to take in the purple mark that stood out like a goldfish in a sea of minnows, "Please have a seat and we will call you when Dr. Jenkins is ready for you."

Anna thanked the woman and thought to herself that she at least had the name of the person who would determine her fate. For some reason the fact that the woman with whom she would meet was a doctor made Anna even more nervous and intimidated than she already was, and Anna had to make a conscious effort to take deep breaths to still her pounding heart. She did as the woman behind the front desk instructed and stared for about twenty minutes at the emerald, sapphire and violet hues of Monet's water lilies as they danced in all their splendor behind the glass frame.

Finally they called Anna's name and directed her through a set of double glass doors to a room with an open door. Inside the room, a spectacled woman, Anna presumed the woman was Dr. Jenkins, sat staring at the computer screen in front of her. She didn't look up, so Anna rapped lightly on the wooden door.

Chapter 40

The knock startled Dr. Kathleen Jenkins and she uttered a hasty, "Ms. Parke. Come in."

Kathleen had been here since about 5 o'clock this morning, maybe even earlier. Her boyfriend, Frank, wasn't too happy about it either. He already felt that she spent entirely too much time and expended entirely too much energy with work-related matters. He was so angry that he wouldn't even kiss her goodbye as she slunk out of bed when it was so dark outside the window that it felt like midnight. She understood his frustrations, of course she did. But what she never told him outright, was that he would always come second. Her patients came first. And in Kathleen's mind, that was how it was supposed to be.

Regardless of what Frank thought, she got here as soon as she could after Gerry Andrews, one of the night-time orderlies, called her to report that Mrs. Hattersly was found in a seizure state after taking too much clozapine. It is highly rare to overdose on clozapine, even if a patient has an unlimited supply. But Mrs. Hattersly did not have an unlimited supply, maybe, *should not have had* is the more appropriate phrase. The facility heavily regulates its medications–heck, all substances, even Tylenol, are kept in a bank-sized safe in the lab and patients are on strict regiments; they are only given their carefully measured doses by trained staff members. It's not like the patients have bottles of their anti-psychotic pills in their medicine cabinets! So now, Kathleen not only had to figure out how to get Mrs. Hattersly back on track therapeutically, she also had to address the glaring problem of how in the world did the patient in question get her hands on so many pills?

Kathleen couldn't help feeling like a failure in the case of Mrs. Hattersly. She always took it personally when her patients experienced set-backs. She didn't have any children of her own, even though Frank would have been more than happy to help in that regard. Her patients were her children, her babies. She loved them fiercely and was vigilant when it came to their safety and well-being.

Kathleen had almost forgotten about this meeting with this woman. What was her name? Anna? Yes. Anna Parke. Honestly, it was a terrible time. She really needed to focus on the Hattersly case. But now, she had to put

Mrs. Hattersly and her overdose aside and discuss yet another seriously ill patient: Jacob Parke.

She gestured for Anna Parke to occupy the seat opposite and across her messy desk piled with stacks of papers.

"Please, bear with me for a minute," Dr. Jenkins said, "I'm just finishing up an urgent matter."

"Of course," the young woman replied.

The young woman's intense gaze made Kathleen feel unnerved as her neatly manicured nails beat a soft tattoo on the wireless keyboard. She just needed to finish this last sentence for the Hattersly incident report.

"Alright…done," Dr. Kathleen Jenkins said, "Now, let's have a discussion about your request to meet Jacob Parke."

She had no time to beat around the bush. Kathleen focused her keen eyes on the girl sitting across from her. *She looks innocent enough. Let's just see what she wants.*

"Thank you for agreeing to meet with me Dr. Jenkins," the girl–Ms. Parke–began. "I didn't even know that I had an uncle until recently."

"How about you explain to me why you would like to see Mr. Parke," Dr. Jenkins asked. "That seems like a logical place to begin. Your request is unusual; most people who request to meet with our patients have an established relationship with them."

Kathleen watched and listened as Anna Parke bumbled her way through an explanation. The young woman did the best she could to account for why she sought a meeting with Jacob Parke. She spoke about her unaffectionate mother and her meeting with Janine Harper–a woman with whom Kathleen was intimately familiar. Ms. Parke continued to relate her hope to have some sort of family kinship with the only surviving bit of her bloodline, of her personal need to learn as much as she could about her history. She rambled on and on, and the more she spoke, the more wary Kathleen became. Jacob was a sick individual. She wasn't so sure this girl would help his situation. To Kathleen, this all sounded like a lifetime's worth of drama. Although she did wonder about that birthmark on her face, but not enough to ask about it.

Dr. Jenkins cut Anna off with a matter-of-fact and emotionless response, "Ok. I see that you have many emotions about this and I understand on some level your perceived desire to meet with Mr. Parke. I think I should share some information with you before we go any further."

She continued, "My job and responsibility at our facility is to look after the best interests of our 28 residential patients. I meet with each of them regularly, along with their therapists and psychiatrists and any other specialist associated with their cases, approve medication regimens, and keep tabs on their daily routines. In short, I am a very busy individual and take great pride in what I do. I have known Mr. Parke for the last ten years, ever since I first accepted this position and know every detail of both his personal and medical life. He has absolutely no idea of your existence."

At this point, Anna Parke jumped in, "Yes of course. As I explained earlier, I myself only just found out about my connection to him."

Dr. Jenkins went on as though Anna hadn't even spoken, "So now, I must decide whether or not your presence could have any benefit to Mr. Parke. This may sound cruel, but you as an individual, and your individual needs and desires, are of no concern to me and do not function in my position here."

Kathleen could see tears forming at the corners of the girl's eyes, but that didn't matter to her. Anna Parke was not her patient. Jacob Parke was. She had absolutely no intention of signing off on a meeting between the two unless she could be convinced that it was in the best interest of her patient. Then again, she was at a dead end with Jacob. Could a visit from this girl help? She tapped her pencil absently on the desk in front of her.

Kathleen went on, "Jacob Parke has not had a visitor in a long time and despite my reservations–I am sorry to say that I do indeed have reservations about allowing you to meet him–there may be some merit in him meeting a family member who has no association with his past. A short visit may prove therapeutic for him. I could be wrong of course. And I also cannot promise that Mr. Parke will provide you with whatever it is you are seeking Ms. Parke, but I will approve a short supervised visit…so long as Mr. Parke himself agrees."

Kathleen thought to herself that it wasn't going to take only Jacob Parke's agreement. She would gauge his reaction, his body language, what he said and how he said it. She would go from there.

"Oh my gosh! Thank you so very–"

Anna Parke's gratitude was cut short.

"Before you thank me. Let me tell you a bit about the patient in question and then you can decide if you would like to go forward with the schedule. It is important that I provide you with all details so that you can make an informed choice," Kathleen spoke gravely and to the point.

"Ok," said Ms. Parke even though she did not appear ready to hear what Dr. Jenkins had to tell her.

"Mr. Parke has had a troubled history, some of which it is clear you have gleaned from your visit with Janine Harper. But Janine Harper herself suffers from manic episodes and she is not always the best source of information. I would like to take you through Jacob Parke's file," she said as she plunked a heavy stack of papers down in front of Anna.

Another mysterious file folder of information.

It was clear that the girl had no idea what she was looking at, but as Kathleen spoke, the girl began to make sense of the documents laid out before her. The doctor guided her visitor through Jacob's internal workings, at least from her clinical perspective. Mr. Parke, as Dr. Jenkins referred to him, was 76 years old and in the early stages of dementia, which only enhanced his many psychiatric diagnoses.

Kathleen continued, "As you can see from the psychiatric reports in front of you, he is often confused and flip-flops between moments of lucidity and moments of cloudiness. Sometimes he appears completely unengaged and his eyes become unfocused and hazy and at other times he chatters incessantly about whatever it is that pops into his mind."

Anna flipped through the documents as Kathleen instructed. The doctor felt as though she was giving a guided-tour through her patient's mind.

Dr. Jenkins continued, "Since I have known Mr. Parke, he has maintained his innocence in the murder of his own parents and generally refuses to speak about his younger sister, Beverly, who I suppose is your mother?"

Kathleen looked up at this point to see her visitor nod slightly.

So she continued, "Anytime she does come up at therapy sessions his mood turns sour and he quickly withdraws into himself."

Next, the doctor gave Ms. Parke insight into Jacob's rages directed towards his girlfriend Janine and explained why she was no longer permitted visitation rights. Dr Jenkins also mentioned that Jacob maintained a relationship with Rebecca before her overdose and before his dementia took such a stronghold on his brain.

At this point, the girl asked a surprising question: "Do you believe him, about his innocence regarding the murder of his parents?"

"It is not my position to believe or not to believe, only to treat, but I do know that Mr. Parke believes it. I am certain that he is truthful when he defends himself…but he is not always accurate in his recollections," she vaguely replied.

Kathleen believed this with all her heart. She was not here to judge her patients–her babies–but to care for them. Most of them didn't have many people championing for them–a role Kathleen inhabited with ardor.

It looked like Anna Parke wanted to say more, but she didn't. Maybe she didn't want to appear pushy or ungrateful. Afterall, Kathleen was helping her out. This girl needed her.

In order to provide the full picture, Kathleen was forced to drone on for about twenty more minutes about Jacob Parke's medication regimen and sleep habits and general paranoia.

When she was done, she looked straight at this girl, this Anna. Kathleen's piercing blue eyes focused intently on the young woman's, and she said, "Would you still like to move forward with the process of meeting Mr. Parke?"

The girl did not hesitate. It seemed as though she was undeterred in her pursuit and this impressed Kathleen. She thought the girl would have shied away after she heard the ugly truth about her relative.

"Yes," Anna replied, "I would very much like to meet my uncle."

"Very well then," Dr.Jenkins replied, mild surprise playing in the corners of her eyes. "We will have to lay down some ground rules for your meeting, but before we talk specifics I think it necessary to gain permission from Mr. Parke himself. I have a session scheduled with him this afternoon and I will broach the subject of your potential visitation. Based upon his response, we will go from there."

"Okay. Thank you."

The doctor continued, "If you will leave me your cell phone number, I will call you either later this evening or tomorrow morning to update you on Mr. Parke's decision."

The girl eagerly wrote the digits on the back of Dr. Jenkin's business card. She wrote the numbers large and clear. She accepted Dr. Jenkins' firm and deft handshake and walked out of the Ithaca Psychiatric Institute the same way she had entered.

Kathleen was left with an uneasy feeling. On one hand, she hoped that Jacob refused such a meeting. It would certainly make her life easier. It troubled her to think that this girl, Anna Parke, would bring more family drama into her patient's life. On the other hand...could this hidden niece be the key? Could she help coax Jacob Parke out of his shell? She didn't know the answer to this as she reread the notes she took on the Hattersly matter. Kathleen just didn't know.

Chapter 41

It boggled Anna's mind to think that she had just been in the same building as her uncle. So close, yet so far away.

So now it was out of her hands; Anna assumed that she passed whatever test Dr. Jenkins had conducted and now it was up to Jacob himself. She felt frustrated by the process, but it was the only way.

There was a light drizzle drifting down from the gunmetal clouds, but the hints of sunshine in the distance promised a clear afternoon. Anna had no plans, but knew she needed to do something, anything to stop her mind from concocting fantasy scripts of Dr. Jenkins' upcoming session with her uncle. She had no control over Jacob's thoughts nor any desire he may or may not have to meet his long lost niece, so it was best not to dwell on what she could not control. She passed a small souvenir shop with sweatshirts of all hues boasting the motto "Ithaca is Gorges," and decided to visit some of the waterfalls for which the small city is famous. Anna doubled back to that small store and purchased a small paperback book providing directions and descriptions of each of Ithaca's over one hundred and fifty waterfalls.

She sat on the small wooden bench outside the shop and flipped through the opening pages of the guide book that outlined the history and unique geography of this small city. The introduction explained how Ithaca and much of the surrounding areas was literally carved out by glaciers over a million years ago, creating the gorges advertised on so much of the tourist paraphernalia adorning the storefront windows. Apparently in the 1800s, local entrepreneurs, including the ivy league school namesake Ezra Cornell, first realized the economic potential of the water power surrounding them, which put the town on the map and lured businessmen to the area.

Although Anna found this information slightly interesting, she was much more enamored with the actual waterfalls as opposed to the economic development of the area, and she quickly flipped past the historical information to read the descriptions of the falls that were within walking distance from where she currently sat. She decided to first head to Ithaca Falls, which according to the pamphlet is “one of the most impressive waterfalls in the entire region” and which was situated less than a mile away.

Anna leisurely strolled through the shopping and business districts and past Cornell University, impressive and stony in its elite little privileged world, until the buildings grew sparser and the nature around her grew denser. She came upon a wooden sign that read ‘Ithaca Falls’ accompanied by a small diagram illustrating the trail that would take her there. Two point three miles round trip and the difficulty rating was deemed moderate. Anna thought that she could handle this; she didn’t regularly exercise, but the cardiovascular benefits of not owning a car were not lost upon her trim physique. She set off down the quiet leaf covered trail listening to the voices of the trees surrounding her. They regarded her with curiosity and murmured their greetings; they brushed their branches against her jeans, but Anna, proficient in ignoring the lure of the majestic oaks and the mighty pines, walked on. She was able to compartmentalism their whispers and put them somewhere in the back of her mind as she walked along the noiseless path. She found that the more she ignored the chattering trunks and branches, the softer their calling and conversations became and the less she had to contend with the unnerving peculiarity of her ability.

The sound of the pounding water slamming against the rocky base was audible before she even saw the waterfall. Anna turned a bend in the trail and before her stood Ithaca Falls in all its misty glory. The water cascaded down a rocky stairway and Anna stood awed by the immense power of nature; she felt small and insignificant in the face of such grandeur. For a moment she held her breath in the face of such aching paralyzing beauty. Anna tentatively made her way down the boulders and wobbly rocks that surrounded the pool at the base of the falls. She sat down on a large, smooth, gray sandstone boulder, careful not to slip; a wrong step could result in a broken ankle or worse. At her vantage point she was able to feel the misty coolness of the falls against her face.

Did she dare step in? Wade into the depth of the unknown? Just like the glaciers had taken this land, blundered into, and turned it into something awe-inspiring, could the truth of her past shape her life into something meaningful and worthwhile? There was only one way to find out.

She removed her sneakers and peeled off her sweaty socks, setting them aside and rolled up the ankles of her jeans to reveal smooth pale calves. She let her naked feel dip into the pool of Ithaca Falls; the cool crisp water felt divine as it splashed lightly over her dry skin. The misty morning drizzle had cleared and the afternoon was temperate and mild. She wiggled her toes, finding comfort in the gentle bubbles the movement produced.

She laid back on the strong rock, feet still in the water and stared up at the cloudy sky. Was Jacob looking out his barred window at the same peaceful sight? She tried not to think about her phone, silent and still in her coat pocket. She stayed that way for a long time, allowing her thoughts to flit and flutter around like butterflies in the wind.

At some point, she decided it was time to move on and Anna reluctantly put her damp feet back into her socks and shoes. She said a silent farewell to Ithaca Falls and wound her way back to the main road. She visited two additional waterfalls: Buttermilk Falls with its massive rainbow cascade and Lucifer Falls with its narrow height before the afternoon turned into early evening and she thought it best to head back to Ithaca Commons. She didn't want night to find her stumbling around unfamiliar hiking trails in the darkness.

She desperately hoped that Dr. Jenkins would have called by now, but as the minutes ticked away and her cell phone read seven-fifteen, Anna became more and more certain that no call would come tonight. In her naive experience, doctors didn't make return phone calls past five o'clock. Maybe tomorrow. After all, tomorrow is another day.

Anna treated herself to a nice dinner at an Italian restaurant named Antonio's. The warm, crusty bread with a salted olive oil dip reminded her that she hadn't eaten since breakfast and she ordered a steaming plate of pesto gnocchi with sauteed broccoli on the side. The meal was a far cry from her usual dinners and she enjoyed the sophistication of her food. The Cabernet she ordered, just a glass...not a bottle, was peppery and rich, hues of smoky vanilla and black current danced upon her tongue. Normally, this one glass of wine would have only whetted her appetite for more alcohol, and she would have sought out a local watering hole in which to drink the night away, but tonight she felt subdued and decided it best to retire to her hotel room.

The meal was delicious and the evening was clear and cold–the stars shimmering their fiery brilliance above. Her satisfied and full belly brought on a rare sense of optimism and Anna felt hopeful that Dr. Jenkins would call in the morning with good news. And that drop of positivity allowed her to pass the nighttime hours restfully.

The next morning Anna allowed herself to sleep in; however she immediately regretted her decision when she awoke to the clock that read 10:10am, checked her phone and saw that she had a missed call and a voicemail from a local number. Her heart went into her teeth when she heard Dr. Jenkins' voice sounding faraway and formal over the small speaker. She cursed herself for having missed the call for which she had been both dreading and anticipating. Dr. Jenkins left her personal office number and Anna immediately punched the numbers into her cellphone to return the call. Dr. Jenkins had left no clue about Jacob Parke's reaction to a possible meeting with a niece he never met in her message, so Anna held her breath and crossed her fingers as she heard the telltale sound of the ringing line.

Just when Anna was sure that no one would answer and that she would be beginning a frustrating game of phone tag with this busy individual, she heard the unmistakable lilt of Dr. Jenkins' educated voice, "Dr. Jenkins, Ithaca Psychiatric Facility."

"Oh, Dr. Jenkins, hello! I didn't think you would pick up! It's Anna Parke."

"Hello Ms. Parke, I was just about to leave the office for a patient meeting."

"I'm so glad I caught you! Do you have any updates on your session with my uncle?" Anna tentatively ventured.

"The short answer is that, yes, we may continue with scheduling a meeting. There is much more that we need to discuss but at the current moment I simply do not have the time to provide specifics."

Anna could feel her pulse throbbing in her neck; her heart was hammering.

The doctor continued, "You may see Mr. Parke tomorrow at two-thirty in the afternoon. I will be the supervising administrator during your encounter. But first I would like for us to meet one-on-one to go over some protocols for your visit. There are some ground rules that must be laid. Please arrive at our facility promptly at one-thirty. I will be expecting you."

"I will! Thank you doctor. I very much appreciate your help," Anna gushed.

"Goodbye Ms. Parke."

"Goodbye."

And with that, Anna pressed the red 'end' button on the screen and inhaled a few deep breaths to calm her trembling soul. She tried to imagine what this 'encounter' as Dr. Jenkins kept calling it, would be like, and couldn't envision any realistic possibilities in her head. She thought that she should write down some of the questions she had for her uncle, but then thought better of it. She felt that she would be better off simply letting conversation flow naturally…if there was indeed any lucid conversation at all. Based upon Dr. Jenkins' assessment of her uncle's mental state, she couldn't be guaranteed any meaningful engagement whatsoever.

Anna had a whole day in front of her to agonize over the endless possibilities that tomorrow might bring. She knew she had to keep both her body and her mind active in order to help the time pass by. She had no idea how she would spend the hours, but she had to do something. Normally she would get lost in the cool comfort of a bottle, or the warm arms of a handsome stranger, but she felt very distant from the life she had lived up until a few weeks ago—a life that was turned upside down by the contents of a dusty cardboard box, quiet and unassuming in the corner of a messy apartment on the other side of the universe.

Mercifully, the time passed quicker than Anna anticipated and after a light lunch, light meaning barely eaten, Anna found herself again in the waiting room of Ithaca Psychiatric Institute anxious to meet a second time with Dr. Jenkins. Anna decided on a sensible and plain outfit that she had agonizingly packed with this exact meeting in mind: plain light, loose fitting jeans, a maroon v-neck sweater and black boots. She didn't know what "guidelines" needed to be ironed out nor what "precautions" Dr Jenkins would insist upon, but she again stared at those wispy water lilies on the wall in front of her.

Finally, at one-thirty on the dot, she was told to go on ahead to the doctor's office; Dr. Jenkins was ready to see Anna.

Chapter 42

Dressed in a crisp navy pants suit, Dr. Jenkins didn't get up to greet Anna when she walked through the doorway and sat down in the designated chair, but she did eye Anna with a newfound appreciation as she slowly settled herself into a seated position. Kathleen felt well-rested and fresh; things with Frank had been better, at least for the past day or so and he did agree to kiss her goodbye as she walked out of the door this morning. The doctor's eyes wavered for a moment to Anna's cheek, but quickly snapped back to her eyes.

"Do you feel comfortable with your decision to go ahead with the visitation?" Kathleen asked.

"I'm not sure," Anna Parke replied truthfully, "but I know it is something I have to do. You mentioned that there are certain guidelines and protocols that you would like to establish in advance?"

Kahtleen always tried to keep it short and simple when it came to patient visitations.

"Yes. I must insist that you follow certain rules during your meeting with Mr. Parke. As I have mentioned previously, it is my priority to ensure his emotional safety and if the visit seems to be erring in the wrong direction, I will not hesitate to insist on an immediate halt."

"I understand," replied Anna.

Kathleen could tell that she meant it. She had the keen understanding that this young woman, no matter how much she hoped for insight into her family, had no desire to cause Jacob Parke any unwarranted distress.

"Ok. Well, I informed Mr. Parke that a young woman would like to see him. I did not tell him who you are or that you are his kin. I will leave that to you. I do not know how he will handle the information, his reactions are oftentimes unpredictable. The information might cause him to become distressed, or he may show no visible reaction at all. Do you understand?"

"Yes. I understand."

"I have three rules that I expect you to follow. I will keep them short and simple," Kathleen Jenkins went on. "Rule One: do not mention anything about his trial. The memory is painful for him and he feels both betrayed and wrongfully accused."

"Ok," said Anna simply

The doctor could sense that this disappointed Anna. Of course the girl would want to discuss the trial. But Anna's wants did not matter much to Kathleen as she continued.

"Rule Two: Do not mention the death of his daughter, Rebecca. It is a fact that Mr. Parke has not accepted and denies to this day. It is a suppressed memory and a major trigger for him."

Before Anna could respond that she understood, Dr. Jenkins laid out the final rule, "It is best that you do not ask about his relationship with Janine Harper. As I'm sure Janine told you, she is no longer permitted visitation with Mr. Parke; her presence is acutely upsetting to him."

"Ok," Anna responded, "I promise to adhere to your guidelines.

The doctor continued, "In my opinion, it is best if you allow Mr. Parke to guide the conversation. He may or not be responsive. I cannot always predict his behavior. He took his first dose of Abilify approximately 90 minutes ago, which typically helps to stabilize his moods. I will give you facial cues that will help you read the situation. And just to reiterate Ms. Parke, I reserve the right to terminate the encounter at any point. If you agree to these terms, we may proceed."

With a deep breath in, Anna clearly stated, "I agree to these terms."

Dr Jenkins provided Anna with a statement to sign that basically outlined what they had just discussed. Anna accepted the blue fountain pen that the doctor extended to her over the desk and signed her name on the allotted line.

"Ok. You may proceed back to the waiting room. When Mr. Parke is situated, I will personally escort you to him."

When Anna Parke exited her office for a second time, Kathleen once again (she had contemplated this over and over again since she first discussed the meeting with Jacob) toyed with the notion of calling it all off. Maybe Jacob Parke was too fragile to handle this after all.However, there was something about this girl that stopped her. Something honest and genuine and pure. Kathleen sincerely hoped that she would not live to regret this.

Chapter 43

Anna did as she was told, trying to ignore her heartbeat which was surely audible to everyone in the waiting room. She folded her trembling hands in her lap in an attempt to still her jittery fingers and closed her eyes in an effort to engage in some mindful breathing. She wished that she took more to the few yoga classes she registered for a couple of years back; the meditation techniques definitely would have come in handy at this moment. To the casual onlooker she had a semblance of calm, but inside she was an absolute disaster. She couldn't ever remember feeling as intensely nervous as she felt at this moment.

Anna wondered if Dr. Jenkins sensed how nervous she was. Despite her hard exterior, Anna liked the doctor and appreciated the fact that she was given a chance. It was obvious that Dr. Jenkins cared about her uncle and wanted to see him heal. Anna also truly hoped that her being here, her meeting with her uncle, wouldn't cause him any harm or distress. Yes, Anna yearned for information, but not at the expense of Jacob's mental state.

She sat like that for quite some time. A part of Anna hoped that they forgot about her or that Jacob Parke changed his mind or that Dr. Jenkins decided against the visitation. But about forty minutes later, Dr. Jenkins herself appeared before Anna in the waiting room and guided her past her private office, down a long corridor, through a set of double hospital doors and into a small cafeteria with three tables that looked very much like those one would find in any high school in the country. Dr. Jenkins guided her into a seat on one of the benches and the table farthest to the left.

"I am going to bring in Mr. Parke now. Do you have any last minute questions or concerns?" The doctor asked.

Anna had so many questions and concerns that she couldn't possibly verbalize at this moment. She felt that if she opened her mouth she would have ended up talking herself out of the meeting all together, so she simply shook her head to indicate that no she didn't have any questions and yes she was ready. Anna wiped her sweaty palms on her soft jeans and watched as Dr. Jenkins walked to a door on the other side of the cafeteria, heels clicking on the tiled floor, to bring in her waiting uncle.

Chapter 44

A memory:

It was 1990, Thanksgiving. Eight-year-old Anna Parke was seated across the dinner table from her mother, trying not to let the fork scratch too loudly at the delicate white plate with the blue daisy pattern around the border placed in front of her. Upon the plate was a dollop of creamy mashed potatoes and two slices of turkey with a thin ribbon of golden crust scalloped around the edges.

Anna was remembering yesterday, when her teacher asked her class to write journal entries about their holiday plans. The students were allotted fifteen minutes to compose their entries and were then asked to share with their deskmates. Anna's deskmate was a sweet freckle-faced boy, named Andrew, with thick black eyelashes outlining deep emerald eyes. Andrew wrote about his family's tradition of waking up early on Thanksgiving morning to participate in a football game at the local field with his five older brothers, nine cousins and three uncles. Anna noticed his excitement at the possibility of being allowed to kick the field goals now that he was almost nine-years-old. His green eyes sparkled with anticipation at the thought. Anna imagined that she was the sixth child in Andrew's family. How lovely the holidays must be! How filled with chatter and warmth!

She imagined squishing around a cramped table and vying for food amongst a boisterous family.

When Andrew was done sharing his journal, which took up almost three pages in his black and white marble notebook, Anna ashamedly shared her measly paragraph, which featured watching the Macy's Thanksgiving Day Parade on the television and ended with a quiet meal, just Anna and her mother. Once she read her piece, Andrew asked, "Don't you have any cousins or brothers or sisters or anything?"

"No. Just me and my mom," Anna replied.

"That's boring!" Andrew interjected, with the honesty that comes so easily from the young, not realizing how deeply his comment cut into Anna's heart.

So as Anna sat across from her mother, quietly and dutifully, she asked, "Mom, do we have family? Other than me and you, I mean?"

She couldn't explain what had made her so bold to ask such a forthright question to her icy and rather frightening mother.

"No Anna. And the sooner you get used to that fact, the better you'll be. The only person you can depend upon in this life is yourself," Ms. Parke replied.

And to show her daughter that she was finished with the conversation, Beverly Parke rose from her seat, scraped her uneaten meal into the garbage can, rinsed her plate and placed it pristinely in the drying rack, and retired to her bedroom, leaving Anna alone at the table, wondering what she had done wrong. Just another Thanksgiving in the books for Anna Parke.

Chapter 45

Jacob Parke entered the room, shuffling along, eyes fixated on something at the far corner of the ceiling, escorted by a security guard on one side and Dr Jenkins on the other. The guard, who was ultimately hospital security, wore gray slacks and a navy blue collared shirt with an ID badge fastened to the breast pocket. While the guard guided him by his elbow towards where Anna was seated, Dr Jenkins was on the patient's other side talking furtively into his ear. Anna wasn't sure what she was saying to him, but her body language told Anna that she was worried. From across the room, Jacob Parke looked like any elderly man, gray thinning hair, slightly hunched, with half moon spectacles sliding down his prominent nose. However, when Jacob Parke was seated directly across from Anna at the cafeteria table, so close that she could reach out and easily grasp his sun-spotted arthritic hands, Anna was struck by the family resemblance. He had the same heart-shaped face as her mother and even though his eyes were cloudy and distant, the hazel hue and wide crescent shape made her feel like she was gazing at an older version of Beverly Parke–had she been given the chance to grow older.

Once Jacob was situated, the guard took his place against the far wall, eyes alert for any potential problems;

Anna hoped that he wouldn't be present for their visit, but he didn't make any movement to leave the room. Dr. Jenkins took a seat behind Jacob, facing Anna; she clearly picked her spot strategically so she could non-verbally communicate with Anna without her patient knowing. Even though Anna understood the necessity of both Dr. Jenkins' and the security guard's presence, she felt clumsy and awkward and wished for more privacy with her uncle. She did not desire to be on display.

Jacob had not yet even looked at Anna; instead his eyes remained engrossed on some mysterious focal point on the ceiling. At one point Anna actually looked behind her to see if there was indeed something up there. Something exciting and absorbing and wonderful to distract her uncle so thoroughly. Nothing… at least nothing that she could see with her own eyes. Dr. Jenkins gave Anna a brief nod telling her that time was ticking and that she should go ahead. Anna wasn't quite sure what to say or how to begin. She felt on display, like a rare oddity in a curio cabinet. Jacob seemed completely uninterested in what was happening around him, completely removed and unaware. Anna knew she had to try something…it was now or never.

"Hi," she ventured. "How are you?"

Silence.

"Thank you for agreeing to see me," Anna tried again.

Nothing, silently moving lips, eyes fixed above her.

"My name is Anna Parke and this may be hard for you to believe, but I'm your niece…you're my uncle…" She trailed off.

No response.

She continued, "I didn't even know I had an uncle until I saw your name in a newspaper article."

At that moment, Dr. Jenkins shook her head 'no' as if to tell Anna that she was treading on dangerous waters and that she should proceed with caution.

Anna changed her tactic, "Beverly was my mom. I say 'was' because she died a few weeks ago."

At this point, Jacob's faraway glare vanished and he looked directly at her, staring straight into her soul. Eyes blazing and aware and lively. Anna was profoundly sure that she woke him from whatever trance he had been in up until this moment.

Still more silence.

Anna went on, "My mom and I weren't on very good terms. She never told me that she had a brother. I wasn't there when she died."

At this point Jacob Parke started to speak, his voice shaky and trembling at first, but clearer as he continued ,"Beverly. Beverly. Is that you? Did you come at last?"

"No, I'm Anna, Beverly's daughter, your niece. Beverly is dead."

In a sudden moment of clarity, Jacob Parke reached out and seized Anna's wrist, his untrimmed fingernails like talons into her tender flesh, "How could you, Beverly? How could you do that… how could you do that... to me?" Anna tried unsuccessfully to free her arm from his grasp

Terrible sounds were emanating from Jacob Parke's throat, sobs, anguish, tears were seeping out of the corners of his rheumatic eyes. He gripped her harder, surprising strength surging from his hand.

"No…I'm not Beverly. I'm Anna! Your niece! I would have come earlier if I knew you existed," Anna felt like she had to defend herself. She felt her face turning crimson and hot; she desperately tried to contain her emotions. She tried to pry her uncle's fingers from her arm. Her breath ragged and gasping.

Dr. Jenkins started to rise; she gestured to the security guard who became more alert and attentive as the conversation progressed.

"Wait, please!" Anna said to the doctor.

Jacob's rantings continued, "The tree…The tree knows.. it knows.. it saw…the tree knows what you did!"

Jacob rocked and rocked and rocked on the hard cafeteria bench, repeating his nonsensical mantra, his incantation over and over, louder and louder

"The tree knows. The tree knows. It saw. It knows. The tree. The tree knows. It knows!"

"What does the tree know, Jacob?" Anna asked, searching his face, trying to help his eyes once again focus on her. She no longer felt the pain radiating from her wrist; she didn't notice the small beads of blood seeping from his stronghold.

Getting up from her seat to take action, Dr. Jenkins interrupted, "Anna, this is quite enough. Mr. Parke is clearly distressed. This meeting is terminated."

"What tree Jacob? What does it know?" Anna yelled as both the doctor and the security guard helped Jacob to his feet and loosened his grip on Anna.

"Windsom trees. The black tree. The big black tree.. the dead tree. With the long arms. The dead tree with the black arms, it knows, it knows...The black tree. It knows..."

And with that last outburst, Jacob Parke was brought to a standing position and led back through the same cafeteria doors through which he had entered and Anna was alone again in the echoing room.

It took Anna quite some time to catch her galloping breath. She remained seated and placed her forehead on the cool countertop in front of her, waiting for her pulse to slow, waiting for the blood to stop pounding in her head. Her mind was spinning and she suddenly had a raging need for fresh air; she felt as though she would vomit if she did not escape this cement tomb.

Dr. Jenkins breezed back through the doorway with a bottle of Poland Spring, cold based upon the cloudy condensation on the ribbed plastic, and a small first aid kit. She sat down directly next to Anna and wordlessly attended to her inner wrist; Anna had no idea she was even bleeding, but as she inspected her skin, the half-moon nail marks made by her uncle were blatantly visible, three of them, red and raw. The sting of the rubbing alcohol on her tender skin was somehow calming to Anna; it gave her something else to absorb her concentration.

"Mr. Parke has been sedated," Dr. Jenkins told Anna.

Silence.

"So, I guess I screwed that up," Anna finally muttered.

"You did nothing wrong Ms. Parke. I take the blame. It was an error in judgment. I thought that your visit might prove therapeutic for Mr. Parke," the doctor said simply, "I was wrong,"

Anna got the distinct impression that Dr. Jenkins did not often admit her mistakes and she respected her even more for doing so now. A small silver lining in the face of such a mess.

Anna turned to face the doctor, her eyes wide and glistening, "What was he talking about? About the tree?"

The doctor replied," Ms. Parke, it is often difficult to interpret the verbal expressions of individuals like your uncle, individuals that have experienced acute trauma accompanied by psychosis. Mr. Parke's dementia also impacts his communication."

"Yes, I understand all that. But has he ever elaborated on what he means when he talks about the trees?" Anna responded.

"I'll put it this way Ms. Parke," the doctor began, "Since I have known your uncle, he has maintained his innocence in the deaths of his parents. He believes that one tree can prove this claimed innocence. This notion is a trapping of his delusion only. Like I have told you before, my job here is not to judge, nor to vindicate, only to treat."

Anna's mind was spinning with endless possibilities. Did Jacob have the same curse (she had come to view it) as she had? Was it a weird family inheritance? Some sort of genetic mutation? Did the trees also talk to him? She had ignored and disregarded her odd capability for years now and she didn't know that she was ready to hash it out again logically and in conjunction with the bizarre scenario in which she found herself now. Or was Dr. Jenkins right? Were Jacob's rantings about the tree mere lunacy? The coincidental manifestations of a diseased mind. These thoughts swam around Anna's tired brain as she spoke with Dr.Jenkins.

Finally, the doctor said, "I must excuse myself Ms. Parke. I need to go check in with your uncle."

"Yes. I understand that," Anna replied. "Is there any chance that I can come back"

"I'm sorry, but I cannot allow a follow-up visitation at this point. If anything changes, I will not hesitate to give you a call."

"Thank you," Anna said to the doctor, crestfallen. "I appreciate you taking this chance."

"Goodbye Ms. Parke. Be well. And if I may offer some advice: I think it best you drop this issue entirely. Don't put too much credence into your uncle's puzzling and enigmatic comments."

And with that, Dr. Jenkins breezed out the door at the far end of the cafeteria, ready to attend to her patient, leaving Anna alone in the white-tiled room. Despite her coldness, Anna felt sad to see her go.

Anna saw herself out of the building feeling defeated and tense. She didn't know exactly what she hoped her uncle would provide, but it definitely wasn't this. Maybe some part of her wished for some sort of family relationship, some sort of connection, someone who could understand the nuances of the Parke family, but with each step she took away from the Ithaca Psychiatric Center, her hopes receded like the ebbing tide and were replaced only with bitter loneliness and disappointment. So that was it, the Parke legacy, just her and her wasted uncle.

Chapter 46

Jacob Parke sat in his room at the end of the day. It must have been an exciting day; his heart was pounding in his chest. Lub Dub, Lub Dub, Lub Dub, Lub Dub. And was he crying? Why, yes. He was. He was crying. He raised a shaking hand to his wet cheeks. Why was he crying? Hadn't he been sitting in this room for hours, ever since the nice lady came to take him somewhere? Where did he go? Where was that lady now? She was just talking to him, just a few minutes ago, talking to him, talking to him. Talking to him about a girl. What girl?

He commenced his rocking. Back and forth, back and forth, back and forth. Lub Dub, Lub Dub, Lub Dub, LUb, DuB, LUB DUB. Why was his heart still pounding? He was dying. His heart was killing him, killing him, killing him. Where was that lady, that doctor? He needed her now, now, NOW!

He pressed the red button in his room, the button above his bedside table, the EMERGENCY button. The one he was told only to push when there was an emergency. This WAS an EMERGENCY! He held it down for 1-2-3 seconds. No one answered and he was dying, dying, dying. 1-2-3-4-5 seconds. Dying and nobody was here. Not the lady–the doctor maybe she was, not the girl, not Janine, not Rebecca–his Rebecca. Oh it hurts. How it hurts.

He crumpled to the floor grasping his chest.

Swallowing air.

Gulping.

A fish on the floor.

A gulping guppy…

Flopping.

Squeaks of rubber.

Turning door.

Opening.

Man in green scrubs, rushing over, rushing over, rushing over.

"Mr. Parke,calm down. Breathe," the man in the green said kneeling beside Jacob.

"But I'm dying, my heart is killing me! I pressed the button for 1,2,3 seconds, 1,2,3,4,5 seconds."

"You're not dying. You're having a panic attack. This happens to you Mr. Parke. Breathe."

"I pressed the button for 1,2,3,4,5 seconds. I. Can't. Breathe."

"You can. Breathe with me. I'll help you. In…and out. Good. In…and out."

"But the tree knows. I'm dying."

"You're not dying. Don't worry about the trees now, Mr. Parke. Keep breathing with me."

"THE tree…not trees. The TREE…" insisted Jacob.

"Ok. Nevermind that now. In…and out. Good. And again. In…and out."

Jacob breathed. In…and out. In...and out.

"Do you feel better?" the man asked.

Jacob did feel better. His heartbeat steadied, Lub-Dub, Lub-Dub, Lub-Dub. Even. Calm. In…and out. In…and out.

The green man asked again, "Mr. Parke, do you feel better?"

"Tell Anna the tree knows.The Windsom tree."

"Who's Anna?" the man in green asked as he helped Jacob Parke back into his recliner.

"Anna Parke. The girl. The young girl."

Another tear on his cheek. A tiny sliver of clarity broke into Jacob's jumbled thoughts and he glanced down at his hand where he was able to see a trace of blood underneath a few of his fingernails. Was he bleeding? He brought his fingers up to his nose to inhale the metallic scent. Not his blood. Then whose? The girl's…Anna's blood. Parke blood.

"Is Anna Parke related to you? She has your last name," the man in green asked as he filled a tiny plastic cup with water and handed it to Jacob.

"Yes. She's my…my…my…sister. Not my sister. Not my sister. God no. NOT my sister. Not Beverly..not like Beverly at all. Beverly's daughter. Beverly's dead. Her daughter is alive. My daughter? Rebecca…" he was becoming confused again.

Jacob had the feeling that something very important happened. Something profound and significant and … and…hazy.

"Well isn't that something," said the man in green as he went to exit Jacob's room.

"Huh?" Jacob uttered in an attempt to hold him there. He needed to tell him something, but…it floated away.

The man in green looked back one more time as he edged out of the room.

"You ok now, Mr. Parke?" he asked over his shoulder.

"The tree knows,"Jacob nodded as he spoke. "It knows. The black tree, the dead, dead, dead, dead tree. The tree knows."

A dreamy look crept up into his eyes and his rocking commenced. The clarity that had been quivering on the horizon sank back into the depths of Jacob's broken mind. Whatever he knew, or thought he knew, faded like the setting sun.

Chapter 47

After her wrecked meeting with her uncle, Anna went back to the Residence Inn and began gathering up her few personal items and clothing that she brought with her on this excursion. What she had packed with such care and consciousness, she now threw into her duffel bag in a tangled mess. Suddenly, she needed to get out of this town as soon as possible. She checked out of the hotel and went immediately to the bus depot, not even bothering to stop for lunch or even a coffee.

On the ride back to Windsom, Anna stared gloomily out the window watching the sights pass her by. She felt distinctly different than she had a few days ago when she boarded this same bus with so much unadmitted hope. She felt older and tired and decidedly more alone than she ever had in her entire life.

She slept most of the bus ride away and when she got back to Windsom, she exited the Greyhound in a misty drizzle. She made her way back to her apartment, which smelled sour and stale when she entered. She hadn't bothered to tidy up the place before she left and now she wished she had. No one likes returning home to a sinkful of dishes and dirty laundry. Anna didn't have the heart or intention to do those chores tonight, so instead she plunked herself down on her sagging sofa in front of the dreaded dollhouse and stared into the tiny detailed rooms of her childhood. The headless Anna remained seated on the front porch. She picked up the brother doll, the doll that she now thought of as Uncle Jacob. The pink smile painted on his porcelain face looked so happy and confident, sure in his role with his family and secure in his foothold on the earth. If only the real Jacob was as healthy. With a sigh, she placed the figurine back in his rightful place and lost herself in a mindless television show, anything to stop the flood of thoughts that crashed over the shores of her mind, and anything to block out the calling of the trees outside her window. They were more persistent than they had been in recent years. She didn't know if she could face what they had to tell her.

Chapter 48

A memory

The sun shone through the leaves, hot and oppressive in the late afternoon sky, blazing red like a hot coal. Anna had dozed off leaning against the large evergreen tree relishing the comfortable shade it provided on this mid-August scorcher. She had wandered farther into the woods behind her house than she ever had before and was confused by the labyrinth of trees, bushes, and brambles that seemed to stretch out endlessly before her. She never intended on falling asleep, just resting for a bit, but the cool shade on her burning cheeks was too sweet to resist and before she knew it she fell into a deep slumber.

Now, wide-eyed, she was no closer to winding her way back home than she had been before her nap. She rose from the floor, gently swatting at the pine needles that stuck to the back of her denim shorts with the pink and silver rhinestones outlining the pockets, her favorite clothing item to wear as an eight-year old little girl. Anna tried placing her hand on the sturdy tree trunk to get a sense of her location and maybe receive some guidance from this friendly companion, but the waves the tree emitted were hazy and dull. Confused.

She wove her way west, what she hoped was towards home, as the ruby orb in the sky sunk lower behind the horizon. Twilight was upon her and she was beginning to worry. The jitters and swaying of the rustling trees told her to beware.

At that moment, a yellow-eyed wolf emerged from the woods and stepped into the clearing about twenty yards in front of her. Its gaze bore into her eyes and dared her to move. Its pink tongue lolled from its mouth, pulsing and dripping with saliva in the gentle breeze. Anna had seen wolves before in movies and heard stories about them in those old fairy tales she used to read in the library. Little Red Riding Hood *stuck out to her at this moment. But she never thought that she would come face to face with such a creature in real life. But here was this wolf, right in front of her. The growl resonated deep within her chest. A twinge of fear made its way up Anna's spine and into her scalp; she was frozen to the floor, rooted to the ground.* Should she run? Could she dare move? Could she possibly outrun such an agile and terrifyingly beautiful specimen? *The wolf took a few confident paces towards her, wordlessly telling her that she had encroached on his territory. He owned these woods, not a pipsqueak of a girl with leaves in her mousy hair. Anna took a tentative step backwards, and as she did so the wolf bared its sharp canines and uttered a guttural growl unlike anything she ever heard before. The echo reverberated deep into her terrified mind. She felt the tree trunk, rough and jagged through the thin material of her t-shirt against her rocky spine.*

The wolf crept forward again; Anna watched him inch closer and closer with a rising dread. Her eyes darted up and down, back and forth looking for an escape, anything to help her in this crucial time of need.

The animal continued in its pursuit. In Anna's heightened state of terror she could make out the wolf's oscillating pupils. At this point, had Anna reached out her trembling arm, she could have touched his wet nose. Panic. Anna closed her eyes, clenched them shut, unable to look, unable to watch how this gruesome scenario would play out. She opened them for what she believed was one final time. One final time before–

At that moment, the wolf's steady gaze became distracted and he took his fierce glare from Anna and directed it upward. Anna did not know what captured the wolf's attention, but it began to retreat, first one step, then two.

Anna risked a look. From her vantage point, with her back against the base of the trunk, she saw branches and leaves and bits of the evening sky, but what she also saw, what she would pretend she didn't see and what she would deny to herself that she had seen in the years to come–it was too odd, too strange, too overwhelming for comprehension–was something entirely and wholly otherworldly. She saw the branches of the evergreen tree all united into a single form bearing down on the wolf, an enormous leafy dagger menacing and black, reverberating with unsung danger. As she gazed up at this incredible sight, she felt, deep within her bones, that she would not be harmed.

Whimpering sounds were audible in her periphery and when she directed her gaze hesitatingly back towards the wolf, she noticed that his mannerisms had changed. His tail was now between his hind legs, his head lowered, and his eyes remained averted. He continued to skulk his way backwards until he was up against a particularly overgrown section of the forest, at which point he simply vanished into the darkened greenery.

Gazing back up, Anna noticed that the leaves and branches had returned to their rightful position except for one, a large bottom branch which descended like a knotty rope and gave her a gentle shove in her lower back in the opposite direction. Silently telling her the correct path to take home.

She wound her way back through the forest and by the time the grass became level and she could see the rise of roofs in the near distance, she convinced herself that It was a raccoon instead of a wolf and that the wind caused the tree to form such an odd shape. She almost believed it.

Chapter 49

Upon waking up the next morning, sweating on the drooping sofa, the events that occurred in Ithaca felt like a cruel dream. Anna actually hoped she had concocted the whole crazy tale in her slumber, but when she saw that ominous newspaper article on her coffee table, the one that started her on this deranged journey in the first place, she stopped trying to convince herself. She was scheduled for a shift at The Food Mart in an hour; calling out sick was not an option after her requested "vacation time" so despite the melancholy that seeped into her bones, she set about getting herself ready for work.

Her messy apartment was beginning to make her feel anxious and unsettled so she made a pact with herself to clean the place up once she returned from work. Plugging in the toaster (Anna always unplugged the toaster oven after she used it; she never trusted that it was actually off) she toasted herself an English muffin, waiting for it to turn brown and crispy. She slathered a bit of butter on the cratered surface and ate it quickly, accompanied by an icy glass of tap water. After a quick shower, and a fleeting glimpse at the dollhouse, Anna was out the door and on her way to work. It all felt quite surreal to her, after so much had happened in her personal life she was expected to just go back to her mundane routine? While Jacob Parke ranted and raved in the looney bin, while Janine Harper and her cat hid away in the crowded apartment, and while Rebecca wasted away in the cold hard ground, Anna scanned the groceries of Windsom's finest.

Her shift went as expected: she evaded her boss' well-intentioned inquiries about her time off and dwindled the hours away in her maroon apron behind the beeping cash register. Anna declined both breaks (down time only took her thoughts away to dark places) and by five o'clock, her boss had to remind her that her shift had ended and that it was time for her to go home.

Typically, she would have wandered into Don's with the intention of having just one drink, which would undoubtedly turn to two and then three and then four, after all it was happy hour, but drowning herself in alcohol wasn't appealing to her lately. In fact, since she learned about her uncle, she cut down on her drinking–not purposely at first, but maybe subconsciously she felt as though at least one of the remaining Parkes had to be stable. She doubted whether or not her current status could even be defined as such. So instead of finding comfort in the cool green bottles and glasses filled with amber liquid, she slowly made her way home.

She stopped in at Lee's Chinese Kitchen before going upstairs to her apartment to buy a quart of wonton soup and an egg roll for dinner. She ate her meal quietly at her small Formica kitchen counter; the dim lighting made the soup look extra yellow. The egg roll was crispy and satisfying, and the duck sauce added a sweetness that was just right.

No matter how much she tried to distract herself, her mind kept returning to all that had occurred in the last few weeks: the unpacking, the endless calls made to various psychiatric facilities, her trip to Schenectady, the bowling alley, Janine, Dr. Jenkins, but most consistently, the pale face of her uncle seemed imprinted on her consciousness. She gazed down at her forearm and could still make out the scabbed crescent fingernail marks, pink half-moons on her pale inner wrist. And those words, the words he uttered over and over again, "The tree knows, The tree knows, the black tree, Windsom tree."

And despite Dr. Jenkins' cautions, it was these words to which her mind kept returning. She couldn't help feeling that her uncle was trying to tell her something, communicate some lost message. He had gazed so clearly and intensely into her eyes as he spoke. The cloudiness was gone and the haziness and the rocking. He seemed lucid and clear. He seemed alive and alert and quite sane as he spoke about the tree. And the more Anna tried to push these thoughts out of her jumbled head, the more certain she became that her instincts were correct. *"Windsom trees, black tree, the dead tree with the long arms, the Windsom tree."*

As she gazed out the foggy window, seeing her washed-out expression highlighting the dark purple imperfection on her skin, Windsom trees called out to her. *Did she dare listen? Did she dare answer the calls that she had been resisting for years?* Suddenly a feeling of absolute terror washed over her, chilling her blood and freezing her very pulse. Anna knew what she needed to do.

Chapter 50

A memory:

It was late afternoon one day in 1998. Anna returned home from Windsom High to an empty home, which was unusual because Ms. Parke was rarely ever out. At first Anna was excited to have the house to herself. She turned on MTV and watched the music videos, at full blast–something her mother would never have allowed. If Anna wanted to listen to music, she did so quietly, wearing headphones in her own bedroom. Soundgarten's "Black Hole Sun" was on and Anna was mesmerized by the psychedelic images that flashed upon the television screen, a dripping Barbie Doll toasted on a spit over an open flame, grins dripping off faces, large, bulging blue eyes. She thought to herself what a gift Chris Cornell's voice was, sweet and raw, piercing in its severe perfection.

At six o'clock she reheated some leftovers in the oven (Beverly Parke didn't believe in microwaves), and ate her spaghetti with jarred marinara sauce on the front porch, watching the evening darken as the minutes ticked by; it was a windy evening, leaves danced down Ackerly

Lane making soft scraping noises on the pavement. Anna was just about to go inside when she saw a dark figure emerging from the woods. She squinted her eyes against the dimness until she was able to perceive the slight, wispy silhouette of her mother, barefoot, walking slowly towards home. Anna didn't call out to her mother, nor did she walk down the stone pathway to greet her. Something about Ms. Parke's deliberate stride scared her a bit, which was of course silly. There was nothing even remotely scary (this kind of scary) about her mother, aside from her obsessive cleanliness and bitterness–traits that were more unpleasant and frustrating than they were frightening. Instead, Anna remained seated on the white wicker rocking chair by the front door as Beverly Parke made her way up the front porch steps.

Anna's surprise must have shown clearly on her face because Beverly Parke spat out, "Don't stare at me like that Anna."

"Were you in the woods?" Anna responded.

"That's none of your concern," her mother responded.

Anna wanted to further the conversation but did not know how to proceed and her mother's body language certainly did not exactly invite questions. She wanted to know what her mother was doing in the woods and why she was so late and why she hadn't come home earlier to make dinner like she normally did and why it was ok for her to go to the woods but not for Anna.

But instead of asking any of these questions, Anna said, "I ate the leftover pasta. There's still some more if you'd like it."

Beverly Parke did not acknowledge this comment and walked right past Anna and into the home they shared. As she strode by, Anna noticed two tiny green pine needles entwined in her mother's loose bun, vibrant green against auburn hair. How did those get there? She followed her mother into the house, not even daring to pluck the contraband from her mother's twisted hair. She let the matter drop, there was no other option, but Anna remained confused for the rest of the evening and her dreams were frightening and strange, tinged with green pine needles like fingerprints across her uneasy mind.

Chapter 51

Once a mind alights upon its purpose, very little can be done to deter that mind's eye from what it is meant to do. So it was with Anna Parke on that dark, cool fall evening in late October. There would be no sleep tonight. Anna had a mission. The trees murmured their incessant summons, *"Come to us. We have a story to tell."*

Anna was ready to hear it. She feared what knowledge those tall guardians would instill upon her; there was an undeniable aura of dread emanating from those woods. Yet, she knew it was time. It was time for her to accept her birthright, to acknowledge what was weird and strange and magical. She had to open herself up again, bind herself to those strings that she attempted to sever for the past decade or more.

She quickly pulled on a pair of worn jeans, stretched her arms through a soft sweater, and laced up her brown leather boots. She raced out of her apartment before she could talk herself out of it, before her logical mind could take over the reins and guide her back to her stuffy apartment.

The night air felt invigorating: fresh and cool and electric. Main Street was quiet, just a few crispy leaves scudding across the sidewalk. Anna's feet instinctively lead her in the right direction. As she hurried along, she thought again about her uncle's words, "Windsom tree, Black dead tree, The tree with the long arms. The tree knows." She would hopefully soon be able to accept her uncle's mutterings as either lunacy or logic. Dr. Jenkins would undoubtedly disapprove of this errand; she would call Anna foolish for "giving credence" to her uncle's ravings. But, what would Dr, Jenkins say about Anna's perceived ability to communicate with the trees? Would Dr Jenkins have Anna confined to a neighboring cell–two Parkes sharing the same delusions of insanity? Probably. But nonetheless, this was something Anna had to do.

Her feet carried her to Ackerly Lane and she walked past her childhood home. The 'for sale' sign was still jutting out of the front lawn, which was slightly overgrown having no owner to keep the grass consistently mown. Her mother would have been horrified to see traces of weeds growing in the flower garden. Despite the realtor's promise that the home would sell soon and for over-market value, there had surprisingly been no takers and lately Chris Reilly, her realtor, was pressuring Anna to lower the asking price. Anna wasn't against this plan, but had been too preoccupied to return the nagging phone calls. Pausing for a moment on the sidewalk, Anna stared into the darkened windows. She didn't have fond memories of her life in this home, but nonetheless, a sense of nostalgia swept over her, powerful and insistent, as she scanned the familiar facade.

Anna didn't allow herself to linger long. The voices of the trees were loud now, echoing in her mind, drowning out the familiar pull of memory. She walked along until the toes of her boots brushed up against the rough edge of the woods. She stepped over the threshold and entered the very place she had been avoiding since childhood, and instead of the terror that she anticipated, her surroundings provided her with a serenity that she didn't know she needed. Opening her arms wide, Anna welcomed the familiar smells and sounds and sights. She felt home.

Meandering through the windy, soft, sweet-smelling, paths, Anna was struck by how much she missed this place. She brought a flashlight with her, but the silver light of the moon through the leafless branches guided her way. Serenaded by the hoots of owls, by the crunching of fall leaves under her boots, and the faraway howl of a bobcat, she searched for her uncle's tree. She felt in her soul the message of the trees; *"Keep going,"* they said. *"You are almost there."*

As Anna wound her way deeper and deeper into the Windsom woods she sensed that she was getting closer…to what exactly she couldn't quite tell just yet, but she felt a prickle on her scalp that made the tiny hairs on her arms stand at attention. Gooseflesh, her mother had called it. Her uncle's words echoed in her psyche, *"the black, dead, tree… the tree knows… the tree with the long arms…"* The brambles of the baby pine trees and the undergrowth of the forest scratched at her exposed hands. Later on, she would find the fine red scrapes.

The trees opened into a small clearing. In the center were the remnants of a campfire: gray ashen logs crisscrossed like legs in the middle, surrounded by larger mossy rocks and stones. What should have been regarded as a beautiful place to settle down for an evening in nature felt all wrong to Anna. Something felt off, that was the only way she could describe it. Something felt wrong. Maybe it was the way the surrounded trees seemed to tilt away from this space; maybe it was the off-putting reflection of the moon on the dewey pine needles at her feet, or perhaps just a sinister aura, Anna couldn't be sure, but suddenly she wanted to get away from here as quickly as possible. Yet, despite the wrongness of the place, she was quite sure that she was close to whatever it was her uncle was trying to tell her and what the trees promised to reveal. She felt a stillness in her heart, a quiet voice in her soul said, *"Take your time. Have a look around. You are right there."*

As she scanned the edges of the clearing, one particular tree held her attention, or maybe the remains of a tree was more accurate. It wasn't much more than a tall stump, jagged and rough, with scraggly outcroppings growing from the center hollow. This stump was onyx, almost as if it had been burned in a fire. It looked like it was made of igneous rock spewed out of some earthquake at the beginning of time. *The black tree, the dead tree, the tree with the long arms…*

She cautiously approached, feeling an almost magnetic pull. This was definitely right… yet oh so wrong at the same time. Standing directly in front of this relic of a tree, she heard its forceful drone pulsing in her core, *"I have a story for you, I have something to show you, I know.."*

Despite feeling an almost palpable aversion to this tree, despite the feeling of her gorge rising in her throat, bitter and acidic, Anna held out both hands and placed them on the center of the stump's charred surface. The moonlight acted as a torch, blazing white in the inky sky.

As soon as her palms encountered the bark, Anna felt an almost electrical current surge through her body. She threw her head back, eyes bulging, glued to the bright orb shining in the black velvet above her.

What happened to Anna Parke on this baleful night as her hands remained affixed to this grotesque artifact was nothing short of other-worldly.

She was transported back in time; she saw the tree in all its former beauty, a friendly maple, tall and straight in the sparkling sunshine which cast a million reflections on its glistening leaves. The tree was massive; certainly the largest she ever saw in these woods behind her house. As she gazed up, she noticed how the thick rough trunk–larger than even two people together could reach their arms around–split into a Y with two enormous outcroppings, each one smaller, but only slightly, than the broad trunk to which her hands were affixed.

As she admired this colossal specimen, her thoughts were interrupted by a family emerging through the clearing. First a father, dressed in hiking boots and cargo pants, topped with a fisherman's hat. Next a mother: brunette and lively, albeit stern, in similar attire. Following the two parents was a teenage boy, muscular and alert, his heart shaped face and smiling eyes were a dead giveaway. It was Jacob Parke, a young, healthy, stable boy in his prime. The mother and father who preceded him into the clearing were Irving and Estelle, Anna's grandparents. And before Anna had time to fully process what she was witnessing, a younger girl, eyes downcast and somber emerged from the brush: Beverly Parke. Anna's breath caught in her throat. The resemblance between the young girl that she now saw directly in front of her, and the mother she knew her whole life up until she had left her childhood home, struck her in the soul with a punch that she could never have anticipated. Anna closed her eyes for a moment to still her rapid breathing.

It was clear that this family could not perceive Anna Parke standing there; they seemed to look right through her as they surveyed the area. And something told her that if she removed her hands from the trunk, the vision, or whatever this was, would be terminated, it would vanish, along with the electric current that was connecting them; so she remained, frozen in position, arms outstretched.

While the family went about setting up their tent, chatting merrily, and arranging their sleeping bags, Anna noticed that Beverly Parke remained distant.

"Beverly, how about you come help us instead of sitting on that log," Irving Parke instructed his daughter.

Beverly made no motion to move, so with a roll of his eyes, Anna's grandfather gave up. Watching the family dynamic made a few things crystal clear to Anna. Most importantly, Jacob was clearly the favorite, adored by his doting family, while Beverly remained on the outskirts, no longer even trying to become one with the cohesive group.

As Anna watched her own family, she desperately wished to interact with them, yet something in the waves emanating from the tree told her to remain silent and to stand where she was.

The afternoon and early evening passed by quickly and Anna wondered if she was viewing this scene in some sort of sped-up motion, like a movie reel accelerated. She strongly believed that she had not yet seen whatever it was that she was supposed to see.

Now the Parkes were gathered around the campfire, again, Jacob conversing with his parents in an affable, easy dialogue, while Beverly remained quiet, morose, nose buried in a book of which Anna couldn't quite make out the title. From where she was, Anna couldn't hear the details of the conversation; she only heard the rise and swell of friendly voices and the halting and unsuccessful attempts of the parents to engage their daughter as well. Beverly seemed bored, distracted and wholly disinterested in her family's discourse. Anna wondered what caused her mother to respond this way.

Anna was aware of a general feeling of fatigue in her extremities, yet she dared not shift her rigid stance. The ruby globe in the sky blazed as it slowly began its descent behind the horizon.

The family in front of her (it felt as though Anna was watching some sort of theatrical performance–this couldn't be real, could it?) began to settle in for the night; they lined up their flannel sleeping bags in a row, the parents and older son cuddled closely together; the wayward Beverly a few feet away. Anna could perceive the heavy breathing of slumber as the solicitude of the forest pressed in upon her.

Just as Anna thought that the scene had ended, that the curtains had fallen, indicating the end of the performance, Anna perceived the shadowy figure of Beverly Parke slithering soundlessly out of her sleeping bag. Her family was asleep, snoring into the darkness–serene in their blissful dreaming. For a long time, Beverly stood there, barely moving, staring down at her sleeping kin. Finally, she moved towards the blue canvas tent, soundlessly rummaging in her leather backpack for what it was she was looking for. What she pulled out of her sack gleamed in the bright moonlight and even from Anna's vantage point, the item was clear. A sturdy hatchet, smooth, metallic and ominous. Beverly contemplated this item for just a moment before placing it into the next duffel bag...the bag with the University of Pennsylvania patch roughly sewn into the stiff material.

Once this task was complete, Beverly went back to her position, directly and imperceptibly in front of the row of sleeping Parkes, lined up like oily sardines in their rectangular tin.

Anna watched with a growing horror, wishing to scream out, yet paralyzed in her frozen purgatory. Beverly Parke's back was to Anna, but what she witnessed next was a scene out of a horror movie. Anna was minutely glad that she wasn't forced to watch from the other angle…she was terrified of the expression she may have seen in her young mother's eyes. However, oftentimes the imagination is much crueler than reality.

She was dimly aware of the trail of salty tears running down her cheeks as she watched her mother raise her spindly arms. Beverly Parke's long dark hair spun around her like a vortex in the wind that she seemed to summon from the depth of the trees. Her family stirred in their sleep, disrupted by the sudden change in atmosphere. Anna saw her mother's head tilt upwards; Anna was able to perceive inarticulate gibberish spewing from Beverly's snarled lips, teeth bared. The rest of the family was awake now, confused in their state of grogginess, mouths formed into large Os, staring up at their daughter.

Jacob Parke moved more swiftly than his parents and quickly pushed his sleeping bag down so he could escape from his flannel tomb. He called out, "Beverly, No. Stop." And he ran forward towards her as if to tackle her to the forest floor.

But he was too late. Beverly made a quick motion with her arms, a slicing motion, and the tree–this massive specimen–seemed to understand her command, like an obedient dog responding to its master. Anna glanced upward to witness the spectacle. The tree to which her hands were affixed seemed to cry out in betrayal and misuse. In a burst of flame and lightning, one of the outcroppings of the trunk–one of the arms of the Y-shape, at least twenty feet long, thick and powerful–snapped from the trunk and came crashing down upon the unsuspecting Parkes.

Thudding to the ground with such force, the ground literally reverberated under Anna's trembling feet. Anna perceived some muted screaming, followed by softer gurgling, choking sounds, followed only by portentous silence that engulfed her as she watched the rest of the scene unfold before her.

Jacob flew forward landing right on top of Beverly; they tumbled together to the ground in slow motion as Anna's voice failed her once again. On the floor, tangled together like shoelaces, Beverly and Jacob Parke rolled within a foot of Anna's feet. Jacob quickly dislodged himself from his sister's body and raced back to inspect the carnage. Beverly remained on the forest floor, eyes up and Anna could almost swear that she saw her at that moment...their eyes locked and the coldness and evil that Anna perceived within those glassy orbs took her breath away.

Horrified, Anna looked up to see Jacob Parke trying unsuccessfully to move the enormous limb from his parents' bodies. His complexion turned crimson from the effort and he was panting ragged breaths of strain as he heaved his shoulders and pushed with all his might. He paid no attention at all to his sister, who had sprung up like a rabbit from the soft floor and ran swiftly and soundlessly back through the clearing the way the family had come hours before.

After about twenty minutes of effort, Jacob succeeded in moving the massive appendage enough. Just enough to see. In agony, Anna saw him crawl around to the other side and inspect the remains of his crushed parents. From her vantage point, Anna could not perceive exactly what he witnessed, but she could tell that Jacob made some frantic efforts to revive them, first his father and then his mother. But when Anna Parke watched her uncle collapse in tears, head in hands next to what were surely at this point, his parents' corpses, she knew that Jacob had given up whatever slim hope he held within him when he tried with desperation to move the tree in the first place. The sobs of sadness and rage that he cried on that dreadful evening will haunt Anna for the rest of her life.

Anna remained transfixed, wishing to all the powers in the heavens that she could go and comfort her uncle. Anna lost track of all time as she watched her sobbing uncle and instead of offering solace, she watched in horror as police officers arrived at the scene, with Beverly Parke in tow. Beverly, who had apparently called them to report that her brother was a murderer.

Beverly Parke had faux tears running down her face and pointed a straight arm at her brother. While one police officer roughly placed handcuffs on the screaming Jacob Parke, the other officer rifled through the duffel bag, the one with the University of Pennsylvania patch sewn roughly on the front flap. The officer gingerly removed the gleaming hatchet from the pack, which seemed to solidify in their minds the culprit behind the gruesome scene.

At this point, Anna screamed out, "No. No. You have it all wrong. How can you possibly believe that Jacob did this?" But no one heard her voice or perceived her presence at all. Anna tasted her own salty tears as she opened her mouth. She opened her mouth so wide that the corners of her mouth began bleeding as the raspy screams wracked her body as though she would split open at the seams. She saw Jacob Parke protest. He pushed one of the officers hard enough in the chest to send him sprawling backwards, but a seventeen-year old boy is no match for two policemen.

The officers led the handcuffed Jacob Parke back through the clearing, not realizing at all the magnitude of their actions. Not realizing at all their terrible mistake. Anna discerned the sound of sirens in the distance.

Beverly Parke remained behind, alone in the dark woods. The young girl wiped the tears away from her cheeks with the sleeve of her shirt and calmly went about packing up her possessions, including the novel that she had been reading earlier that evening. Anna heard Beverly humming as she gathered her belongings and Anna felt a terror so severe rising within her that it took just about everything she had not to fall down in a bundle of shaking nerves. Just as Beverly Parke was about to disappear down the path towards home, she turned around and once again locked eyes with Anna. Beverly smiled a tiny smile, lips barely curling up at the edges.

And then, she simply turned her head and walked slowly away from the clearing, leaving Anna alone in the moonlight. That smile stayed with Anna…she recognized that smile. She had seen it many times before. It was a victorious smile. A smile that said, "Now what. I win. Don't you know? I always win."

CHAPTER 52

Peeking through the tiny sliver of a bedroom door left ajar, Anna watched greedily, fascinated by her mother's vulnerability in the seemingly mundane activity of dressing after a shower. For most girls, witnessing their mother in various states of undress is commonplace. But, nakedness was not celebrated in Anna's household and Beverly Parke placed the concepts of privacy and decorum on a pedestal to be honored above all else. Never did Beverly Parke allow the bathroom door to slip open while bathing, so careful was she to fasten the bedroom lock while dressing. But on this day, Beverly was careless and Anna relished a fleeting moment to witness her mother unguarded. Part of the appeal was curiosity. The curiosity of knowing what a grown woman looks like, and not the grown women pictured in magazines and in the movies, but a real woman. All young girls feel an urge to know what they might one day look like once adolescence fades away like a ship slowly disappearing over the horizon. But a bigger part of Anna's motivation was purely seeing her mother at ease, doing a simple task that most mothers perform naturally. Beverly Parke never relaxed around Anna, never let down her stony wall to expose what was real and true about her–if there was anything real and true about her–and because of this, Anna felt as though she lived with a stranger.

Anna's eyes were drawn to the stretch marks, purple in hue against Beverly's pale skin. They looked like claw marks, jagged and parallel coursing across her mother's deflated belly. Anna felt a sense of misplaced pride seeing those marks, knowing that she had made them. That she had clawed her way into Beverly's life while she was still inside her womb, regardless of how unwanted she was. To Anna, they were proof. Not that she needed proof to know that Beverly was indeed biologically her mother, but Beverly acted so un-motherly most of the time that seeing those marks insisted on a connection that Anna wished she experienced. Anna so often felt that Beverly tried to deny this connection, deny her motherhood, deny her. But as Anna watched her mother, she guessed that nature has a way of exposing truths that people would rather hide, and no matter how much Beverly may have fought against her truth, the evidence was right there, written in red ink on her hollow abdomen.

At this moment, Anna mused that motherhood might mean more than pushing a squirming, wiggling baby through a distended and throbbing vagina. Yes, that act is the beginning, but Beverly seemed to view it as the end. It was true that Anna was no longer physically inside of her mother, feeding off her like a leech, but they were stuck with one another, for better or worse. A life sentence.

At this moment, as Anna dazed into her own subconscious thought, a shrill and volcanic voice brought her back to reality.

"What do you think you're doing? Are you watching me?" spat Beverly Parke.

Anna was discovered. Beverly stormed over to the door as she pulled her bathrobe protectively across her chest. Anna's feet wouldn't work; she couldn't run. Instead, she remained there, frozen, transfixed, mumbling her defense behind numb lips.

"I asked you a question Anna. Why are you spying on me?" she hissed.

"Um–"

Anna couldn't think of a word to say–no explanation, clarification, rationale, nothing to lessen the blow of Beverly's outrage. In Beverly's mind, Anna had broken a golden rule. Anna had blatantly and profoundly crossed the line of what is tolerable and appropriate and decent.

Anna tried again, "Sorry mom, I mean, I saw your door open and—"

"And…and what? You just thought that you would stop in for a peep show? How dare you violate my privacy in this way? What is wrong with you?"

"I was walking to my room…I saw those marks on your stomach…" Anna blurted out before she could swallow those words.

Beverly's rage was nearly palpable and Anna stood there sweating under her mother's scrutiny.

"You gave me those marks Anna. You! And that's not the only thing you ruined. Do you think they are ugly? Are you criticizing me?"

"No, mom..I didn't mean it that way. I was just wondering about them. I never meant to make you upset. I'm sorry," Anna continued on.

"Well at least my marks can be hidden. What about that disgustingness on your face?" Beverly responded with a gleam of victory in her eyes.

At this point in time, Beverly rarely brought up the unsightly port wine stain that took up most of Anna's right cheek (although soon the blemish would become yet another source of daily contention in their already suffocated relationship). Such specific remarks were used only when Beverly really needed to make a statement, when she really needed to put her daughter in her place. And now was the perfect time for cruelty. Anna could perceive the gleam of a smile, that victorious smile, playing on Beverly's thin lips. Anna brought her palm up to her face and wavered on her feet confused, not truly knowing what her next move should be, not really knowing what to say next.

"Go to your room," Beverly said.

Anna was grateful for the opportunity to escape, and she did as she was told. She felt Beverly's eyes boring into her back as she scurried down the hallway, feet pitter-pattering on the aged oak floors, and returned to her own bedroom, slowly closing and locking the door behind her. *Good*, Beverly must have thought. *Let her run away.*

Once Anna was safe in her bedroom, she thought again about the stretch marks on her mother's body and remembered how, just a few minutes earlier she had thought about motherhood being akin to a life sentence. Never before had that thought felt more true, more real. One can never fully escape her parentage, can she?

She fell asleep dreaming about that smile. That cold, hard, humorless smile. That smile, most of all, she couldn't forget

Chapter 53

Now

Now alone in the clearing, the image of her smiling young mother began to fade, and with that fading mirage, Anna noticed the tree crumbling and shriveling against her smooth palms. She felt the rough, healthy bark turn slimy and black. It was as if the tree became diseased, rotten once her mother had forced it to commit this bitter act. With a sneer of revulsion, Anna removed her hands from the charred surface and found herself once again staring at the tree's remains.

Now back to her present world, Anna's mind raced. Her face was soaked from the tears that she had shed and from those still running down her face. Her uncle, her mother, her grandparents. She paced back and forth, thoughts swimming around in her jumbled head. Rage, sadness, confusion, her emotions battled for position in her pounding heart. It may have provided Anna with a degree of comfort, knowing that her own absent father saw, within Beverly, a glimpse of her true nature, but not much. And at this moment, Anna never could have known the degree to which Beverly Parke had unsettled her long lost lover.

Maybe she would have been better off not knowing...but she could not 'un-know' the horrors that the tree revealed to her and for one moment, for one moment before logic could regain power, she felt a hatred for her uncle so deep it threatened to drown her in its black sea. How dare he rattle her world like this? Or maybe she was more angry at herself; she had willingly engulfed herself in this mess. But once the rage cleared, she felt only sorrow settle in the depth of her soul and the sadness and sympathy that she felt for her uncle overcame her like nightfall settling over a distant land.

She felt a sudden and powerful urge to get out, to leave these woods and hide herself in the comfortable cocoon of her safe apartment. She needed time; she needed to think. However, before she did so, her eyes alighted on a shiny something buried within the depths of the stump. Had the moon not been shining just so, she would have undoubtedly missed it. Reaching her hand inside the oily remains of what was once a healthy, living tree, she pulled out a silver case, slightly smaller than a shoe box. It looked like a mirrored jewelry case, but larger. The box was tarnished and cracked, and covered in dirt, but still mostly intact. Even despite its antiquated beauty, the item made her skin crawl. She needed to get out of here. And no matter how much Anna wanted, needed to know what the box contained, her urge to flee was more pronounced than her curiosity, so Anna shoved the box inside her backpack and ran towards the exit of the woods.

The trees swiftly passed her. At one point, her foot caught within a soft, rotten fallen log and she tumbled to the wet ground with a thud. Once she rose, brushing the dirt and leaves from her legs, she continued her desperate escape. Anna felt like a fugitive fleeing the scene of a crime, which she supposed she was in some odd way.

The trees helped guide her in the right direction and before long, she emerged, gasping, onto the concrete of Ackerly Lane. Anna had a painful stitch in her side and stumbled along, not daring to rest–not daring to look back at the woods from which she emerged. She was too afraid to face the trees once again; she knew she could not bear to be the recipient of any more secrets tonight, maybe not ever.

She slowly made her way towards Main Street, her mind still racing. It was nearly four o'clock in the morning when she stomped her way back into her apartment and collapsed upon her unmade bed. Anna didn't even bother removing her muddy boots or wet jeans before she fell into a deep unrestful sleep.

The box remained hidden deep within Anna's knapsack during Anna's slumber, just waiting to be opened.

Chapter 54

Anna opened her eyes to the glare of the bedside clock reading three-thirty in the afternoon. She could not remember the last time she slept so late. Her head throbbed and as she rose from a lying position, she realized that she was still wearing the clothes from last night. The comforter and sheets were dirty with mud and wet leaves and Anna cringed at the thought of visiting a laundromat today. As she rubbed the sleep from her eyes and ran her fingers through her tangled hair, visions of last night came back to her full force. She felt her chest compress with the memory and for a moment she tried to convince herself that it had all been a bizarre and terrible dream.

However, as Anna stood up, and more and more of last night's strange occurrences danced across her eyelids, she could no longer avoid them. Now that she could think more rationally a few thoughts stood out in her mind like lighting bolts: her uncle was innocent and more coherent than anyone had ever given him credit for; her mother was the true criminal in the Parke family legacy–a thought she put away for the time being because it was simply too raw, too bloody to dwell on at the moment.

Because Anna could not yet mentally compartmentalize the troubling facts about her own mother, she forced her thoughts towards her innocent uncle, wasting away in an Ithaca insane asylum, ranting about trees–his one source of possible vindication. How many people and loved ones had dismissed his words, chalking up his comments about the trees to mere delusion? How long Jacob Parke had swallowed his past until it bubbled over, frothing like boiling water in a tea kettle! He tried to push it down and live a normal life with Janine Harper, Anna now saw, but the past always surfaces, even when one believes it to have sunk into the murky depths of time. What kind of responsibility did Anna have to her long lost uncle? Did she have the guts to try to vindicate him?...and thus incriminate her recently-deceased mother? And who would even believe her? “The tree told me,” seemed like a sentence that would never be given much credence by any sane human being. This was all too much for Anna to take in, and she desperately wished she had a sister or a close friend in which to confide. But Anna Parke was alone–alone with the demons of her birthright.

And as much as Anna forcefully pushed these thoughts away, her mind kept returning to her mother, Beverly Parke–the little girl with the swirling, vortex of hair who caused so much destruction such a long, long time ago. Some facts became clear to Anna on that cool afternoon as she rambled around her apartment looking for anything to keep her mind distracted from the thoughts that impaled her. She thought of how her mother had commanded that branch to snap, of the power that emanated from those hands, of the evil of which her own mother was capable. She and her mother shared the uncanny and troubling connection with the trees that surrounded them, that much was clear. Anna remembered a time in her childhood when she told her mother about an odd experience she had in the woods; how her mother had reprimanded her! What had been running through her mother's mind when Anna uttered these words? Like mother like daughter? That maxim sent shivers down Anna's spine; she had spent so much of her life trying not to follow in her mother's footsteps. And yet, here she was.

Anna's mother had always been cold, which would be putting it mildly, but the thought of Beverly Parke murdering her parents and framing her brother was a hard pill for Anna to swallow. Yet, the proof could not be ignored; Anna witnessed the act with her very own eyes, a drama that would forever be imprinted upon her soul. It made sense why Beverly Parke kept to herself, why she refused to discuss her parents, why she kept her only living family member a secret, why she had forbidden Anna to venture into the Windsom Woods. At this point, Anna felt a sudden rage forming in her stomach, like a tree taking root in her very being. She felt as though she had been robbed of something very dear...and that the thief in question was her own mother.

As these thoughts bubbled in Anna's mind, Anna paced around her apartment in such a disoriented way that it was no surprise that she tripped over a soft object and tumbled to the floor, hitting her elbow on the corner of the end table situated next to her bed. The impact sent a sharp jolt of pain coursing through her body. Gripping her elbow she looked around to find the source of her fall and her eyes alighted upon her backpack, which in last night's exhaustion she failed to hang up when she returned to her apartment in the wee hours of this morning. As she gazed upon her dirty knapsack she sat bolt upright remembering the glittering box she dislodged from the depth of the tree stump. She hastily unzipped the bag and rummaged through. Her hand hit a solid, smooth edge and she eagerly pulled out the treasure.

In the brightness of her apartment the box didn't look as shiny as it had in the moonlight of the woods, and its mirrored surface was badly cracked and rusted, but her impression was the same: a jewelry box, complete with a snap closure and claw-legged feet. It must have been quite beautiful years ago and had it been in better condition it would have undoubtedly been considered a valuable antique.

Slowly, sitting on her bedroom floor leaning against the nightstand that had pained her elbow, still dressed in last night's dirty clothes, Anna unclasped the closure and opened the damaged lid. It emitted a muffled creak as it moved up to position. As Anna gazed inside she felt a sudden dread, and for a moment she was tempted to close it up, and throw the box along with whatever it was that was inside it right into the kitchen garbage, but Anna could do that no more than she could have avoided the pull of the trees last night.

Anna didn't know what she expected to find inside that glittering box on that late fall afternoon as she remained seated on her bedroom floor, but when she peered in, she was disappointed to see only a wad of folded up papers rubber banded together. The rubber band immediately snapped in Anna's fingers as she attempted to open the parcel; it was old and dry. As she unfolded the bundle she realized that the papers consisted of a series of correspondence along with articles torn from old books, the edges jagged and rough. Attempting to smooth the deep grooves and creases in the flimsy sheets, Anna gingerly pressed them open using her thighs as an ironing board.

Anna quickly rifled through the papers and from her rough perusal it looked as though the letters were all addressed to her mother and were sent from Jacob Parke. It felt wrong to Anna to read what were undoubtedly personal letters; it felt as though she were ransacking a stranger's underwear drawer, but at the same time she believed she was supposed to read them. She felt that her uncle wanted her to read them. Hadn't he communicated this desire during their bizarre encounter? Afterall, her mother was dead; whatever contents these letters contained, Anna was the closest surviving kin to the individual to which the letters were intended. Anna needed to know.

So, with a shiver up her spine, Anna began reading and then re-reading the letters,one by one as afternoon turned into evening and the sun gradually set behind the horizon.

The first letter was sent to Beverly Parke on September 17th,1957 from the Half-Moon Juvenile Detention Facility. Anna did some quick mental calculations and came to the knowledge that this letter was composed and sent almost a month after the untimely deaths of Irving and Estelle Parke. Anna remembered her visit to the Half-Moon Juvenile Facility; Jacob was taken there immediately upon arrest and spent significant time there (was it seven years?) both before and after his guilty sentence.

The letter read:

Dear Beverly,

I know we have never been close, but I am still your older brother. I am here in the Half-Moon Juvenile Facility awaiting my trial. It is strange to think that I should be beginning my classes at the University of Pennsylvania. But instead I am here. I know you hated all the college talk. You never said it, but I always saw the way you would roll your eyes and leave the room anytime mom and dad spoke about my future.

I've had a lot of time to think and I realize that it must have been difficult for you in our house. I should have made more of an effort to be a better and more present older brother to you. I am sorry for that.

I am told by my lawyer that you have declined to testify in my defense. Maybe it is a blessing that you have declined because I am afraid of what you might say.

How did that hatchet get into my backpack? Did my eyes deceive me about what I witnessed in the woods that night? I have nightmares Beverly. I have nightmares about what I saw you do. If I hadn't woken up, I also would have been crushed alongside Mom and Dad. Maybe that was your intention all along. I'm not sure what goes through your head...Maybe I have always been too afraid to ask.

I am writing you this letter to beg you to reconsider testifying on my behalf. Or to at least consider coming to my trial. My lawyer, Mr. Denson, feels that it would look better for me in the eyes of the jury if I had a family member on my side.

I have so many questions about that night. I miss mom and dad. The thought of being implicated in their murders is almost too much for me to handle.

Please write back, Beverly. My future depends upon it,

Sincerely,

Jake

Anna read this first letter at least three times and each time she read it she could do nothing to stop the tears from trickling slowly out of the corners of her eyes. She felt so many emotions jumbled together in her very core; they threatened to overwhelm her. Anna admired

Jacob for containing the rage that he must surely have felt for his younger sister. But then again, he was asking for something. He was asking her to do what was decent and right.

The next letter was sent two weeks later. It was shorter and slightly more desperate, filled with subdued anger and melancholy.

Beverly,

Considering I have not received a return letter or any news at all from you I can assume only two possibilities. One: You did not receive my letter, however I don't think that this is not the case. The second possibility is that you have refused to be involved in my trial and have officially turned your back on me. I am not completely surprised although I am heartbroken.

What have I done to make you hate me?

My trial is officially underway and I sense the jury turning against me. They see me as a privileged, know-it-all, spoiled brat who is simply looking for his parents' small inheritance. Maybe you agree with them!

The hatchet that was found in my backpack seems to be the nail in the coffin and no one believes my defense that I honestly do not know how it got there.

You seem to be viewed as the angel of the family and the judge feels that it would be immoral to get a summons for your testimony as you must be grieving the deaths of your parents. Ha! If they only knew.

Please please please reconsider Beverly. I am the only family you have.
-Jake

Following this, the next letter was sent on October 6th, 1957.

Dear Beverly,

I have been officially convicted of murder. Me, Jacob Parke, all-American teenager, a murderer. But you must know this already. It was a surprise to see you in court last week. I knew that you had declined to testify on my behalf, but I had no idea that you would testify against me! How could you tell those lies! That you saw me cut the trunk of that tree, that I intentionally killed mom and dad! I wish I could say that I am shocked, but something in my soul expected this. I can't imagine how the jury could even believe your story. How could I possibly chop through such a thick trunk with that measly hatchet?

Today I opted to give my final, closing argument. Even though Mr.Denson advised against it, I think even he sensed that the jury had already made up its mind.

I think I went overboard. I talked about you and what I saw. The vortex and the fire and the waving hand motions. But, everything I said contradicted your testimony and they didn't believe me. I must have sounded totally crazy in my closing argument because when the jury returned with their guilty verdict, instead of sentencing me to time in Attica, they sentenced me to ten years in some psychiatric facility. So, that's where I will be. Instead of going to college and graduating and finding a job, I will be wasting away in some padded cell. Is this what you wanted? Please answer me. You owe me at least that and so much more; Please help me understand why you did what you did and how our relationship went so horribly wrong. Please, Beverly. I am all you have left!

Your Brother,

Jake

The letters continued. There were about twenty of them written at various points throughout the next ten years. Some of them were angry, raging against Beverly and demanding that she vindicate him. Others were sad and somber begging Beverly to come visit. It was clear to Anna that Beverly never responded to any of Jacob's letters, nor did she go visit him.

The letters also revealed some insight regarding Jacob Parke's trial and sentence. The idea that any investigating officer would automatically believe that Jacob could have physically done what he was accused of doing was gnawing at Anna. Also, didn't it all seem too perfect? A tree trunk falling perfectly on sleeping parents? How could any police officer think that a teenager could have orchestrated such a perfectly planned symphony? But the letters revealed how such a story could have come to pass as truth. Beverly's testimony excused the shoddy police work. The precinct didn't need to investigate how a seventeen-year old boy could possibly chop through a thick tree trunk with a mere hatchet. They didn't need to account for the precision and accuracy that such an endeavor would have required. They had a crying "innocent" little sister who told them all they needed to know. Even a small investigation would have found holes in her story. This thought stood out in Anna's mind as she continued to rifle through letters and documents before her.

Anna also puzzled over Beverly's purpose in saving such incriminating artifacts. Had her mother considered the letters to be some sort of trophy? Don't murderers keep souvenirs of their crimes? Was that what this was? Reminding Beverly of her success? Or, deep down did Anna's mother possess some human capacity for love? Anna wasn't sure and Beverly was long gone...as proven by the vat of ashes that remained hidden in the depth of Anna's closet.

She felt a sudden and intense rage towards her mother. For the coldness and the judgment and the isolation. How dare she play with her family's future? With their lives! Anna found this new image of her mother exceedingly difficult to reconcile with the one she had built up in her mind and experienced first hand as a lonely child desperate for approval. She had so many questions. It was clear from the letters that Beverly had some sort of resentment built up towards her brother, a palpable jealousy about his academic and athletic success? Maybe. Was that the rationale behind her actions? It seemed so extreme, so calculated and cruel.

Aside from her mother's capacity for murder, Anna also tried to grasp the alien powers Beverly possessed. And consequently the alien powers Anna herself had stifled within her own being. What a family legacy!

Glancing down, Anna realized that there was more in the bundle of papers. Underneath the letters were three articles torn from some publication written many years ago and hastily stapled together. The pages were yellowing and faded. Anna sensed that if she handled them without the utmost delicacy they would disintegrate in her grasp. At various points throughout the articles, someone had underlined and jotted hasty notes in the margins and Anna could immediately tell by the lettering that that someone was her mother.

All of the articles were published in some medical journal titled *The Medicine Behind The Mind* as evidenced by the footnotes scrolling across the bottom of each page; the date of publication was not included. The first article was titled, "The Dark Side of Nature: Quelling the Call," written by a Dr. Martin Prince.

Ever since the beginning of time, nature has called to mankind. The intensity of the call varies from individual to individual depending on certain psychological markers that will be examined later on in this dissertation. Only a select few possess the ability to answer that call in a true and intentional way. The Native Americans referred to this ability I will call it as Unci Maka Kae or Earth Manipulation. Those who possessed this ability in the native tribes were revered as godlike figures and offered sacred positions in leadership roles.

However, as we have come to learn more about Earth Manipulation through analysis of the native tribal heritage, it is clear that there is little to be admired in such individuals and more to be feared. Take the example of Chief Amitola of the Lakota lineage. He was revered as a Wakan Tanka and named as Chief Spiritual Advisor for his community. Based upon their historic manuscripts, Amitola used his water manipulation powers to drown all of the children born out of Lakota-Lakota jointure as the society highly valued what they referred to as "pure-blood" Lakonan lineage. Stories like that of Amitola and others like him must make us pause to consider the dangers of Unci Maka Kae.

Although it is less likely in our modern society to be endowed with Earth Manipulation tendencies, there are certain markers both physical and psychological of which caretakers may take note

Those with Earth Manipulation abilities are often quite literally and physically marked. It is reasonable to assume that something within the very genetic makeup of Earth Manipulators results in physical manifestations, possibly as a warning for the rest of mankind. These marks may take the form of birthmarks or moles, areas of increased or absent skin pigmentation, unexplained scars, or any other dermatological defect.

After Anna read this paragraph, she stopped in her tracks. Her mother had marked this section with a large bracket and underlined the entire paragraph with a thick, dark smudge. Unconsciously Anna's hand was drawn magnetically to the dark port wine stain adorning her cheek. Her mark. The cause of her estrangement from her mother. Could it also be the source of her connection to the trees? The paragraph went on to discuss in detail the various physical defects associated with what Dr. Martin Prince called “Marks of Earth Manipulation” and how to tell an ordinary skin imperfection from the more sinister counterpart.

After this, the article went on to discuss the proper course of action if a skin marking was found and if the defect was present in conjunction with Earth Manipulation.

Looking back at the infamous Chief Amitola. All drawings depicting him, most of which were etched into buffalo skin, depict a discernible and dark blemish on his upper left pectoral muscle. If you suspect that either yourself or your offspring possess a mark associated with this sinister genetic malformation, the best course is to expediently remove the flaw. However, in my experience it is best to excise the blemish after puberty. It has been proven that such marks may re-establish themselves if removed prematurely and possibly enhance in nature.

This section was also underlined and there was a small note in the margin. *Call the dermatologist immediately for Anna’s birthmark!!*

This side note written in Beverly Parke’s shorthand made a few factors crystal clear to Anna as she remained hunched over these artifacts trying to make sense of her life. One: Beverly Parke knew that Anna possessed some sort of ability to communicate with nature–a fact that Anna herself couldn’t quite grasp even though the truth blazed like fire across her brain. Two: Beverly Parke actively tried to suppress any abilities that Anna may have possessed by forcing her into having her port wine stain removed. Anna cringed as she remembered the awkward encounter with the dermatologist years ago and her hasty escape from the out-patient facility. Three: Beverly Parke had a hidden life in the woods behind Ackerly Lane throughout Anna's entire life, a life she tried to hide. A life that had too many parallels to Anna's own past to thoroughly digest at the moment.

As Anna flipped the page over in hopes of reading more of Dr. Prince's theory on Earth Manipulation, she realized that the article was not whole and Beverly Parke had not bothered to tear out the remainder of the publication.

The next article was taken from the same publication, but titled, "Spiritual Implications" and written by Judy Collins PhD. Like the first, this article was also incomplete, as if Beverly Parke only bothered to tear out the section she found valuable.

Those possessing spiritual and psychic abilities have been glamorized in our modern society; however, what people fail to discuss is the possibility that these abilities are evil and alarming in nature.

Over the course of time, many have speculated about the reality and truthfulness of spiritual and other-worldly abilities and why only certain individuals claim to possess such tendencies. Science, specifically the illustrious Dr. Kinder and his theory on Biotechtonics, has proven without a doubt the existence of such supernatural powers; however Kinder, along with many other well-known theorists in this field have neglected to uncover the inauspicious implications associated with such inclinations.

Anna read on as the article continued to discuss the dangers of what Dr. Judy Collins referred to as 'supernatural tendencies' and what Dr. Prince would undoubtedly have referred to as 'Earth Manipulation.' As she read and thought, Anna became more and more convinced that by saving these articles, not only was her mother investigating her own tendencies, but Anna's as well. Did her mother possess the 'sinister side of spirituality?" She must have. What else could account for her manipulation of the tree to cause the deaths of her family members? Was Anna herself guilty by association? Was Anna's ability sinister as well? She didn't think so; after all, her own abilities seemed paltry and weak when compared to her mother's as displayed in that unearthly vision. But Anna's scalp began to prickle at the thought.

The final paper in the stack was one last excerpt; this time from an article labeled "A Child's Gift: Oddities and Abilities in Youth" published anonymously. The beginning and end of the article were not included in Beverly Parke's collection, yet the few paragraphs that Anna read only increased her sense of confusion and growing melancholy.

Oftentimes children possess extreme powers that gradually extinguish themselves as youth merges into adulthood. Typically, logic, maturity and downright skepticism are enough to naturally quell any odd or sinister inclination that a child might exhibit. However, in rare cases, more must be done to fully stamp out supernatural abilities before they take root and weave themselves into a child's genetic makeup.

It is of the utmost importance that caregivers recognize the pull towards the spiritual within their offspring. While this notion sounds simple enough, the signs and symptoms are not always as obvious as one might believe. Let's examine the case of Danica DeMorra, a young girl from the suburbs of Des Moines Iowa. I will not reveal her specific location out of respect for her and her family's privacy.

Mrs. DeMorra contacted me with concerns about her 7 year old Danica, who was reportedly capable of summoning the wind, in other words, Aerokinetic Wind Manipulation. When I went to examine the child, it was clear that her mother was correct in her assumptions and that Danica was a formidable youngster with enormous power. I thought it best to act expediently because a regression would be unlikely considering Danica's strength.

Mrs. DeMorra and I discussed a course of action to help extinguish Danica's inclinations, which included guided neglect along with other methods outlined previously in this publication. I left the family confident that Danica's abilities would gradually diminish with our planned approach.

I continued to follow-up with the DeMorra family and I was dismayed to learn that Mrs. DeMorra was not acting with the required vigilance and that Danica's inclinations were only growing stronger with each passing week. I decided the best approach would be another personal visit. When I arrived at the DeMorra residence I was told by Mr. DeMorra that Danica had accidentally killed herself using her manipulation powers and that as a result, Mrs. Demorra had been committed to the local psychiatric family in a neighboring town.

And that was it; Anna felt almost thankful that the remainder of the article had not been included in this awful stack of memories and research. She didn't want to read anymore about poor Danica DeMorra nor her mourning relatives, nor about the concept called "guided neglect." Anna shuddered to think about the implications of that term. She didn't want to see anymore of Jacob's desperate pleas to his cruel and calculating sister.

It was evening now, and Anna straightened up her neck and head for the first time in hours and felt a palpable knot in her left shoulder blade as a result of her hunched and awkward position. She folded the stack of articles and letters back into their original position and returned the bundle to the mirrored treasure box that still had bits of dirt and grime etched into its crevices. Anna closed her eyes for a minute trying to process some, heck, any of the insights that she gleaned over the course of the last twenty-four hours. It felt like the world was slipping from her grasp as she saw, over and over again in her mind, the swirling vortex of her mother's dark hair as she commanded the tree trunk to snap, thus ending the lives of her parents and thus imprisoning her brother.

It made sense why her mother had waged the war against Anna's birthmark–to remove the outward mark of her strange ability and hopefully cure her of her manipulation powers. To suppress whatever magic Anna had hidden within her. But what Anna was still unsure about was why her mother had killed her parents and turned against her brother. Had Beverly been that insecure and troubled as a child to undertake such a criminal act? Anna supposed so; yet it was difficult for Anna to process. She supposed that some things were better left unknown. But what plagued Anna's mind most intensely, was what she could possibly do about it. She felt an urge to set the record straight, to vindicate her uncle. She needed to see Jacob Parke again. She needed to tell him that she understood and believed him. Would it even be possible for Anna to make this happen? Dr. Jenkins had taken a chance on Anna once, and it hadn't worked out well. Would she be given a second chance?

Anna, still dressed from last night's excursion, desperately needed some air. Her apartment felt hot and stuffy, like a tomb. Anna rushed out the door not even bothering to lock up; no one wanted any of her measly possessions. As she walked up and down the dark curvy streets of Windsom, New York, she tried to imagine what life was like for young Beverly Parke. What it was like for her mother to grow up in the shadow of her perfect brother. What it was like for Beverly to possess such a powerful and dangerous ability. All sorts of stories and possibilities unfurled like flower petals in Anna's mind as the cool night air blew steadily against the back of her neck. Anna couldn't possibly know the truth of Beverly's youth, nor how close her imaginings were to her mother's reality. But by the time Anna wound up back at her apartment late that November evening, she felt as though she knew. And that was all that really mattered.

Chapter 55
Then- Beverly Parke- 1945

"Which school looks most appealing to you, Jake?

"Georgetown has an excellent baseball program."

"But SUNY Binghamton is offering a full scholarship. Maybe we shouldn't cross it off the list just yet."

"Cornell is only about two hours away; and they have an outstanding pre-Med reputation."

No matter what she does she can't drown out the constant buzz of her parents and her perfect brother having this conversation downstairs. Perfect Jacob Parke with his perfect grade point average and his perfect athleticism. Accepted to all the schools he applied to and still agonizing over his final decision. It's almost 7 o'clock and if she doesn't head downstairs and start packing her bag she'll never make it to school on time. But she just can't bear to overhear this back and forth in any closer proximity than her tiny upstairs bedroom.

And then as if on cue, "Beverly, come down and grab some breakfast honey, or you'll be late!"

Beverly is actually surprised that her mother even notices that she's still home; she gets so caught up in her brother, the golden child.

She stomps down the stairs purposely, knowing full well that it drives her parents crazy, but that's fine by her.

"Honestly Beverly, why must you scamper around so?" Her father begins.

She has on her favorite plaid skirt, red and black checkered, and white stockings with an old pair of saddle shoes that she spent half of last night polishing and cleaning. Hopefully today she can avoid the standard jeering comments about her old, hand-me-down, thrift store clothing. Middle school kids can be cruel about things like that, a fact that her parents either don't understand or don't care about. Estelle and Irving Parke are nothing if not practical. There is a piece of toast intended for her, burning and forgotten about in the brand new stainless steel contraption sitting on the kitchen counter. She ignores it and grabs her satchel bag instead. Her parents bought it for her at the Salvation Army for two dollars in late August in anticipation of her 8th grade year at Windsom Middle School. It never lost its stuffy old-person smell–a combination of mothballs and lint.

Beverly doesn't bother with breakfast and doesn't say goodbye; over the past few years her attempts at both greetings and goodbyes have been met with only the briefest of acknowledgements. It's hard to notice Beverly Parke in a family where the superstar older brother gets most of the attention. This is a fact she wouldn't even mind if that older brother wasn't such a creep.

It is a beautiful April morning, the kind of morning that really reminds a person that winter has officially ended and that spring will soon bloom, soft and warm, in upstate New York. Ackerly Lane is quiet as usual; the grass is so wet it looks as though it has been slathered in oil. The air smells clean and fresh. This is the best part of Beverly's day, her daily walk to school, this quiet block full of life. Once she approaches school, it won't be as quiet. The click of her short, blocky heels gives her a satisfied feeling. Maybe today won't be so bad.

Before the thought even finishes, she hears a leering voice in her ear, "Hey Bevvy."

"Bevy Bevy where's your Chevy?" another voice adds in.

Still with that stupid taunt. Can't they come up with something more creative? She doesn't have to turn around to know the owners of those voices. Troy and Dan, two boys who have been merciless ever since the 3rd grade and who have gathered most of her classmates under their wings and in unison against her. She's not even sure what she ever did to make them hate her so much, aside from wearing out-dated clothing. Beverly figures that for them, that's enough.

She knows it's best if she doesn't respond; any display of emotion only provides additional fuel, a fact she's learned the hard way over the years. But they circle around her on their shiny Schwinns, a blur or metallic blue and red and silver.

"Hey Bev, my grandmother has the same bag."

A sea of giggles. As she approaches the school, more kids turn around and snicker at the spectacle. Troy and Dan are the popular boys: Troy's father owns Amos' Drug store, a respectable money-making business, and Dan's father is running for mayor this term, a position which he will most likely win. Do their successful upstanding fathers know what pieces of shit their sons are? Beverly thinks probably not. Or maybe worse, maybe these boys take after their old men, maybe they're the spitting image. After all, you know what they say about the apple falling from the tree.

The next part is torture, pretending to ignore the stares and jeers and taunts as the kids all line up in front of the school awaiting the opening bell. Whoever created this system surely did not consider the social problems it could cause for the outcasts. Some of Beverly's most humiliating moments have occurred right here, waiting for the doors to open. As the students of Windsom Middle School linger around in anticipation of yet another school day, Beverly feels a shot of pain bloom on her upper back. And then another poke, this one sharper than the first. One of her classmates, or maybe more than one, has started throwing rocks. She sends up a secret prayer that the doors will open soon, before the next rock strikes her head or somewhere similarly painful.

Thankfully, as if on cue, the doors open and the students begin shuffling into the 8th grade hallway to drop off and pick up their school books at their lockers. Beverly's locker is easy to spot. It has a huge pink smear across the front; it used to say Beverly Eats Shit; however, the custodians, in their attempts to erase the slur, created a discoloration the color of Pepto Bismol.

She swaps out her math book for her Social Studies and literature textbooks, the subjects she must endure before lunchtime, and heads to Study Hall, room 302, on the opposite side of the building. Study Hall is the one period without assigned seating, so Beverly likes to get there first in order to secure an inconspicuous seat in the back. She slides into the brown wooden seat just as announcements begin blaring over the speaker.

Good morning Windsom Middle School. Today is Monday, April 18th. We have some exciting news to share with you. Windsom High has just announced that the Valedictorian of this year's graduating class is none other than Jacob Parke! Many of the teachers here remember having Jacob in class and we are very proud! Congratulations to his family and teachers! In other news, Cheerleading tryouts for next year will take place….

The announcements drone on.

"Can you believe Jacob is related to her?!" She overhears Sheila Whitemore, dressed in her perfectly pressed pink skirt whisper to freckle-faced Kimberly Preston. "I mean, he's so cute and Beverly is just so…so, weird."

Kim glances over her shoulder, and she and Beverly make eye contact. Sheila and Kim giggle quietly together at their blatant rudeness. Their comment is mean, but not surprising. Since elementary school it has mystified Beverly's classmates that she can possibly be related to Jacob Parke. All the girls want him and all the guys want to be him. He is Windsom's pride and joy, the poster child for this stupid town. The perfect scholar athlete. He stands in stark comparison to her own mediocrity. She's not a terrible student; she could perform much better in school if she tried harder. She's also not the klutz everyone thinks she is. She can throw almost as hard as some of Jacob's teammates, a fact that remains hidden due to her hatred for organized sports. But every time her teachers ask her, “How’s Jacob doing?” Or attempt to lure her into a conversation by saying, “Gee, your brother made quite the play in yesterday’s game against Syracuse! He seems to be getting better and better” it makes her want to disappear. Discussing Jacob’s stellar academic and athletic records at home is already too much. She doesn’t need to hear any more about him outside of home, especially from well-meaning educators attempting to “pull her out of her shell.” She’s perfectly happy in her own little world, well, as happy as she can be. Or maybe that’s just what she tells herself. Most lies are told for self-preservation anyway.

The rest of the day progresses as usual with Beverly being mostly successful at remaining invisible, aside from the few taunts and jeers directed her way. At lunch she sits in the library and quietly eats the bruised apple that she dug out of the depths of her bag, wishing she had remembered to grab her lunchbox out of the refrigerator. Even the puny chicken-salad sandwich that her mother threw together last night would be preferable to this.

Finally, after tortuous periods of Social Studies and Latin, the three o’clock bell rings signaling release. Beverly inhales a deep breath of relief and rushes to her locker to pick up the books she needs for the two hours of homework she’s been assigned. She knows she has to make the locker trip a quick one because once the teachers pack up their belongings and leave for the day, her classmates become much bolder.

"Hey, Beverly," Sage McGovern jeers, "Want some bubble gum?"

"No thanks, Sage."

"Well here's some anyway!"

And with that ominous retort, Sage spits her wad of pink Bazooka directly into Beverly Parke's hair. She can feel her face burning as she sees not only Sage's laughing face, but the giggling of her cronies, Sue Dansforth and Patricia Cullen. As Beverly reaches up to disentangle the gooey glob, Sage reaches her hand out to press the gum further into her scalp, further and deeper. She can feel the stickiness taking hold at the roots of her hair. She slams her locker closed and races out of the school with the sounds of the chuckles behind her growing fainter.

She doesn't allow herself to stop to catch her breath until she is around the block from her house. Untangling the bubble gum at the moment is a pointless task, it will definitely require scissors and a comb, neither of which she has. She can't even cry anymore; incidents like this occur so frequently, she's grown used to them

Beverly turns the corner of Ackerly Lane and sees her brother, her *perfect* brother, already home from school playing basketball outside with his friend, Derek. Her dad is still at the office and mom is at her weekly sewing circle meeting with some of the other women and won't return home until about five o'clock. Trying to avoid conversation, she scampers up the front steps, but it seems as though Derek has other plans.

"Hey Beverly," he says, "Nice outfit."

For someone who is graduating high school his comment is juvenile and stupid, but apparently enough to make her brother laugh, which was probably Derek's goal in the first place. Like so many others, Derek's main aim in life is to impress Jacob.

"Nice acne," Beverly responds. This is a sore spot with Derek, and she knows it. Then Mr. Perfect chimes in.

"Aren't you going to congratulate me on getting named valedictorian?"

"No." Not a chance she's going to congratulate him. His whole life has been one big chain of congratulations. Beverly refuses to hop on the bandwagon.

"So angry!" Derek says faking concern."Aren't you proud of your brother?"

"Not particularly," she retorts, trying to dodge his encroaching body.

"Who twisted your tit?" He moves directly in front of her, blocking her way into the house. Derek is large and muscular, albeit covered in pimples. She can see the perspiration on his upper lip and at his hairline. His red hair blazes against his pale skin. Her brother does absolutely nothing, just watches the exchange with a sort of bland indifference.

"I'm really not in the mood Derek. Get out of my way."

His searching glance finds the gum smeared into her hair and she sees a smile play across the corners of his mouth.

"Did you have some trouble in school today Bev? Or maybe you just don't know how to chew your gum. I can show you if you want." And then Derek takes his grimy, sweaty hands and presses them around her mouth forcing her jaws open and closed in a pantomime of chewing.

She plants both hands directly on his chest and pushes as hard as she can. He's like a brick wall; he doesn't so much as budge, but his amusement is mixed now with something bordering on excitement and he wraps his arms tightly around her and lifts her off the ground. She can hear Jacob dribbling the basketball somewhere down by the end of the driveway.

"I'll help you get that gum out of your hair, silly Beverly."

He carries her into the house as though he owns it and they stumble into the kitchen locked in a sort of strange embrace. Derek grabs the chicken shears off the counter and holds her with one strong arm. He uses his free hand to grasp her hair so tightly it burns. In seconds he shears off a quarter of her hair, right down to the very roots. The snipping sounds crisp and loud. Beverly does all she can to fight against him, but he outweighs her by at least a hundred pounds and towers over her by more than a foot.

"Stop! Stop you asshole!" A comment that only seems to fuel the fire as she watches the brown ribbons of hair fall like dead leaves to the white tiled floor.

Her face burns with shame and anger.

Now finished with the chopping, he holds her arms back with one hand. He uses his other hand to grope up under her shirt, twisting and pulling, scratching her skin with his meaty hands and rough fingernails. She kicks and screams and squirms, but it's no use. She turns my face away, unable to watch.

"Now who's twisting your tit Beverly?" He whispers fiercely into her ear as he presses himself against her.

Jacob's unexpected voice acts as the force to make Derek stop, so she supposes she should feel relief. She doesn't know what would have happened had her brother not arrived at this moment, but she can imagine nothing good. But Jacob's next comment is so venomous and cruel it hits her like a punch in the belly.

"I never knew you liked older guys Beverly!!"

Derek laughs and the cruel glint in his icy blue eyes lessens a bit.

"Yeah Jake, I think your sister likes me."

Beverly's shock is so utter and so complete that she is speechless. How could her own brother say something so stupid and cruel? Beverly and Jacob clearly do not have a close relationship, but he is still her older brother. He can't deny that fact. How did it get turned around this way? Did he not see what was happening here? Did he not see the extent of the violation? Could Derek's body have blocked Jacob's view so thoroughly? Or did Jacob just not care? Maybe it's more possible that Jacob didn't want to see the truth. Admitting the truth would be harder for Jacob, more complicated. Had Jacob already calculated what admitting the truth would have cost him? Beverly has many criticisms of her older brother, but stupidity is not one of them. After all, isn't denial easier than acknowledgement?

As Derek releases her to follow Jacob out of the house he whispers almost imperceptibly in her ear, “We aren’t done yet Bevy.”

Silence.

She’s left to catch her breath, which feels like sandpaper rubbing against her dry throat. She pulls her broken blouse tight against herself and suddenly she can’t stop shivering. Out of the corner of her eyes she catches the curling remnants on the floor; she had almost forgotten about her hair.

She races to the bathroom to examine the damage. Glancing at herself in the bathroom mirror is more painful than she thought. She is an absolute mess; her face is bright red and tears burn streams down her cheeks; there are crimson fingernail marks that bloom angrily across her chest and stomach. The skin below the small swell of her left breast is so raw and red she can almost see beads of blood forming below the surface. But the most striking aspect about her appearance, of course, is her hair. Derek has chopped off a good portion of the hair above her right ear. There is a square, a patch about two-inches by four-inches that has been cropped almost to the scalp. It will certainly take some clever manipulation to hide the visual damage. At least the gum is no longer a problem. And now the tears come harder. Bitter and salty. She can’t tell if the tears are in response to Derek or her brother’s cruelty–Jacob surely knew what was occurring less than ten feet away from him–or if she is feeling sorry for herself, but either way, now that the tears have started flowing it is impossible to pull them back in.

Oh no. She hears her mother's voice. Can the sewing circle be over so soon? "Goodbye Derek, have dinner with us tomorrow," she calls as she walks through the front door.

"I'd love that! Thank you for such a kind invitation!" Derek responds in his honey sweet voice. "Bye Jake. See you tomorrow in school. Tell Beverly I said goodbye," spoken louder, for her benefit.

The sarcasm isn't lost on her, even though the conversation is muddled by the bathroom door.

How am I going to explain my appearance to my mother? Will she ever believe me?

"How was your day, Jacob?" Mom asks.

"My day was great! Coach Healy thinks that the University of Pennsylvania will offer me some scholarship money. And they finally announced that I am the valedictorian! I officially beat out Ronald Joyce!"

"Amazing news Jake! All your hard work has finally paid off. I'm so proud of you!" Beverly can hear her showering hugs and fresh kisses upon Mr. Perfect.

"And...Oh Jake, if your heart is set on the University of Pennsylvania, your father and I will make it work"

"Really mom?"

Maybe if she sneaks out now, no one will see her. They always get so engulfed in college talk. No such luck. As soon as her mother hears the door creak, "Beverly, is that you? Come out of the bathroom!"

Her mother's eyes widen as soon as she takes one glimpse and the girl's messy appearance.

"Beverly!" she says harshly, "What happened to you?"

And before she can respond, before she can say what happened or concoct some story to explain her hair and blouse–which is torn at the collar from Derek's assault–Jacob opens his mouth and says, "Beverly was trying to look cool in front of Derek."

Beverly saw the apology in his eyes, but it meant little to her.

Bullshit, Beverly thinks to herself. *He knows what a piece of garbage his friend is…but he covers for him anyway.*

"No," she yelled. "That is not what happened! Jake–"

"Grow up Beverly. You're too young to date anyway," Jacob interrupts.

"Young lady! I thought you were more responsible and mature than this! I am flabbergasted!"

"Mom, he's lying!"

"How dare you accuse your brother of such an outrageous thing! Get up to your room Beverly. I don't want to see you for the rest of the evening! You have completely ruined what should be a celebratory evening."

And with that, Beverly's mother turns around to begin dinner preparation. Jake's puppy dog eyes regard Beverly one final time before he busies himself with his schoolwork.

Instead of storming up the stairs, Beverly flies out of the house not even bothering to close the front door behind her. She needs air. She needs to be alone. She needs the trees. She can hear her mother calling her name, but pays no attention to her cries.

She is done with these people…her classmates, her teachers, her parents, and especially her brother. The humiliation that had just occurred is just one more line on a long list. One more item on a shopping list. One more red gumball in an entire dispenser.

The Windsom Woods open their arms to embrace her as she crashes into their soft, sweet comfort. She doesn't need to bother hiding her disheveled shirt anymore. In fact, as moves deeper into the woods, she removes it–no one is here to see. The gentle breeze feels glorious on her scratched chest, it kisses her wounds, healing her from the outside in. The trees bend towards her, urging her on. She runs until she can't breathe anymore and then collapses at the base of a giant oak. The roots feel her anger and sadness; she feels them pulsing beneath her outstretched legs. They want to help.

Reaching her hands up to the sky, the branches come down to meet her, winding their soft tendrils around her wrists, forearms and shoulders. Their caress eases her racing thoughts and calms her jumbled soul. Her tears are wiped away by the velvety spring leaves sprouting from the wooden arms. The branches continue to weave their way around her body–down her bare neck and chest, easing the rage that is bubbling in her intestines like an angry sea. She is cocooned in branches and leaves, in comfort and calm and cool.

"We will help," the trees soothe.

"We are here."

"Trust in us."

This is not the first time, not even close, that the trees with their thick honey-suckle sweetness have come to her rescue. Over the years their connection has deepened. She can feel their presence in every corner of her soul and being. She has long ago gotten used to the strangeness that occurs on her solitary visits to the Windsom Woods. Things beyond words, beyond belief, beyond logic. And as she sits here, engulfed in this odd yet familiar embrace, she knows what she has to do.

Chapter 56

Now

Anna couldn't possibly know the entirety of Beverly Parke's story. She couldn't possibly know how lonely her mother felt as a child, or how badly she was abused by her peers, how deep her resentment became for her parents and brother, nor how strongly she was connected to the very same trees that called persistently to Anna herself. But Anna's musings on her midnight walk, coupled with the insights revealed in Jacob's letters and the vision that possessed her in the woods, provided Anna with enough clarity. Enough to guess at the shadow of the truth about her mother. And that was all she needed. This truth and clarity allowed Anna to view the situation in a more productive and logical manner.

She was left again with the urge to visit her uncle; the need to confirm his story and assure him of her belief in him was all she could think about. Even if it meant betraying a mother who was really no mother at all. Jacob Parke needed vindication; he needed someone to believe him instead of dismissing his ravings as the trappings of hysteria. But how could Anna navigate Dr. Jenkins and her protectiveness over her patient? Does her uncle even possess the capacity for clarity or has insanity eaten away too much of his deranged mind?

Despite it all, Anna knew she had to try. She owed it to her family, to her uncle, to herself to take this matter further no matter how much it all terrified her. Doing nothing wasn't an option for Anna Parke as she gazed at her flawed reflection in the shiny bedroom mirror, the jagged mark, blatant and glaring. Maybe she could even help her uncle by simply letting him know that she believed in him. Belief in a person is akin to a superpower.

Tomorrow she would contact Dr. Jenkins. She would plead with her, beg her, to give her one more chance to converse with her uncle. Maybe she could extract the last remnant of Jacob Parke buried inside his diseased mind. Maybe there was still some hope left for him. For them.

She finally stopped shivering. While the memory of the woods remained sharp as needles in her mind's eye, (the vortex of dark hair and the snapping of the tree limb-dare she even think!), having a plan–even if that plan was a long shot–provided Anna some much needed peace. Anna was able to sleep, albeit not restfully, and that was good.

Chapter 57

Anna was plagued with dreams that caused her to whimper in the wee morning hours, but despite waking with a terrible, drilling headache, the dusky sunlight that shone through the front window felt refreshing. A new day.

She wasn't scheduled for a shift at The Food Mart, which gave her an open day to try to get in touch with Dr. Jenkins. And hopefully, fingers crossed, Dr. Jenkins would be willing to give Anna a second chance.

She knew that calling the Ithaca Psychiatric Hospital before nine in the morning would be a fruitless endeavor; no front desk took early phone calls. In terms of doctor's offices, personal matters, no matter how urgent, must wait promptly until nine o'clock in morning and must be resolved by five o'clock in the evening. If only life were that easy, that neat.

So Anna tried to busy herself with tidying up her apartment while the minutes ticked slowly by. Her apartment was in desperate need of a good cleaning and at seven thirty in the morning, Anna tied her hair back, filled up a bucket with warm, soapy water and got to work on the tiled kitchen floor. It felt good to be productive and it helped to still Anna's restless mind.

Anna almost didn't realize when the tiny clock on the counter read nine o'clock; she was so engulfed in what she was doing. The apartment was cleaner than it had been in months, maybe years and Anna felt a twinge of subdued pride in the work that she had done.

She plopped herself down on the living room couch, pulled out her cell phone and punched in the number to Dr. Jenkin's personal line, the number the doctor had given her days ago...Had it only been days since she visited her uncle in Ithaca? It seemed like a lifetime ago. As she listened to the ringing on the other line, she gazed into the rooms of the dollhouse that remained spread out before her. Anna had no idea what she would do with this relic, but she couldn't quite bring herself to pack it up. It was too beautiful in its detailed delicacy. Too filled with childhood memories that have been flooding back with increasing frequency, welcomed or not. Her eyes searched specifically for the figurine which she now thought of as Jacob. If only the real Jacob was as pliable and obedient as the ceramic boy of this childhood realm.

The answering machine picked up the open line and Anna heard Dr. Jenkins' recorded voice, formal and clear, "This is Dr. Kathleen Jenkins. I am currently out of the office. Kindly leave your name and contact information so I can return your message." Beep.

So, Kathleen is her first name. To Anna, Dr. Jenkins looked more like an Alice or Maureen.

"Hi Dr. Jenkins. It's Anna Parke, I assume you remember me," Anna rambled. "I know my meeting with my uncle didn't go as well as we hoped, but I was hoping you would grant me one more conversation with him. I left you my contact information at our meeting. I found out more information–" and then the answering machine cut her off. Anna cringed as she pressed the button to end the call.

Her recording would undoubtedly come off as desperate. She sighed and thought that she would try again later if the doctor didn't return her call in the next couple of hours.

The swirling vortex of hair kept creeping into Anna's periphery like a pet who had misbehaved but is trying to get back into his owner's good graces. The screams. Jacob's attempt to stop his sister from her destruction. The darkness. The sound of the snapping limb, too perfect with its smooth cut. The dying tree. The black, charred, oily stump. The glint of the handcuffs as they closed around Jacob's thin, pale wrists. Rebecca. The old man tucked away in a psychiatric center ranting about Windsom trees. The thoughts plowed into Anna, insistent and relentless, and Anna thought she would surely go crazy waiting for Dr. Jenkins' phone call.

Cleaning provided a surprising reprieve, so Anna continued her crusade, this time focusing on the tiny, pink and black tiled bathroom. Musingly she thought about who would select such a grotesque color combination. She kept her cell phone on the ledge of the bathtub never allowing it to leave her field of vision. She would be lying if she said she didn't check at least five times to make sure the ringtone was on the loudest volume setting.

Anna felt slightly indebted to her neat freak of a mother as she scoured her apartment until it was almost unrecognizable. As she hauled a large bag of recyclables, namely empty beer cans and liquor bottles, over her shoulder and down the narrow staircase she tried to remember the last time she had a drink. She couldn't remember, and this was highly unusual. Anna's relationship with alcohol had progressed over the past few years. Anna couldn't quite remember exactly when the daily beer after work turned into a habit that consumed not only a case of beer per week, but a few vodka bottles as well. She wouldn't have gone as far as to call herself an alcoholic. But if she continued on her path, that nomer would be more fitting, certainly within the next few years.

However, as Anna took stock of her life over the past few weeks, it seemed as though she had accidentally kicked the habit. Who knew it would be that easy. She supposed that she had other things to occupy her mind, which would be putting it lightly.

Her cellphone took this moment of contemplation to announce its presence with a loud, blaring ringtone. Anna quickly pulled it out of her back pocket and her breath caught in her throat as she saw the familiar number. It was Dr. Jenkins.

"Hello?" She said as she slunk down to a seated position on the bottom step of the staircase. She dropped the bag of recycling between her feet.

"Hello. Is this Ms. Parke?"

"Yes. It's Anna. Hi Dr. Jenkins."

"Hello Ms. Parke. I received your message about scheduling a second meeting with your uncle–"

"Yes," said Anna. "I'm sorry if my message seemed scattered and confused. I am really hoping to try again."

"Ms. Parke–"

"Please, call me Anna."

"Ok. Anna. May I be frank with you?" Dr. Jenkins asked.

"Always."

"I am sorry, but I can not endorse another meeting. Your uncle was highly agitated after your visit. He required medical sedation in fact. Since your visit his verbalizations have increased in frequency and urgency."

"I understand your reservations. But I really believe that Jacob was trying to tell me something. His 'verbalizations' as you call them made sense to me. I found out more insight into his situation and past—"

Dr. Jenkins interrupted, "Ms.—Anna. I specifically cautioned you about searching for hidden meaning in Mr. Parke's puzzling words. It will undoubtedly lead you down the wrong path."

"With all due respect Dr. Jenkins, I can't believe his comments about the trees are simply a manifestation of insanity."

"We do not use the word 'insanity' here. It is outdated and—"

"I'm sorry Dr. Jenkins," Anna pleaded. "Please reconsider. I think that I can actually help my uncle if he feels heard and understood. Maybe the fact that everyone dismisses him has only increased his mental…" Anna searched for the word, "instability."

Dr. Jenkins was quiet. Anna could almost hear the wheels in the doctor's mind turning, processing.

And then with a sigh, one last attempt, "I cannot let this go Dr. Jenkins. Let me try again. Please."

Pause.

"I have a suggestion," Dr. Jenkins finally uttered.

Anna's ears perked up.

"I will allow you written correspondence with Mr. Parke. Write him a letter. I will read it to him at our therapy session. I will gauge his reaction and we will go from there. It is the best I can do," Dr. Jenkins concluded.

And although this was not entirely the response for which Anna had hoped, it was the best she was going to get. A tiny sliver of sunshine. A pine needle stuck in velvety hair.

"Yes. Dr. Jenkins. I will write the letter today and put it in the mail. You should receive it by the end of the week."

The thought of waiting so long was maddening to Anna, but it would have to do. It was all she had.

"Ok. Anna. I suggest you choose your words with care. Goodbye."

"Goodbye Dr. Jenkins. And thank you."

Chapter 58

Kathleen Jenkins sighed as she hung up the phone. This whole situation was beginning to take up too much time. Time she didn't have. She glanced at the endless stack of paperwork laid out in front of her. She hadn't even left the office until ten-fifteen last night in hopes of making a dent in it. Had the stack grown since then? That couldn't be possible, could it?

Last night Frank was furious with her for coming in so late. This lateness was the most frequent topic of their chronic arguments. When she walked in the door of their condo, she could see the remnants of the romantic meal her boyfriend had prepared. She even smelled the faint scent of recently extinguished candles. *Oh Shit!* Was today their anniversary? It was. And she had forgotten all about it. When she saw Frank's hurt and dispirited eyes, she knew that this relationship was destined to end as all the others had. A person could only really have one monogamous relationship right? And Dr. Jenkins was already married to her work. Her patients were her children and that was the sad, but necessary reality. *I'll call him once I'm done with all this paperwork*, she thought. *I'll make it up to him…I always do.*

She picked up the first file from the stack on her desk. MaryBeth Brandley. The small colored photo of the woman glared back at her. Dr. Jenkins clearly made out the pain in the old woman's eyes. The paper asked for Dr. Jenkins to sign off on a new medication regimen. Apparently, the daily dose of Clozapine was no longer adequately stabilizing the woman's extreme mood swings. In other words, her disease had grown either resistant to the current dose, or progressed further. With frustration and disappointment, Dr. Jenkins thought about the endless counseling sessions, the family interventions, the intensive psycho and behavioral therapy tailored specifically to Mrs. Brandley.

Lately, with more and more frequency, the doctor wondered if her efforts here made any difference at all in the lives of her patients. When she accepted this job, her mentor, Dr. Haji (her professor at the Fordham University) warned her that the burnout rate for doctors working in such intensive facilities is high. Could that be what Kathleen was experiencing? Burnout? She signed the paper, placed it back in the manila folder and moved on.

As she worked through the paperwork, in the back of her mind, Anna Parke had taken up residence. Another patient. Another obligation. But just maybe, this honest woman with her simple request could do what Dr. Jenkins could not for Jacob Parke. Help him.

Chapter 59

While Dr. Jenkins sat, pouring over her paperwork, Anna sat, pouring over a blank computer screen. One letter. That was her only hope of reaching her uncle and convincing Dr. Jenkins that she should be granted additional access to him. She had never been great with words; she was much more successful at appreciating the words of those long ago literary masters who wrote in their flowery, magical language. The idea that so much should rest on what she could manage to scratch out on a piece of paper almost brought a fresh wave of tears to her eyes. The stakes were certainly high.

After finishing the job of taking out the recycling, Anna sat down at the kitchen counter and pulled out her old laptop that hadn't been charged in weeks. As she plugged the charger into the device, she had a sudden change of heart and decided on a handwritten letter instead. So much more personal than an email and she had read somewhere that handwriting sheds insight on inner emotion, which was exactly what she needed now. She needed her uncle to really hear her.

In the top kitchen drawer Anna kept a yellow legal pad and an assortment of writing utensils that mostly went unused. Her fingers closed around a black Bic pen and as she scribbled a few test circles on the soft paper to coax the ink to flow more freely, her mind raced. So much to say. How should she begin? Dare she hint at what she saw in the forest?

Her first attempt at a letter was long and rambling, filled with nostalgic sentiment about wanting a family and a Parke legacy gone wrong. After she re-read what she wrote, she angrily tore the sheet out of the pad, crumpled the paper into a tight ball and tossed it directly into the plastic trash can that stood on the other side of the kitchen counter. It was all wrong. The next five letters joined the first. They all felt forced and desperate. This was proving to be a harder task than she had expected.

Anna decided to change her tactic. If the detailed and lengthy approach felt wrong, she would try again, this time keeping her words and emotions brief.

Dear Jacob-

I believe you. The tree knows the truth. I heard its story. I heard ***your*** *story. I know about your sister, Beverly. I want to help. I hope you will agree to see me again.*

Sincerely,
Your niece, Anna

She read it again. It was pitifully short compared to her prior attempts. The words weren't special nor showy or elaborate, but they felt honest and real. Her only hope was that Dr. Jenkins would agree. Carefully, Anna tore the slice from the legal pad and folded it once and then again. She had no stamps, heck she didn't even have an envelope. When was the last time she actually mailed something? A trip to the local post office was necessary to complete this first leg of her task. Then it was out of her hands.

She slid the folded note into her back pocket, grabbed her sweatshirt and purse and before she had any more time to agonize over her course of action, she locked up and headed out the front door and onto Main Street. The post office was only a few storefronts away.

The tinkling bells announced her arrival and Lacey Macquade looked up, her blue eyes brightening when she saw Anna.

"Anna. Hi dear. How have you been?"

"Hi Mrs. Macquade. I've been ok. Thank you."

Anna knew that she needed to keep her answers brief, or she would surely be here for the duration of the day learning all about Mrs. Macquade's postal woes.

"I'd like to buy an envelope and book of stamps, please," Anna said.

Mrs. Macquade instructed her where she could find the required items and Anna walked out of the post office empty handed, aside from the small booklet of stamps with brightly colored fall-leaves adorning each tiny square. It was done. Now she had to wait.

Her gait slowed now that she had mailed the letter and Anna felt a slight sense of ease. Rambling slowly down Main Street, Anna was able to appreciate the beauty of the town's quaintness. This town with its memories and ghosts. She wondered if her late grandparents had frequented this post office. Had Jacob Parke enjoyed a strawberry ice cream cone from Chilly Scoops with his childhood friends? A strong sense of nostalgia assaulted Anna, a terrible longing for the family she only began to know years after their existence. Except for Jacob...except for Jacob, in spite of the odds, he was still very much alive, just a few hours away.

Anna walked past Don's Place; Don himself was in the doorway fixing the hinges on the brown, splintered doorway. Don was always proud of the 'Open 24 Hours a Day' sign displayed in the storefront window and Anna was not too proud to admit that she had been drinking at this very establishment at times when no respectable individual should find herself at the local bar.

"Anna. I haven't seen you in awhile," Don greeted. "Come in, have a beer with me."

Normally Anna wouldn't even require such an invitation. She would have had one foot already across the wooden threshold. Yet something about her newfound sobriety felt refreshing and healthy.

"Thanks Don. Not today."

With a hint of surprise playing at the corners of his eyes," Ok. If you change your mind, you know where to find me."

"That I do, Don. See you later."

And Anna kept on walking, her chin raised almost imperceptibly, back towards her apartment. She didn't have any plans for the rest of the day and it was just about noon.

The day was glorious. Fall had fallen, full and bright in Windsom, New York. Autumn was in the musky-sweet smell of the breeze and in the comforting click of boots on pavement. The whispering of the trees calmed to a murmuring drone in Anna's ears, quiet and subdued. And while they continued to summon her, the urgency in their calls had softened. They already revealed their tale. She didn't know if she could bring herself to return to the woods behind Ackerly Lane even though something in her very core desperately urged her to do so.

Chapter 60

Over the course of the next few days, as Anna's letter transitioned from postal worker, to mail carrier, to office mail assistant and finally to Dr. Jenkins, Anna tried to find peace and calm. Working at The Food Mart, with all its mundane responsibilities allowed her some distraction from the endless contemplation of the strange turn her life had taken. She so artfully sculpted her life into a semblance of normalcy. But fate came knocking; so had the trees.

Anna no longer even felt the pull towards Don's. She couldn't and wouldn't allow alcohol and all its fuzzy comfort to drown out the urgency of her mission. The need to see her uncle was almost palpable and the minutes passed by slowly for Anna Parke as she awaited word from Dr. Jenkins. Words that she hoped would bend in her favor. *Please, Dr. Jenkins. Please, give me one more chance.*

No longer was Anna able to fight against the thoughts that continued to slam against the inner workings of her brain. While scanning whole milk along with assorted produce and canned goods across the rubber belt and over the electronic code reader, Anna replayed that fateful night spent in the woods over and over again. She committed to memory almost every word written in Jacob's letters to her mother; she poured over them every night in the dim evening light of her bedroom desperately wishing there were more. Desperately searching for hidden meaning. And those articles, which revealed a young mother searching for answers regarding her own child's hidden gift sent shivers down her spine. Rebecca haunted her nightmares–impossibly, beautifully young and troubled with a hypodermic needle poking out of her pale inner arm. But it was the face of her uncle, his blazing eyes and wrinkled forehead that stood out most brilliantly in her mind's eye. Her innocent uncle, just wasting away. Her innocent uncle that she could perhaps help by showing just a tiny bit of faith in his convictions.

It was four whole days before Anna's phone rang displaying once again Dr. Jenkins' office line. Four agonizing days of waiting and hoping and doubting and second guessing. Maybe her letter was juvenile and stupid and had been crumpled up and tossed in the trash as soon as it was read. Maybe. Anna almost gave up all hope even before the doctor's educated voice came through, clean and clear, over the open phone line.

"Dr. Jenkins?" Anna said upon answering the call.

"Yes. Hello Anna."

Right to the point, "What did my uncle say?"

"Before we discuss this specific matter, I'd like to provide an update on your uncle since your visit."

"Ok. Tell me," said Anna without any use for the normal and expected pleasantries.

"Since your visit, Mr. Parke has shown increased agitation, but of a more consistent, specific, and coherent nature. He continues to talk about the trees and unlike in the past, once he starts on the subject, it is almost impossible to deter him from his course. He has begun to make mention of his sister, your mother, Beverly and his anger towards her, which has subsided over the years, has returned full-force."

"Dr. Jenkins—"

"Please let me finish," Dr. Jenkins cut in with an edge and intensity that surprised Anna.

She continued, "Despite his increased agitation and anger, over the past five years, this has been the most lucid he has been in at least 5 years."

Dr. Jenkins allowed this fact to sink in. Anna absorbed it.

"And it was for this reason alone that I decided to present to him the letter you composed," continued the doctor.

"Okay," said Anna. "What was Jacob's response?"

"Well, he was uncharacteristically subdued. I reminded him of your visit and repeated the fact that you are not his sister Beverly, but his sister's daughter- his niece. He showed an emotional response. He manifested actual tears, which he has not done since I've been part of his care team. He repeated the utterance, 'She believes me' over and over again."

Anna listened to Dr. Jenkins' words quietly and intensely.

The story continued, "I told him that you have requested another visit and stressed the fact that this consultation could only occur, would only be permitted to occur, if it did not impede his progress here nor cause him any emotional distress."

"And what was his response to another meeting?"

"He has insisted that you be permitted a visit. Towards the end of our conversation, his clarity began to waver and his impulsivity began to hamper our discourse. He began to revert back to his typical rocking and muttering. However, he gave the clear opinion that he would like to move forward with another scheduled visitation."

Anna was floored, "Okay! Thank you! I'll be there tomorrow!"

"Just hold on, "Dr. Jenkins interjected. "This is highly unusual! I am not completely comfortable with this. It's clear that you have an underlying agenda and I am not convinced I want to be part of it. To be very honest Anna, I'm very much torn about whether I should allow this relationship to progress any further than it already has. I am worried that it will cause harm to Mr. Parke, both mentally and possibly physically."

This ominous concern about Jacob's ability to inflict harm on himself was not lost on Anna and this sudden burst of emotion was clearly uncharacteristic of Dr. Jenkins. Her professional exterior had cracked open revealing a genuine and compassionate protectiveness over her patient. This only enhanced Anna's opinion of the doctor, even though it may not help her in her cause.

"Dr. Jenkins," Anna tentatively began. "I also want to see my uncle make progress and heal and function normally and fully. I am not trying to detract him from his course. I believe, from the bottom of my heart and soul and being that we can help each other." And then she added, "He is my family. The only one I have"

With a deep sigh and intense hesitation, Dr. Jenkins finally said, "Alright Anna. I sincerely hope I do not live to regret this decision. You may visit next Wednesday, October 30th at ten-am sharp."

"Thank you. Truly. Thank you so very much," Anna said right before she ended the call.

And for the first time since she unpacked the cardboard boxes that used to take up space in the dusty corner of her apartment, Anna felt a small weight lift off her shoulder. She wasn't happy; no, happy would not be the correct choice of adjectives to describe her feeling about being given access once more to her uncle, it was more a sense of ease. The images of the swirling vortex of hair, and the handcuffs glinting in the moonlight, and the eerie eyes that peered out of her mother's pale face and directly into her own remained etched into her consciousness, nagging at her mental well-being. But that sense of hope that had dimmed almost to blackness in her mind, that tiny flicker of a flame had been rekindled within her. And this miniscule thing allowed her to find the strength she needed to endure the wait of the next few days.

In her silent apartment, Anna peered into her lovely dollhouse. The only surviving artifact of her lonely childhood. Even though her living room was now spotless after her recent cleaning crusade, she couldn't quite bring herself to re-pack this beautiful item into the shadowy depths of a box. It was too special, too dear. With its sloping, shingled roof and intricate decor, it undoubtedly belonged in a place where it could be admired and gazed upon: appreciated. The figurines remained in their rightful place, oblivious and smiling in their glossy, ceramic ignorance. Well, all smiling except for little Anna, headless and solitary, seated on the wicker rocking chair. Outside and alone.

Chapter 61

The days passed by, as days always do. Anna hadn't mustered up the courage to go back into the woods even though the trees throbbed their gentle hum, pulsing through her abdomen. Anna submitted her second request for time off and come Tuesday afternoon, she found herself back on that Greyhound bus once again, this time harboring a slightly different sense of anxiety and dread than the anxiety and dread she felt just weeks ago on her first visit to Ithaca. She watched the mountains and quaint towns pass her by as she played out endless scenarios of how her second meeting with her uncle might unwind. She hoped it would be better than last time.

She reserved herself a room at the same hotel and was actually given the keys to the same room. Maybe this room was specially reserved for young women attempting to solve old murders and vindicate innocent family members. The thought made her laugh quietly as she plunked her duffel bag on the exact same chair it had occupied a few weeks ago. Dejavu.

Anna didn't feel the urge to visit the waterfalls again, nor to venture into the picturesque college downtown area with its trendy boutiques and overpriced souvenir shops. Instead she ordered Dominos pizza to her room–a thin crust medium pie with pineapple, and an order of cheesy bread, warm marinara sauce on the side for dipping. While she waited for her food, she pulled on a pair of soft sweatpants, slightly pilled from years of wear and her favorite long-sleeve t-shirt and snuggled up under the rough hotel bedding.

Anna did not feel very much like an adult as she tuned into the movie playing on the one cable television channel that the hotel room offered: *Clueless.* God, she loved this movie. Nor did her college freshman dinner, even though it arrived, warm and crusty and satisfying. She felt more like a little girl. A little girl pretending to be a woman. Yet she certainly had been endowed with an adult task. Could she see it through?

Her face, reflected in the rectangular mirror over the bureau, was pale and tired, the wine stain well-defined and dark. She thought about the article she found in that beautiful, but worn trinket box in the charred tree stump on that fateful night spent deep within Windsom Woods. The article explained that physical markings often accompany what was referred to in the excerpt as "Earth Manipulation." Anna wondered how powerful her small ability could have been had it been nourished as opposed to quelled. Was the scientist author correct in his belief that those with Earth Manipulation tendencies lean towards the sinister side in life? Couldn't her connection to the trees be viewed as a beautiful gift instead of the curse that her own mother clearly believed it to be? The curse that her own mother so vividly and blatantly possessed? Maybe there was some defiant part of her, some unknown and subconscious motivation for her to resist the removal of this mark. Maybe she wanted to keep this strange bond to those tall, stately figures that have played such an odd and confusing role in her life thus far. She didn't know the answers to these thoughts as she folded up the pizza box so it fit neatly into the small plastic receptacle that passed as a trash can in the sparse hotel room. Maybe she never would.

Despite all of the anxiety she felt regarding her meeting with her uncle, the hotel bed was warm and she was tired. She could not predict what tomorrow would bring nor could she control what was going to happen in that harshly-lit cafeteria, sitting across from her uncle. This thought brought her some comfort and allowed her to pass the nighttime hours restfully. No use worrying over what you can't control, right? If only that maxim was that easy to follow.

Chapter 62

Eight o'clock in the morning came, brilliant and cool. Anna was already in the midst of getting ready for the day: she turned the water in the hotel shower to steaming hot. The streams streaked her skin with red blooms of scarlet. Her plan was to arrive at the Ithaca Psychiatric Facility with time to spare. She definitely did not want to be late.

She was dressed and ready by eight-forty-five, and on bus number four, headed in the right direction by nine on the dot. Anna had just enough time to scarf down an apple and chewy Quaker granola bar before the hiss of bus brakes and the swish of the opening bus door informed her that she had arrived at her destination. It was now or never.

Walking up the circular, paved driveway and into the breezy waiting room was surreal to Anna. It seemed as though her last meeting with her uncle was yesterday. It was hard to believe that more than two weeks had passed since her first. The half-moon fingernail marks on her inner arm were barely perceptible anymore. Time certainly heals all wounds...well most wounds she guessed as she approached the reception desk.

Seated again, this time in front of not Monet's 'Water Lilies' but next to 'Poppies,' Anna settled down to wait for Dr. Jenkins' summons. It was nine-forty-three.

At five past ten, Anna found herself back in the green-tiled cafeteria, seated across from Dr. Jenkins, finally seeing the real doctor. Underneath the white coat and gold-rimmed spectacles and the cultured speech was Katherine, a woman who cared immensely for her patients and who put her whole being into her role at this small upstate facility. Her hard exterior cracked and it was clear to Anna that she was struggling and torn about her decision to allow this second visitation to occur. The doctor no longer put the default Ms. in front of her name, and was now comfortable with calling Anna simply, Anna. At this moment, Anna felt truly connected to Katherine Jenkins in a way that surprised her, as if an invisible web had bonded them to one another.

This time, Anna began, "Hi Dr. Jenkins–"

And it was the doctor's turn to correct, "Please, Anna. At this point, call me Kathleen."

"Ok," Anna continued. "Thank you so much Kathleen for allowing me this meeting. It means a lot to me. I know you care about my uncle. He is lucky to have had you looking after him for so long."

And then, simply, "It's my job Anna."

But Dr. Jenkins had gone above and beyond her 'job' concerning Jacob Parke. Anna wondered briefly if the doctor was ever truly able to disconnect herself from her work or if visions of her patients haunted her dreams at night, once she went home to enjoy a quiet evening away from this place curled up on her sofa with a glass of red wine in her hand. Dr. Jenkins wore no wedding ring, nor did photographs of children adorn her desktop.

"Is there anything you would like to discuss before I escort your uncle in?" the doctor continued.

"No," Anna replied. "I'm ready."

No lecture, no ironing out of rules this time.

Dr. Jenkins rose from her seat and after casting one more furtive glance at Anna, approached the door and opened it.

Jacob Parke shuffled through the cafeteria doors. This time, no security guard held his left elbow, just Dr. Jenkins walked with him, looking worried and anxious as she assisted him into a seated position opposite Anna at the table. He was clutching a battered manila folder to his chest. Dr. Jenkins stepped back and took her seat behind Jacob. This time, Anna did not mind her presence and was in fact comforted in knowing that someone else had a stake in what happened here in this echoing room.

Their eyes met.

Jacob looked straight at her today. Directly into her eyes, into her soul. He was not distracted like last time, nor did he focus on some imaginary point above and behind her. They remained like that for a moment in time that felt like eternity. Lost in some thought with the world spinning around them. Wheels turning, pondering the role that they would each inhabit in one another's lives, in one another's hearts. Anna didn't quite know how to begin.

Jacob took that burden from her shoulders when he uttered, soft and wavering, "You believe me."

"Yes. I believe you Jacob," Anna offered back.

She instinctively reached out to grasp one of Jacob's hands that remained affixed to the folder, still against his chest. He flinched backwards at her touch as if zapped by some electronic jolt. He likely had felt no human connection nor warmth in decades. Her touch rattled him and Anna immediately withdrew her hand. *Too fast* Anna thought to herself. Dr. Jenkins shifted uncomfortably in her seat. Jacob commenced with his rocking, back and forth, back and forth, back and forth. He was slipping.

"I know the truth, Jacob. I saw the truth," Anna began again.

More rocking, back and forth. Back and forth. More rapidly now.

She continued tentatively, "The tree showed me."

Dr. Jenkins cast a wary glance at Anna as she spoke those words.

Again Jacob uttered, "You believe me."

"Yes, Jacob. I believe you. I saw my mom. Your sister. Beverly. She scared me," Anna didn't know how else to convey what she had seen in the woods.

Certainly Jacob did not require a summary. He was there. He lived it.

"The tree knows," he uttered in a knowing tone. He nodded his head and Anna nodded back, showing him that she understood. Showing him that she believed him. A conspiratorial nod of two individuals who shared a hidden knowledge.

Jacob's rocking slowed slightly, an undulating pendulum in time.

Anna went on, bolder now, “There has to be a way to prove it. Maybe there is more evidence. Fingerprint evidence. Science has come a long way since your trial and we could reopen your case to prove your innocence.”

To this suggestion, Jacob simply shook his head slowly from side to side. The sadness and conviction in his eyes told Anna all she needed to know.

“No more,” was all he replied.

And then again, louder still, “No more.”

Jacob was not looking for freedom, nor vindication. Maybe at some level he knew that he could never survive on the outside. That he could never escape the walls of his sentence. That he could never escape the walls of his diseased mind. What would be the point of putting him through the trial experience again? Anna was angry at herself for not seeing the logic of the situation before. Anna remembered the sadness and desperation and rage in Jacob’s letters to his sister Beverly. What had he said? “I’ve never been a good brother to you.” Something to that effect. Maybe he felt that he had gotten what he deserved.

Suddenly Jacob stopped rocking and removed one hand from the folder that remained tightly in his grip. He laid his arm out, palm up on the cafeteria table. An invitation. Anna slowly placed her own arm on top of Jacob’s and interlaced her own fingers with his. Her uncle. He was here, after all.

They stayed like that for a long time, gazing into one another's eyes, envisioning the life that could have been, the relationship that just opened up its first tentative petals. Was it too late for them? Anna didn’t think so.

Anna risked a glance over Jacob's shoulder at Dr. Jenkins who remained silent throughout this encounter. Anna saw tears swimming in her eyes and she knew that the doctor would not regret allowing them this time together.

After a while, Jacob laid the folder down in front of Anna. When Anna moved her hand to reveal its contents Jacob stopped her and shook his head. *Not yet* his movements said. *When you are alone*. And with a final squeeze of her hand, Jacob turned around to face the doctor indicating that the meeting was over. Dr. Jenkins wordlessly escorted Jacob out of the small seat and back through the same set of double doors he had entered over an hour ago.

"Can I come back?" Anna asked Jacob.

She didn't want to say goodbye again, not after they finally connected. Anna's heart broke as Jacob walked away from her.

After she uttered those words, Jacob cast one last look over at Anna and the hint of a smile played at the corners of his lips. One smile. A tiny thing. Yet at the same time it meant everything. That small trace of miracle told her all she needed to know.

Chapter 63

Now alone, Anna opened the thin manila folder that lay in front of her. A beautiful little girl smiled back at her from the glossy photograph that fluttered to the floor. Anna bent down to pick it up. She examined the rectangular image. The brown-eyed little girl revealed a toothy grin and even though Anna had never been accurate in estimating children's ages (maybe as a result of never having kids of her own), she guessed the little girl must have been about two years old. She turned the photograph over and written in pencil on the back was: Sophie Parke. Sophie Parke?

Mind racing, she placed the photograph back on the table looking once again at the child's rosy-cheeked, happy face. Anna reluctantly turned her attention back to the folder and the one remaining piece of paper in it.

A letter:

Dear Dad-

I know that it has been months since my last visit. To be honest I have purposely avoided seeing you. How selfish am I? I know how much you depend on my visits. I haven't had the courage to allow you to see me. I haven't had the courage to tell you what I need to say.

I've been in a bad way. You know my habits. I am not proud of them, but I can't seem to break them. Yet, something new has happened..has happened to me and by default something has happened to you. At my last visit I think you may have suspected, even though I couldn't say the words. You looked at me and I saw it in your eyes. Even now I almost don't have the guts to write what needs to be said and I am tempted to crumple this pathetic letter into a ball and light it on fire with the matches that are buried in my pockets. Those matches have been used for far worse purposes than this.

I'm just going to write it. Dad–I had a child. It's almost incomprehensible. A beautiful little girl. I cried when she was born, mostly because I knew I couldn't keep her. What kind of mother would I be? A junkie, high school drop-out. No money, no home. I am so sorry to have kept this from you! I am ashamed of myself and who I have become.

Before I handed over my tiny, little girl, I gave her a name. Sophie. I've always loved that name. I was promised that someone would adopt her and that she would be safe and well-cared for. I asked to be sent updates and photographs. I hope to send one along in the near future. I also hope to come soon to visit you...when I can. When I can bear to sit across from you and face you in person. I love you dad. And I'm sorry that I have become such a screw-up.

-Rebecca

That was it. Nothing else in the folder. Just two small items. Two small items that shook up Anna's already shattered reality. There were no words. No words that Anna could even muster up in her clouded brain to fully convey the depth of emotion she felt as she read those last few words of Rebecca's letter to Jacob. She gazed back at the photograph. Rebecca's daughter, Anna's cousin, Jacob's granddaughter. This artifact must have come from Rebecca, from one of the "updates" she had requested concerning the whereabouts of her own daughter. Had Rebecca ever made it back to see her father before she overdosed? Or had heroin robbed them both of a final goodbye? There was no way to know. Only room to ponder these troubling questions and Anna quickly discovered that sometimes the imagination can be crueler, greedier than reality.

What Anna would do with this new knowledge, this uncovered branch that extended her family tree further than she could have dreamed, she did not yet know. Yet she did know that Dr. Jenkins would soon sweep back into the room to discuss the encounter that just occurred and Anna was very much interested in hearing her perceptions.

So Anna gingerly placed both the photograph and the letter back into the folder and tucked the parcel away in her own bag, which had unassumingly fallen to the floor at her feet. But even though it was out of sight, it certainly was not out of mind. It seemed to Anna that with each chapter in her story that closed, yet another one was nudged open and Anna truthfully did not know how many more secrets she could stand.

With much effort, Anna brought her attention back to the present as she saw Dr. Jenkins' slim figure emerge again through the doors at the other end of the cafeteria.

Chapter 64

Anna was only able to hash out bits and pieces of what had occurred over the last weeks in small chunks over the course of the next few days. Any time she tried to think about too many facets of her story, she developed a throbbing headache starting first at her temples and then spreading like wildfire throughout her brain. God, she could use a drink. In a moment of weakness, Anna purchased a six-pack of Coors at the drugstore, but as she walked back to her apartment with the contraband hidden in a brown paper shopping bag, she placed it gently in one of the metal trash receptacles that dotted Windsom's Main Street. Up until recently, she wouldn't have thought twice about downing all six of those bottles, and then maybe walking over to Don's to finish the night with a few vodkas. She hadn't exactly been an alcoholic, but she had certainly been walking a hazy line. And even though she felt a brief regret as she walked away from the comfort that drunkenness could have offered her at the moment, and despite her jumbled mind, she felt a sense of pride that she was able to do such a thing.

She was able to think clearly and rationally about her mother, that seemed within her mental capacity, but anytime her thoughts alighted on Rebecca, or harder yet, Sophie, something in her just shut down, like an overheated computer. It was too much, too bitterly sad.

Her last encounter with Dr. Jenkins also bothered her. After Anna explored the papers that Jacob relinquished to her, Dr. Jenkins returned to the cafeteria, as Anna knew she would. The doctor would undoubtedly want to debrief with Anna what had just occurred. Dr. Jenkins had never seen the folder before and inquired about its contents. Anna lied to her. She told the doctor that the folder contained only the letter that she herself had written to her uncle, nothing more. Lying never came easily to Anna and being dishonest with this woman who had taken such an honest and keen interest in her uncle did not make Anna feel good. Anna wasn't sure if the doctor actually believed her, something in the tilt of her glare told her that there was doubt hidden beneath the surface, but she didn't push the issue. Dr. Jenkins was too delighted in Jacob's newfound ability to form a connection to call Anna on any suspected dishonesty. She was already in the midst of rethinking a treatment regimen for him. A treatment regimen in which Anna herself agreed to be involved.

Anna wished that she could feel only contentment regarding her family. She certainly looked forward to being part of Jacob's rehabilitation. Yet, the information about a little cousin, tucked away in some unturned corner of New York, nagged at her happiness. What was she like? Did she look like Jacob?

It wasn't until a week later that she decided on her next step, only after she crossed other options off her mental list, one of which was to do absolutely nothing. As appealing as this thought seemed, she could no more forget about what she had learned than a flower could close itself to the rain, every pore in her body thirsted for information. She also sensed that her uncle wanted her to do something. That he needed her to pursue this further. Why else would he have given her that folder? It was a challenge. A challenge that she had to accept.

Janine Harper was Anna's next stop. When Anna had met with Janine weeks ago, she sensed that Janine was withholding information. It was time for Anna to confront this woman about Sophie and her whereabouts. Anna felt unreasonably angry at Janine. How could she allow her only granddaughter to be placed in the foster care system? Surely Janine could have helped her wayward daughter by accepting her own flesh and blood into her home. Anna knew that she needed to give this old woman the benefit of the doubt, that there could possibly be more to the story than what emerged at face value, but the bitter seed of resentment had taken root within her. And Anna craved a face to face confrontation.

It was a Tuesday in late November and Anna was working her typical shift at The Food Mart. She couldn't completely ignore her responsibilities. She still needed the paycheck. The customers were shopping for their Thanksgiving essentials: cans of cranberry sauce and boxes of turkey flavored Stovetop stuffing were flying off the shelves with the usual rapidity of the season. Anna thought the holiday season as good a time as any to arrange to drop in to see Janine. Like herself, Anna assumed that Janine had no family obligations.

Anna had two off days approaching. She was given time off for Thanksgiving even though she hadn't asked for it. Anna was typically the sole employee without family obligations. Adam must have felt guilty for putting Anna on the schedule for yet another holiday. What he didn't know was that Anna preferred the routine of work to a solitary holiday spent in her empty apartment.

But this year, Anna would take advantage of the days off. While most people were settling down and making final preparations for a day spent watching football and eating a golden-crusted roast around a dining room table crowded with loved ones, Anna would be on the bus headed towards Schenectady to once again pay a visit to Janine Harper. Maybe she should have asked Janine for her phone number when she went to find her the first time. That way she could at least call before showing up unannounced again, but she was fairly sure that Janine would be there. Where else would she go? Like Anna, she had no family.

Anna had explored more of central New York in the past few weeks than she had in her entire lifetime; she never dreamed that her adventures would have led her down such a confusing road into her own identity. But now that she was on that road, that strange and sad and at times, riveting road, she needed to reach the final destination...even though at this point she couldn't be quite certain what would lie at the end.

Chapter 65

Standing once again on the rickey plattform outside the blue, splintery door, Anna hesitated before she knocked. Although she still felt a subdued anger towards Janine, the intensity of the emotion subsided when she took in the meager accommodations in front of her. Like Anna herself, Janine led a tough life, possibly tougher than Anna's, and had endured much tragedy. Anna couldn't imagine what it was like to lose a partner to mental illness and a daughter to drug addiction. Janine may have had her own reasons for withholding the knowledge of Sophie Parke's existence and Anna almost felt guilty for showing up here so unexpectedly and on Thanksgiving no less.

After a timid knock, Anna heard footsteps on the other side of the door. Then the door opened, sticking a bit on its rusty hinges. When Anna brought her gaze up, she was surprised to see a young shaggy-haired man in front of her wearing a Pink Floyd t-shirt and flannel pajama pants. The smell of marijuana emanated from the small opening.

"Can I help you?" he said groggily.

"Um. Yeah..." Anna trailed off. "I'm looking for Janine.."

"Who?"

"Janine Harper. She lives here," Anna replied.

Looking down she noticed Janine's black house cat weaving himself through the young man's ankles and staring at her with his enigmatic emerald eyes.

"Not anymore, I guess. I moved in last week," the man replied.

"But–" Anna protested. "That's her cat."

"Hendrix?" he said looking down at the diminutive companion. "The night I moved in he was pawing at the door. I took him in. He's pretty cool."

Anna was flabbergasted, "A woman named Janine Harper lived here! I was just here a few weeks ago! The apartment was filled with things–"

She peered over the man's shoulder to see a newly painted and nearly empty living room with only a blue tye-dyed tapestry hung up on the wall and a black futon caddy-cornered near the kitchen.

"Never met her. You can ask the landlord. He owns the bar downstairs..last name is Hadman, or Hadley..something like that," he offered, trying to be helpful.

"I will. Thanks–"

"Will," he offered. "And Happy Thanksgiving."

"Thanks, Will. You too," Anna replied as he closed the door softly against her perplexed expression.

Anna felt dizzy walking down the steep flight of wooden stairs. She came here with such conviction and confidence–conviction and confidence that was now whittled down to sheer disappointment. She circled back around to the front of the building. Even though it was only ten o'clock in the morning, Anna was surprised to find the door to Stout's propped open.

She imagined that such a place had a different sort of holiday tradition. Establishments such as Stout's have their own families that congregate in solemn and sometimes defiant solidarity around the bottle. Anna had spent many a holiday at Don's surrounded by the locals who simply had no other place to be. There was something comforting in sharing the loneliness of strangers when the rest of the world was filled with holiday zeal. The sort of people that gather at pubs like Stout's or Don's on the holidays are no less a family than the traditional sort. In some cases, they deal more in truth, honesty, and reality than conventional families. There is no pretense or hierarchy. No stuffy conventions or polite conversation. No rules about avoiding talk about politics or long-held familiar grudges. Any and everything is up for grabs and as the drinks flow freer, so does the laughter. But even so, the overt merriment is tinged with a sense of disillusionment that threatens to turn the tears of laughter into tears of despair at any moment.

Walking through the open door of Stout's, Anna saw that the bar was completely empty. She glanced at the wobbly wooden tables stained with shiny circles from many years of un-coastered perspiring pint glasses. There was no bartender behind the vinyl countertop with a backdrop of jewel-colored liquor bottles. The place smelled of dirty taps and stale beer with the hint of disinfectant spray; combined Anna recognized the smell from Don's.

"Hello?" She called to the air.

No answer.

She tried again, "Excuse me…Is anyone there?"

"Yes. Be right with you," came a raspy voice.

Chapter 66

George Hadley wondered who could possibly be calling him from the other side of the door at this time. Recently, he took down the 'Open 24 Hours a Day' sign displayed in his window. He was too old to work around the clock and it was getting harder and harder to find honest people willing to bartend for the small paycheck he offered. In recent years, there wasn't as much money to go around. Recession maybe. And then there was the business of this damn fryer. He had been putting off buying a new one, but today it seemed that the old thing might have finally cooked its last batch of wings. Now, he stood over the old appliance, fiddling with the knobs, trying to wipe away the accumulated grease.

"Excuse me. Is anyone there?"

Again that call.

George put down the dirty washcloth and walked through the swinging doors leading from the back kitchen to the bar.

When he emerged into the dim pub, he noticed a young lady standing uneasily near the brown-lacquered bar. That bar was his prized possession. In fact, in his younger years, George made that bar himself out of a cross-section of an old pine tree that he had chopped down from his own property a few miles north.

"What can I do you for?" he said, taking his rightful position behind the bar. "We don't open for a few more hours, but I'm happy to fix you a drink if it pleases you. Take a seat"

He slid a cardboard coaster with the word 'Budweiser' to her across the counter top.

After a brief hesitation, the girl said, "Just a coke, please."

George recognized that pause. It was the pause of someone making the conscious decision to *not* order booze. It wouldn't have been the first time he had served someone a stiff drink at ten o'clock in the morning and over his career as a bartender here, he had seen many a customer fall off the wagon. He didn't judge them. He understood that life had its ups and downs and that sometimes the bottle helps smooth over life's little wrinkles.

"Bottle or fountain?" George asked.

"Fountain please," the girl responded, more sure of herself this time.

Maybe this one would stay on that wagon after all.

George went about selecting a pint glass off the drying rack, filling it with ice, and using the soda dispenser to top it off with the syrupy liquid. The rush of the carbonated liquid made a hissing sound as it lapped against the side of the glass.

George watched the girl grimace as she took her first greedy swallow. Oops. He forgot to clean the taps last night. Hopefully it didn't taste too bad. At Stout's, most Coke's were ordered simply to accompany vodka or rum and George supposed the stale taps didn't matter much in that case. George didn't really know though, he was not much of a drinker himself.

"Thank you," she said as George went about wiping the bar top and rearranging some of the bottles behind him from the night before.

"My pleasure Miss," he responded in an affable, easy tone."We were packed last night. Thanksgiving Eve is always busy."

After he deposited the washrag in the sink, George turned around and looked at the girl who sat there quietly picking at her fingernails. She looked sad. Maybe not sad, maybe troubled was the better word. She was a cute kid about the same age as his granddaughter.

To break the silence he said, "I'm George Hadley," and he extended his hand across the bar.

"I'm Anna," she responded simply, extending her own hand to shake his.

"What brings you to town? You don't look familiar."

"I was coming to visit Janine Harper…your tenant."

"I'm sorry miss, but Janine no longer lives there," he vaguely offered. He didn't think it was his place to offer more. Janine never had visitors and it was odd that this young girl seemed so earnest and eager to see her. George thought that he was the only friend Janine had and he was sure that the old woman had had no family.

"Yeah. Will, the guys upstairs, told me. Where did she go?" she asked.

George Hadley ran his hand over his chin stubble and said, "Gee, I didn't know she had any family."

To which this girl, Anna, responded after a pause, "She didn't even know about me until recently."

George noticed that the girl neither confirmed nor denied a family relationship, and he didn't want to press the issue. After all, the girl looked distressed. He decided to tell her what he knew.

"Well in that case," began Mr. Hadley, "I best be honest. Janine died two weeks ago. She was a pretty ill woman. I'm so very sorry for your loss."

The girl contemplated him for a few moments. He felt awkward having to break this news. George himself still felt emotional about Janine's death. Hell, he had known her for decades.

Finally she spoke, "I had no idea. I just saw her a few weeks ago. She seemed– ok!."

"Yeah. Janine was pretty tight-lipped about most personal matters. Although over the years we got to know each other pretty well. I'd call her my friend…one of the few I have left. And I think she'd say the same for me. She lived up there ever since she was a kid you know," he explained.

It looked like the girl was trying to choose her words carefully. George could tell that she had many questions swimming around behind those pretty eyes. For a moment, George noticed that odd marking on the girl's cheek.

"How did she die?"

"Sudden heart attack, it seems. At least that's what the coroner said."

Now it was this girl's turn to tell George, "I'm sorry for the loss of your friend."

"Yeah. Me too. I'll miss her. Janine used to come down here a few times a week and sit at the bar with me. You're sitting in her seat, actually."

George noticed the girl squirm a bit after he said that.

"Where is she buried?" the young lady asked.

George told her that Janine rests in the tiny cemetery on the top of the hill. He didn't know the name, but it was a few blocks over. She couldn't miss it if she headed west up Franklin.

The girl continued to drink her soda and George allowed her to do so in silence. He wasn't much for small talk and he had to admit that having this girl here made him miss his friend even more.

Finally, the girl spoke again and said, "Janine had a granddaughter."

"Yeah," said Mr. Hadley, "Sophie. I'm surprised she told you about her. She never talks about her. I thought I was the only one who knew."

Chapter 67

Still sitting at the bar–apparently in Janine's old seat–Anna was struck silent by the news of Janine's death. Another leaf of tragedy in the Parke family story. Janine was taken by a similar force that took her mother Beverly. Was there some symbolism there? She would ponder that fact later. But now, she needed information. She also needed a drink. She knew that the ache could be dulled with booze, but she had already ordered a coke, and was proud of herself for doing so. Sobriety had served her well for the past few weeks, and she needed a clear head to process whatever was coming.

Anna hadn't corrected Mr. Hadley about the fact that Janine wasn't the one to inform her of Sophie's existence; Jacob was. But she didn't think the small dishonesty mattered much anymore. She thought about asking Mr. Hadley if he had known her uncle but decided against it. That didn't matter now. She focused on what did.

"You and Janine talked about Sophie?" Anna asked.

"Only once, and only after she drunk a few beers late one night after all the customers left. Her daughter took off a while back and Janine seemed so sad that I guess I just remembered the conversation," he explained.

"What did she say about her?" Anna boldly inquired.

Mr. Hadley elaborated, "Just that she was placed in some foster care home in Albany, some place with God in the name; I'm sorry. I can't remember the name. Janine said that Rebecca refused to let her be a part of the baby's life."

"That's so sad," Anna said. She didn't exactly know how to keep the conversation afloat.

"Yeah. It really broke her heart. Janine had this one small photograph of Sophie. Cute little baby. Janine could have been a good grandmother, you know, if things were better between her and her daughter. That was about 8 years ago now."

So it wasn't Janine's refusal that caused Sophie to end up in foster care. Anna felt almost embarrassed for misjudging the situation. Clearly, Rebecca felt that this was the best scenario for her own daughter.

"Yeah, I bet she would have, Mr. Hadley."

Comfortable silence ensued.

"Thanks for the soda and the conversation," Anna said as she got off the stool and wrapped herself in her winter coat. It was chilly outside in central New York.

"Glad I could be of help," Mr. Hadley replied. "Happy holiday."

"Same to you. Take care."

And Anna exited Stout's and emerged into the crisp late morning Thanksgiving air. She knew what would come next. What she had to do next. What she had to do not just for herself, but for Janine, and Rebecca, and

Jacob. *To Albany*, she thought to herself as she headed away from the building. *To Albany*.

Chapter 68

The next day found Anna in the state's capital. Albany was a bustling albeit not very beautiful city, teeming with people racing to and fro and cement buildings that rise like trees from their concrete beds. Once in 6th grade, Anna had taken a school field trip to tour some of the government buildings she now saw again with adult eyes, but other than that one organized visit, Anna had no other experiences here and was not at all impressed with its stony and forbidding facade.

After she had left Stout's earlier today, Anna found the correct bus and rode the twenty miles southwest in quiet contemplation. Before she had boarded the blue and red bus, she went to visit Janine's grave, to pay her respects one final time.

The headstone had not yet been placed (if there would even be a headstone) and instead Anna stood in front of a rectangular dirt patch. The thought of Janine's body lying in rest six feet below the surface brought a wave of sharp grief to Anna. The woman had lived through such heartache and tragedy and this measly plot of earth was all she had to show for it. Anna said a silent and tearless farewell. She considered how Jacob might react when he eventually learned of Janine's passing. Yet another question to which she had no answer.

Now in Albany, Anna once again played the role of detective in her own life story, a role she had come to like less and less as the weeks passed. Yet, she had located Jacob and Janine, and now it was time for her to find Sophie.

She hadn't yet reserved herself a hotel; she couldn't quite bring herself to think that far in advance, but when she exited the bus onto Lark Street, she set out in search of a quiet place to do some research. She didn't know what her intentions were with Sophie, but she felt a yearning deep within her bones to meet her.

Located on Henry Johnson Boulevard, the Albany Library was a modern, mirrored monstrosity that stood in stark contrast to the quaint Victorian library of her childhood. Taking in the crowded tables on the first floor, Anna rode the elevator to the second floor in hopes of finding a corner of privacy. The second floor, though still filled with people–eager college students diligently searching databases for coveted sources, the casual readers sipping their lattes while devouring the latest Stephen King masterpieces–had a few empty seats. Anna plopped herself on a rather stiff and uncomfortable chair in front of what looked to be a brand new Dell computer and pulled up the search window.

Her very first search provided a list of foster care agencies in the area. While scanning the list of names, Anna was shocked to discover that Mr. Hadley had not been so far off the mark when he told her the name of the agency. Or at least he had the God part correct. Towards the bottom of the page, Anna's eyes alighted on the name: Partners of God. Next to the institution's name was the contact information. Could this be it? This was as good a place as any to begin.

After purchasing a small green tea from the library's coffee shop, Anna left the library and sat on a small wooden bench on the street. The tea sent steaming tendrils into the crisp air. She took a tentative sip and punched into her phone the numbers she had written hastily on the back of her hand.

A friendly voice answered on the second ring, "Hello. Partners in God. How may I help you today?"

"Hi. My name is Anna Parke. I'm looking for information regarding my cousin, Sophie Parke. I was recently told that she was possibly placed in your care about eight years ago," Anna explained carefully.

Talking about her story and discoveries no longer inspired within Anna the shock and horror that it had a few weeks ago. She also learned that directness was always the best and most expedient in the end.

"Well. Ms. Parke. Sophie is indeed registered with us. But, I'm sorry, we are not allowed to provide information regarding our youngsters to unauthorized callers," the woman replied. BINGO!

Anna anticipated such an answer. In this case, she was almost happy to learn that there were such safeguards in place and that her small cousin wasn't in the evil orphanage of her nightmares. Hopefully this institution did not hire Miss Hannigan-like figures who profited from others' misfortune and used the money to fund a never ending supply of booze. *Annie* was all Anna really knew about orphanages. As a child she would watch the movie on repeat, enthralled with the music and the happy ending where the little orphan girl gets to live with Daddy Warbucks in his million dollar mansion. But Anna was quite sure that if a Miss Hannigan didn't exist, neither did the billionaire hero who rescued children from their misery.

Surprising herself with her poise, Anna replied, "Yes. Thank you. I'm prepared to submit myself for any interview or background check required. I would very much like to meet her.

And so it was that Anna Parke endured interviews and paperwork and applications and all of the necessary protocol. She was able to begin the process that very day in Albany when she had her initial inquiry meeting. But it wasn't until four weeks later, when Mrs. Morrow at the agency called her with the news that she had been added to Sophie Parke's contact list, that she learned about her cousin.

Sophie Parke was nine years old and was currently living with a foster family in Clifton Park, a suburb of Albany. The family apparently cared for three other children aside from Sophie. Anna was also provided with the name and contact information of this foster family: The Pickards: Amy, Daniel, and Kelsey–their daughter. The family had been notified of Anna's existence and were expecting her call.

So many steps of Anna's extraordinary journey thus far had begun with a phone call. Such a simple thing.

Now she found herself here, in her apartment still wearing her Food Mart uniform, staring at the phone number she wrote down on a blue post-it note that could connect her to yet another small branch of her family, another facet of her story. The trees outside, in the not so distant distance, sent out their message: she was on the right path.

Chapter 69

Next Tuesday was the date decided upon by Anna and Amy for a first meeting. Anna was surprised by the ease in which she found Sophie. Compared to the difficulty she encountered in locating her uncle, this seemed like a walk in the park. Amy was excited and eager to set up this meeting. She thought it would do Sophie good to meet a blood relative.

On the phone she explained how Sophie had yet to secure a permanent adoption placement. She told Anna a bit about the nine year old in question. Sophie was apparently a headstrong and keenly intelligent little girl, traits that appeared off-putting to some inquiring couples. The Pickards were Sophie's third placement since she was registered at the agency. Amy didn't give the details as to why the previous two placements hadn't worked out and Anna didn't ask. Anna wanted to form her own opinions of the little girl and remain untainted by others' experiences with Sophie.

"Sophie got close once, a few years back," Amy explained. "But after the final encounter, the family backed out of the agreement."

There's that word again: 'encounter.' Such a coldly clinical word. Amy did not elaborate on this fact and Anna thought it best not to ask. Anna couldn't imagine the disappointment that young Sophie must have felt when she heard the news that her adoption would not be finalized. Although Anna yearned to ask Amy more questions about Sophie: *What was she like? What hobbies did she have? Did she like school?* She decided against it. Anna would rather meet Sophie herself before forming any concrete opinions.

After ending the phone call with Amy, Anna felt a growing sense of excitement about meeting the young girl. She felt her pulse fluttering like tiny butterflies taking flight within her belly.

In her eagerness, Anna briefly considered writing to her uncle to tell him what she planned. Dr. Jenkins called her the other day with a promising update regarding Jacob's progress. Anna had actually been invited in for another visit with him in two week's time. A visit to which she very much looked forward. Yet, she decided it would be best to deliver her uncle the news in person. Too much too soon isn't always a good thing. Jacob was still healing after all.

Anna also had a missed call from the realtor regarding the property on Ackerly Lane. Anna did not return the phone call and pledged to take care of that bit of business when she returned from Clifton Park.

Chapter 70

Anna arrived bright and early to the Pickard residence located at 175 Woodward Way in Clifton Park. She took off from work at The Food Mart for three days and arranged for accommodations at the local Courtyard Marriott. Her boss was accommodating though surprised by Anna's sudden need for time off. Over the past month, Anna had fleetingly begun to consider looking into more meaningful employment opportunities, but couldn't fully process what that could entail in her current situation.

The home on Woodward Way was picture perfect. A beautiful Cape Cod shaded by large, mature trees, bare against the sunny Saturday December sky. In the holiday spirit, the Pickards had decorated their property with plastic Santas and white wicker reindeer. Standing on the front stoop Anna took a deep inhale before ringing the bell.

Within seconds the red-painted, wreathed door swung open and a smiling woman stood in the bright rectangle. Her teeth were so white and straight and her outfit was put together with such care and style that Anna felt disheveled and plain in her presence. But, the woman's reassuring demeanor and kind words pushed away any feelings of insecurity that Anna felt.

"Hi. You must be Anna. I'm Amy," the woman said, reaching out to hold Anna's gloved hand. "Please come in. It's cold out there!"

Anna stepped through the threshold and glanced around the rosy living space. There was a fire blazing in the brick fireplace casting its warmth into every nook of the room, which looked to have been taken in entirety out of *Good Housekeeping.* The decor was stylish, but not flashy and Anna briefly wondered what it would have been like to grow up in such a place.

"Thank you for letting me come meet Sophie," said Anna.

As Anna spoke, Amy's husband entered from the kitchen wearing an apron, "Hi Anna," he said. "It's so nice to meet a relative of Sophie. I'm Dan," he said, reaching out to shake Anna's hand.

His cerulean eyes and dimpled cheeks took Anna's breath away a bit. As he spoke, Anna took in his athletic build and tanned complexion; his thick salt and pepper hair looked like it was cut every week. Anna wondered what would inspire such a perfect couple to pursue what was surely the messy business of fostering children. Anna hoped that the reason behind their decision was motivated by kindness and generosity. The more she spoke with Amy and her husband, the more sure she was that their motivations, whatever they were, were genuine and good.

"I'm making Saturday sauce in there," he explained. I better make sure it doesn't boil over. I'll be back," he said coolly as he headed back to his task.

"He makes sauce every Saturday," Amy explained. "Don't tell him I said this," she said conspiratorially, "but we get kind of sick of it." She giggled good-naturedly.

Anna was beginning to like the Pickards more and more as the minutes passed by, even though they seemed impossibly perfect.

Amy continued, "Sophie is downstairs in the basement, playing with our other three kids–I don't like to call them fosters," she said. "I know we spoke on the phone about Sophie's–" she struggled for the word, "situation," she finally decided upon. "She has lived here for the past year and a half and has experienced some heartbreak within that time. She experienced heartbreak before that too."

Anna assumed that Amy was referring to the almost finalized adoption of which she told Anna on the phone when they spoke.

"Sophie has her ups and downs emotionally. She excels in school and has a vivid imagination, yet socially–it is a bit harder for her," Amy explained.

"Thank you very much for all you do for her," Anna responded. "She is lucky to have you. I first learned of her existence only recently. And from what I have been told, Sophie did not have a very auspicious start to life either."

"Yes. I was told about her mother," Amy said with tears swimming in her deep brown eyes. "I can't help but feel like a failure for not having secured her a permanent home."

Anna tried to reassure her that it was not her fault, but she saw that Amy had her own demons regarding

Sophie and that there was nothing that Anna could say to ease her feelings of guilt.

Amy swatted at her tears and took a minute to compose herself before saying, “Shall I call Sophie up to meet you?”

“Yes please,” Anna said without hesitation.

A few minutes later, Anna found herself seated across the dining room table from a little girl. A little girl about whom she knew so little in the grand scheme of things. Yes, Anna knew of her past, but how much does an individual’s past define one’s life? Anna didn’t know the answer to that question.

Sophie did not have much to say, wouldn’t even look up from her hands that were anxiously engaged with the small plastic doll in her lap and Anna found it difficult to start conversation with Amy’s well-intentioned prompting.

Finally and thankfully, Amy excused herself by painstakingly saying, “I’ll let you two ladies chat.”

Maybe she sensed that her presence was not helping the situation.

Once Amy left the table, Anna was able to truly observe Sophie and she took in the little girl’s appearance. Sophie was small for her age, Anna thought, with curly, shoulder-length, brown hair and clothes that hung a bit on her delicate frame. She had wide eyes lined with thick lashes, a delicate sloping nose dotted with freckles. She was truly a beautiful little girl.

Anna tried again to engage her, “Does your doll have a name?”

Nothing.

Anna continued, “When I was your age, I loved dolls.”

No response.

“I had this beautiful dollhouse that my grandfather made that looked exactly like my own house. I actually still have the dollhouse,” Anna rambled. “It’s on the coffee table in my apartment in Windsom. I don’t really know what to do with it.”

“I have a dollhouse,” said Sophie tentatively, still not glancing up.

“You do?” Anna asked.

“It’s in my room. Want to see it?” Sophie surprised her by saying, still not glancing up.

“I’d like that,” Anna replied.

And Sophie got up from the table and ran up the stairs. Anna followed.

Chapter 71

Amy Pickard tried not to listen in on the conversation that ensued between Anna and Sophie on the other side of the wall, but she couldn’t help trying to decipher the rise and swell of voices. Amy and her husband had been fostering children for about ten years now. They started with the agency when it seemed impossible for them to get pregnant with their own child. They supposed it would fill a void.

It was a hard time for Amy, hard for Dan too… but he wasn't the one who had to endure the IVF treatments, the hormone therapy…the miscarriages. God those miscarriages still haunt her. Especially the last one. Amy had been almost 23 weeks pregnant when the bleeding began. So much blood…soaking through her silk nightgown, the sheets, the mattress. She had read in one of those pregnancy books, *What to Expect When You're Expecting,* that at 23 weeks, her baby was the size of a mango. Amy had just ditched her own pants for the cute, overpriced pregnancy jeans with the elastic waistband that she bought in the maternity section at Bloomingdale's. And then the bleeding started and didn't stop. It felt like she bled for months. She went to the hospital for a uterine scraping. They had to scrape her squashed mango out of her diseased womb. She could actually feel her baby leaving her. She cried and cried and cried.

Kelsey was their miracle. Amy and Dan had stopped even trying to have a baby. Amy stopped tracking her periods and propping her hips up on pillows after Dan climaxed inside of her; she stopped the acupuncture and the diffusing of essential oils. It was all too painful, too disappointing. When she found out she was pregnant with Kelsey, Amy didn't tell Dan until she was almost 16 weeks along. He was so happy…Amy herself was terrified. She refused to learn the gender, to consider names, to muse on what sports and activities their child might enjoy once he or she was old enough. She refused to get her hopes up. Amy dealt with her pregnancy with as little emotion as possible, with a cool detachment intended for self-preservation. She doted on her treasured foster children and loved them like her own.

It wasn't until she pushed Kelsey into the world in a burst of excruciatingly beautiful pain that the love truly began. And that love was intoxicating and extreme and overwhelming in its simplicity.

She and Dan raised their daughter and loved their daughter alongside the broken children that came to their home. Children from all walks of life, from all manners of tragedy and circumstance.

And now one of those little souls had been given the gift of a real blood family relationship: a cousin. She hoped that Anna Parke didn't go running like so many of the others. Sophie had a good heart even though she might seem a little rough around the edges. But who could blame that little love? She had been through so much in her short life.

Amy rearranged the pictures on the bookcase and tried to imagine what was happening on the other side of that wall. Should she have told Anna Parke more about some of the difficulties that Sophie experienced? Should Amy have mentioned the fact that Sophie recently got suspended from school for pushing a girl in the hallway? Yes, the girl deserved it, but Sophie must learn how to control her temper. It is something she had been working on in her weekly therapy sessions.

Amy sighed as she picked up a framed photograph of her family: herself, Dan and Kelsey smiling at the beach five summers ago. She hoped Sophie could one day know what family means. That Sophie, and all of her foster children for that matter, could learn that a mother isn't supposed to overdose on heroin and leave her child to fend for herself in a difficult and unfair world. Maybe this woman, Anna Parke, could help Sophie in that regard. Amy didn't know what the future held for any of her foster children, hell, even for herself. Unfortunately, time doesn't have a road map. But that hope buoyed her up as she heard footsteps scampering up the center staircase.

Chapter 72

Anna found Sophie sitting criss-cross on the wooden floor of a little girl's room. Her room. Before her was a plastic dollhouse, nothing like the wooden beauty of Anna's childhood, but by the way Sophie gazed into the diminutive toy, Anna knew that the feelings of wonder and longing were the same. Anna sat next to Sophie on the floor while Sophie picked up each doll and introduced them.

"This is Amy," she said holding up the 'mother' figurine, "and this is Dan, and this is Kelsey–she's at ballet rehearsal right now."

Sophie held up the little girl figurine turning her head to its rightful position on the swivel neck.

"Where are you?" Anna asked.

"I'm not here," said Sophie matter-of-factly with the detached emotion that only a child could muster.

Anna thought that had she majored in psychology in college instead of business, she could more accurately interpret Sophie's playworld and her own absence from it. But Anna made the assumption that even though the Pickards were a lovely and inclusive family, Sophie knew that her own life was separate from them.

Finally, Sophie risked a glance at Anna. The little girl studied her in silence for a moment or two and Anna fought against the urge to avert her eyes or adjust her position. She stared into Sophie's dark eyes while the child explored her face.

"What's that?" Sophie asked. "That mark on your face?"

There was no disgust or judgment in her question, merely curiosity.

Anna reached up and placed her hand on her birthmark. She sometimes forgot that it was even there.

"The doctors call it a nevus, or a port wine stain. I've had it since I was born," she explained simply. "My mom wanted me to have it removed," Anna continued, not knowing exactly what urged her to go into such detail with Sophie.

Sometimes children inspire confidences that adults restrict.

"Oh," said Sophie. "Purple is my favorite color."

And that simple acceptance meant so much to Anna at that moment. That simple acceptance compared to her own mother's disdain, that it brought warm tears to Anna's eyes.

Anna changed the subject to ease her aching heart, "Maybe you can come see my dollhouse one day," Anna said tentatively.

An invitation.

"Can we go tomorrow?" Sophie asked with honest enthusiasm.

"I'd like that," said Anna.

"But first," Sophie interjected, "Can we play with my dollhouse for a little bit?"

And the two girls, strangers up until only a half an hour ago, sat side by side, on the wood floor, spinning stories and weaving dialogue, laughing like old friends as the afternoon slipped peacefully by.

Chapter 73

When Anna asked Amy for permission to take Sophie for the day back to Windsom and then return her late that evening, she expected more push-back, not because Mrs. Pickard was difficult or unyielding, but because Anna was unsure what the protocol was for such adventures and Anna was a new contact on Sophie's "approved visitor" list. Anna was, in fact, the only individual on Sophie's "approved visitor" list. A fact that evoked a deep sense of sadness within Anna.

Amy couldn't give Anna leave for such a trip the day after their initial meeting, even though Anna would have preferred that to having to wait a week, so that Sophie would not miss a day of school. But Mrs. Pickard did promise to contact the agency on Monday (they did not answer phone calls on weekends) and inquire about Anna's request.

The Thursday after her visit with Sophie, Anna got a phone call from Amy, who excitedly informed Anna that her request had been granted and approved for this coming Saturday. Since Anna left Sophie on Sunday afternoon–after having spent the entire afternoon on Saturday with her and after enjoying a pancake breakfast with the Pickards, complete with real maple syrup, on Sunday morning–the little girl had not left her thoughts. Anna found it difficult to focus on anything aside from her deep, brown, contemplative eyes that seemed to reach into the depth of Anna's soul and awaken some hidden part of her. Sophie, though somber and subdued, was curious and intelligent in a humble way and Anna enjoyed passing her hours with the child. Anna yearned for their next visit and felt the small prickles of excitement bubbling within her when she thought about spending an uninterrupted day with Sophie in Windsom. It amazed Anna that Sophie had lived through such turmoil and tragedy. What a strong little person.

Anna knew she had to arrive in Clifton Park on the early side on the appointed Saturday. She would unfortunately have to depend upon public transportation, which was often unreliable and time-consuming, but Anna tried to view this fact in a positive light. She would have much down-time with her cousin and instead of focusing on driving and navigating, she could spend the bus trips to and from Windsom getting to know her. Anna didn't have an exact itinerary planned. Sophie was excited to simply see where Anna lived and play with the dollhouse that Anna had described to her in detail during their few phone conversations over the course of the past six days. Hopefully Sophie would take the lead.

Anna hopped on a six o'clock bus Sunday morning. She couldn't remember the last time she had awoken so early, but she felt refreshed and excited to begin her day. She would hopefully arrive in Clifton Park at about seven-fifteen and she hoped to take the nine o'clock bus back to Windsom with Sophie in tow. Today would certainly hold the record for the most bus trips she had been on in a single twenty-four hour period. But Anna didn't mind.

Walking up the stone walkway of the Pickard residence, Anna was able to make out Sophie's pale face in the front bay window. It looked as though she was already dressed in her winter coat; she was set to go. Sophie opened the front door before Anna even rang the bell, her mouth formed into a wide smile. Anna noticed that she had one deep dimple on her left cheek. Anna was smiling too. She was surprised by how much joy she took in Sophie's company.

"Goodbye girls," Amy called as Anna and Sophie walked back down the narrow path.

Anna didn't hear the rest of Amy's words because Sophie had casually slipped her mittened hand into Anna's and the warmth of the sweet touch was slowly traveling up Anna's forearm directly into her heart.

It was a cold, blustery December day and Sophie's cheeks, the one body part that peeked out from her winter ensemble, were red as the two waited for the nine o'clock bus to arrive after a quick bite to eat at the Dunkin Donuts directly across from the bus stop.

The bus was on time and Anna and Sophie arrived back in Windsom at around ten-forty. Sophie looked around her with wonder as they walked the short distance from the bus stop to Anna's apartment. Sophie had begun to warm to Anna and the little girl, though still reserved and tentative, started to smile more often and talk more about her interests, which included playing with her dolls, especially her dollhouse, riding her scooter fast up and down the street, and spending time with Kelsey, who she referred to as her sister-friend.

After the girls removed their outer layer of coats and hats and gloves, Sophie looked around Anna's apartment. She seemed to consider each item in turn, committing it to memory. Finally, her searching gaze landed on the dollhouse and her eyes lit up. She slowly approached it, running her fingers over the rough surface of the corrugated roof, covered with tiny brown wooden shingles. Peering inside the treasure, Sophie explored the furniture and noticed that the blankets and pillows actually came off the brass four-post beds, found that the kitchen cabinets opened to reveal delicate, hand-painted plates and cups, observed the fabric curtains and the miniature porcelain bathroom sink and the impossibly tiny toys stacked in the corner of the little girl's bedroom. This was a far cry from her own plastic toy in her home in Clifton Park.

"Wow," she whispered as she explored the plaything. "It's beautiful."

"I've always thought so too," replied Anna, seeing the dollhouse for the first time again through Sophie's eyes, filled with wonderment.

Sophie picked up one of the small figurines, "What happened to her?"

The memory flooded back to Anna as she said, "I was angry one day and I broke her. I stepped on her and she broke. I felt guilty about it. I still do. I wasn't always the happiest kid. Sometimes I felt lonely."

"I feel lonely sometimes," said Sophie.

And because she made this confession with such openness, and with such sadness, Anna did not push the issue nor ask any follow-up questions. She was not going to pry into Sophie's mind uninvited.

So instead, Anna said, "Should we play?"

And that's what the two girls did. They lost themselves in the magical world laid out in front of them.

After a while, Sophie said, "Your house looked like this when you were a kid?"

"Yes," replied Anna. My grandfather built this dollhouse as an exact replica of the house I grew up in."

"Where is that house? Sophie inquired.

"It's actually right in Windsom. Just a little bit away," Anna said tentatively, knowing exactly where this conversation would lead.

"Can you show me?" Sophie responded.

And even though Anna felt a terrible anxiety about going back to Ackerly Lane, about going home, she would not deny this girl access to her past. Anna realized that the past, and the home was as much Sophie's as it was her own. So Anna replied, "Of course. Let's get our coats on."

The two girls walked the short distance, from Main Street to Anna's childhood home. Anna told Sophie about her grandfather, Jacob who grew up in the house too and who first told Anna about Sophie's existence.

"I'm really glad he told me about you, Sophie. I never had much family," Anna confided.

Something about Sophie inspired Anna to talk about her past and her childhood dreams. It felt healthy and therapeutic and right.

They stood, side by side, at 43 Ackerly Lane, staring in silence at a place that was both new and old at the same time, a place in which both Anna and Sophie were rooted, connected. Sophie marveled at the similarity the real 43 Ackerly Lane had to the miniature displayed on Anna's coffee table.

"Wow," the little girl marveled. "It's just like the dollhouse."

"Yes," Anna responded. "It's exact."

It was remarkable to compare the two, even for Anna.

"Can we go in?" asked Sophie

Anna took out her key chain and plucked out the key to the front door that was now in need of a fresh coat of paint. They walked up the front path and Anna let Sophie in. Into the house and into her past.

Chapter 74

It had been almost eight years since Anna stepped through the threshold of Ackerly Lane. The furniture and personal items had been cleared, yet Anna swore that the living room still smelled of Windex and the kitchen still smelled of the lemon disinfectant and bleach that her mother obsessively used to clean the tiles. Beverly would have been happy if the same cleaning supplies could have scrubbed the birthmark off Anna's complexion. She could still see her mother, standing by the sink, frantically scouring the remains of dinner off the earthenware plates. Standing in the bare kitchen, Anna shuddered to think of her mother. Of what she had done and of what sat in hiding behind her stony veneer.

Anna and Sophie ended the small tour in what was Anna's childhood bedroom, also empty and desolate, aside from the lace curtains that remained outlining the picture window. Sophie pushed the curtains aside, revealing the line of dense forest and trees surrounding the periphery of the backyard. Anna had been so preoccupied with Sophie that she didn't notice the quiet drone of those trees, but when Sophie opened the window, the call was almost deafening. Loud and demanding. Magnetic and Insistent.

"Let's explore," Sophie said.

And before Anna could say no, or protest, Sophie ran down the center staircase and out of the house towards the entrance to the Windsom Woods. Anna followed closely at her heels. Sophie's hair bounced against her back as she ran, tendrils flying in the windy afternoon.

Without even thinking, Sophie crossed the threshold to the woods and disappeared in the trees and underbrush.

Anna called her name, loudly, "Sophie. Sophie! Come back."

From a short distance within the woods came the giggling reply, "Anna, come in. Come find me!"

With the briefest of hesitation, only for a moment, Anna stopped short, almost falling over her clumsy booted feet. But then, she let herself go. She let herself enter the woods once again. The trees approved of the decision and urged her on.

Anna caught a glimpse of Sophie's orange coat a few yards away.

"Sophie!" Anna sighed, bent over and panting next to a tall spruce a few feet away from her young cousin. "You scared me! The woods can be dangerous if you aren't careful, "Anna continued.

"Not to me," Sophie replied.

Such an odd response. Anna looked up. Sophie was standing a few feet away, her back was to Anna. The wind had blown the little girl's hair over her right shoulder revealing a strange, dark marking right behind her left ear. A marking that Anna recognized, a marking that Anna knew. She remembered something she had read a few weeks ago, or maybe it was months ago, years ago. Something that she had read while she was hunched over on her bedroom floor:

> *Those with Earth Manipulation abilities are often quite literally and physically marked. It is reasonable to assume that something within the very genetic makeup of Earth Manipulators results in physical manifestations, possibly as a warning for the rest of mankind. These marks may take the form of birthmarks or moles…*

But before Anna could say anything about this mark, before Anna could even open her mouth to speak, Sophie raised her hands up to the sky, her head thrown back.

On that cold, cold, December afternoon as Anna Parke watched in fascination from behind, the trees responded to Sophie's call. And their response was kind and good and sweet. The scene was nothing like the awful, fearful vision she witnessed while affixed to that oily stump on that fateful night. Sophie's touch was pure and innocent and honest. Caressing and tickling and playful. Tears emerged from the corners of Anna's eyes as she watched such beauty. And at that moment, she knew, she knew from the depth of her being, that the connection that both she and her young cousin possessed, Earth Manipulation or *Unci Maka Kae* or whatever other name could be applied, was not evil. No, it wasn't evil at all.

Chapter 75

On the bus ride back to Windsom, after dropping off Sophie in Clifton Park late that evening, Anna felt a terrible emptiness steel over her. What a day it had been. Anna reflected on the rest of her day with Sophie in the quiet solitude of the empty, dark bus. The cousins spent the rest of the afternoon exploring the forest and basking in the power of their shared touch. Sophie was delighted to find that Anna shared her unique pull towards the trees, and although significantly more subtle than Sophie's ability, Anna stopped resisting the urge to block out the call that she felt deep within her bones. She let the trees pull her, spur her on, and for the first time, her soul was at peace. It was only once the girls' noses were drippy and cold that they left the comfortable woods to find warmth in steaming mugs of hot cocoa at the Windsom Diner.

During her shift the next day at The Food Mart, Anna couldn't stop thinking about Sophie, about their next communication, their next outing. Anna thought that Sophie might like to visit that new indoor amusement park that opened about 45 minutes north of Windsom. Maybe she would ask Amy for permission to take Sophie there next weekend. Anna wondered how much it cost to purchase an admission ticket to that place...probably more than she could afford. Maybe it was time to start looking for a better job.

There was a thought coming to her, coming to her through the air, a thought traveling through the storefront window pushed on by the not so distant trees. When the thought first entered her mind, Anna tried to beat it back, dismissing it as foolish and improbable, but once she ran out of excuses, she knew her path.

Once the thought held her, Anna could find no rest. She spent a sleepless night turning her future over in her mind, in her heart. At nine o'clock sharp the next morning, Anna punched some numbers into her cellphone. The numbers connected her with the Partners of God Foster Care Agency.

"Hello. Partners of God Fostercare. How may I help you?" said the breezy voice on the other line.

And with a newfound confidence, more sure than she had ever been about anything in her life up to this point, "I'd like to fill out an adoption application," Anna Parke replied.

Chapter 76
Later

Ten o'clock in the morning, Anna found herself curled up on the living room sofa, scrolling through her jumbled inbox. She couldn't remember the last time she actually read any of her emails and at the moment, she was wishing she had not been so neglectful in emptying her mailbox. There were over two thousand unread messages, mostly junk. However, there was one email to which she quickly attended, while the morning stretched lazily out before her. She had been asked to digitally sign off on her official application for a management position at The Food Mart. Her boss, Adam, had recently announced his retirement–it was about time–and Anna had basically been guaranteed the job. This new employment opportunity was in no way her dream job, not even close. Even at almost thirty years old, she still had not fully defined what career path she wanted to pursue even though she had some ideas skating around her brain. Lately Anna thought more and more about the foster care system and these innocent children wasting away behind its paperwork and protocols. She thought of Jacob and Dr. Jenkins. She thought about Janine and Rebecca. Anna humbly thought that she might make a difference somehow. Perhaps by going back to school to study social work. At the moment, that dim hope had begun to gather speed in Anna's mind. The thought excited her. Was it even possible for her to start over? She was starting to think that yes, maybe it was.

Even though a new career path was years away, as Anna finished the task of digitally signing her promotion paperwork, she thought to herself that it was at least a start, a beginning, a step in the right direction.

Anna glanced briefly in front of her; next to the dollhouse, shining in the morning sun filtering through the front apartment window, stood the copper, silver-rimmed urn containing Beverly Parke's ashes. Last night, Sophie came across the object when Anna sent the girl into her closet in search of an extra sweatshirt. It was drafty in her apartment; a fact that the 1920s steam radiator heating couldn't quite combat. Sophie had appeared in the living room, wearing Anna's tie-dyed sweatshirt hanging down to her knees and holding the vessel carefully with both hands. Anna was surprised to see it; of course she knew the urn was there, but she much preferred it buried in the shadowy depths, covered with clothes and spare blankets. That way she didn't have to think about the woman that it contained. When Sophie asked about it, Anna was brief, but honest. Sophie accepted Anna's explanation with one last searching glance and then placed the item gingerly in the place it now stood, forbidding and dark. It took Anna a few moments of quiet deliberation to decide what was to be done with such a haunted item. After she delivered Sophie back to the Pickard home, she would once again descend into the woods behind Ackerly Lane. The trees no longer invoked such a sense of anxiety and unease within her. Not after her afternoon with Sophie. She would scatter her mother's ashes at the base of the forbidden tree, forever silent, forever buried. The plan provided Anna with a deep sense of peace and finality.

She had finally come to terms with her mother, in all her flawed glory. Gradually, since she had met Sophie, Anna's anger towards her mom had packed its bags and slipped unwittingly into the starry sky. She was not aware of the fading until she looked upon the urn containing those ashes, held tightly in Sophie's small hands and was surprised to find no knot in her chest, no rage blooming in her belly. Maybe that's how acceptance happens, not as a big flashy epiphany, but quietly, unassumingly.

Once the matter of the urn was settled, Anna turned over on the soft cushions lost in thought. She was trying to be quiet; she didn't want to turn on the television or go about fixing breakfast. She didn't want to wake the small sleeping child, entwined in the comforters of Anna's queen-sized bed. The door of the bedroom was slightly ajar, and Anna could just make out the tiny upturned nose and wide set eyes of Sophie Parke, peacefully sleeping the morning away. Even though the adoption was not yet finalized, Anna was granted permission for a sleepover with her soon-to-be adopted daughter. It was still weird for Anna to think of Sophie in those terms. The girls stayed up late last night, watching *Snow White and the Seven Dwarfs,* and then *Who Framed Roger Rabbit* and pigging out on microwave popcorn and Hershey Kisses. There were still remnants of shiny metallic wrappers scattered like leaves under the coffee table. Gazing at the tiny dreaming face, Anna felt a surge of love so strong it almost brought a fresh wave of tears to her eyes; she felt the thickness gather deep within her chest. She had certainly shed many tears since she unpacked those boxes in the corner of her apartment, the corner where Sophie's backpack now stood.

It was hard for Anna to absorb how drastically her life had changed in such a short span of time. But the change felt welcome and right. Exactly two months had passed since Anna began the process of adoption, which Anna was warned would be a lengthy and drawn-out experience, but Anna didn't mind the wait. Amy was accommodating in allowing Anna ample time with Sophie and on the days they did not see one another, they spoke on the phone in the evenings. Anna didn't know the first thing about motherhood, and she did not exactly have an exemplary role model to follow, but she had faith that she and Sophie would figure it out together, in time.

As she deleted each message in order, her mind wandered to a time just a few weeks ago, when Anna went for the third time to see her uncle. The progress he had made since their 'breakthrough meeting' as Dr. Jenkins titled it, was remarkable and the administrators and doctors were beginning the discussion of transferring him to a less restrictive facility. Anna could even say that she and Dr. Jenkins, Kathleen, had become sort of friends. They developed a mutual respect for one another and Anna viewed the doctor as her teammate, so to speak. Kathleen had even begun to reveal some of her own personal life to Anna, telling her that she was now prepared to dedicate more time to Anna's uncle because she had just come out of a relationship.

Jacob was mostly quiet during Anna's visit, as he had been the previous time, and the two spent long moments of togetherness gazing into one another's eyes, silently trying to come to grips with their shared, albeit tragic history. Anna told him about Sophie and her plans for adoption. He didn't say much in response; he never did, but he let Anna talk. When he heard the news, he just smiled, wide and bright. It was the first time Anna saw him smile fully and she noticed that the small gesture changed his entire face, lit it up from within. She saw the young boy he once was, she saw him with all his flaws; she detected the playfulness that was hiding in the depths, buried under years of trauma. She briefly discussed with Dr. Jenkins the possibility of bringing Sophie along on one of her upcoming visits, a possibility that Dr. Jenkins promised to consider in the coming weeks, assuming that Jacob continued to move in the right direction. But she was optimistic. Optimistic–such a new word to Anna.

An incoming phone call scattered Anna's thoughts. She picked up the phone quickly, without noticing the incoming caller, trying to silence the ringtone before it could disrupt Sophie. She closed herself outside of her apartment to take the call in the dimly lit stairwell.

"Hello," Anna spoke.

"Hi. Anna. I've been trying to get in touch with you. It's Chris."

"Chris–?" she responded, trying to place the name.

"Yes. Chris Reilly, your realtor," the voice responded.

"Oh, yes. Chris. I'm so sorry," Anna apologized.

"No worries, no worries. Anyway, I have some news for you. A young couple just put in an offer for the property on Ackerly Lane," he informed her.

The word 'property' sounded so alien, so clinical. It suggested nothing of the life that had been lived behind those aging plaster walls. The past that had unfurled there behind the closed doors.

Chris continued, "It's a fair offer Anna–five thousand over asking price."

Anna didn't respond right away.

"Anna? You still there," asked the realtor breezily.

"Yes. I'm here Chris. Sorry. I was just thinking," she responded.

"What's there to think about?" he said. "It's a no-brainer!"

Anna took a moment to consider the sleeping child on the other side of the door, the life that had just begun to blossom in the face of a past filled with such loss and sorrow, and she imagined that her response was inevitable. That fate had a way of righting all wrongs and bringing her full-circle, back to the place it had all begun. Back to the place that *she* began. Back to Ackerly Lane, the old house outlined by the woods.

Anna quickly imagined the conversation she wanted to have with Chris. But instead of allowing her words to remain locked up forever in her mind, unspoken and regretted, she uttered them aloud over the phone.

They came out timidly at first, but as she gathered momentum, she spoke more and more confidentially.

"You know Chris. I think I've changed my mind," she finally said.

"*Changed* your mind? About the offer?" he asked, puzzled.

"No. I think I've changed my mind about selling," Anna said with a finality that seemed to emerge from the very core of her being.

She felt a sudden and potent possessiveness over her childhood home; she would not, absolutely could not, part with it.

"Well, Anna..I've put a lot of time into selling the property. We have a binding contract. You can't just change your mind," Chris responded.

Anna knew that she was in a sense screwing him over. She understood his annoyance and anger. But she really didn't care.

"Yeah. I understand that you're annoyed. And I'm sorry. I really appreciate all the hard work you put into selling my home, but I *can* break the contract. And that's exactly what I am going to do."

"There are fees that you will incur in doing so, Anna. A contract is a legal document," Chris Reilly persuaded.

"I'll pay whatever fee is required. I just can't sell my home, Chris," Anna said. "I hope you understand."

"Ok. If you are sure that this is the route you would like to pursue–I guess I will deliver the news to the Julians. They are not going to be happy when I tell them that–"

"Great. Thank you Chris," Anna interrupted. "I'll stop in sometime this week to pick up the keys."

And then she almost apologized once again, but she closed her mouth instead. She would no longer apologize any more for her life and for her decisions.

When she ended the call, a smile played upon the corners of her mouth. She remembered the damaged little girl that she once was, so lonely and eager for acceptance, so willing to do whatever was necessary for any display of paltry affirmation. She felt decidedly different now, older, as she slowly opened the front door of her apartment and re-entered her living space.

Gazing once more into the dollhouse–this artifact from her past that once again resurfaced–Anna opened up the Amazon icon on her cell phone and in the search bar on the top of the screen she typed in *porcelain figurines.* She needed to purchase two new dolls for Sophie. She needed a new Anna doll, one without a crushed face, and a little girl doll. A Sophie. A doll that belonged inside the house, a doll that belonged with Anna.

She heard Sophie's soft voice call out, "Good morning Aunt Anna."

Anna walked over to the voice and leaned against the doorway gazing into her bedroom. She saw Sophie, her soon to be daughter, sitting up in bed, hair disheveled and couldn't keep the smile off her face.

"Good morning Sophie. How did you sleep?"

"Really good," the little girl responded, "Can we play again this morning with the dollhouse?"

"Of course, Sophie. I'd like that."

While Sophie re-organized the bedrooms in the dollhouse, visions of the future danced upon Anna's mind as she went about toasting and buttering bagels. Once the adoption was final, she and Sophie would move together into 43 Ackerly Lane and begin a new life there–a fresh start. Anna would restore the dollhouse to its rightful position in what would undoubtedly be Sophie's bedroom. The girls would embrace the magic of the trees, and rejoice in their shared secret deep within Windsom Woods. And they would be beautifully, extraordinarily happy.

Epilogue

Surrounded only by the cawing of the chattering gulls overhead, Mia Rossi stood securely on the shore. Her light denim jeans rolled up so the cool Atlantic could lap at her pink-painted toes and sun-browned ankles. Her hands remained buried deep in her pockets against the cool spring breeze that blew her long dark hair against her cheeks; a curly tendril flew into her mouth, sticking to the glossy lipstick she applied about an hour before.

Gazing out over the glistening sapphire expanse laid out before her, Mia's mind wandered to a dream she had last night. Mia rarely remembered her dreams, but there was something about the young woman in the vision, who seemed to stare into her soul–a woman who had emerald-green pine needles stuck into her tangled hair and a striking purple mark that stood out like a bluejay amongst ravens upon her pale cheek. It felt as though the woman understood her; Mia felt comfortable in her presence. In the wee hours of the night, the magical time where fantasy takes flight, Mia could have sworn the woman was trying to tell her something, trying to connect with her in some intangible way. But as the hours ticked slowly by, Mia felt more and more sure that it was just a silly dream, a result of too much Netflix before bedtime.

Sighing, the dream slipped away from Mia as she lost herself once again in the azure depth in front of her. Crashing with fervor on the sandy coast, the foamy waves sent a mist of seawater up to Mia's damp cheeks. She could taste the salt on the tip of her tongue.

Up until recently Mia viewed the ocean as a mere luxury. A commodity that increased the value of homes and tourist destinations around the globe. But lately, the sea at the end of Minnesota Avenue in Long Beach, New York had become more of an enigma to her. Coming to her in soft droves through the air, she heard the waves crashing even when she was nowhere near them. Sometimes that crashing reached a near violent pitch, causing her to grip her ears to lessen the intensity of the noise. However, no matter how tightly she closed her ears, or the front door of her small second story apartment, or the crumbling, chipped windows in her bedroom, the sound and volume of the crashing waves remained unchanged.

And this is what brought Mia to the edge of the Earth and the start of the ocean not only this afternoon, but many afternoons of late. She spent hours contemplating the sights and sounds of the sparkling blanket that reflected a million prisms into the cloudless sky.

As Mia turned to leave, the wind caught and lifted the front of her light linen shirt revealing for less that a moment, a small brown jagged mark, slightly larger than a silver dollar on the slight curve of her hip; it almost looked like the drip mark that melted dark chocolate would make upon the ground.

Mia continued to head towards her apartment, no closer to solving the mystery that seemed to hold her in its grasp. No closer to discovering the source or purpose of the relentless sound of the crashing waves that seemed to beat upon the shores of her mind. She had another fleeing image of the girl from her dreams; the purple imperfection, almost the color of her favorite cabernet, marring her complexion.

Even when Mia entered her apartment, and closed herself in the cool comfort of her bedroom, the waves commenced their unabating echo. Were they calling out to her? Summoning her for some hidden purpose? Laughing humorlessly to herself, Mia tried to dismiss the notion as fantasy, but she couldn't help feeling that there was some tiny nugget of truth in the notion. She read somewhere once that all humans feel a connection to the sea...something about the saltwater within us aching to return to its native tributary. Could that be what she was feeling now?

Just as she dismissed that thought, her mind shifted to fixing dinner. Yet, deep within her, the pulsing of the waves commenced again, more palpable now and in a kind of syncopated rhythm. At that very moment the blinds covering the window at the rear of her apartment snapped open in a gust of wind and banged noisily against the pane, revealing a nearly unobstructed view of the Atlantic. Stopping in her tracks, she cautiously approached the window, drawing closer and closer yet, pulled by an almost magnetic force. A sense of raw, unadulterated fear gripped her as she bent down to peer out over the neat row of houses and fences. Overhead the sky turned a steely gray and electrified thunder clouds rolled in across the horizon covering every inch of the May sky in a gunmetal blanket. Mia could just make out the jagged, irregular streaks of lightning playing within their stormy depths. The ocean swirled and burbled with turmoil and Mia could perceive dark sinister shapes below the surface. Falling to the linoleum floor, Mia grasped her ears tightly as the voice of the ocean–she knew now with certainty it was the voice of the sea, some primeval growling that had been awakened by a mysterious catalyst–slammed against her tired mind.

There was no use resisting anymore; she was consumed. What possible fight could a single human put up in the face of the mighty powers of Mother Nature? Absolutely none.The ocean would have its say. Whether Mia liked it or not, the ocean would have its say.

The End

Thank Yous

There are so many amazing people who have encouraged me along my writing journey. First off, I would like to thank my amazing husband, Brian, who shows me unfailing support and love each and every day. He was my first reader and my springboard, giving me the confidence to actually finish my first manuscript.

To Dave Goldman, who provided his invaluable time, advice, and support for this project. He loves Anna Parke as much as I do and without him, her story would probably never have seen the light of day. She and I are both humbly grateful.

To Danielle Jump, for creating the beautiful image that adorns the front cover. Your creativity, patience and artistry are astounding.

To Monica and Dena–my friends and early readers. You helped me feel comfortable sharing my work. Thank you for the encouragement and helpful suggestions.

I started writing this manuscript for no other reason than to prove I could. As an English teacher, I am so used to analyzing the works of the literary greats; this was my chance to craft something of my own. Anna's story was written during off periods at work, in the parking lot of my son's martial arts studio, in metal bleachers at little league games, in the lobbies of our family pediatrician and orthodontist offices, in the echoing, chlorine-odored corridors of swim meets, and at countless other parenting obligations.The bits and pieces, odds and ends, came together in a way I didn't expect…in a story about a broken girl who finds herself. Thank you for taking the time to read my story. I hope you enjoyed the ride.

Made in the USA
Middletown, DE
30 October 2023